CRIME
OFFICER
STOP

A KILLER'S *Obsession*

D.R. BROOKS

A Killer's Obsession

(Killer's Game Duet Book 1)

First Edition

ISBN: 979-8-9944813-0-1

Editor/Proofreader: Alysha Thornton at Athorntonedits

Cover designer: Fay Lane

Interior formatting & design: 3Crows Author Services

Thank you for taking the time to read my book, and an even special thank you to my beta readers who helped me along the way.

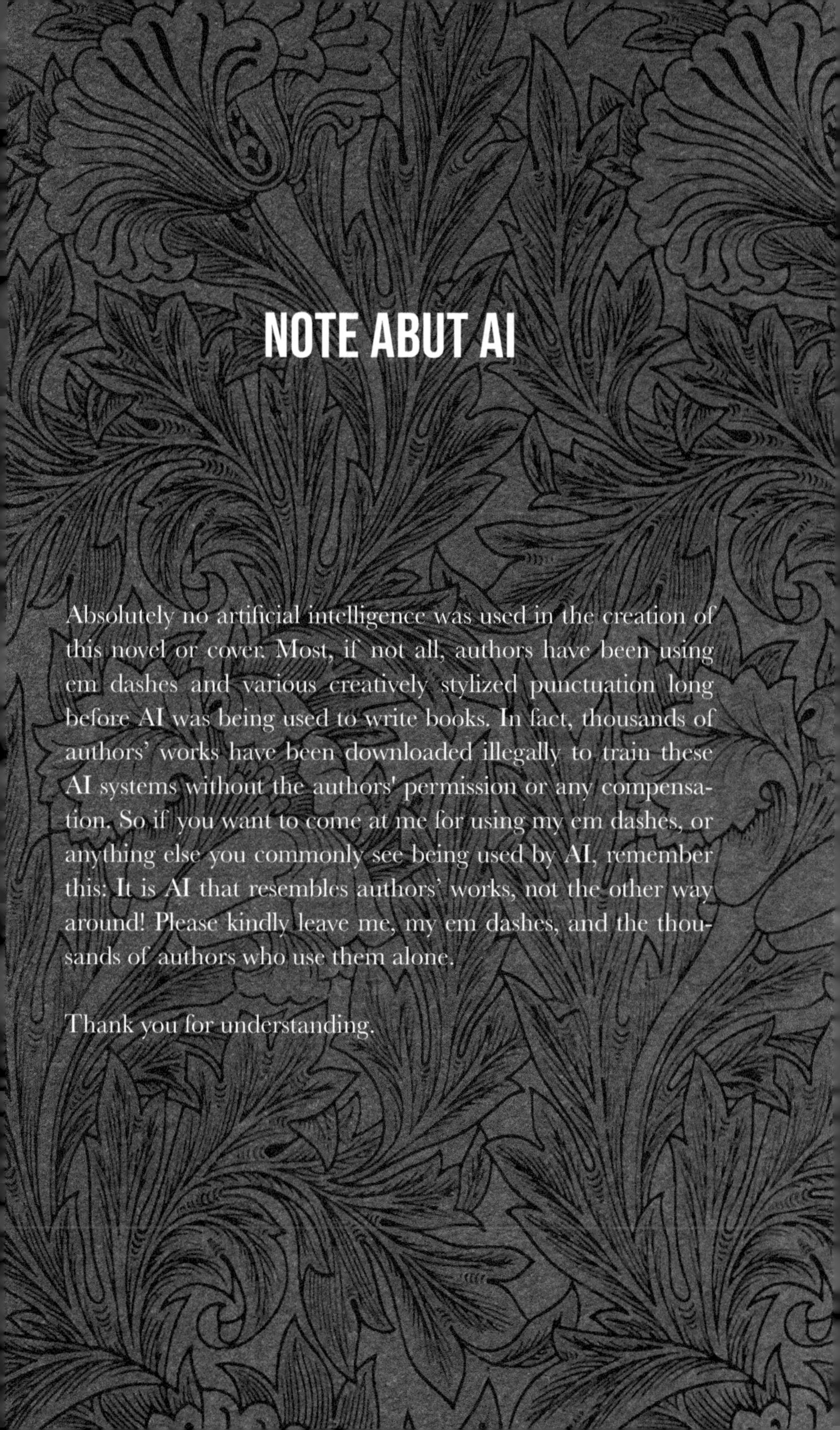

NOTE ABUT AI

Absolutely no artificial intelligence was used in the creation of this novel or cover. Most, if not all, authors have been using em dashes and various creatively stylized punctuation long before AI was being used to write books. In fact, thousands of authors' works have been downloaded illegally to train these AI systems without the authors' permission or any compensation. So if you want to come at me for using my em dashes, or anything else you commonly see being used by AI, remember this: It is AI that resembles authors' works, not the other way around! Please kindly leave me, my em dashes, and the thousands of authors who use them alone.

Thank you for understanding.

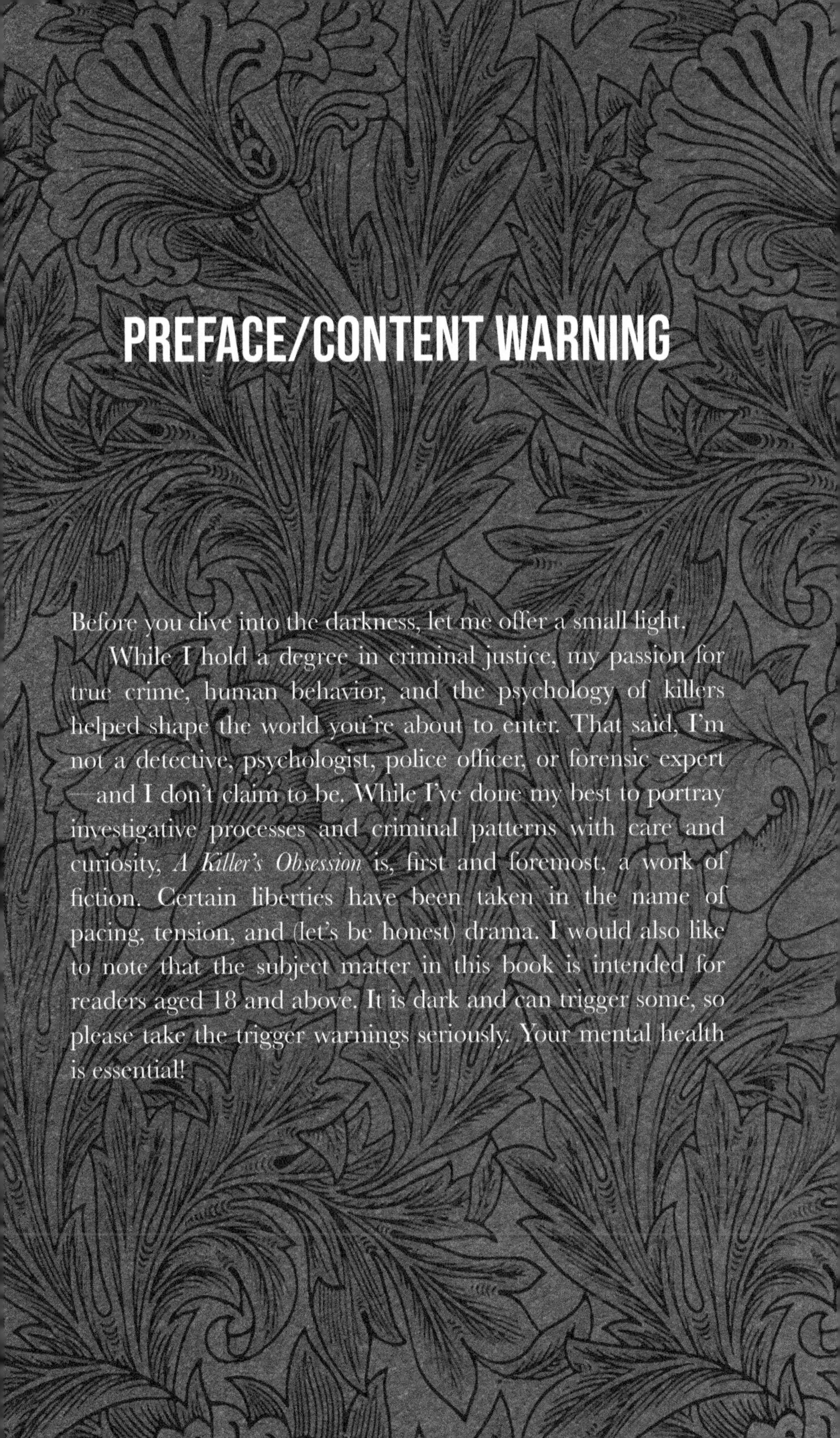

PREFACE/CONTENT WARNING

Before you dive into the darkness, let me offer a small light.

While I hold a degree in criminal justice, my passion for true crime, human behavior, and the psychology of killers helped shape the world you're about to enter. That said, I'm not a detective, psychologist, police officer, or forensic expert—and I don't claim to be. While I've done my best to portray investigative processes and criminal patterns with care and curiosity, *A Killer's Obsession* is, first and foremost, a work of fiction. Certain liberties have been taken in the name of pacing, tension, and (let's be honest) drama. I would also like to note that the subject matter in this book is intended for readers aged 18 and above. It is dark and can trigger some, so please take the trigger warnings seriously. Your mental health is essential!

MESSAGE TO MY FAMILY:

I absolutely love and appreciate all of your support, and I can't wait for you to get your hands on a copy. However, fair warning—this isn't your average, clean-cut slasher. There are, *ahem,* explicit scenes tucked in... so read at your own risk. Don't say I didn't warn you.

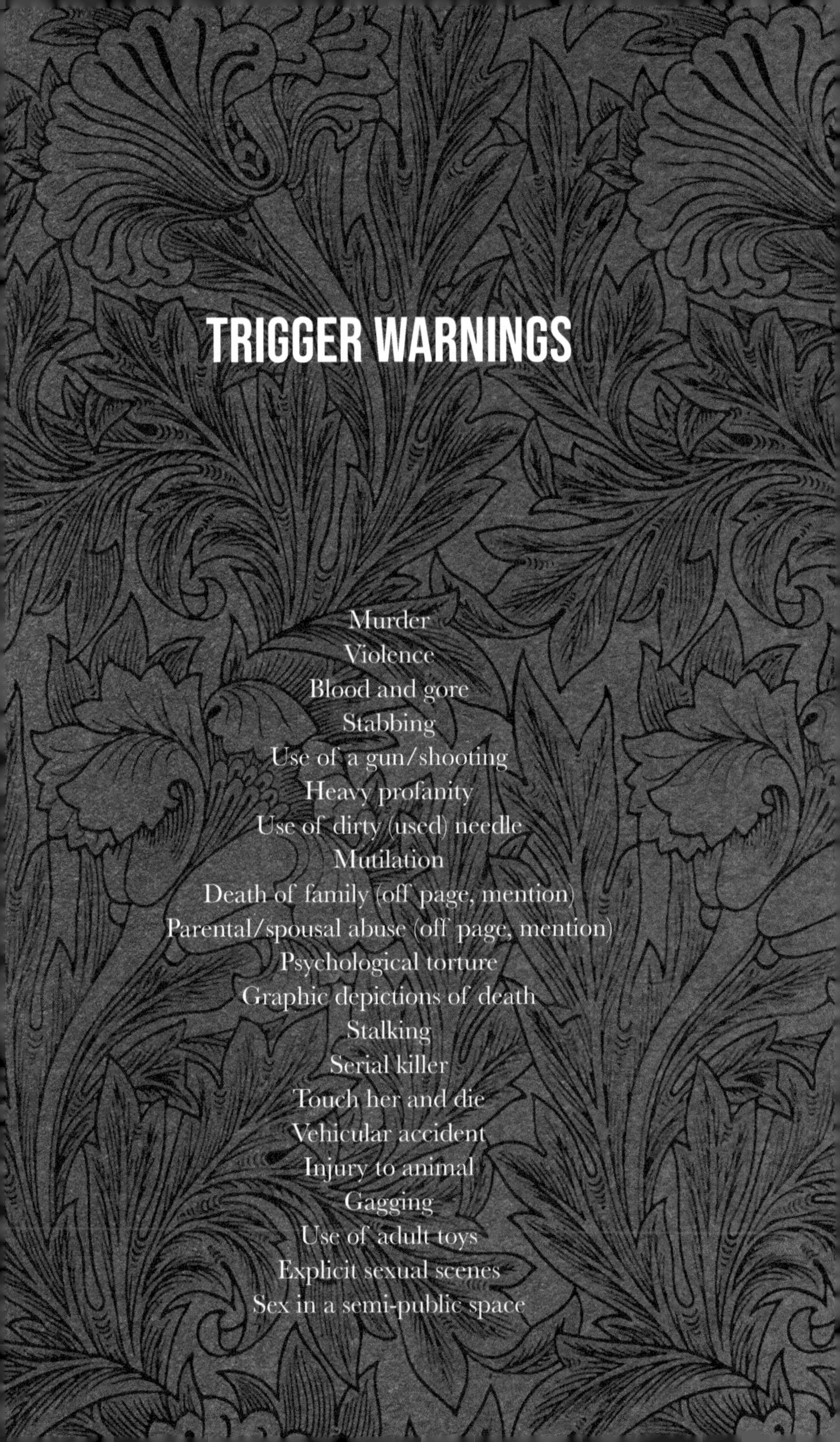

TRIGGER WARNINGS

Murder
Violence
Blood and gore
Stabbing
Use of a gun/shooting
Heavy profanity
Use of dirty (used) needle
Mutilation
Death of family (off page, mention)
Parental/spousal abuse (off page, mention)
Psychological torture
Graphic depictions of death
Stalking
Serial killer
Touch her and die
Vehicular accident
Injury to animal
Gagging
Use of adult toys
Explicit sexual scenes
Sex in a semi-public space

Oral sex
Fingering
Hand necklaces
Restraints
Masturbation
Kidnapping
Home invasion
Strangulation
Obsession

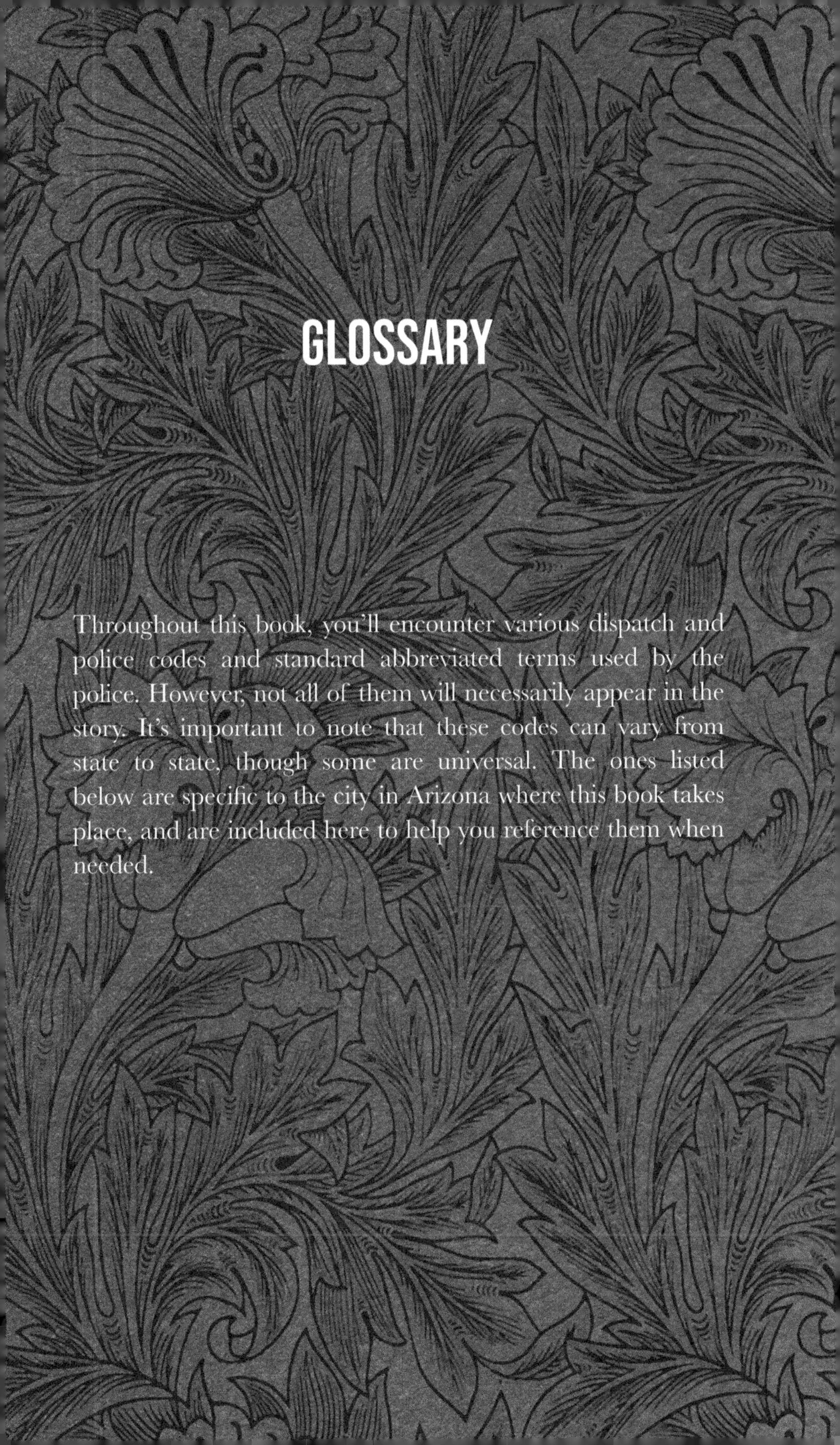

GLOSSARY

Throughout this book, you'll encounter various dispatch and police codes and standard abbreviated terms used by the police. However, not all of them will necessarily appear in the story. It's important to note that these codes can vary from state to state, though some are universal. The ones listed below are specific to the city in Arizona where this book takes place, and are included here to help you reference them when needed.

Code 1: Clear to receive confidential message
Code 2: Urgent response
Code 3: Emergency response
Code 4: No further assistance needed
Code 7: Out of service to eat
10-1: Receiving poorly
10-2: Loud and clear
10-3: Stop transmitting
10-4: Message received/OK/Acknowledged
10-7: Out of service
10-8: Back in service
10-9: Repeat message
10-18: As soon as possible/Immediately
10-23: At the scene
10-26: Detaining subject - expedite response
10-33: Disturbance
10-39: Major incident (Units not involved, remain 10-8 and 10-3)
10-40: Prowler
10-43: Armed robbery
10-47: Lost/Missing Person

10-51: Auto accident - without injury
10-52: Auto accident - with injury
10-53: Fatal auto accident
10-59: Ambulance
10-72: Rescue/Paramedic Unit
10-81: Stop and Field Interview (probable suspect)
10-82: Stop and Arrest
10-84: Backup Unit
10-99: Officer urgently needs assistance/Respond code 3

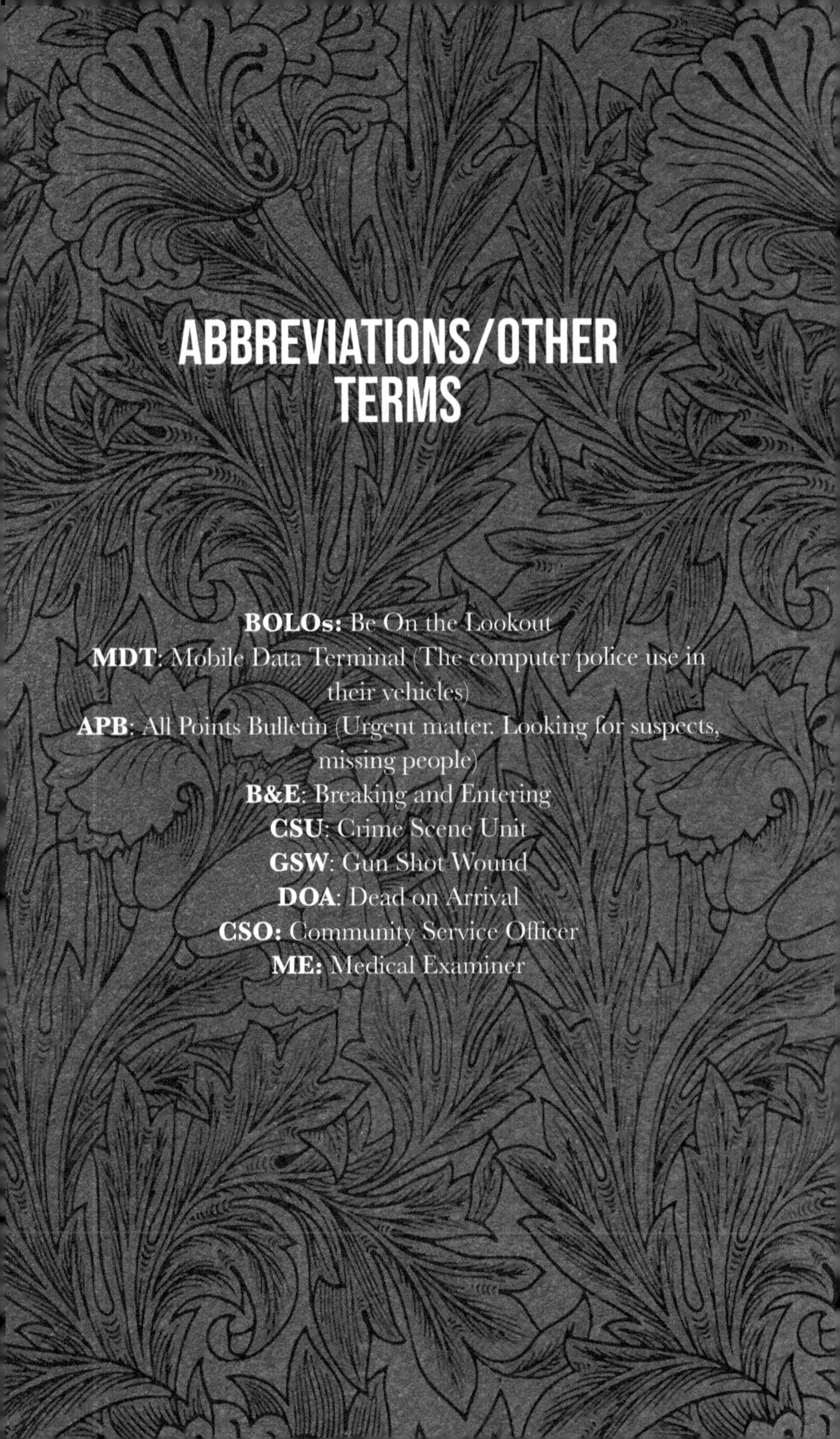

ABBREVIATIONS/OTHER TERMS

BOLOs: Be On the Lookout

MDT: Mobile Data Terminal (The computer police use in their vehicles)

APB: All Points Bulletin (Urgent matter. Looking for suspects, missing people)

B&E: Breaking and Entering

CSU: Crime Scene Unit

GSW: Gun Shot Wound

DOA: Dead on Arrival

CSO: Community Service Officer

ME: Medical Examiner

FINAL GIRL (too pretty to die) -- PI3RCE
Nightmare -- Halsey
Deadly -- Catch Your Breath
Atlantic -- Sleep Token
Red Vineyard -- Diggy Graves
Machinehead -- Bush
KNIVES -- Neoni
Like A Villain -- Bad Omens
Numb -- Sleep Theory
Ghost Inside The Shell -- Catch Your Breath
Dark Signs -- Sleep Token
Heads Will Roll -- Yeah Yeah Yeahs
Climbing Up the Walls -- Radiohead
Blood On White Satin -- Naomi Scott
Can u see me in the dark? -- Halestorm, I Prevail
GODDESS -- Written by Wolves
Fire Up the Night -- New Medicine
Paranoia -- Neoni
Paralyzed -- Sleep Theory
Never Say Die -- Neoni
Strong for Somebody Else -- Citizen Soldier

PIECES -- Daughtry
I am not a woman, I'm a god -- Halsey
If I'm There -- Bad Omens
Kill of the Night -- Gin Wigmore
Run For Your Life -- K. Flay
Die Trying -- New Medicine
Game of Survival -- Ruelle
Follow You -- Bring Me The Horizon
Motley Crew -- Post Malone
Coming Undone -- Korn
I Am the Fire -- Halestorm
Irreplaceable -- Citizen Soldier
Duality -- Slipknot
Getting Away With Murder -- Papa Roach
Monsters -- Ruelle
Even If It Kills Me -- Papa Roach
Puppet -- Diggy Graves

For those who crave a love that doesn't cage you,
but arms you.
Who doesn't pull you from the fire,
but stands in it with you,
gun drawn, heart wild,
ready to kill for your next breath.

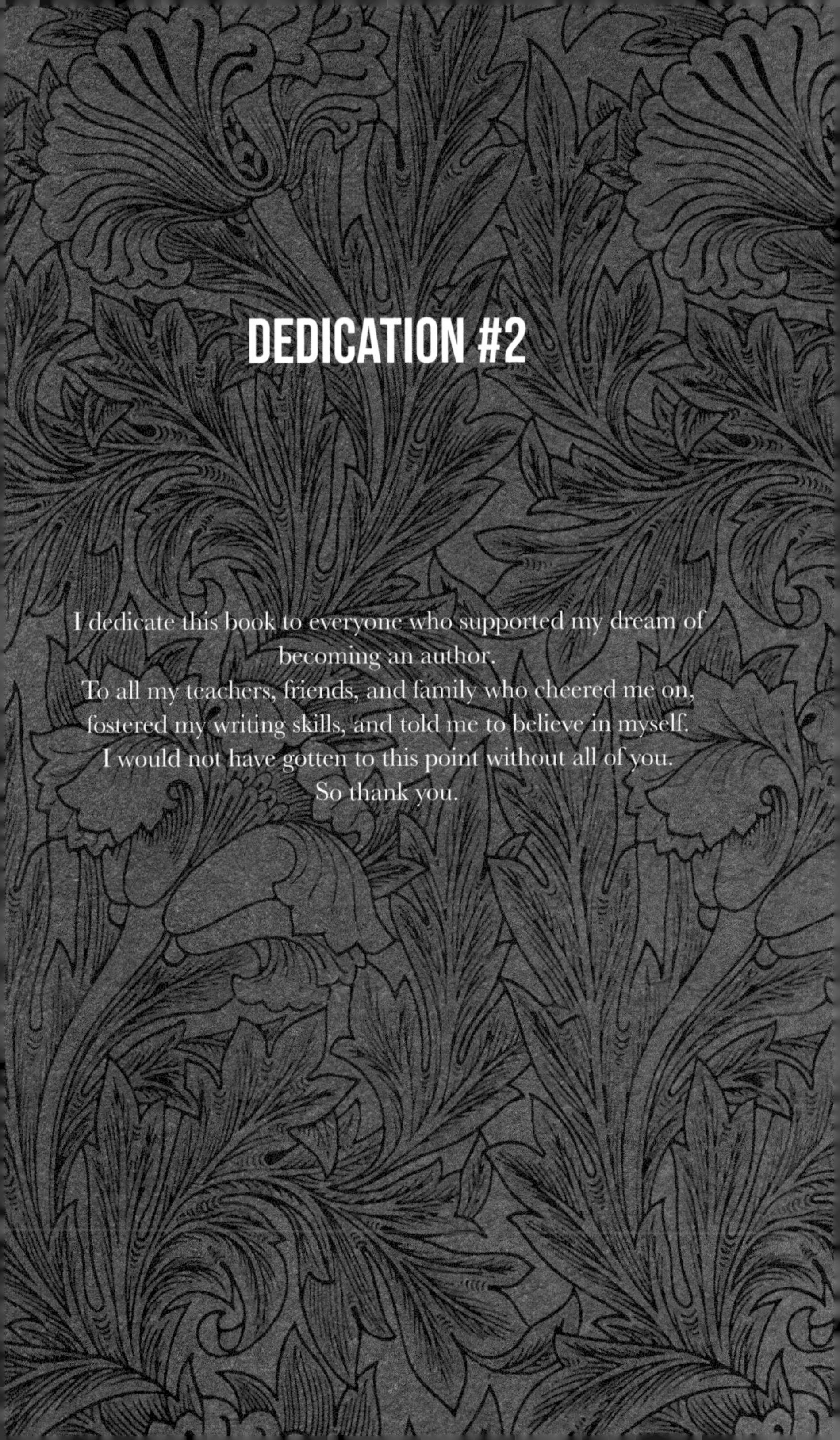

DEDICATION #2

I dedicate this book to everyone who supported my dream of becoming an author.
To all my teachers, friends, and family who cheered me on, fostered my writing skills, and told me to believe in myself.
I would not have gotten to this point without all of you.
So thank you.

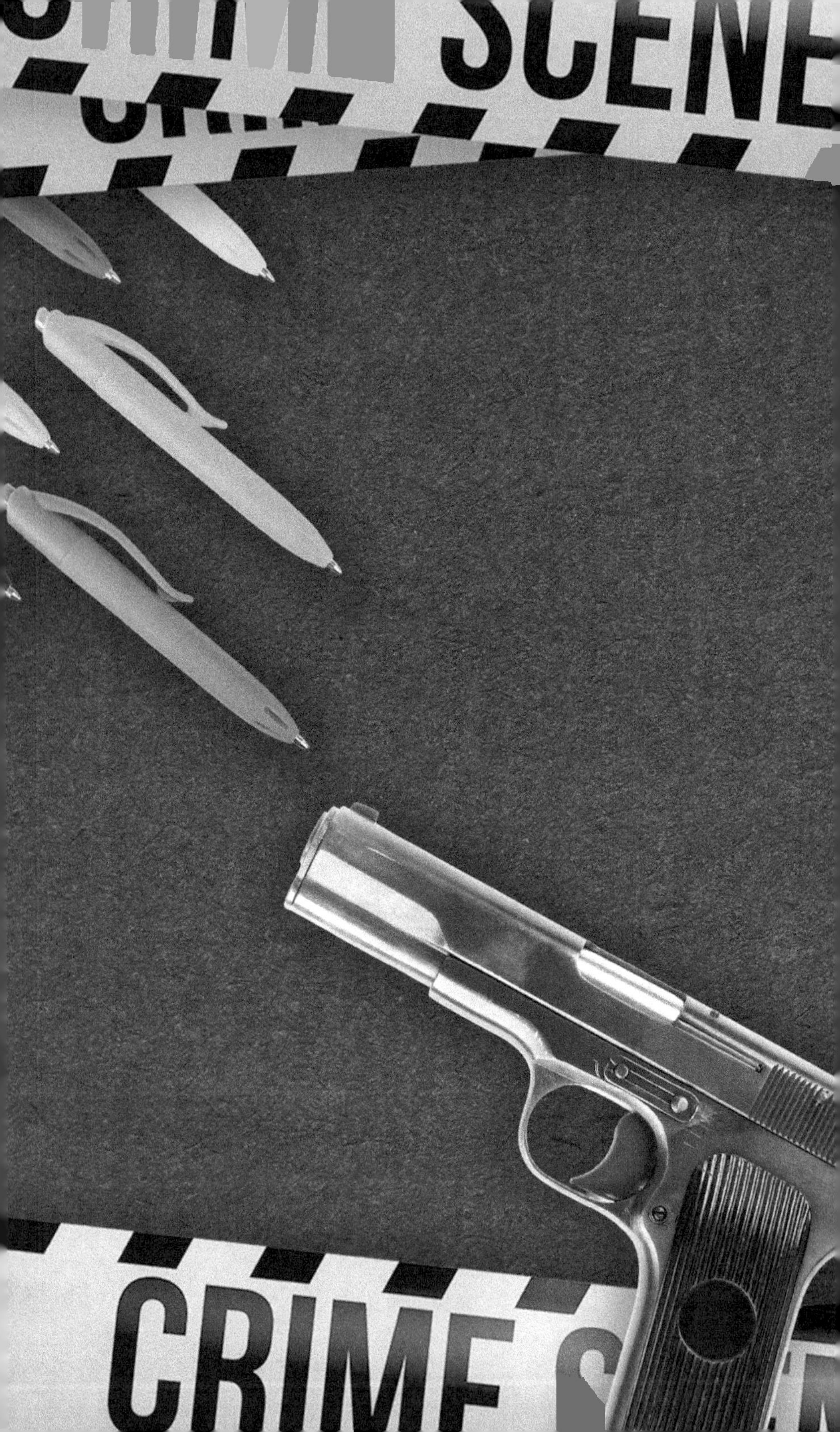
SCENE
CRIME

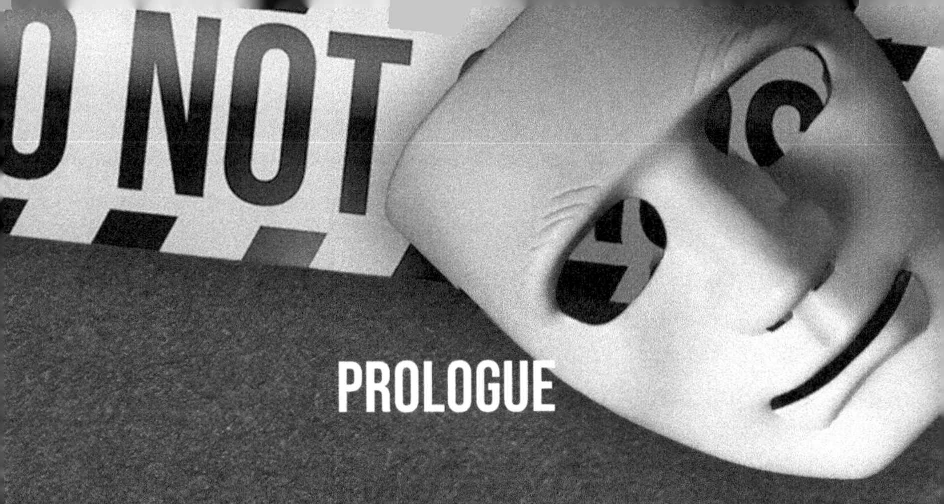

PROLOGUE

THE WARM AIR still carries the scent of rain and sun-baked pavement, thick with humidity left behind by the storm that swept through earlier. It clings to my skin, heavy and damp, and the wind that whips around the corners of the buildings offers no relief—only swirls of heat laced with the earthy tang of wet asphalt and desert dust. My boots splash through shallow puddles along the sidewalk, sending lazy ripples through the watery reflections of amber streetlights overhead. The asphalt glistens beneath me, scattered with broken patches and the occasional billow of water stirred by a passing breeze.

The last traces of daylight are long gone, swallowed by the thick, charcoal sky. What remains is the unnerving and heavy quiet. There are no voices, music, or even the distant shuffle of other footsteps. Just the occasional car rolling by with tires hissing over wet pavement, headlights sweeping briefly across the street before vanishing around a corner.

I shift the straps of my book bag higher on my shoulders, wincing as it digs into my skin. It's too heavy—stuffed with textbooks, my laptop, and everything else I've dragged around all day. The weight is a constant reminder of how long this day has been. Ahead, my apartment building looms like it's barely holding itself together. Faded, cracked, and crumbling at the edges, just like most of the forgotten buildings on this side of town. Stone Ridge Heights has been clinging to existence for years. It sits awkwardly on the edge of campus, not quite university housing but close enough to draw in broke students and low-income tenants desperate for cheap rent. With its age and reputation, you'd think the city would've torn it down by now, but because it still gets business, it still stands. Unfortunately, though, no one seems to care enough to fix it up.

The street leading up to it is deserted—no joggers trying to hit their step count, no drunk students staggering home from off-campus parties, not even the guy who lives on the second floor who usually chain-smokes on his balcony. Just me, dragging my feet toward a half-condemned building, and a kind of silence that feels less peaceful and more tired. Like, the whole block is just as worn out as I am.

As I approach the side entrance, the flickering fluorescent light above the door hums faintly, casting sporadic flashes of dim illumination over the chipped stucco and the cracked, crumbling concrete steps. I pause for a second, catching my breath, sweat and humidity sticking to the back of my neck.

I sigh and reach for the handle. It's warm from the day's lingering heat but slick from the earlier rain. It slides beneath my fingers with a faint resistance as I yank the door open. I wedge my foot into the gap before it slams shut again. The hinges groan loudly, the sound echoing through the silence like it resents being disturbed.

Inside, the stairwell hits me with its usual blend of mildew, damp concrete, and someone's stale weed. The door slams shut behind me with a metallic clang that echoes off the walls, trapping me in the thick, musty air. I groan, press the back of my hand to my nose, and try not to gag. The smell's awful, and the stuffiness in the stairwell has somehow made it worse. I shift the straps of my bag again, hiking it up as far as they can go on my shoulders.

Four flights of stairs wait ahead, stretching upward into dim, flickering light. The elevator's still broken. Surprise, surprise. It's been out for weeks—just another casualty of the building's long list of ignored maintenance issues. People complain daily, their voices growing more impatient by the hour, but management does what it always does: absolutely nothing. We're used to it by now. Broken promises and busted utilities are, to some extent, part of the charm.

I stand at the base of the stairwell for a second, steeling myself. My fingers tighten around the straps of my bag as I look up the stairs. The overhead fluorescents flicker and hum, throwing warped shadows across the cracked walls like they're trying to set the mood for a horror movie.

And honestly? They're doing a pretty good job.

With a resigned sigh, I start my climb. My boots hit the steps with soft, steady thuds, echoing up the narrow stairwell. Each step feels heavier than the last, my muscles protesting the effort. The weight of my bag pulls at my shoulders like an anchor, dragging the last bit of energy out of me. I'm tired (more than tired), and it shows in every inch of my body.

When I reach the fourth floor, I'm breathless and sore. My legs ache like I just hiked a mountain instead of a busted apartment stairwell, and sweat clings to the back of my neck, making my shoulder-length dirty blonde hair stick uncomfortably to my skin.

With a sharp exhale, I shrug off my book bag and let it drop to the floor with a loud, satisfying thud that echoes down the hall. The release of that weight is a tiny victory, and I savor it for all of two seconds before peeling off my red university hoodie. It's lightweight, but the fabric clings to my damp arms like shrink-wrap. I tug it off and toss it over my shoulder, rolling my neck and shoulders to shake out the tension that's settled deep in my muscles.

Crouched beside my bag, I unzip it and shove my hand in. Digging through the clutter, I push around empty gum wrappers, condoms, crumpled receipts, a few rogue bobby pins, and at least three pens that have no business still existing. My fingers sweep through the chaos, brushing past old granola bar crumbs as I mutter under my breath, searching for the familiar loop of my lanyard.

Just as I'm about to give up and dump the whole thing out, a sharp creak cuts through the silence behind me.

I freeze.

My breath catches, fingers tightening around the edge of my bag as a chill creeps up my spine. I don't move. I just listen—eyes scanning the murky corners the overhead lights don't quite reach. Another groan follows, quieter this time. My heart stutters, pounding harder now as I straighten up slowly. I glance behind me, every muscle tensed. Nothing. No movement, no voices, just that familiar hum of cheap fluorescent lights and the faint echo of my own breath.

I swallow hard and exhale slowly, trying to will my pulse back into something manageable. "Jesus," I mutter, my voice low and unsteady. "It's just an old building. You've lived here for how long now?"

And then, like some horror movie timing joke, a sudden blur darts out from the far end of the hallway.

I let out a sharp gasp, practically leaping back against the wall as a small tabby cat streaks past me, its tail flicking like a whip as it bolts down the stairs that I had just come from. My heart slams against my ribs so hard it hurts, and I let out a breathless, shaky laugh.

"A cat," I whisper to myself. "I almost had a heart attack over a fucking cat." Still rattled, I bend down and yank my red and blue university lanyard out of the bag. My hands are trembling as the keys jingle in my grip. I rise slowly, eyes darting back toward the hallway, just in case.

It's quiet again.

I step forward quickly, not wanting to give my brain any more time to spiral, and make it to my door. The key sticks like it always does, and I jiggle it until I hear the deadbolt finally give way with a dull click. I shove the door open and pause, one foot inside, one still in the hallway.

Just one more glance. I can't help it.

I look back down the corridor, eyes lingering on the edges, the shadows, the places where sound shouldn't come from. Everything looks normal. But that doesn't stop my skin from crawling.

Finally, I step inside and shut the door behind me, the click of the lock oddly satisfying. I flip the deadbolt and slide the chain into place for good measure. Just the sound of it settling into the track makes me feel a little safer, a little more in control.

I turn away from the door and reach for the light switch. With a soft click, a warm, golden glow spills across the living room, stretching over the worn-out, eggshell-colored couch, the cluttered coffee table, and the stack of dishes I still haven't dealt with in the kitchen. The tension that's been coiled in my shoulders since I stepped into the stairwell loosens just a little. I let out a long breath and feel my body sag with it, like I've been holding it all in without realizing.

"Meow!"

I don't even have time to set my bag down before Calypso, my chubby calico cat, trots over, tail high, weaving eagerly between my legs. Her steps are nearly silent on the hardwood, but her meows are anything but subtle, and they bring a much-needed smile to my face.

"There you are," I murmur, crouching to scoop her up. She's warm, soft, and smells faintly like clean linen—probably from her favorite spot in the laundry pile I have yet to fold. I bury my face into her fur, breathing her in like a comfort I didn't know I needed until now.

"Hi, Calypso," I whisper, pressing a kiss to the top of her head. She purrs loudly, already licking my cheek with that gritty little tongue of hers. I laugh softly and set her down, giving her one last scratch behind the ears before she rubs against my calf and trots a few steps ahead, clearly not done with our quality time.

I toss my hoodie onto the arm of the couch, partly covering the spot Calypso's shredded with her claws, then kick off my boots and shrug my bag from my shoulders, dropping it beside the coffee table with a soft thud. Calypso trails me as I make my way down the narrow hallway, meowing like I've been gone for days instead of hours, and when I don't scoop her up, her protests only get louder.

"You're so needy," I chuckle, bending down to stroke her back. She presses into my hand as I reach for my bedroom door, twisting the knob and nudging it open with my shoulder.

I trail my fingers along the wall until they find the switch. A soft click, and warm light spills across the room, revealing its usual chaos—blankets tangled halfway off the bed, laundry overflowing from the hamper, and a pink glittery dildo perched unapologetically atop a stack of smutty romance books on the nightstand.

Calypso glides in ahead of me, her tail swaying with lazy confidence as she hops onto the bed without hesitation. She makes a beeline for my pillow, circles twice, then flops down like royalty returning to her throne. The purring starts almost instantly.

"Of course," I mutter, smiling despite myself. "I sleep there, you know."

She doesn't care. She never does.

But before I can move to shoo her off, a sudden chill brushes across my bare shoulders—cool, sharp, unexpected. I freeze, a ripple of unease crawling down my spine. My eyes snap to the window across the room.

The dark purple curtains sway gently in the breeze, shifting in slow, uneven waves that stir the quiet room. They brush against the wall, and the blinds behind them tap lowly against the pane, just enough to catch my attention. Just enough to make my stomach tighten.

The window's open.

But I don't remember leaving it open.

Goosebumps ripple down my arms as I cross the room, each step heavier than it should be. My fingers brush the curtain's edge, and I ease it aside, leaning close to peer out. I duck my head out and glance around.

The balcony is empty. Just my old lawn chair, its fabric so frayed and torn it's practically begging me to finally throw it away. A chipped coffee cup—which I forgot to bring inside—sits abandoned on the concrete, filled to the rim with old coffee and rainwater from the storm this afternoon. The thin, rust-speckled railing lines the edge of the narrow platform, offering absolutely zero comfort or sense of safety. The fire escape ladder is pulled up and secured in place, waiting to be lowered when needed.

I scan the street below next. A few cars are parked along the curb, their windshields reflecting faint streaks of yellow from the nearest streetlamp. Around the corner, headlights glow in the distance, but there's no movement. No figures standing in the shadows. Nothing looks out of place.

But something *feels* out of place.

There's a weight in my chest I can't quite name—a slow-building pressure, like someone is pressing their palm against my sternum from the inside out. My hands grip the windowsill as I linger longer than I need to. I can very clearly see that no one is lurking on my damn balcony, but still, the feeling doesn't dissipate.

I pull back inside and shove the window closed harder

than I mean to. The loud *clack* of the glass and frame slamming together makes me jump—and it startles Calypso too. She hisses from the bed, bolting upright with a flick of her tail, clearly offended.

"Sorry, baby," I murmur, securing the window lock with a sharp *click*. My fingers linger on the latch for a second longer than necessary before I finally draw the curtains shut, the fabric falling still against the wall.

Maybe I did leave it open. Maybe I was in too much of a rush this morning and forgot. Or perhaps it's just my nerves being… my nerves.

I stand there momentarily, staring at the closed curtains, my hand still resting on the fabric like I'm waiting for something else to happen. But the apartment is still again, and Calypso has already returned to her loaf position on my pillow, her tail flicking lazily as she settles.

Shaking the feeling off, I run a hand down my face, dragging the lingering tension with it. "It's nothing," I whisper to myself. "You're just tired."

And I am. My entire body feels like it's moving on a delay—like I'm wading through mud, and every step is just a second too slow. My thoughts are hazy, and I can't tell if I'm just exhausted or if the unease from earlier is still hanging on, pressing down behind my eyes. Probably both.

Definitely both.

All I want to do is rip off my tank top and leggings, faceplant into my bed, and disappear into sleep. But as if on cue, my stomach lets out a loud, miserable growl, echoing through the quiet apartment.

So much for collapsing into bed.

I glance over at Calypso, still curled on my pillow like she's the one who paid rent this month. "You hungry, baby?" I ask, my voice softer now. She lifts her head, stretches out her chunky little body with a satisfied groan, then hops down from the bed in one graceful leap.

She trots ahead, tail flicking as if to say, *finally*, and I follow her out into the dim hallway. We make our way into the kitchen, and I pick up her food bowl from the floor before flipping the overhead light on. The soft glow floods the space, illuminating my overflowing sink, a counter cluttered with several boxes of food—their contents long gone—unopened mail, and a half-drunk coffee I never finished this morning.

I sigh, setting Calypso's bowl on the counter before moving to the pantry. I scan the shelves, eyes skimming past cans of soup, a half-eaten, forgotten bag of stale Great Value mini marshmallows, two boxes of Kraft Mac and Cheese, and a box of Cinnamon Toast Crunch cereal. I've already had mac and cheese three times this week, and I'm out of frozen dinners, so cereal will have to do. It's the only thing that sounds remotely appetizing tonight.

I grab the cereal and a can of chicken-flavored Friskies off the bottom shelf for Calypso and set both on the counter. She immediately starts meowing like she hasn't eaten in a week, her little paws kneading at my leg as I pop the lid off the can.

"Chill, Caly," I mumble, wrinkling my nose at the smell. "It's coming."

I dump the wet food into her bowl, the slop hitting the dish with a wet *plop* that makes me grimace. She doesn't wait. As soon as I set it down by her water dish, she dives in with all the grace of a raccoon in a trash can. I can't help but laugh softly as she inhales her food.

Another loud, angry growl rips through my stomach, cutting through the quiet and reminding me (loud and clear) that I still haven't eaten. I sigh, turn away from Calypso, and curse under my breath.

Every *single* bowl I fucking own is piled in the basin, teetering dangerously like a Jenga tower of bad decisions and laziness.

I stare at it for a second, weighing my options. I could do the responsible thing and finally wash all of them… or I could do the bare minimum and pretend I'll handle the rest tomorrow.

Bare minimum wins in the end. Shocker.

I grab the least offensive-looking bowl and a spoon from the mountain of ceramic shame, then snatch my Scrub Daddy (that has seen better days) and the bottle of Honey Berry Hula-scented Gain dish soap from the corner of the sink. The scent is the only cheerful thing about this situation. I scrub until the dried-on cereal from a few days ago finally surrenders and rinse the bowl clean, followed by the spoon.

Once satisfied, I set them down next to the box of Cinnamon Toast Crunch, which was waiting on the counter, then tear the last few sheets off the paper towel roll. I dry everything halfheartedly (bowl, spoon, and hands) before balling the damp towel and tossing it toward the overflowing trash can like I'm shooting a free throw.

It bounces off the rim and lands on the floor, rolling a few feet away from the can. Of course it does.

I shrug. Whatever. I'll take the trash out in the morning. Maybe. Probably not. We'll see.

I pour a generous amount of cereal into the bowl, and the sweet smell of cinnamon and sugar immediately triggers another rumble in my gut. I pop a few pieces into my mouth straight from the bowl, then pivot toward the fridge to grab the milk.

Just as I'm reaching for the handle, my phone rings.

I pause, letting the fridge door fall shut with a soft thud; the condiments in the door rattle when it closes. I slide my phone out of my back pocket and glance at the screen. *Unknown Caller* flashes on the screen. I hesitate for a second, thumb hovering over the red button, but curiosity gets the better of me.

I press the green one instead, then balance my phone between my ear and shoulder as I reopen the fridge to get the milk.

"Hello?" I say, drawing the word out slightly, already bracing for a spam call—or worse, someone asking about my car's extended warranty.

Static.

I set the milk down on the counter, confused by the silence, and pull the phone away from my ear to glance at the screen. The call's still connected, the seconds ticking upward. I press the phone back to my ear, my brows furrowing.

"Hello?" I repeat sharply, impatience bleeding into my voice.

Still nothing. Just silence—an uncomfortable, almost intentional kind.

I wait another beat, tension creeping into my shoulders. "Who is this?" I ask, speaking louder this time, already annoyed at myself for bothering to engage. I start to lower the phone from my ear, ready to end the call and move on, when I hear it.

Heavy breathing, slow and deliberate, fills the silence.

My skin prickles, goosebumps forming on my arms as unease twists through my gut. Anger quickly overtakes the initial flash of anxiety.

"Piss off, whoever this is. This isn't funny," I snap, irritation slicing my words.

The breathing continues, unchanging, and my irritation deepens into disgust.

I jab my finger hard against the screen, ending the call before tossing the phone roughly onto the counter. "Asshole," I mutter under my breath, shaking my head to dismiss the lingering chill at the base of my spine. But that's what I get for answering unknown calls.

I grab the milk again and pour it hastily into my cereal bowl, some splashing over the edge onto the counter. *Great. Just what I needed.* With another irritated sigh, I shove the milk back into the fridge, kicking the door shut with my heel. I swipe the bowl off the counter, milk dripping down one side as I head toward the living room.

I glance back at my phone one last time before leaving the kitchen, half-expecting it to light up again. It stays dark and silent. Good. Hopefully, whoever the hell that was got the hint.

I set my bowl down on the cluttered coffee table and fish around for the Roku remote, finally spotting it partially hidden beneath an old notebook, another stack of mail, and a half-eaten bag of Salsa Verde Doritos. Dropping onto the loveseat, I tuck my legs under me and set the remote in my lap as I reclaim the bowl, spooning a generous bite of cereal into my mouth. Cinnamon and sugar explode across my tongue, briefly calming my jittery nerves. I take another bite, then turn on the television and click Netflix.

I scroll idly through the app, barely registering the titles flicking past, before I spot *Supernatural* and select it without hesitation. It's my comfort show. I always feel better when watching my boys.

"What season tonight, Calypso?" I ask absently, glancing toward the kitchen as Calypso wanders into the living room. She jumps gracefully onto the back of the couch and stretches out behind me before kneading my hair.

I chuckle quietly, reach behind me, and scratch gently behind her ears. "How 'bout season three?" Calypso purrs loudly in agreement, settling comfortably as I click on season three and hit play on the first episode.

I'm barely five minutes into the episode when my phone buzzes again, sharp and intrusive from somewhere in the kitchen. The upbeat tones of "Final Girl" by PI3RCE cut through the dialogue between Sam and Bobby, right in the middle of a conversation about Sam's obsession with breaking Dean's demon deal.

I sigh and pause the episode, eyes narrowing toward the kitchen like I can glare the sound into silence. My brows pinch as I debate whether it's worth checking. After a beat, I shake my head. Whoever it is can wait. I'm officially done with mystery callers tonight.

I unpause the episode and crank the volume a little higher, loud enough to drown out any other noise trying to get my attention.

But barely another minute passes before my phone starts again, this time rapidly chiming with multiple text alerts in quick succession. Annoyed, I groan loudly, slamming the remote down beside me on the couch.

"Seriously?" I mutter, irritation sharpening my voice as I shove myself up off the cushions. "This better be good."

I march back to the kitchen, cereal forgotten on the coffee table. Snatching my phone off the counter, my stomach tightens when I see messages from Unknown plastered across the screen. A prickle of apprehension runs down my spine as I unlock my phone, quickly tapping open the text alert.

My stomach drops as I read the messages, one after another.

UNKNOWN:

Have you ever felt that subtle, creeping sensation prickling along your spine, that someone's unseen gaze is fixed on you?

You should listen to that feeling.

You put all that effort into locking your doors and windows. Such a waste of time.

I found a way inside long before you ever realized something was wrong.

You're going to look real pretty in red, I can already picture it.

My breath catches sharply in my throat, and my heart starts beating a frantic rhythm in my chest as I stare down at the messages. I read them once, then twice, my eyes darting across each word, desperately searching for some sign that this isn't real—that it's just some twisted prank from someone with a messed-up sense of humor.

But even as I tell myself that, unease tightens around me like a vice. The apartment suddenly feels too quiet, too still, the walls pressing closer than they did a few seconds ago. My stomach knots uncomfortably, dread pooling deep inside me.

Who the hell is this?

With trembling fingers, I open the message app again, thumbs hovering uncertainly over the screen. My thoughts race, panic clouding my head. Should I even reply? Am I just giving them exactly what they want by engaging with them?

But I have to know. I *have* to know if it's a sick joke or something more serious.

Taking a shaky breath, I force myself to type, my thumbs stumbling awkwardly over the keyboard as the words appear on the screen:

ME:

Who is this? What do you want from me?

My finger hovers over the send button, hesitating. Then, heart hammering against my ribs, I press send and hold my breath, waiting.

Instant regret washes over me as several more messages quickly flash across the screen.

UNKNOWN:

I want to carve out your insides and paint the walls with your blood.

My knife will look real nice coated in your blood.

A sob catches in my throat as I hastily dial 911, my hands trembling as I press each button.

Calypso hissing and growling snaps my attention away from the phone as the operator answers. My heart jolts painfully in my chest, and I whip around, eyes landing on

Calypso, crouched low, ears pinned back, and the hair on her back raised as she faces the living room.

Then my gaze shifts, following hers, and the world seems to freeze.

A dark figure stands motionless in the center of my living room, silhouetted by the dim glow of the hallway light behind it. The closet door hangs wide open behind the intruder, shadows spilling out like ink.

"Oh god," I choke out, my voice strangled, barely audible.

My whole body trembles violently, knees going weak as I stumble backward, pressing myself flat against the kitchen doorframe. Fear rushes through me, cold and consuming, locking me in place as I stare at the faceless shape in my home.

The large figure stands rigid, its head tilted slightly to the side, as if it's curious or fascinated by my terror. The expressionless white mask glows faintly under the dim lighting, cold and emotionless, sending ice racing through my veins.

"911, can you state your emergency?" The operator's voice crackles urgently through my phone, distant and muffled by the roar of blood pounding in my ears.

My gaze drops from that empty mask to the glinting blade hanging loosely beside the intruder's thigh. Panic floods my chest, squeezing the air from my lungs. The knife shines ominously, catching the dim glow of my television, its sharp edge gleaming like a promise.

"Hello? If you need help, say something, or press a key," the operator says, their calm voice sharply contrasting with the nightmare unfolding before me.

My breath comes in shallow, desperate gasps. All I can manage is a strangled whimper as the intruder slowly—deliberately—raises the blade, pointing it toward me like a silent threat.

"H-help," I choke out, the word barely audible, breaking into fragments as terror overwhelms me.

My hand goes limp, and the phone slips through my trembling fingers, clattering loudly against the wood floor. The sound echoes through the sudden silence.

My only lifeline skids just out of reach.

Screams erupt from my throat, and without a second thought, I turn towards the front door and attempt to open it, forgetting that I had put the chain in place. "SHIT!" I cry out as I fumble with the chain, sliding it halfway before I'm grabbed from behind, a gloved hand pressing firmly against my mouth to silence the scream that attempts to break loose. I thrash in the intruders' arms, muffled screams slipping past the hand.

"Shush," they whisper-growl harshly into my ear as a long and serrated hunting knife moves into my view, the tip pointed at my chest.

"P-please!" I cry out, my plea stifled beneath the glove. Tears roll down my cheeks as I catch a distorted view of the intruders and my reflection in the blade.

"It will all be over soon," the intruder's low voice growls in my ear again, followed by a dark chuckle. I continue to thrash and claw at the hand as they raise the blade several inches off my chest.

"Please, no!" I cry out as the intruder swings the blade down, missing their mark and instead driving it deep into my shoulder.

Another scream erupts as searing pain tears through me. The blade digs into my clavicle as it is pushed deeper into my shoulder. The intruder's grip on me loosens, and I drop to the floor, the blade still embedded in my shoulder. Tears continue to flow down my cheeks as I reach for the knife's handle, my fingers wrapping around it. But before I can pull it out, the intruder kneels into me, their knee digging into my stomach as they wrap their fingers around the handle tightly, crushing my fingers with a bruising force before quickly ripping the blade out of my shoulder, blood splattering against the white mask.

I let out another bloodcurdling scream upon its removal; however, my screams are cut short when the blade is once again driven into me, this time dead center between my breasts. Blood rises into my throat. I gag and cough, spitting blood as the knife is ripped out again, only for it to be driven into my body several times more.

The distant wail of sirens, the terrified scream of my cat, and the sickening sound of my own flesh tearing are the last things I register before the world around me dissolves into darkness.

Del
F12
PgUp
PgDn
Home
End

ONE
RAELYNN

TWO WEEKS EARLIER

THE DISTANT BLARE of car horns and the rising wail of a siren slice through the last thread of sleep, pulling me into the day whether I'm ready or not. It isn't the soft, sunbeam-through-sheer-curtains wake-up I always imagine for the start of senior year—but then again, nothing about real life ever is. Still, it does the job.

I lie still for a moment, my heart fluttering with nerves, adrenaline already kicking in as if it knows today matters. My sheets are twisted around my calves, my pillow is hanging on for dear life at the edge of the mattress, and my brain is already buzzing—new professors, heavier course loads, internship hours to juggle, graduation dates circling closer every time I blink.

Senior year. My last first day. The words feel dreamlike and heavy at the same time.

I stare up at the ceiling and count four slow breaths, then four more, trying to iron out the tightness cinched beneath my collarbones that I can't quite name—part anticipation, part fear. I want to be excited, and I am, but it's the kind of excitement that comes with pressure. This year is everything. I need to finish strong. I need to prove to myself that I can do this—that all the late nights and breakdowns and doubts haven't been for nothing.

Rubbing my face, I try to push through the lingering haze in my head. It's not quite exhaustion—more like the buzz of a brain that never fully powered down. Nerves, probably. I barely slept, too keyed up thinking about today, about everything riding on this final year. I shift beneath the tangled covers, rubbing the grit of sleep from my eyes.

Thud.

The sound is sharp enough to jolt me fully awake, and I glance over the edge of the bed to see my forensic psych textbook, *The Criminal Mind*, sprawled across the hardwood like it dove for freedom. The cover is half open, pages crumpled, a few of my sticky notes fluttering loose like white flags of surrender. I'd been pre-reading it last night, trying to get ahead before classes officially start. Apparently, the book had other plans. It's not the first time it's launched itself off the bed mid-sleep, and at this rate, it probably won't be the last.

The noise startles Max, my black labrador, who had been passed out in a warm heap at the foot of the bed. His head jerks up fast, ears twitching and eyes wide with sleepy confusion. He lets out a low grumble, almost a growl, and shifts to look at me like he was asking: *What the hell was that for?*

"Easy, buddy," I murmur, reaching out to run my fingers gently over the top of his head.

His stiff posture eases as I scratch behind his ears, lazy circles that always seem to melt the tension right out of him. His eyes flutter half shut again, and he huffs softly through his nose before dropping his head back onto the blanket.

"Good boy," I whisper, barely loud enough to register in the quiet morning air.

Once his breathing evens out and his eyes close fully again, I lean over the edge of the bed and grab the book that startled him in the first place. The glossy black cover catches the faint morning light filtering through the blinds, giving it a cold, metallic gleam. Sometime in the middle of reading, I must have dozed off. It would explain the awkward position I woke up in and the ache in both my back and my neck.

Sighing, I sit back, thumbing through the dog-eared pages before tossing it onto my nightstand, where it lands with a soft *thunk* among a pile of half-used notebooks, pens missing their caps, granola bar wrappers, and a cup of tea from yesterday that I never finished.

I reach for my phone, which is partially buried beneath the crumpled edge of my pillow, and tap the screen with a sluggish thumb. The display flares to life, way too bright for my tired eyes. I squint at the numbers.

6:36 a.m.

Ugh. That awful in-between time—too late to justify falling back asleep, too early to face the day with anything resembling grace. I sigh through my nose and glance at the flood of unread notifications lighting up the top of the screen. Texts, emails, calendar reminders. All of it waiting to drag me back into reality.

I rub the heel of my palm against my eyes, chasing away the last wisps of sleep clinging to the edges of my mind. My phone slips from my hand and lands on the nightstand with a soft *clack*—less a surrender and more a momentary pause—just a breath before the rush.

For a few more seconds, I stay still, listening. The world outside is already stirring—muffled conversations drifting from cracked windows, engines rumbling to life, and the soft patter of leftover monsoon rain needling the glass. It's peaceful. I could stay buried under the covers a little longer, listening to the remnants of the yearly monsoon and let the warmth wrap around me like a shield—but not today.

Max stirs behind me, letting out a soft snore as he burrows deeper into the covers, completely unbothered by the world starting to spin around us. I glance over my shoulder and smile faintly. Must be nice.

I sit there for a moment, elbows resting on my knees, letting the cool air pull me fully into the present. The nerves are still there, tugging at the edges of my stomach, but they're wrapped in something steadier now. Something closer to purpose.

It would be so easy to crawl back under the covers, to let myself hide in the warmth for just a little longer. But I've waited too long for this day—this year. And I'm not going to miss a second of it.

Time to move.

With a soft groan, I grab the textbook off the nightstand and shuffle over to my desk, dragging my feet across the cold floor. The surface is a disaster zone—stray highlighters and uncapped pens scattered like confetti, balled-up Post-its with half-baked ideas, and a lineup of empty soda cans standing like a row of tiny, metallic tombstones.

My laptop is still sitting where I left it, propped open and waiting. I swipe the trackpad, and the screen glows to life—Ghostface stares back at me, blade raised, like he's daring me to survive another semester. It's dramatic, but fitting. He is my little tribute to the part of me that finds solace in horror, blood-splattered stories, and fictional psychopaths who probably need prison time.

I stack my laptop on top of my textbooks, my hand smoothing over the mosaic of peeling Dutch Bros stickers, dark romance quotes, and true crime decals that toe the line between quirky and concerning.

It's a strange, chaotic little collection—but it's mine. A reflection of the pieces that make me who I am: caffeine-driven, criminally curious, and entirely too invested in fictional morally gray (teetering toward morally black) men with knives.

I slide everything into the main pocket of my book bag, zip it closed, and rest my hands on top, fingers tapping a quiet rhythm as if my nerves are trying to find their beat. After a second, I take a breath and straighten up, rolling my shoulders back.

Today's going to be good. I can feel it.

I step away from the desk and circle around it, heading for the door. My hand finds the knob—I twist, pull, and yank it open. I barely have time to take a single step before Max launches off the bed like a missile. His paws hammer the hardwood, nails clicking frantically as he barrels past me in a blur of black fur.

"Max!" I call after him, but he's already halfway down the hall.

The rapid *click-click-click* of his nails against the hardwood echoes through the apartment, each step full of urgency. He doesn't hesitate or glance back—just makes a beeline for the front door, his nose pressed hard into the seam. He paws at the bottom corner, claws scratching against the base like he's trying to dig his way through.

The second I step into the living room, my eyes land on the chaos—and I mean *chaos*. It looks like a garbage can exploded in the middle of the apartment. Empty cans of Vanilla Coke and Mike's Hard Lemonade are scattered across the coffee table like confetti from a party we forgot to clean up. A Domino's box sits wide open, a single sad, half-eaten slice of pepperoni still inside, surrounded by a pile of discarded crusts like some kind of greasy pizza graveyard.

Tessa's signature move. She *always* leaves the crusts, and it drives me insane. I actually like the crust (love it, even), but I'd already inhaled four slices last night and figured five would officially launch me into food coma territory. Still, seeing them just sitting there, untouched, feels personal.

But it's the popcorn that takes the prize. There are pieces *everywhere*. In the cushions of our dark gray couch, under the table, even in the cone of the damn floor lamp. I told her to clean it up, especially since she's the one who flinched so hard during the first jump scare that she launched the entire bowl, scattering pieces like the timer ran out in the game of Perfection. But I should've known better. She probably ignored me on purpose. Her passive-aggressive revenge for forcing her to watch *Friday the 13th Part VI: Jason Lives* with me. Her version of a fuck you without saying a word.

Classic Tessa.

She's my complete opposite in every way, which makes it a minor miracle that we haven't killed each other. It could be that we've been friends since we were kids and her family took me in (which makes us more like sisters at this point), so we were already accustomed to each other's quirks, but still. She's bright and bubbly, sunshine in pastel floral Vans, always humming while she is painting or sketching something with her headphones in. Happy-go-lucky to a fault. She can't even *look* at fake blood without gagging, and yet somehow ended up best friends with a girl whose bookshelves are filled with serial killer profiles and forensic textbooks.

I'm the quiet one. The introvert. The girl who finds comfort in silence and studies murder for fun. Tessa can't go five minutes without background noise—and yet, she's the person who knows me best.

Don't ask me how it works. It just does.

I rub my temples, trying to stave off the headache already threatening to bloom behind my eyes. Between the disaster zone that used to be our living room, the four hours (give or take) of sleep I barely scraped together, and the lingering buzz of nerves still dancing under my skin, it's shaping up to be a *stellar* morning.

With a sigh, I tiptoe my way across the minefield of rogue popcorn kernels, doing my best not to crush them underfoot. They crunch *anyway*, of course, and I wince with each step like the sound is personally attacking me. I make it to the coffee table and reach down to scoop up a couple of empty cans, but

I barely touch the first one before Max lets out a sharp bark from behind me.

I glance over my shoulder to see him pacing near the door, tail wagging like crazy, nails tapping impatiently against the hardwood.

"Okay, okay, I hear you," I mutter, dropping the cans back onto the table with a metallic clatter. "God forbid the prince has to wait five more seconds to do his business."

Max barks again, louder this time, then scratches at the front door and spins in a tight circle like he's about to explode if I don't move now.

I give the mess one last glance—mentally adding it to the list of things Future Raelynn will deal with—then head to the door. I grab his leash off the hook beside the door and clip it to his collar, the container of doggy bags clinking against the chain. The second the clasp clicks, he's bouncing in place, nails skittering on the floor.

"Let's go, you bossy little shit." I chuckle softly.

The moment I crack the door, he lunges forward, dragging me into the humid morning.

The air outside is heavy with desert rain, thick with the sharp scent of creosote. It clings to my skin, sticky and electric, as if the storm still lingers in the atmosphere, waiting to crack open the sky again. The sidewalk steams faintly beneath the first hints of rising sun, and somewhere nearby a cicada buzzes like a live wire.

Max's tail wags like a propeller as he trots down the walkway, his nose glued to the concrete as he gets to work cataloging the universe. I let him do his perimeter checks—every bush, every patch of damp grass, the utility box that apparently holds dog secrets, until finally, he circles the little strip of gravel he considers his, squats, and handles business. When he finishes, I tear a bag free from the container and scoop it up. Holding the bag between two fingers, I toss it into a trash can as we circle back toward the apartment. The second we're inside, he's already pawing at me to unclip the leash.

"Hold on," I say, fiddling with the clasp.

The moment he is free from the leash, he rockets forward like he's been shot from a cannon. His destination is obvious before he even hits the coffee table—straight into the Domino's box.

"Max—don't you dare!" I shout, lunging after him.

Too late. His snout disappears into the box, tail wagging wildly in proud defiance as he inhales stale pepperoni like it's gourmet.

"Goddammit," I mutter as I wrestle the box away with a glare before he can devour the rest of Tessa's crust collection. He looks up at me with zero shame, licking his chops like *he* had a great start to the day. "You're lucky you're cute."

He lets out a happy huff and trots toward the couch like he owns the place. Which, honestly, he kind of does.

Max hops onto the couch and curls up against the arm while I begin to gather the stray cans. Behind me, the chorus to "Heads Will Roll" begins. Tessa's alarm clock. It plays for all of ten seconds before it is cut off. If I knew my best friend, she probably snoozed the fucker. Anything for a few extra minutes of sleep.

Rolling my eyes, I grab the last of the cans, balancing them inside the pizza box, and saunter into the kitchen. With my foot, I press on the pedal of the garbage can. The lid springs open, and I dump the cans and crusts into the half-full bin. Then I fold the pizza box in half and shove it in, compressing it and the rest of the trash to make room.

Next, I grab the broom propped against the wall beside the trash bin and return to the living room. Max is standing up on the couch, hoovering up popcorn pieces from the creases of the cushions. I don't stop him either. He's making my job easier; besides, I'm rather surprised he hadn't noticed the kernels before he laid down.

As Max continues cleaning the couch, I start sweeping the pieces off the floor. We barely got to eat the damn popcorn before Tessa threw it everywhere, and if I had let Max out, I probably wouldn't be sweeping up the mess right now. But Max is a menace when it comes to people's food. You can't eat in peace with him around. He will actively try to take whatever you are eating out of your hand. Unfortunately, I have not been able to train that out of him. The little shit learned that habit from his previous owner. So to avoid fighting off my dog, he lies in my room while we eat.

Roughly five minutes pass by, and the living room looks halfway decent. I still have to go in with a mop and some cleaning spray later, but right now it's okay. Max is back to lying down, snoring like he works full-time. I giggle softly as Tessa's alarm clock goes off again. It is shut off almost immediately.

"You better not have snoozed that shit again, Tess," I call out as I make my way into the hall and head toward her room. I press my ear to the door briefly, listening for any sign that Sleeping Beauty has risen.

Silence.

"Tessa Vaughn, I swear to God," I say, stifling a laugh as I throw open her bedroom door. "Bitch, get the fuck up," Amusement laces my voice as I glance toward the bed, where a lump is buried under a floral comforter, a tangle of fiery red hair peeking out.

"Fuck off," she mumbles sleepily from under the covers.

"Woman, get up. You've been hyped about the first day of classes for *weeks*," I say as I stride toward the bed. Without hesitation, I grab the end of her comforter and yank it off in one swift motion. Tessa lets out a dramatic squeal, scrambling to snatch it back but missing entirely. She flops into herself with a groan. "Maybe you shouldn't have downed half a six-pack of Mike's Hard Lemonade last night," I tease, balling the comforter in my arms like a prize.

An arm shoots up from the bed, her middle finger raised high.

"Right back at you," I shoot back, grinning when she drops her arm and finally sits up. Through the blanket-snatching commotion, I hadn't even noticed Tessa's disheveled appearance. "Tessa, fix your damn shirt," I say through giggles. At some point in the night, her red tank top had shifted, leaving her right breast completely exposed through the armhole, her nipple perked from the sudden chill. Tessa looks down and giggles before sliding her tank top back into place and smoothing it down. It does absolutely nothing to hide the hardened peaks.

"What time does your first class start, Rae?" Tessa asks as she grabs her round black wire-framed glasses off her nightstand and puts them on.

"Nine, but you know I like getting to campus early. I have this class with Austin, Khloe, and Marlena, and they also like getting there early."

Tessa nods and slips off the bed, adjusting her Winnie the Pooh sleep shorts so they are no longer bunched between her ass cheeks when she rises.

"What time does yours start?" I ask as I finally toss the comforter back onto the bed. Grabbing the end of the comforter again, I shake it out until it covers the bed—my half-assed attempt to make the bed for her.

"Nine thirty," she responds. "If you're making me go early, can we at least stop at Dutch Bros to grab some extra-large coffees? I'll pay."

A smile forms on my lips at the word coffee, and Dutch Bros Coffee is a definite need this morning, and I would never say no to free. "Yes, we can do that," I reply as Tess disappears into her closet.

"Cool. Now get out so I can get dressed," she orders.

I don't bother replying. Instead, I spin on my heel and walk out, shutting the door behind me with a soft click.

Before heading to my room to get dressed, I detour into the kitchen. I grab Max's bowl from the floor and set it on the counter, then open the pantry and pull out a can of Nutrish—Chicken and Veggies, his favorite.

The second the can cracks open, Max trots in like clockwork, tail swishing, eyes locked on his prize. I empty the food into his bowl and use the lid to break it up, the scent already making his nose twitch and drool dribble from his lips. I set the bowl on the floor, and he dives in without hesitation. Smiling, I give his head a quick pat and finally head to my room to get ready.

Another difference between Tessa and me is that she is organized. Everything has a place, and god forbid her clothes not be hung up. Meanwhile, my room is chaotic. My laundry is hardly ever hung up. My clean laundry perpetually sits on my lounge chair, while my dirty laundry overflows the basket. I absolutely hate doing laundry, but my procrastination always bites me in the ass when I go to find a pair of clean leggings, only to find there aren't any. Fortunately, I did laundry recently, and several pairs of leggings sit upon the mountain of clothes.

I grab a pair of black leggings off the top of the pile, digging carefully through the rest until I spot my red cold-shoulder top and tug it free. Both go onto the bed with a lazy toss. Then it's back into the chaos—my hand diving into the mountain of laundry in search of a clean pair of panties and whatever socks I can scavenge, matching or not.

A few minutes of rummaging later (after nearly knocking the whole pile to the floor), I manage to pull out a pair of plain black panties and, miraculously, a matched set of socks. The miracle is slightly less impressive when I remember I bought half a dozen pairs of the same Walmart dollar-bin socks—blue, with little cats and coffee cups.

I toss the underwear onto the bed and peel off my pajamas, slipping them off along with yesterday's panties. Then I reach for my favorite bra, still draped casually over the back of my desk chair. It's black, soft, wire-free, with delicate lace stitching across the cups. Comfortable and cute—what more could I want?

I clip it in place, adjust the straps, and slide the panties on. Then come the leggings, which I shimmy into with practiced ease, followed by the top. I pull it over my head, smoothing it out, and sit on the edge of the bed to tug on the socks.

Once those are on, I reach for my combat boots and drag them closer with my toes. I lace them up fast—muscle memory by now—then get to my feet and head toward my vanity dresser.

It's the first time I've seen my reflection today, and… yikes.

I look like shit.

The bags under my eyes look even worse against my fair skin and emerald eyes—darker, more pronounced, like little bruises from another restless night. My hair's doing whatever it wants, wild and slightly frizzy, and the haze of not enough sleep clings to my face like fog. No surprise there. My circadian rhythm is trash. I stay up too late, wake up too early, and keep pretending I'm built for it.

Spoiler alert: I'm not.

But hey—I'm dressed. That's half the battle, right?

I sigh and glance at my reflection one last time. "Definitely going to need Tessa's concealer," I mutter to myself.

Grabbing my brush off the dresser, I pull it through the tangles of my dark brown hair until it looks less like a bird's nest and more like intentional chaos. Once satisfied, I set the brush down, scoop my phone off the nightstand, and head for the hallway.

"Hey, Tess?" I call out, knocking lightly on her bedroom door.

"Come in!" she replies.

I push the door open to find her sitting on the edge of her bed, tying the laces of her pastel floral Vans. She's dressed in her usual sunshine-in-human-form vibe—white frayed shorts and a baby blue blouse dotted with tiny purple flowers. Her hair is twisted into a bun, held in place with a clean paint-brush stabbed right through the center.

"What's up?" she asks, finishing one shoe and lifting her other foot to start on the next.

"Can I borrow your concealer?" I ask, already anticipating her answer.

Tessa glances up with a soft smile, her turquoise eyes bright behind the black frames of her glasses. Her lips are tinted a slightly darker shade of pink. She never goes full glam, never covers up the constellation of light freckles scattered across her cheeks. Just mascara, a dab of concealer here and there, and that signature lip tint she swears is magic. Tessa's always been about enhancing what's already there—natural beauty with a little edge.

"Of course." She rises to her feet, smooths her blouse, then glides across the room to where she keeps her makeup—a little wicker basket on top of her dresser. "Want me to help you put it on? I can also braid your hair if you want; it looks a little frizzy today," she says as she plucks the small bottle of concealer from the basket.

A smile forms on my lips as she walks over to me. "I'd love that."

Tessa doesn't bother hiding her excitement and immediately shoves me down into her desk chair. "How much time do we have before we absolutely have to leave?" She sets the concealer down on the desk and drags her fingers through my hair, snagging on a few stubborn knots that have me wincing.

"Uh," I mutter, tapping the screen of my phone. The lock screen lights up, revealing a shirtless guy in a Ghostface mask, caught mid-stride with a machete in hand—equal parts horror and thirst trap, frozen in pure chaotic kink. I avert my eyes from the image and glance at the clock at the top of the screen instead.

7:43 a.m.

"About forty-five minutes, why?" I ask, drawing out the word.

"I was thinking a French braid would look cute and that shit takes a minute," she says as she toys with a strand of my hair.

I was starting to regret letting her do my hair, but there was no turning back now. "Fine, but hurry. You're cutting into coffee time," I say as she begins the braid.

"I'll be quick. I promise," she reassures me.

Thankfully, she kept to her word. She was quick. Several *hair-pulling* minutes later, Tessa spins the chair around so that I am facing her and fluffs her work before reaching for the concealer. "It's a good thing we share a similar skin tone," she muses as she applies it to my under eyes.

It takes a couple of coats to *truly* hide the deep-set bags, but when she is finally done, I look as normal as can be. The purple bruising still pokes through the layers, but not enough that anyone will notice.

My hair definitely looks better and more contained now that it's braided and no longer a frizzy mess. "Thanks, Tess," I say warmly, turning away from my reflection.

"No problem, babe," she replies, her lips curled into a bright smile, dimples and all. "You ready to go?"

I nod. Coffee was calling me by my full government name.

TWO
RAELYNN

IT WAS JUST after eight thirty when Tessa and I finally pulled into the Highland Avenue parking garage, and closer to eight forty-five by the time we stepped into the heart of campus. The university is already wide awake—buzzing, crowded, and pulsing with that chaotic energy unique to the start of a new semester.

That early-semester buzz hangs thick in the air. Cars crawl through the traffic loop like they are wading through syrup, hazard lights blinking in frustration. Students weave between bumpers and each other, book bags thumping against their spines like metronomes, iced coffees gripped like lifelines, the plastic sweating in the rising heat. The sidewalks are flooded with motion—everyone headed somewhere, but most look like they aren't entirely sure where that is.

The real chaos comes from the freshmen and transfers—faces full of hope and confusion, their confidence already cracking under the weight of real schedules and actual campus sprawl. Some cling to printed maps as if they are sacred texts. Others walk in hesitant zigzags, eyes glued to campus apps, trying to make the little blue dot point them in the right direction. A few have already surrendered and huddled at the temporary info booths scattered across the quad, looking for someone, *anyone*, to point them in the right direction.

I remember that feeling all too well. That overwhelming cocktail of excitement and dread, adrenaline tangled with uncertainty. Everything felt too big, too fast, and way too easy to mess up. I spent my first week terrified I'd end up in the wrong class or miss a building entirely.

It's nostalgic now… in that mildly traumatic, *I-survived-so-it's-fine* kind of way.

Sometimes I wonder what my parents would think if they could see me now—

my last year of school, inching toward a career in law enforcement, I never got the chance to tell them about.

I still catch myself imagining their reactions, the advice they might've given, the pride I hope they would've felt.

It's a quiet ache, imagining the words I never said and the moments that never came.

Wistfulness is all I have of it now, those almost-memories sitting in the spaces where real ones should've been.

I take a long sip from my Dutch Bros, draining the rest of the crafted blend of hazelnut and Irish cream, and toss the cup into a nearby trash receptacle. "I will see you later, Tess," I say, briefly turning towards her.

"We're still on for lunch?" She takes another sip from her coffee.

"Of course. I will probably extend an invite to the others, though."

"I figured you would," she says, her lips curling into a smile.

"I'll see you later, babes." I smile in return and start towards the Koffler Building, where my Criminology class is held.

Palms stand at attention along the walkway, tall and sparse, tossing narrow shadows that miss you by inches. Beds of brittlebush and agave shoulder the paths, gravel raked into tidy ripples around them. Bikes blur past in tight zips—thin tires whispering—while skateboard wheels chatter over expansion joints. Someone's blasting indie pop from a Bluetooth speaker; another circle of students practices a clumsy hacky sack routine between backpacks.

I half-jog up the steps to the building, dodging a guy with headphones who's somehow taking up the entire staircase. Reaching the lecture hall door, I grab the handle, yank it open, and slip inside as quietly as possible, though the creak of the hinge still sounds way too loud in the half-lit room.

Showing up ten minutes before class might *sound* like good timing, but in reality? It's a rookie move—especially when it comes to seat selection. I'm one of those students with very specific preferences: not front row, where you're in direct line of fire for eye contact and pop questions, but definitely not dead center either, where you're boxed in on all sides and stuck for the duration. No, I like the sweet spot—just a few rows back, near the aisle. Easy in, easy out. Prime real estate.

But with time slipping through my fingers this morning, I already know those seats are long gone.

It's not a massive space, maybe two hundred seats at most. Cozy compared to the cavernous lecture hall I had for Economics last year, which housed five hundred students and felt like a full-blown stadium. This room, at least, feels slightly more manageable, even if it's already buzzing with energy and low-level panic.

I pause just inside, scanning the rows for a familiar face. For a few seconds, all I see are strangers—some hunched over their phones, some flipping through syllabi like they've already accepted academic defeat, and others whispering to each other with that awkward, *first-day-small-talk* energy.

Then I spot them.

Halfway up the tiered seating, three blondes clustered right in that ideal zone I would've claimed for myself. Relief rushes through me like a deep breath I hadn't realized I was holding. I weave my way up the aisle, careful not to knock over anyone's coffee or bump a laptop with my bag.

"Khloe!" I call out, just loud enough to cut through the ambient chatter.

Khloe Wilson turns to the call of her name, and her baby blue eyes light up when she sees me, her lips curling into a big, glossy, pink grin. Her dirty blonde hair is tied up into a high ponytail, complete with a red bow studded with clear rhinestones. Her sunglasses sit perched on top of her head, and she is wearing a red university tank top featuring the university's mascot—a wildcat—frayed denim shorts, and red Converse sneakers. Her whole vibe screams school spirit and confidence.

"Rae!" she squeals, like we haven't seen each other in a year instead of just a few weeks. Her voice draws the attention of the other two sitting with her, Austin Whitmore and Marlena Beckett, the inseparable couple of our group. High school sweethearts. Disgustingly adorable. Practically married.

Marlena stands to greet me; her platinum hair is pulled into two pigtails, with a small section of hair pulled forward to frame her face. She's wearing a pale pink summer dress, girly and casual all at once, and somehow not wrinkled at all, which I respect because I woke up barely holding my life together. I haven't seen her or Khloe since right after my birthday in June—life got busy, and our schedules never lined up.

Austin flashes me a smile from his seat. He runs a hand through his mess of blonde curls, then adjusts the gray t-shirt tucked into the waistband of his jeans. A black cowboy boot pokes out beneath the hem as he stretches his leg into the aisle and props open his laptop like he owns the place—which, to be fair, is kind of his vibe.

I drop my book bag on the floor and hug both girls quickly before settling into the seat next to them, just in time for the professor to walk in.

"Tessa and I are grabbing lunch at the Cactus Grill later," I whisper as I fish out my laptop. "You guys should come."

"What time?" Austin asks in his thick southern accent, already slouched deep into his seat.

"After her second class. She gets out around 12:50, so... one?"

"That works for me," he says, glancing at the girls. Marlena and Khloe nod in agreement.

"Sweet," I reply, finally flipping open my laptop. The screen lights up, and I take a breath, settling in.

Silence settles over the lecture hall as the professor finishes setting up his PowerPoint. His black hair, streaked with gray, is neatly slicked back. He's dressed in a white button-up shirt with the sleeves rolled to his elbows, revealing an array of black and gray tattoos on both arms; the designs are indistinguishable from where I sit. Black-rimmed glasses frame his face, and a short, neatly trimmed beard, stippled with gray, sharpens the angles of his jaw.

"Good morning and welcome to Criminology 101. I'm Professor Mark Henley," he begins, stepping away from the podium with his hands tucked casually into the pockets of his black dress pants. His voice carries easily across the room—calm, steady, but commanding. "This course is designed to provide you with a rigorous, analytical exploration of crime and criminal behavior—grounded in theory, informed by empirical research, and relevant to contemporary issues within the criminal justice system. As upper-division students, you're expected to go beyond surface-level understanding."

He scans the room as he speaks, pulling a clicker from his pocket and advancing to the next slide. His eyes flick briefly to the screen before returning to us.

"This semester, we'll examine the structural, social, psychological, and economic forces that influence criminal behavior. We'll also critique how society defines, manages, and responds to crime. Our discussions will cover major theoretical frameworks, policy debates, and ongoing challenges within law enforcement, the courts, and the correctional system. This is not an easy subject. It requires you to confront difficult truths—not just about crime, but about power, inequality, and the systems built to maintain them."

For a moment, he lets that sit, then continues. "You are expected to engage critically, read consistently, and contribute thoughtfully. My role is not to provide answers but to challenge your thinking and help you develop the tools to analyze complex issues through a criminological lens. If you put in the work, this course won't just broaden your academic perspective—it'll prepare you for real-world application, whether you're headed toward law enforcement, research, policy, or public service."

He scans the room again and offers the smallest smile. "Let's get started, shall we?"

Returning to the podium, he clicks the next slide and raises his eyebrows slightly. "Can I get a volunteer to tell me, in your own words, why criminology is important in criminal justice?"

Several hands go up—including mine.

His gaze lands on me, and he gestures. "Yes—you."

"Criminology is important in criminal justice because it helps us understand the underlying causes of criminal behavior, not just the behavior itself," I say, sitting a little straighter. "It gives us a framework to analyze patterns, social influences, and systemic issues that contribute to crime. By studying criminology, we can develop more effective prevention strategies, enhance rehabilitation approaches, and create evidence-based policies that extend beyond punishment. It connects theory to practice in a way that's essential for meaningful change."

There's a pause before he nods. "Perfect. Thank you…?"

"Raelynn Carson, sir."

"Thank you, Raelynn," he says, his eyes lingering just for a brief moment before turning back to the screen and resuming the lecture.

An hour and fifteen minutes later, the class finally wraps up. Most professors let students out early during the first week, giving them a chance to ease into things and make a good impression. Not Henley. He used every single second of the period, driving home the significance of criminology and the subfields we'd be diving into this semester. He didn't just touch on theory—he went deep, listing categories, cross-disciplines, and case types. Then came the semester-long research paper: choose a well-known case and analyze it through the lens of a criminological subgenre.

Lucky for me, I already know what I'm doing.

After dismissing us, Henley stays behind to field questions from a few eager students. I pack up my things slowly, half-listening to the background chatter as he gathers his materials, slips his laptop into a worn leather messenger bag, and exits quietly through the side door.

"Okay, be honest," Khloe blurts, breaking the silence as we close our laptops and shove notebooks into our bags. "Did anyone else completely zone out every time Professor Henley spoke, or was that just me? Because… *damn*. That man is ridiculously hot."

I raise an eyebrow as I zip my bag. "You were supposed to be paying attention, not imagining him shirtless."

Khloe shrugs with zero shame. "I can multitask."

Marlena giggles, nudging Austin with her elbow. "Yeah, he's hot, I'll give you that. But soooo not my type. Too serious. He looks like he drinks black coffee and judges your music taste."

Austin smirks, sliding an arm around her waist. "Maybe,

but I couldn't help noticing he kept looking our way. More specifically, at Rae."

I freeze mid-motion, my brows knitting together. "What? Me? Why would he be looking at me?"

"You *did* answer his question like a total badass," Marlena points out, slinging her bag over her shoulder. "Confident, articulate—very *main character* energy."

"So what?" I scoff, but there's a flush creeping up my neck that betrays me. "I just answered a question. It's not that deep."

Khloe smirks like a cat with a secret. "Or maybe he thought *you* were hot, too, Rae. Did you see the way he looked at you? Intense."

"God, I highly doubt that," I mutter before slipping my arms into the straps of my bag.

"You can't tell me the idea of hot, forbidden sex with Professor Henley doesn't do it for you," Khloe teases as we step out into the sunlight. "I've seen your bookshelf. I *know* what you read."

I shoot her a halfhearted glare. Okay—yes, I've read more than a few professor-student dark romances. But real life? Hell to the fucking no.

"No. Just—*no*," I say firmly, shaking my head.

Khloe and Marlena burst into another fit of laughter as they skip down the steps, as if they didn't have a care in the world. This time, I *do* roll my eyes and let it happen.

We head across the quad, weaving between clusters of students taking back-to-school selfies, tabling campus ministries, and one guy aggressively handing out flyers for some back-to-school party.

Khloe loops her arm through mine as we head toward the quad. "So, if not Henley, who *is* your type? Don't say fictional serial killers again."

"I said morally gray men with knives. There's a difference," I deadpan.

"Not much of one," Khloe teases.

Austin snorts behind us. "You know, most people go for, like… firefighters. Guys with dogs. Not ones with body counts."

"I *like* complexity," I say with a shrug, smirking. "And fictional is the key word. Real murderers are not hot. They're just… murder-y."

"God, please put that on a t-shirt," Marlena laughs. "*Not hot, just murder-y.*"

Khloe pulls her sunglasses down dramatically. "Okay, but if Professor Henley asked you to stay after class to 'discuss your paper' and closed the door behind him… you'd stay."

I pretend to think. "Yeah, and then I'd text you my location in case I went missing."

"Hot *and* responsible," Austin quips. "You're a catch, Rae."

"Don't encourage her," I mutter, fighting a grin.

We reach the shaded area near the Student Union, and Khloe drops onto the concrete bench, sighing like she's just run a marathon. Marlena joins her, pulling her phone out of her bra.

"So, Cactus Grill at one, right?" she double-checks.

I nod as I tug my phone from my waistband and glance at the time. "Yup. Tessa should be out of her art history class by then. She said she'd meet us there and that she'll try to grab us a booth."

There's still about half an hour before my next class—just enough time to mentally prepare myself for the hour and fifteen minutes of boredom that is Public Finance. At least the day ends on a better note with Forensic Psychology.

"Ugh, I'm starving already," Khloe groans, clutching her stomach like she's on the verge of collapse. "If I don't get food soon, I might literally pass out and die in the middle of the Union. And when that happens, Rae, it'll be your fault."

I roll my eyes and slip my phone back into my waistband.

"Please. If you die, it'll be because you tried flirting with Henley or some other guy you thought was hot and forgot to breathe."

That earns a round of laughter and a playful smack on my arm from Khloe. "Woman, I am not that thirsty."

"Khloe," I deadpan. "You are the queen of thirsty. You love to comment on my reading habits, but I've seen your Instagram. Every other reel is a thirst trap from some tattooed biker with greasy hair and a growl."

She gasps, dramatically offended. "Bitch, you're one to talk!"

"Okay, fair," I say, throwing my hands up in mock surrender, laughing. I built my algorithm brick by brick, and I'm not ashamed. Masked men with knives, leather-clad bikers—some of them overlap, and those videos? Chef's kiss. Definitely guilty pleasure and droolworthy.

"I hate to break up this charming roast session," Austin cuts in with a lopsided grin, slinging his backpack over one shoulder, "but unfortunately, I've got class."

Marlena lets out a dramatic little whine and wraps her arms around his waist like it will prevent him from leaving. "Already?" she pouts, nuzzling into his chest.

"You'll survive, baby," he teases, his arms wrapping around her in an awkward but endearing hug.

"I was about to take off, too," I chime in, reaching down to adjust the strap on my bag as he absentmindedly twirls one of Marlena's pigtails between his fingers. "See y'all at one?"

"Wouldn't miss it," Austin says, leaning down to press a soft kiss to Marlena's forehead. "Behave," he adds with a mischievous smirk before giving her a gentle swat on the butt.

She lets out a playful squeak and swats him back. "No promises," she calls as he starts to walk off.

We all watch him disappear into the crowd of students. I glance at the time again and sigh, forcing myself to stand and brush off my leggings. "I should get going too," I mutter. "Gotta mentally prepare myself for Public Finance."

"Let us know if this next professor is as hot as Henley, okay?" Khloe says with a devilish grin, stretching her arms above her head.

I roll my eyes but can't suppress the laugh that bubbles up. "Don't hold your breath," I call over my shoulder as I start toward the Chemistry Building. Their voices and laughter fade behind me, replaced by the low hum of campus chatter and the occasional skateboard clack on pavement.

THREE
RAELYNN

PUBLIC FINANCE IS EXACTLY as boring as I imagined it would be—maybe even worse. Professor Lynn Andrews spends the first thirty minutes walking us through the syllabus in a voice so flat and lifeless it could probably sedate a rabid animal. She's middle-aged and dresses like a strict librarian—perfectly pressed slacks, a stiff white blouse buttoned all the way to her throat, and glasses that rest low on her nose like they're perpetually disappointed in you. Everything about her screams control. Her PowerPoint is color-coded down to the bullet points, her syllabus is a twelve-page manifesto, and her overall vibe suggests she alphabetizes her spice rack and sends back lukewarm coffee just for sport.

When she starts lecturing on how finance plays a "crucial role" in criminal justice—budgeting, resource allocation, grant writing—I try to care. Really, I do. I know it matters. I just wish it didn't feel like being slowly smothered by a weighted blanket of boredom.

Seventy-five minutes of this, twice a week, and attendance is mandatory.

Of course it is.

By the time she clicks to her final slide and dismisses us—

mercifully, twenty minutes early—I'm already halfway packed. My notebook snaps shut, and I shove my laptop into my bag like it personally offended me. I don't even pretend to linger. The moment I'm in the hallway, I pull out my phone to check the time.

11:56 a.m.

I've got an hour to kill before lunch, and honestly, I'm grateful for it.

After barely surviving the soul-sucking monotony of Public Finance, the thought of real food and actual conversation feels like salvation. I could use the break before Forensic Psychology—a class that actually sparks my interest. Something dark. Layered. The kind of material that gets under your skin in the best way. Definitely a far cry from budget spreadsheets and grant-writing lectures that make me want to jam a pencil into my eye socket just for stimulation.

I make my way across the quad, the heart of campus pulsing with midday energy. Students spill out of buildings, clustering in groups, animated by caffeine and shared misery. I weave through them, sidestepping the usual suspects—zombie-eyed freshmen staring at their phones for directions, overly confident skateboarders who think they own the sidewalk, and cyclists who seem to believe bells are optional.

A chime rings out over the loudspeakers, three short bells, followed by the university fight song. I don't even flinch. It's clockwork by now. I hum along as I saunter toward the Union, not really in a hurry.

I don't head straight to the Cactus Grill, though. Tessa won't be out of her art history class for nearly an hour, and I'm not sure what time the others are free. No sense staking out a booth like a desperate lunchroom gremlin just yet.

Instead, I take a detour into the campus bookstore.

It's quieter in here—cooler, too. The air conditioning hits like a wall the moment I step inside, at least ten degrees colder than the lingering summer heat outside. A shiver runs up my arms, goosebumps rising as I adjust to the sudden chill. The chaos of campus life fades behind the thick sliding glass doors, replaced by the soft rustle of turning pages, the occasional ding of a scanner at the checkout kiosk, and the low murmur of voices drifting between shelves. The scent of freshly brewed coffee curls through the air from the Starbucks tucked in the back—rich, warm, and dangerously inviting.

I head toward one of the oversized red leather chairs nestled near the balcony railing, which overlooks the lower level where students pick up their textbooks or seek help with their electronics. The chair lets out a soft creak as I sink into it, worn just enough to be comfortable.

From my bag, I pull out my current read—a dark romance I've been chipping away at between classes like it's contraband. The cover is curling at the corners, spine bent from overuse, the kind of book that's clearly been dragged around and loved a little too hard. I flip to the chapter I marked and skim the first few lines before letting myself sink into it completely.

Obsession. Violence. A dangerously charming man with a crooked smile and blood on his hands.

Precisely the kind of escape I need.

An hour slips by faster than I expect. I slide my bookmark into place, close the book, and drop it into my bag with just enough care to keep the spine from snapping. My phone is the next thing I reach for, and I check it out of habit more than urgency.

Two messages.

The first is from Khloe, ranting about how her juvenile delinquency professor is *not* hot and how disappointed she is. Shocking.

The second is from Tessa.

TESSA:

On my way.

I fire off a quick reply to Tessa and leave Khloe on read. I'm not about to encourage her thirst-fueled professor fantasies this early in the semester.

Tessa responds almost immediately.

TESSA:

Be there in five.

That's my cue to get moving.

I stand, stretch out the stiffness from sitting too long, then head toward the exit. The cool air inside clings to me for a second before the dry heat outside takes its place. I make my way toward the stairs that lead up to the third floor, already anticipating the mixed scents of the different foods offered and the sound of my friends' laughter waiting on the other side.

Marlena and Austin are already waiting by the doors, half-leaning against the metal railing, caught up in their own quiet conversation. Marlena's laughing softly, her eyes bright, while Austin casually twirls one of her pigtails around his finger like it's second nature.

"Hey, guys," I say with a smirk as I saunter up to them.

"Howdy," Austin drawls, flashing me a grin.

Before I can reply, I hear footsteps pounding behind me, followed by the sound of breathless giggles. Khloe and Tessa rush up the stairs, looking slightly winded but energized, like they just sprinted from opposite ends of campus.

"Oh, good—we're all here!" Tessa beams, skipping the last few steps before launching herself at me. Her arms wrap around my neck, nearly knocking me off balance.

"Whoa!" I squeak, laughing as I steady myself. "Hey, Tess."

She loosens her grip just enough to let me breathe, and I return the hug. Her enthusiasm is impossible not to love.

"Hey, Rae," Tessa greets warmly as I fall in step with her and Khloe. "How were your classes?"

"Criminology was solid," I say, brushing a strand of hair out of my face. "Public Finance, though? Absolute ass."

Khloe perks up instantly, a hopeful glint in her eye. "Was your professor at least hot?" she asks with a giggle as we weave toward the growing line outside The Cactus Grill.

I shake my head, holding back an eye roll. "Not even close. Picture a strict librarian with a monotone voice, glasses sliding down her nose, and zero tolerance for joy. That's her."

Khloe groans dramatically. "Ugh, the worst kind. What a waste."

"Seriously, she reminded me of Mrs. Wade," I add with a visible shudder. "Remember sixth-grade math? The way she'd just… stare at you until you wished you could disappear?"

Tessa makes a face. "Don't remind me. That woman hated *everyone*. Like she woke up every morning actively choosing misery."

"I lost count of how many times I got in trouble with her," Khloe chimes in.

I give her a knowing look. "Khloe, you were always in trouble with everyone. But yeah… I think she hated you the most."

She grins, unfazed. "True."

We all laugh, that strange kind of middle school trauma bonding that somehow never loses its sting—or its humor.

The line shuffles forward faster than expected, and before long, we've swiped our meal cards and stepped into the buffet-style dining hall. Usually at this hour, all the booths are filled (typically by a single person who could have sat *anywhere* else but chose not to), but we score big because there's an open booth in the back corner by the big bay windows that overlook campus. It is partially shaded by the heritage tree outside, but sunlight filters through just enough to give the table a soft, warm glow.

We toss our bags into the booth to claim it before scattering in different directions, each of us heading toward our preferred section of the buffet.

Forensic Psychology is a breath of fresh air after the slow death that was Public Finance. It's a hundred times more bearable—maybe more. Doctor Howard Lowell is sharp, animated, and actually seems like he *wants* to be there, which already puts him in the top five percent of professors I've had.

He doesn't waste time with the syllabus either. "You're adults," he says, pacing in front of the whiteboard. "You don't need me to walk you through information you're perfectly capable of reading."

Instead, we dive straight into a quick lecture on how television *absolutely* butchers forensic psychology. He throws out examples from *Criminal Minds* and *Mindhunter*, pointing out all the inaccuracies with just the right balance of sarcasm and actual insight. I'm hooked almost instantly. Fifty minutes fly by, and before I know it, the class is over.

When I step outside, the sun is lower in the sky but still blazing. The air has that sticky, post-monsoon weight to it, like the heat is clinging on for dear life. Just ahead, I spot Tessa perched on a stone bench a few feet from the building entrance, earbuds in, completely in her own world.

She's bobbing her head and singing—*loudly*—to "Nightmare" by Halsey. Her voice is unmistakably off-key, but it's full of conviction. I've heard the song enough times to know the lyrics by heart, even from her slightly tone-deaf rendition.

Tessa's amazing at a lot of things. Singing is *not* one of them. And thank God she knows that and still doesn't care. Sing your heart out, baby—even if you sound like a dying cat.

Giggling softly to myself, I approach her. I gently tap my fingers on her shoulder. She jumps, startled, before pulling one earbud out and turning. When she sees it's me, her whole face lights up. "Hey!" she grins, yanking out the other bud and stuffing both into their pink JLAB case. Without missing a beat, she tucks the case straight into her cleavage like it's a built-in pocket.

I raise an eyebrow. "Is that the official headphone storage unit now?"

She smirks. "Hey, it works."

I have to agree with her there. God didn't give us cleavage to not shove shit into them. It's not like we get pockets in our clothes anyway.

"How long have you been sitting out here?" I ask as she stands up, swinging her strawberry-printed book bag over her right shoulder.

"Not long, maybe ten, fifteen minutes?" she replies as we start moving toward our garage. "How was your class?"

"It was a thousand times better than Public Finance," I say with a dramatic sigh as we fall into step beside each other. "It was actually interesting. Doctor Lowell knows how to keep people awake—shocking, I know."

Tessa grins. "So it wasn't soul-crushing? Progress!"

She suddenly skips a few paces ahead of me, then spins into a couple of light twirls. She moves like someone who can't stand still for too long, like the world might lose momentum if she doesn't add a slight motion to it.

Chuckling, I pick up my pace to catch up.

"What about you?" I ask. "How were your classes?"

She shrugs, but she's smiling. "Honestly? Not bad. Studio was fun. My professor actually has a personality, which is rare, apparently. Art History, though? Bit of a drag. I think the only exciting part was when someone in the back fell asleep and snored so loud the professor stopped mid-sentence."

I laugh. "At least it wasn't *you* snoring this time."

She gasps, hand over her chest in mock offense. "Excuse you! I don't snore. I breathe with *style*."

Rolling my eyes, I grin. “That’s what you’re calling it now?”

“Absolutely.” She links her arm with mine and leans into me dramatically. “But seriously, I think this semester’s going to be good. I can feel it.”

I nod, tipping my gaze up toward the sky as we walk. The sunlight’s gentler now, filtered through the late afternoon haze, casting everything in a soft, golden glow that makes the campus look almost peaceful.

“I hope so,” I say with a slight chuckle as we exit the bypass and cross the street toward our parking garage. “It’s our last year. I’m seriously praying it doesn’t go to hell.”

FOUR
RAELYNN

THE SUN HASN'T EVEN DRAGGED itself over the horizon by the time my alarm tears me out of sleep, the sharp opening riff of "Machinehead" by Bush shredding through the last scraps of whatever dream I was having. I jolt upright with a groan, fumbling blindly across the nightstand until my hand smacks against my phone and finally silences the noise. My eyes crack open just enough to squint at the glowing screen—5:15 a.m. The numbers blur for a second before my brain accepts them. Too early. Far too early.

Another groan slips out, this one louder, as I let the phone drop back onto the nightstand with a dull thud. I flop onto my back and stare at the ceiling as if it might take pity on me and reverse time. Mornings and I have never been on good terms, but mornings before sunrise? That's just cruel and unusual punishment.

And today of all days, I have to be at the department by six thirty sharp. Sergeant Rodriguez, my internship supervisor, insisted I come in early for my first official day. She said she wanted to give me a full tour and ensure everything was in order—badge access, paperwork, the whole shebang. And, even though I'm just an intern, I still have to sit through roll call like everyone else, which means pretending to look alive in front of a room full of actual officers.

I'm already regretting not begging for the afternoon shift instead.

I linger in bed for another five minutes, staring at the faint cracks in the ceiling and questioning every life decision that led me to this ungodly hour. Eventually, with a sigh, I peel back the comforter. Max lifts his head from the blanket nest at the foot of the bed, blinking at me with the kind of sleepy judgment only a dog can pull off. When I swing my legs over the edge and stretch, joints popping, Max hops off the bed and shakes himself awake, tail wagging halfheartedly.

My outfit is waiting on the dresser—a rare stroke of foresight courtesy of the slightly more responsible version of me from last night. I'd gone for what I considered *semi*-professional attire—emphasis on semi.

Leggings, a dark blue blouse, and my boots.

Leggings are the only bottoms I'll tolerate. Jeans? Absolutely not. I can't stand the stiff fabric, the pinch of the zipper, the way the waistband always feels like it's plotting against me. Leggings, at least, give me comfort—even if I have to accept the cruel lack of pockets as the trade-off. The boots are practical, sturdy, and ready for whatever today decides to throw at me. What exactly that might be, I don't know. But still. Better prepared than not.

On top of the blouse and leggings, I'd stacked a clean pair of panties, my favorite bra (though, truth be told, it probably needs to see the inside of the washing machine soon), and a pair of socks—mismatched, because that's all I managed to grab from the drawer before collapsing into bed. Even now, I can't summon the energy to fix it.

No one's going to see them anyway, so who cares?

I scoop the pile into my arms and pad across the room to the door. The second it cracks open, Max darts past me, nails clicking against the floor as he heads down the hall toward the living room, tail now fully awake and wagging. He plants himself at the front door of the apartment, nose pressed against the wood, as if sheer willpower will get him outside faster.

I detour to the bathroom first, setting my clothes on the back of the toilet and flipping the shower handle. The pipes groan, then cough themselves awake, steam curling from the spray as it heats. With that going, I cross the hall into the living room. Tessa's slippers sit by the door, and since she's not awake to complain, I slide my feet into them.

Max is practically vibrating now. I grab his leash from the hook, the roll of bright blue poo bags clipped to it rattling faintly as I snap it onto his collar. His whole body wiggles, nails scrabbling against the laminate as he dances in place.

"Alright, alright," I mumble, still half asleep, tugging the door open.

The air outside is already warm, thick with the stillness of the desert. The complex is quiet. The kind of quiet that only exists in the thin hours before dawn. Streetlamps cast hazy halos over the sidewalks, their light catching the trimmed bushes that border the paths and the low stucco buildings arranged in neat rows. The pool area is locked up, chairs stacked along the fence line, and the sound of the fountain near the leasing office carries faintly across the courtyard.

Max bounds ahead to the nearest patch of grass by the parking lot, nose glued to the ground, inhaling a story only he can read. I stifle a yawn, rubbing at my eyes as he circles, sniffs, and circles again.

From the far end of the lot, an engine turns over. I glance up as a car eases out of a parking space, its headlights sliding briefly across the rows before it slips onto the street. The quiet settles again, and I turn back to Max just as he tugs at the leash.

Finally, he squats and takes care of his business. I tug a bag free, the plastic crinkling loudly in the silence, and grimace as I clean up after him. The tied-off bag swings from my fingers as I carry it to the trash can near the walkway.

We linger a moment longer, Max lifting his nose to the breeze like he's debating whether there's more to investigate. "Nope," I mutter, giving the leash a gentle tug. "Sorry, bud. Not today, Mommy's got places to be."

Back inside, I lock the door behind us and unclip his leash. Max trots straight to his water bowl, nails clicking on the floor, before lapping noisily. I rub at my face and head for the bathroom, dragging a hand down my face as I step back into the steam.

Time to make myself look alive.

Nervous energy hums just beneath my skin as I sit stiffly in the lobby of the Westside Division.

The front desk clerk, a stocky man named Thomas—with jet black hair slicked back with enough gel to survive anything thrown at it—greeted me with a warm, practiced smile the moment I stepped inside. After the standard bag check and a pass through the metal detector, I was waved through and told to take a seat.

He'd assured me that Rodriguez would be out shortly. She was finishing up a few last-minute administrative tasks before giving me the full rundown for the day.

That was fifteen minutes ago.

I arrived right at six thirty like I was told, but now the minutes are stretching thin, each one dragging a little heavier than the last. My leg bounces restlessly, the toe of my boot tapping a jittery rhythm against the tile, and my fingers drum against my bag like it's the only thing tethering me to the ground.

The station isn't open to the public yet, and the silence is almost oppressive. No ringing phones. No chatter. Just the soft, low hum of the fluorescent lights overhead and the occasional click of Thomas's keyboard behind the desk. Even the air feels still, as if the whole place is holding its breath.

It gives me way too much time to think.

To second-guess what I'm wearing. To wonder if I'm going to mess something up. To imagine Sergeant Rodriguez walking through those doors and realizing she made a mistake bringing me on.

I shift in my seat, straightening my posture like that'll magically make me look calm and confident, even though my body has other plans, and take a slow, deliberate breath, glancing toward the AUTHORIZED PERSONNEL ONLY door, willing it to open.

Then, finally, the door hisses open, and a woman steps through.

She carries herself with quiet authority—tall, composed, and effortlessly self-assured. Her black uniform is crisp and clean, not a wrinkle in sight, and the gold badge pinned to her chest catches the harsh fluorescent light with a subtle gleam. Her dark hair is pulled back into a sleek bun, and her eyes, a deep brown nearly black, sweep the room with calm precision before landing on me.

"Raelynn Carson?" she asks as she approaches me, her voice steady but warmer than expected.

I jump to my feet a little too quickly, my bag nearly slipping from my lap and knocking against my knee. "Yes—hi," I blurt, the word coming out too fast, too eager. I clear my throat and try to find a shred of composure.

She offers a friendly smile that instantly takes the edge off my nerves. "I'm Sergeant Sara Rodriguez," she says. "Sorry to keep you waiting. We were just finalizing your clearance and access credentials. You're all set now."

"Thank you," I reply quickly, adjusting the strap of my bag over my shoulder as she gestures for me to follow.

"Come on," she says, holding the door open and guiding me through. "I'll give you a quick walkthrough before we get you settled. Things move pretty fast here, but I think you'll get the hang of it in no time. You ready?"

I give her a nervous smile. "As I'll ever be."

She glances back at me as the door clicks shut behind us, her smile pulling into something a little more relaxed and human. "That's the spirit."

Rodriguez leads me deeper into the station, her pace brisk but not rushed. The hallway buzzes with activity—staff moving in and out of rooms, voices exchanging clipped updates, and the low hum of police radios chattering in the background. The air smells faintly of coffee and printer toner, with a hint of something sterile beneath it all.

She glances back at me briefly. "I'll give you a quick overview today, just so you're familiar with the layout. You'll get used to the flow soon enough."

I nod.

We step into the Evidence Room first. It smells faintly of plastic, paper, and something metallic, like pennies and antiseptic. Metal shelving units stretch wall to wall, each one lined with carefully labeled boxes, sealed bags, and locked storage containers. Everything is marked, cataloged, and coded. A technician in latex gloves gives us a nod as he slides a folder into a cabinet.

"This is where all seized property, physical evidence, and documentation are logged and stored," Rodriguez explains. "Chain of custody is taken very seriously—nothing moves in or out without proper documentation."

I nod, doing my best to absorb everything while my eyes dart from shelf to shelf. There's something eerie about seeing personal belongings reduced to sealed plastic bags and barcodes.

Next, we enter the Forensics Lab—a stark, white room that hums with quiet intensity. Sleek computers line one side, and lab equipment glints under the bright overhead lights. There's a distinct chemical smell in the air, not unpleasant, but sterile. Two techs are hunched over a work-station, murmuring as they study something under a microscope.

"This is where we process fingerprints, DNA, trace fibers, and anything else our officers bring in," Rodriguez says, keeping her voice low so we don't interrupt. "We coordinate with the state lab for more complex testing, but most of the preliminary work is done here."

It's fascinating—and a little intimidating. I feel like if I so much as breathe too hard, I'll mess up a crime scene.

From there, we move past the holding cells—Rodriguez doesn't stop to linger, just gives a brief nod toward the area and keeps going—and down a corridor lined with bulletin boards, each one filled with memos, department updates, BOLOs, and mugshots. We briefly go over where ammunition and guns are stored and where officers gather the things they'll need for a shift before finally reaching the room for roll call. It's larger than I expected, with rows of plastic folding chairs and steel tables with wooden tops, arranged in a tight formation and a whiteboard at the front cluttered with shift schedules, recent case numbers, and scribbled notes from the graveyard shift.

"This is where every shift starts," she says, stepping aside to let me take it in. "Briefings, assignments, case updates—it all happens here. You'll check in here most mornings before heading off to your designated tasks. I don't have any tasks for you today, so I'm having you do a ride-along."

The energy in the room is quiet, expectant. Officers are beginning to filter in, some still sipping coffee, while others scan the board or chat in low voices. It's clear this is the calm before the storm.

Rodriguez turns to me with a nod. "Any questions so far?"

I shake my head. "Not yet. Just… a lot to take in."

Her lips curve into a comforting smile. "That's normal. First days are always like that. Don't worry, you're doing fine."

I return her smile, nerves flickering just beneath the surface.

"Have a seat. I'll let you know who you're riding with when I dismiss everyone," she says, gesturing to one of the front tables.

I head to the table closest to me, the one just off to the left of the podium, and settle into the plastic chair. I immediately tug at the hem of my blouse, smoothing the fabric over my front and giving the back a discreet pull to ensure it's not riding up.

Almost like a bell had gone off, officers finish filtering into the room, their casual chatter filling the space as they took their seats. Some carry coffee, and others drop into seats without looking up. The energy shifts quickly from quiet anticipation to something more alive.

Two officers step up to the front of the room alongside Sergeant Rodriguez. One of them—the younger-looking of the pair—immediately draws my attention.

If I had to guess, he's in his late twenties, Hispanic, and stands at least 6'2". His build is lean but solid, with just enough muscle to make his presence known, even through the Kevlar vest strapped to his chest. While some officers chose to wear the long-sleeved uniforms, he has opted for the short-sleeved black uniform shirt, which fully displays the black and white tattoo sleeve of a snake slithering through a garden of roses wrapped around his left arm.

His black hair is cropped short, the ends curling slightly where they meet his forehead. Under the fluorescent lights, his light brown eyes almost appear golden, sharp, and observant beneath subtly furrowed brows. A neatly trimmed beard and mustache frame a jawline so defined it looks carved.

He glances my way—just for a second. His expression is unreadable, calm. Not hostile… but definitely not inviting either. Then, without a word, he turns his attention back to the quiet conversation he's having with Rodriguez and the older officer.

He gives off a grumpy vibe. And if I had to bet, I'd say he's the one I'll be riding with.

Lovely.

Eventually, he and the older officer take a seat at a table behind me, and my shoulders tense slightly as Rodriguez steps up to the podium.

"Alright, settle down," she says, her voice firm but easy. The hum of conversation dies almost instantly, giving way to quiet focus. I do a quick scan of the room—twenty-something officers, all in varying stages of alertness—and then shift my attention back to Rodriguez.

"First things first," Rodriguez says, her voice carrying easily across the room, "we've got a new intern joining us today."

She gestures in my direction—a silent cue to stand. As she continues, I push myself up from the chair, smoothing down my blouse again. "She's here to assist with whatever needs doing and to get a real sense of what the job's like."

I offer a small, slightly awkward wave to the room full of uniformed strangers. "Hi, everyone," I say, keeping my tone as steady as I can, even though there's a small flip in my stomach. "I'm Raelynn Carson, and I'm looking forward to working with you all."

A few heads turn—nothing dramatic—just polite curiosity, maybe mild disinterest.

I give a quick smile and sink back into my seat, doing my best not to look like I'm analyzing every glance thrown my way.

But I got through it—no stumbling, awkward stammering, or spontaneous combustion.

I'll take the win.

Rodriguez spends the next five minutes going over a few

current cases and shift updates—suspected drug activity near the university, a string of break-ins in the downtown district, and a briefing on a recent domestic violence call that escalated fast. Her tone remains composed yet firm, and the room listens attentively. Even the ones who look half asleep seem to take mental notes.

Once she finishes explaining everything and assigning officers to specific areas, she steps down from the podium. She strides smoothly across the room toward my table, her boots barely making a sound against the scuffed tile. Around us, officers begin rising from their seats, conversations picking back up as they filter out of the room to prepare for patrol. The room is nearly empty within moments, except for me and the two officers still seated at the table behind mine.

Grumpy and his partner.

"Miss Carson," Rodriguez starts, "you'll be riding along with Officers Emilio Perez and Jacoby Kline today."

I half-turn in my seat to face them and offer a polite smile. My eyes flick to the name tags clipped to their uniforms, putting names to their faces.

She nods once, then adds, "At the end of your shift, we'll meet and go over your plan." She turns and exits the room, leaving me in the increasingly awkward silence that follows.

Officer Kline is the first to break the silence. He leans forward slightly and extends a hand with an easy, warm smile. "Welcome aboard, Raelynn."

I reach out and shake his hand. His grip is firm and steady, confident without trying to dominate. He gives a single shake, then casually tucks his hands back into the space between his chest and Kevlar vest, like it's second nature.

Like Perez, he has opted for the short-sleeved uniform, revealing a few intricate geometric tattoos that wind down his arms. He looks to be in his late thirties, maybe early forties, and about the same height as Perez, with a broad, solid frame and sun-kissed skin that suggests years spent under Arizona's unforgiving sun. His short-cropped brown hair is peppered with gray, and faint crow's feet frame his gray blue eyes.

There's a rugged steadiness to him. The kind that comes from experience—not just surviving this job, but staying grounded through it.

I turn to offer my hand to Officer Perez, but he doesn't take it. Instead, he stands, stiff and unreadable, and gives Kline a sidelong glance.

"Kline, can you grab our ride-along her observer vest?" he says, his tone flat but laced with annoyance.

Kline gives a quick nod and heads out of the room without hesitation, boots thudding softly against the floor.

I'm barely able to process the brush-off before Perez turns his gaze on me fully. He folds his arms across his chest, and I swear the temperature in the room drops a few degrees.

"If you haven't figured it out yet," he says, tone clipped, "I'm not thrilled about this arrangement."

I blink and my mouth parts slightly, caught somewhere between surprise and irritation. "Excuse me?"

"I don't like babysitting," he adds, not even bothering to mask the disdain.

My eyes narrow, the bite in his tone flaring something sharp in my chest. "Well, don't look at it that way," I say, doing my best not to let the frustration slip too far into my voice. "I'm not here for a joyride, *Officer Perez*. I'm serious about what I'm doing." I say his name like it leaves a bad taste in my mouth. His brows lift slightly, as if he wasn't expecting me to push back. "I'm here because I give a damn about this job and the path I'm on," I continue. "And I'd appreciate not being treated like some kid tagging along for extra credit."

Perez doesn't flinch, but his expression shifts slightly as he studies me, his eyes dark and unreadable.

"Then you should understand well enough that you're not trained," he says calmly, but firmly. "If Kline or I tell you to stay in the car, back off, or leave a scene, you *do it*. No debate."

My jaw clenches. He's already grating on every nerve I have. I'm not stupid. I've done ride-alongs before. I know how to keep myself out of the way, and I sure as hell don't need to be treated like some clueless kid on a field trip.

Before I can fire back, Kline returns, holding a neon yellow vest in one hand. The word "OBSERVER" is printed in bold, peeling black letters across the back. The thing looks like it's been through hell—frayed at the edges, faint stains along the shoulder seams, and the dingy thing had to be slipped on like a t-shirt because the straps had been tied together at the buckle. No one cared enough to try to undo the hellish knot. Kline holds it out with a sheepish grin. "It's seen better days, but it does the job."

I nod, take it from him with a soft sigh already dreading the scratchy material, and slip it over my head. The scent of sweat and something artificially floral itches my nostrils as it falls into place.

"All right, she's ready—let's go," Perez says, his tone clipped as he turns on his heel and strides out of the roll call room without waiting for a response.

I quickly grab my bag and fall into step behind him and Officer Kline, trailing them down the hallway and out into the morning light. It's past 7 a.m. now, and the day is already warming up, the sunlight casting long shadows across the concrete as we head toward the gated lot reserved for police-issued vehicles.

The parking lot is quiet, nearly empty aside from a few crime scene vans parked off to the side and a few specialty units. Only three patrol cars remain; of those, just one is running—headlights glowing faintly against the pavement, engine humming low.

Kline heads straight for it, sliding into the driver's seat with practiced ease, while Perez circles to the back of the cruiser. He opens the rear door and pulls out a folded wool blanket from the trunk. Without a word, he spreads it across the hard plastic bench seat in the back.

I blink, a little surprised by the gesture. I'd forgotten entirely that the backseat of a cruiser has those molded, unforgiving seats that weren't built for comfort—and it hadn't occurred to me until now that I'd be spending the ride-along in the back like an arrestee, not an intern.

"Thank you," I say quietly as I climb in, easing myself down onto the thinly padded blanket. It doesn't do much to soften the seat, but I appreciate the effort all the same.

Perez glances at me, the corner of his mouth twitching faintly. "No problem," he mutters, then shuts the door behind me with a solid thunk.

He circles the car and slides into the passenger seat up front without another word. He then spins the MDT toward him, his fingers already tapping across the keyboard like he's tuning me out completely as Kline pulls out of the parking lot.

I lean back against the seat, hands folded in my lap, and brace myself for whatever the next few hours might bring.

Del
F12
End
PgUp
PgDn
Home
P
L
K
M
N

FIVE
RAELYNN

WE WERE ONLY two hours into the ride-along and had already been on six calls, one of which was a regular traffic stop. The rest of the calls were two domestic violence cases back-to-back and one drunk and disorderly.

Who the fuck is out drinking this early in the morning?

We also had one call about a homeless man dumpster-diving at Circle K and a welfare check on a little old lady who hadn't answered her phone or door for a few days. She was okay, thankfully, just almost entirely deaf and didn't hear the door or her landline. Paramedics, however, did take her in to be checked out.

At each call, a second cruiser pulled up to assist. Kline had explained earlier that they couldn't detain or transport anyone with me in the backseat. Safety and liability concerns. I knew this already, but still politely nodded in understanding.

By the third hour, things began to slow down, and by the fourth hour, Kline and Perez decide to head back toward the station, since my shift is almost over and they know Rodriguez wants to chat with me.

"So," Kline says, breaking the silence as he drives. His

tone is casual, curious. "What made you want to go into law enforcement?"

I glance up, fiddling absently with a section of frayed pieces on the observer vest. Through the metal grating that separated arrestees from officers, I can see Kline staring at me through his rear-view mirror, his expression curious. "Oh… um," I pause, debating on how honest I want to be. "Several reasons, I guess."

Kline hums thoughtfully and returns his gaze to the road. "Care to share?" he asks as Perez turns partially in his seat to look at me. His expression is unreadable.

I shift slightly under his gaze, unease building in my stomach as I sink deeper into the molded plastic seat; the blanket does little to ease the discomfort I'm really starting to feel now. "I'm not sure I want to share," I admit. "It's kind of… personal."

Perez doesn't let up. His eyes narrow slightly. "C'mon. You said you had *multiple* reasons. Give us one."

I sigh internally. I'm not ready to open up about *that* reason, not to them. Not yet. Especially not to *him.*

So I give them the safe version.

"I've always been fascinated by true crime," I say carefully. "I eventually decided I wanted to study it, and in my freshman year, I decided I wanted to be a cop and then work my way up to being a homicide detective one day."

"Homicide, huh?" Perez snorts, like it's some kind of joke. Like he believes I don't have what it takes.

"Yes," I say flatly, the edge in my voice cutting sharper than I intend. "And for the record, I have my reasons. But I'm not exactly eager to share them with someone who's spent this entire ride treating me like an inconvenience."

I cross my arms—not just out of defiance, but to steady the flicker of emotion clawing its way up my chest. Anger, mostly. Frustration. And buried underneath it all, the dull ache of old grief stumbling back after years of trying to keep it contained.

I was only six when my mom was murdered.

And by nine, I had lost both of my parents.

My dad unraveled after her death, piece by agonizing piece. The guilt consumed him—he blamed himself for not being there, for not protecting her. It clung to him like a second skin he could never peel away. The monster responsible—a serial killer, the media nicknamed *The Butcher* for the way he left his victims. Brutalized and in pieces. He vanished after my mother's murder. No trace. No justice. Just a gaping silence that settled over our lives like a shroud.

I was old enough to feel it. Old enough that the trauma of her death etched itself deep inside me, a scar I would carry into everything that came after.

That silence hollowed my father out. It made it impossible for him to look at me without seeing everything he'd lost. He tried to drown it—grief, guilt, memory—in the bottom of a bottle.

It didn't work.

After three years of numbing himself into a ghost, he finally gave up for good. He wrapped his car around a telephone pole on some deserted back road in the middle of the night. The official report called it an accident.

I knew better.

After that, I was passed into the care of my grandparents. They did their best—God, they tried—but by the time I was thirteen, life had taken another swing at me. My grandmother died quietly in her sleep. Peaceful, they said, but it didn't feel peaceful to me. It felt like the world was ripping another piece out of me, leaving less and less behind.

My grandfather tried, but he wasn't equipped to raise a grieving teenager—not mentally, or physically. And before long, the system started circling, ready to scoop me up and spit me out somewhere I didn't belong.

If it hadn't been for Tessa's family, I would've become just another file buried in a stack of forgotten kids until my eighteenth birthday. But they didn't hesitate. They opened their home and hearts to me without asking for anything in return. No conditions. No pity. Just love. Real, stable, unconditional love—the kind I didn't even know still existed.

And because of them, I'm still standing.

A heavy silence inside the cruiser is suffocating. Perez stares at me for a beat, something I could almost mistake as regret flickering across his face. His jaw tightens, then loosens. His lips part like he's about to say something, but whatever it is, he swallows it down and turns back to face forward without a word.

I exhale slowly, feeling the weight of it all settle in my chest again, and lean back against the seat, staring out the window as the cruiser hums quietly beneath me.

An uncomfortable twenty minutes pass by, filled with nothing but the occasional squawk of the radio and the low, steady hum of the air conditioner. No conversation. No acknowledgment. Just silence, heavy and awkward, weighing down the already stifling air inside the vehicle.

Finally, Kline eases the cruiser into the station's parking lot, pulling into one of the reserved spaces near the back entrance. He shifts the car into park and reaches for the radio. "2-Adam-34 is 10-7," Kline announces on his radio.

"Copy that 2-Adam-34," a voice crackles back through the speaker.

Without another word, both Kline and Perez climb out of the vehicle. A second later, Perez opens the back door for me. I glance up at him, my lips pursed. His expression is neutral as he steps off to the side, giving me space to climb out.

"Thank you," I murmur, sliding from the backseat and into the hellish afternoon heat. Going from an air-conditioned vehicle and straight into what can only be described as walking into an oven, nearly has me cursing, but I hold my tongue and immediately start stripping off the stiff and *beyond* fucking itchy vest, wishing I could rip off the rest of this godforsaken outfit while I'm at it. It's *too damn hot* for any amount of clothing, much less this. I will never get used to the heat, despite living here my whole life. Anyone who says they're used to it is fucking lying.

The vest does nothing to help the sensation of overheating. I fold it over my left arm anyway and quickly fall into step behind Perez and Kline, eager to chase the promise of air conditioning as we cross the lot and head back toward the station entrance.

Inside, we wind through the familiar halls—past uniformed officers, department staff, and the low buzz of conversation and ringing phones. Kline leads the way to Sergeant Rodriguez's office, knocking twice before pushing the door open. He steps aside, holding the door with a small nod, gesturing for me to enter.

"Welcome back, Miss Carson," Rodriguez says, glancing up from behind her computer screen. A warm smile spread across her lips.

I smile politely and take a quick scan of the office as I step inside. It's small but clean, with just enough personal touches to feel lived-in. A neat stack of case files sits to one side of the desk. A framed photo of what I can only assume to be her family sits next to a departmental award, and a dry-erase board covered in neat, color-coded writing hangs on the opposite wall. Everything about the space is structured and efficient—exactly what I'd expect from her.

"Thank you," I reply as I lower myself into one of the two sleek, black, cushioned chairs across from her desk, the worn leather creaking softly under my weight.

"I'll take it from here," Rodriguez says, turning her attention briefly to Kline and Perez.

I half-turn in my seat, glancing back just in time to catch Perez staring at me. His gaze lingers for a moment longer than necessary before he shifts his attention to Rodriguez, gives a slight nod, and disappears down the hallway with Kline following close behind.

I exhale quietly and refocus on Rodriguez as she leans back in her chair, studying me with an appraising look.

"So," she says, her voice a little lighter now. "How was your first day out in the field?"

I hesitate for half a second, considering whether I should mention Perez's attitude. But what good would that do? I'm not here to make enemies, and I don't need to give him even more of a reason to dislike me by running straight to his boss.

"It was great," I say instead, and honestly—it's not a total lie.

Sure, Perez's attitude was grating, and there was that one gut-punch moment where grief came barreling out of nowhere and nearly knocked the air from my lungs. But beyond that? The ride-along was the most real experience I've had in the field so far.

Not just simulated scenarios or hypothetical lecture discussions—*real* people, real consequences, real unpredictability.

Compared to my last ride-along, which dragged on for ten uneventful hours with only a handful of low-level calls and long stretches of radio silence, today had been… intense. And constant. And honestly? Kind of thrilling.

"I'm glad to hear that," Rodriguez says, offering a small smile. "You'll have plenty more opportunities for ride-alongs over the next fifteen weeks. But while I've got you here, let's talk about your duties around the station and what areas of law enforcement interest you most, because that's where we'll try to focus your time."

I nod, shifting slightly in my seat to give her my full attention.

"While you're at the station, I'll assign you a mix of responsibilities. Some tasks will be administrative, including filing, organizing case files, and assisting with data entry. You'll assist with logging reports and, occasionally, updating digital records to track property or evidence. It's not glamorous, but it's important."

She taps her pen on a legal pad and glances back at me. "We'll balance that with time in the field. I expect you'll spend roughly half your hours on ride-alongs or shadowing officers in different units. The idea is to give you a full view of the department, not just the flashy parts."

"I'm good with that," I say quickly, then add, "honestly, the two areas I'm most drawn to are patrol and criminal investigations."

Rodriguez smiles like that's the answer she was hoping for.

"We can definitely work with that. I'll most likely pair you with Detective Meyer at some point. She has been a part of the Criminal Investigation Department for some time. She has worked on a wide range of cases, including robbery, homicide, missing persons, and even cold cases. You'll learn a lot from her."

I nod, even more interested now. "That sounds perfect."

"Good," she says, scribbling a quick note on her pad. "We'll get your schedule mapped out by the end of the week. In the meantime, if you have questions or would like to explore other units, such as traffic, forensics, or community outreach, please don't hesitate to let me know. This internship is what you make of it."

Rodriguez finishes jotting down a few final notes before flipping the notepad closed with a quiet snap. She looks up at me, offering a final smile. "That's it for today. You're free to head out," she says with a nod. "First days are rarely smooth, but you handled it well."

"Thank you," I reply as I rise from the chair, the observer's vest still draped over my arm. "Ma'am," I say to get Rodriguez's attention. She looks up at me, brows slightly lifted in question. I hold out the vest.

"Oh! Thank you," she says, reaching for it. "I completely forgot you still had that."

"You're welcome. I hope the rest of your afternoon goes well."

"You as well, Miss Carson. We'll see you on Thursday."

I nod and step out of the office, the door clicking shut behind me. My footsteps echo faintly as I make my way down the hall toward the lobby. A few passing officers offer polite nods as I go, and I return each one with a small smile.

Entering the lobby, I spot Thomas behind the front desk and give him a wave as I pass. He grins and returns it, then continues his conversation with a visitor as I make my way through the crowded space and back out into the heat.

I cross the lot at a steady pace, the heat radiating off the pavement in shimmering waves as I approach my maroon Optima. Key in hand, I press the button, and the doors unlock with a soft click. I slide into the driver's seat, thankful that I don't have leather seats, and press the start button beneath the steering wheel. The engine rumbles to life, and a rush of cool air spills from the vents, sweeping across my flushed skin. I lean back into the seat, letting the air hit my face and dry the sweat that was beading along my forehead as I close my eyes for a second, hoping to decompress and let the weight of the day melt off me.

My mind, however, has other plans.

It's running in a hundred directions, but nearly every thought circles back to him.

Emilio Perez.

Officer Condescending. Mister I-Don't-Have-Time-for-Interns. The embodiment of everything that should make my skin crawl.

He pissed me off. No—he *infuriated* me. Treated me like I didn't belong, like I was just dead weight in the backseat of his cruiser. Every word he spoke carried that same clipped, dismissive tone, and when he laughed at my ambitions

—*laughed*—like they were some kind of fucking joke, I swear I saw red.

And yet, beneath all the irritation and anger, there's something else simmering—a heat that coils in my gut and spreads low and slow, soaking through the fabric of my panties with humiliating ease.

I hate that my body doesn't seem to care that my brain wants to punch him in the throat.

This is what I get for reading too many dark romances and obsessing over morally gray men with emotional trauma and control issues. My type? Apparently, assholes with badges and looks that should be illegal.

God, *why* does he have to be so obnoxiously hot?

I let out a long, exasperated sigh and lean forward, jabbing the touchscreen on my dash to switch from radio to Android Auto. The screen blinks, then loads Amazon Music. I hit shuffle on my "Favorites" playlist.

The opening beat of "Motley Crew" by Post Malone pulses through the speakers, bass thumping in time with my pulse.

Throwing the car into reverse, I ease out of the parking spot, jaw tight and knuckles white around the steering wheel.

I need a distraction. Preferably one that doesn't come with a uniform, a brooding stare, or the power to completely unhinge my thoughts with one fucking look.

ME SCENE
CRIME
OFFICER
STOP
CAU

SIX
EMILIO

I'VE ALWAYS HATED RIDE-ALONGS. They're a pain in the ass—plain and simple. Just another excuse to throw untrained civilians into the middle of situations they've got no business being in. Liability magnets. Distractions. Extra weight in a job that already demands everything you've got. But when your boss tells you to take one, and your overly eager partner agrees before you can object, you don't argue. You grit your teeth, swallow the irritation, and deal with it.

So yeah—I wasn't exactly thrilled when Rodriguez told Kline and me we'd be saddled with a ride-along for the first half of the shift. I didn't bother hiding my annoyance. I didn't *want* to.

But what I didn't expect was that the rest of my shift would be haunted by the girl in the backseat—uninvited, persistent, and impossible to ignore.

Raelynn Carson.

All attitude and sharp edges, stuck in my thoughts like a goddamn splinter the second we dropped her off at Rodriguez's office. I didn't want to think about her, but she embedded herself in my mind anyway, uninvited and stubborn.

And beautiful.

God, was she beautiful. But not in some soft, delicate way—but in that quietly devastating kind of stunning that sneaks up on you and leaves a mark. She had a full color, half butterfly, half cherry blossom tattoo on her left forearm and a black and white lunar moth on her right bicep. Her dark brown hair had been thrown up in a messy bun that *begged* to be undone, strands escaping just enough to tease. I kept catching myself wanting to run my fingers through it, to grip it and see if she'd still glare at me the same way.

And those lips…

When she spat my name out like it left a bad taste in her mouth, all I could do was stare at her mouth. Soft, full, pink. The kind of lips made for kissing. Biting. *Bruising.*

It took every ounce of self-control to will my cock not to pitch a tent in my pants like some hormone-wired teenager seeing a tit for the first time. And the second I caught myself drifting too far into those thoughts, I did what I always do when things get complicated: I shut it down.

Shut *her* down.

I was an asshole to her. No sugarcoating it. Blunt. Cold. Dismissive. Not just because the morning had already gone to hell before she even showed up, but because the second I laid eyes on her, something in me short-circuited. She got under my skin without even trying, and I didn't know how to deal with that, so I defaulted to the only thing I knew: keep her at arm's length. Push before I could be pulled.

She didn't deserve that.

She could've gone straight to Rodriguez with a complaint. Could've thrown me under the bus during her debrief or dragged my name through the dirt for being the exact kind of cop most interns expect to hate.

But she didn't.

And I'll be damned if that didn't catch me off guard.

Especially after I laughed at her career choice, as if it were some kind of joke. Like her ambition didn't matter. Hell, I don't know what the fuck I expected her to say when I pushed, but it wasn't that. Wasn't *her* snapping back with fire in her voice and pain in her eyes.

And that's what did it. That moment. That shift.

I saw it—clear as day—in those hauntingly beautiful emerald eyes. There was more behind her words than irritation. There was weight. Grief. The kind of pain that doesn't come from a hard class or a bad breakup. This was older. Deeper. The kind of ache that nestles into your bones and stays there, quietly rotting you from the inside out. The kind of hurt you carry like a second skin, invisible to most but impossible to ignore once you've seen it.

I don't know her story. I don't know what shoved her toward a career in homicide as if it were her only lifeline. But I know the look of someone who's been through the fire and still has the burns to prove it.

And I hate that I want to know more.

By the time I finished typing up my portion of the shift reports and filing statements, and logging the last of the shift data, it was already creeping past six. My head ached, my shoulders were tight, and the building hum of frustration hadn't quite faded, even after clocking out.

The locker room was in its usual state of organized chaos—officers filtering in and out during the shift change, a blur of banter, boots, and duty belts. The air smelled of sweat, cheap deodorant, and the bitter bite of burnt coffee. Lockers slammed shut, radios squawked, and conversations overlapped in a steady hum.

I move on muscle memory, peeling off my uniform, folding it neatly, and stuffing it into my backpack to wash later. I pull on a fitted black t-shirt that clings to my chest and arms, followed by a pair of dark gray jeans.

I slide my feet into my black Vans, then lean against the

bench for a second, rolling my neck to work out the tension still sitting there like it pays rent.

Across the room, Kline's locker swings shut with a dull clank. He's fastening the buttons to his plain light gray dress shirt when I glance over, his expression relaxed in that annoyingly zen way he always seemed to carry post-shift.

"Kline," I call out, catching his attention as he fastens the last button on his shirt.

He looks over. "What's up?"

"You got plans tonight?" I ask, zipping my backpack shut.

"Nope," he says, lifting his boot onto the bench to start lacing it. "Why?"

"Thinking of grabbing a drink." I pause. "You in?"

Kline raises an eyebrow, his mouth twitching. "Depends. You buying?"

I snort, shaking my head. The corner of my mouth lifts despite myself. "One round. After the kind of day we had? Feels like we earned it."

He finishes tying his left boot, then glances around the half-empty locker room—the last of the shift-change crowd trickling out. After a beat, he shrugs. "Sure, why not."

I slip my arms through the straps of my backpack as he grabs his duffel off the floor.

"Cool," I say, as I head toward the door to the locker room. "Meet you at Zeke's?"

"That works," he replies, slinging the bag over his shoulder and following me out.

We step out into the hallway, the noise of the shift change fading behind us. Outside, the air is cooler than it's been all day—a welcome break after being out in the heat all day in wool uniforms and bulletproof vests. The dry heat still lingers, but it's mellowed, the edge taken off by the slowly setting sun. Streetlights flicker on above us. Patrol units idled nearby, radios crackling faintly, headlights cutting through the dusky haze.

We cross the lot in silence, but my mind's anything but quiet. *She's* still there, pacing circles in my thoughts like she's got a damn key to the place.

Reaching into the side pocket of my backpack, I pull out the keys to my Black Silverado as Kline peels off toward his dark gray Grand Cherokee, giving me a quick chin lift before hopping in.

I climb into the cabin of my truck and fire it up. The engine growls to life, and a few seconds later, the radio kicks on. The chorus of "Numb" by Sleep Theory spills through the speakers, too, on the nose to ignore.

For a second, I sit there, letting the engine idle while I adjust the vents and roll my neck. Then a sharp honk makes me glance up—Kline, already pulling out, his hand stuck out his window as he gives me a wave.

I blow out a breath and throw my truck into reverse, then follow.

About fifteen minutes later (would have been less if I didn't have to make a pit stop at the gas station), I'm creeping into the gravel lot behind Zeke's, which is tucked between a pawn shop and a tire outlet. For a Tuesday night, the place is surprisingly packed. The lot's nearly full, and I have to circle twice before I finally snag a spot near the back, wedged between a rusted-out F-150 and someone's beat-up Impala.

I throw the truck into park, kill the engine, and hop down from the cabin. Gravel crunches under my Vans as I shift my weight and shut the door with a dull *thunk*. I lock my truck, then make my way toward the front entrance. Neon signs flicker above the door—one half burnt-out, the other buzzing like it's on its last leg.

Country music bleeds through the cracks in the door—something twangy and upbeat, paired with the low hum of conversation and clinking glass. The scent of stale beer hits before I even open the door, thick and familiar. Not exactly pleasant but oddly comforting after the day I've had.

I yank the door open and step into the semi-lit haze of the bar. Neon signs flicker above the counter. A TV in the corner is playing some muted baseball game, and the crowd is a blend of off-duty workers, regulars, and a few cops still in partial uniform.

A few familiar faces glance up and nod when they see me, fellow officers already halfway through a beer. I politely nod back but don't stop because Kline's waving me down from a table tucked into the back, already posted up with a half-empty bottle of Dos Equis.

He raises it in salute as I approach and knocks back the rest in one long swig before setting the bottle down with a clunk.

"What happened to me buying the first round?" I ask, a smirk pulling at the corner of my mouth.

"You got the next one, compadre," he replies, flashing a grin.

I roll my eyes and head toward the bar, weaving through tables and elbows as I dig my wallet from my back pocket. The music shifts to something slower, and I signal the bartender before settling against the counter, trying not to think about how much I've needed this drink.

"What'cha havin', darlin'?" the bartender drawls, her thick Southern accent wrapping around the words like honey.

She's older—probably late fifties—with sun-worn skin, red-tinted lips, and a honey blonde bun that looks like it's been through the wringer. Her cherry red top dips low—low enough that her breasts threaten to spill out with every move. A wad of gum snaps rhythmically between her teeth as she polishes a glass with a bar towel that's frayed and stained from years of hard use. Her half-smile is easy but practiced, the kind you earn working dive bars long enough to see it all.

"Two Dos Equis and a shot of tequila, please," I say, sliding my ID and debit card out of my wallet and placing them on the counter with a quiet slap.

The bartender gives a nod without missing a beat. She sets the glass she was drying down, gum snapping between her teeth as she turns toward the fridge behind her.

While she moves, I let my attention drift, half-turning to survey the place. A couple of college kids, repping the university, are hunched over the pool table near the back, cue chalk dusting the air as one lines up his shot. Off to the side, two construction guys in sweat-stained work shirts are locked in a friendly shouting match over the baseball game playing on the TV. They've got enough empty Miller bottles stacked on their table to pass for a sad game of bar bowling.

The bartender pulls two beers out and sets them down on the counter, then grabs a clean shot glass and a bottle of Patron off the shelf, pours an ounce and a half into the glass, topping it with a lime wedge.

"Here ya go, darlin'," the bartender says, pulling me back as she slides the drinks my way.

"Thanks," I mutter, grabbing the shot glass in one hand and the lime wedge perched on the rim with the other. I squeeze it into my mouth, let the bitterness cut through for a second, and then throw back the tequila in one smooth motion, welcoming the burn as it goes down.

She swipes my debit card from the counter, ignores the ID, and runs the payment while I breathe through the heat in my chest. The second she drops the receipt in front of me, I scribble a signature and slide a five-dollar tip her way before pocketing both my cards again.

Grabbing the two beer bottles by the neck in one hand, I make my way back toward Kline. He's already leaning back in his seat, watching me with that easy smirk like he's been waiting for me to hurry the hell up.

I set both the bottles down in front of us. Kline doesn't waste any time and jams a lime wedge into the bottle. He throws it back, taking a long swig as I sit in the chair opposite him. When he finally comes up for air, there's maybe a third left in the bottle.

"Thanks, man," he says as he wipes his mouth with the back of his hand, setting the bottle down on the table.

"Don't mention it," I reply as I shove the lime into the bottle, then take a sip, the bitter aftertaste coating the back of my tongue as I swallow.

We sit in comfortable silence for a few beats, letting the buzz of the bar fill the space between us. Pool balls clack in the distance, country music hums low through the speakers, and the occasional burst of laughter or curse comes from across the room.

Kline leans back in his seat, one arm draped over the backrest, bottle in hand. He takes a long sip, then exhales slowly, the corners of his mouth twitching into a relaxed grin. "You know," he says after a beat, voice low and reflective, "sometimes I forget how damn nice it is to sit down and have a beer without having to watch your six."

I nod, nursing the last few sips of mine. "Yeah. Too many nights end with adrenaline still jacked through my system. It's nice to come down without crashing face-first into bed."

Kline lets out a short laugh, tipping his bottle lazily. "Remember that call a few months ago? The naked guy on the roof, screaming about government drones spying on his cat?"

I smirk around the rim of my beer. "How could I forget? You were the lucky bastard who had to climb up there."

He groans like the memory physically pains him. "Damn rain gutter tried to kill me. I still have a scar on my hip."

I chuckle as he polishes off the last of his bottle and shakes it, the lime inside rattling like a bell. "I'm grabbing another. You want?" he asks, already halfway out of his seat.

I glance down at my empty bottle, then shake my head. "Nah, I'm good. You go ahead."

Kline nods and strolls to the bar, leaning against the

counter with the ease of someone who's been here more times than they'll ever admit. His shirt rides up just enough to reveal the grip of his off-duty piece tucked into the back of his jeans. It's too loud to make out what he is saying to the bartender, but whatever it is, it makes her laugh. Her body language practically flirting back as she slides him a fresh beer and a receipt. I don't catch the exchange, but whatever he said must've landed.

He returns a minute later, a smug grin etched across his face and slaps the receipt onto the table. "Check it out, man."

I raise an eyebrow, glancing down. A name (Vicky) and number scribbled in loopy handwriting. "You got her number?" I say, slight shock evident in my tone. "You gonna call her?" I ask as he goes through the ritual again—lime in, then sip.

"I dunno, maybe." He shrugs. "Depends on how many more of these I have."

I laugh and stand, stretching slightly as I glance at the bartender. Even under the neon lighting from the sign above the bar, I could tell she was flushed. "Well, whatever you decide—wear a damn condom."

Kline snorts into his drink. "Always do, Mom."

"Anyway, I'm calling it. We have an early shift, and I don't like working on shit sleep," I say.

"Yeah, no one likes you when you're tired," he mutters with a smirk. "You become more of an asshole than usual. What the hell was that earlier, anyway? With the intern?"

I tense slightly. The last thing I want is a breakdown of my behavior. "Lack of sleep. And my deep, undying hatred of ride-alongs that you were far too quick to agree to."

Kline gives me a knowing look, smug as hell. "You liked her. Don't gotta lie, Perez."

"I'm not lying," I grumble. Then add, after a pause, "But yeah. I liked her—or at least my dick did. Can't deny that she is hot."

He chokes out a laugh. “So what, that’s your excuse for acting like a dick to her? You get all flustered and revert to middle school tactics?”

I groan, dragging my hand through my hair. “I don’t know, man. She got under my skin. I was a dick because I didn’t know what else to do. I just hope she’ll forgive me and take my lame ass excuse.”

“You’d better hope that excuse of yours comes with a peace offering,” he says, finishing the bottle and then sliding it into the ever-growing pile forming.

“Yeah, well. Good luck with the bartender.”

“You too, loverboy,” he calls after me, already eyeing the bar again like he’s deciding if he’s got one more in him.

I shake my head, chuckling to myself as I head toward the exit. If he actually shows up to shift tomorrow, it’ll be a damn miracle.

Del
F12
End
PgUp
PgDn
Home
P
L
K
M
N

SEVEN
RAELYNN

BY THE TIME I cut across the long, brick-lined green in front of Koffler, the sun is already a fist on the back of my neck. Morning heat rises off the pavement in soft mirage-waves. It's not even nine yet, and I'm already regretting my choice to wear all black. The steps up to Koffler are crowded—the slivers of shade feel rationed—and the soundtrack is first-week chaos: iced coffees clacking ice, syllabus complaints, "what's your major" micro-introductions.

I dodge two guys on skateboards and sidestep a poor soul juggling a melting frappuccino, his cell phone, and a crumbling breakfast burrito like he's in a circus act. I shoulder past with a murmured "sorry" and yank open the door to Room 204.

As soon as I step into the lecture hall, a blast of ice-cold air hits me, and I welcome it. The cool air immediately chills my flushed skin, causing goosebumps to bloom. I let out a sigh of relief as I make my way to my chosen seat, halfway up the tiered rows, and slide in beside my friends. Khloe has toned down her school spirit and decided that chaotic comfort was the choice attire for this lovely morning. She's in an oversized graphic tee with a worn-for-wear skull printed on the front, the collar of the shirt hanging off her right shoulder, a pair of black leggings with little tears in the knees, and her tan Ugg boots. Her hair's loose and wavy, like she rolled out of bed and let the breeze style it.

Marlena, on the other hand, looks like she stepped out of an Instagram ad for fairy grunge. She's rocking a pale blue knee-length dress with soft lace detailing, paired with heavy black combat boots. Her blonde curls are arranged in perfect ringlets that bounce every time she laughs during her conversation with Austin. Compared to them, I look like a half-assed horror movie reject. My favorite *Scream* tee, faded black leggings, and my scuffed combat boots. I tossed my hair into a high ponytail and didn't bother with makeup. I just didn't have it in me this morning—not the time, not the energy, and definitely not the fucks.

After quick greetings, I settle into my seat and slide my laptop out of my book bag.

Henley stands at the front of the room, arms folded, radiating that unreadable calm of his. He's dressed in dark gray slacks, held up by a pair of matching suspenders. His white shirt is crisp with the sleeves rolled to his elbows, revealing his tattoos that decorate his forearms. His jaw is freshly shaved, and his hair is tousled just enough to look deliberate without being try-hard. There's something effortlessly sharp about him, like he walked out of a noir detective film and into our class.

As soon as the clock reads nine, Henley doesn't wait. He dives right into the lecture.

"Today, we start at the roots—where modern criminology first took shape," Henley begins, flipping to the first slide of his PowerPoint. A black-and-white portrait of an old man with wild hair and sunken eyes flashes on the screen.

"If you are going to remember any name this week, make sure it's this one: Cesare Lombroso. The so-called father of criminology," Henley says, his voice smooth and commanding.

"Lombroso believed criminals weren't made, they were born. He believed that one could identify a criminal by studying their physical characteristics, such as sloping foreheads, facial asymmetry, long arms, and large ears. Basically, if someone looked 'off,' he assumed they were dangerous. He called them 'born criminals.'"

He clicks through slides: old anatomical sketches, diagrams of skulls, unsettling mugshots.

"He spent years cataloguing cadavers, measuring skulls, searching for the biological blueprint of evil," Henley continues, his voice even but intense. "It was pseudoscience, obviously. But at the time, it was revolutionary. Lombroso was the first to suggest that criminal behavior had observable, measurable causes. That crime wasn't just a result of sin or poor choices—it could be studied. Predicted, even."

The lecture completely enthralls me, and by the end of it, my Google Doc is filled with bullet points, quickly hashed-out notes, underlined phrases, and several question marks and stars on points I have more questions about and what I thought was important to remember.

At the end of the lecture, Henley goes over the assignment —a short reading, and then a one-page essay in response— then dismisses us with a curt nod.

"Raelynn, can you stay for a moment?" he calls as soon as I rise, my laptop tucked under my arm as I pick my bag up off the floor and set it into my seat.

A few heads swivel my way, and heat floods my cheeks. Of course, Khloe shoots me a look that screams mischief. Her smirk says it all—her brain is already busy spinning some fantasy about a scandalous affair between me and the professor. I'm convinced at this point the woman *lives* in the damn gutter. Sex is *always* on her mind. It does not matter who the subject matter is.

"Not a fucking word, Khloe," I mutter, holding in a

nervous laugh as I shove my laptop into its designated slot and sling my bag over my shoulder.

I make the walk down the steep rows toward him, each step echoing against the tiered floor. Henley leans against the edge of the desk, his arms folded across his chest.

"Hello, Professor," I say, my voice coming out steadier than I feel as I try not to stare too obviously at every bit of this man has to offer. Up close, he is definitely more striking than expected (I do have a minimal view from my seat after all). His eyes are nearly the same shade as mine, though a little duller —like the color had been drained by time or weariness. Faint crow's feet sit at the corners, subtle but present, hints of a life lived with more than just books and lectures.

Barely breaching the collar of his white shirt is the inked head of a snake, its forked tongue stretched toward the delicate skin at his pulse point. It's a detail I never would have pictured on someone so meticulously polished. And there's a faint scar along the underside of his jaw, usually hidden by a beard, but now bare and exposed thanks to a fresh shave.

For a man with the pristine reputation of a respected professor, he carries a surprising roughness. A sharp edge beneath the veneer of academia. It makes me wonder what kind of life he lived before this one.

"I wanted to follow up before I finalize the list of paper topics," he says, pushing off the desk and rising to his full height. His presence feels larger up close. He's easily taller than Perez—6'5" if I had to guess.

"You've proposed focusing your term paper on The Butcher case." It isn't posed as a question. His tone suggests he already knows the answer, but he waits anyway, giving me room to speak.

"Yes, sir," I say. My grip tightens on the strap of my bag. "It fascinates me. It's… important to me."

A flicker crosses his expression—too quick to name. "Important," he repeats, like he's testing the weight of the word. His eyes sharpen, pinning me in place. "You're certain it's the right choice? Cases like this carry… baggage."

The word hangs between us, heavier than it should. My chest tightens. "I can handle it."

Henley tilts his head slightly, as though studying me under a microscope. "I have no doubt you're capable. But I also know that objectivity is harder to maintain when the subject matter strikes close."

My stomach knots. "How did you…?" My question dies on my tongue. Of course, he knows, anyone with a brain can connect the dots.

"I've spent years studying the case," he answers smoothly. "Patterns, timelines, victimology. Connections are easier to see when you've read every detail." He pauses, letting the silence stretch, his eyes never leaving mine. "Your last name isn't one easily overlooked in that context."

The air leaves my lungs in a sharp exhale. My shoulders stiffen, gaze dropping slightly to the side.

"I appreciate your concern, sir," I say carefully, willing my voice not to waver. "But it doesn't change my decision."

Henley regards me for a long moment, unreadable. Then, finally, he inclines his head. "Very well. If you find it becomes… more than you anticipated, my door is open." A faint smile curves at his lips, one that doesn't touch his eyes. "I'd rather you asked for help than carried the weight alone."

"Thank you, sir." The words scrape out of me, eager to be free of his gaze.

I turn sharply, striding for the exit. Even as I push through the side door into the hall, I feel it—the weight of his attention lingering, following like a shadow that doesn't want to be shaken.

Outside, Khloe and Marlena are waiting. Khloe's grin is feral the moment she spots me. "Sooo…" she drawls, leaning in. "What did Professor Tall-Dark-and-Tattooed want?" she asks, following it with a giggle.

Rolling my eyes, I drop my bag on the ground. "He just wanted to make sure I was okay doing my paper on The Butcher. Y'know… because of my connection."

Marlena's lips part with a small gasp. "He knows?"

"It wasn't hard for him to put two and two together," I sigh, lowering myself onto the cement bench bolted to the wall.

Khloe leans in, refusing to let it drop. "So… what did you say?"

"That I appreciate his concern, but I'm still doing it." I shrug, settling back against the bench.

Khloe smirks knowingly. "Of course you did. No one could ever talk you out of anything. You're stubborn as fuck."

I laugh under my breath. "Yeah, that's true."

Pulling my phone from my bag, I double-tap the screen to check the time. I still have half an hour before my least favorite class, and I'm seriously debating whether to show up or not. I was not mentally prepared for it. Just thinking about sitting through seventy-five minutes of that monotone torture makes me want to rip my hair out.

"Hey, I'm gonna go get a coffee, anyone wanna come with? It's on me," I say after a beat.

"Yes, please," Marlena and Khloe say in unison.

I glance at Austin, and he shakes his head after checking his phone. "Nah, I'm good, Rae. I gotta head to my class, but thanks, hun," he says, his lips curling into a smile as he pulls Marlena into him and presses his lips to her forehead. "I'll see y'all later."

The three of us head across the quad, weaving through the usual swarm of welcome tents and overeager campus ministries that always pop up during the first week. By the time we slip inside the bookstore Starbucks, the blast of air conditioning feels like salvation. Only a few people stand in line before us, but at least ten or so more people stand off to the side, chatting idly as they wait for their orders. Unfortunately, I am the only one who has class soon, but I also don't give two fucks about being on time. If *she* wants to mark me absent for being late, oh fucking well. Missing one class won't kill my grade. I can miss up to four times before I get an automatic fail.

After about a five-minute wait in line, I finally order our drinks. I go with my usual grande iced vanilla blonde latte with vanilla cold foam. Marlena decides on a grande matcha latte with strawberry-flavored cold foam, and Khloe orders a caramel ribbon crunch frappuccino in the largest size available, the fucking trenta. I shoot Khloe a heated glare as I pay the tab, then join them at an open table tucked beside the emergency exit.

"Coffee is on you next time," I mutter as I drop my bag onto the ground beside my seat.

She only giggles, clearly unbothered. "Deal."

Almost ten minutes crawl by before my name is finally called. Relief washes over me, and we push away from the table to collect our drinks. Marlena grabs her matcha latte with a bright grin, Khloe clutches her massive frappuccino like it's a newborn, and I secure my iced vanilla blonde latte, straw in hand.

The second we step outside, the heat slams into us like we've opened the door to an oven preheated to four hundred degrees. The blast of dry air steals the breath right from my lungs, clinging to my skin and making the condensation on my cup vanish almost instantly.

"Alright," I sigh, tightening my grip on the cold plastic as I tug the hem of my shirt out, fanning myself with it.

The Arizona sun is ruthless—like the devil's own breath scorching the earth. We're supposed to be easing into fall, but apparently, Mother Nature didn't get the memo. And to make matters worse, the monsoon season has been practically nonexistent this year: hardly any storms, barely any relief—just unrelenting heat.

"I'm off to endure seventy-five minutes of pure torture," I announce, taking a long pull from my coffee. The caffeine is necessary, even if it's already fighting a losing battle against the exhaustion of the day. "I'll see y'all later for lunch?"

"Same place, same time?" Marlena asks, raising her cup with an easy smile.

I nod mid-sip, returning her grin before waving them off. With the sun already prickling against the back of my neck, I start my slow, reluctant trek toward the Chemistry Building —dragging my feet like I'm on my way to my own execution.

I sit cross-legged in bed, the morning sun streaming through the half-open blinds, casting soft streaks of light across my comforter. Max is curled up before me, his massive head resting in my lap. He's snoring gently, his hind leg twitching every now and then in response to some dream he's chasing. I absentmindedly scratch behind his ears while my other hand cradles my phone, thumb flicking lazily through the usual parade of masked men, bikers, book-related posts, and chaotic meme dumps clogging up my feed. It's Friday, and after my alarm woke my ass up, I heavily debated whether or not I wanted to drive to campus for my only class, despite it being one of my favorites.

Clearly, I chose not to, or I wouldn't still be doomscrolling on Instagram.

Neither Tessa nor I have to work. Her parents are the reason for that little miracle. They cover the rent on our apartment, the bills, groceries, and practically everything else we could ever possibly need. They insisted on it from the start, wanting us to focus on school rather than worrying about making ends meet. Her dad is a trauma surgeon at the university hospital, and her mom owns a veterinary clinic, so money's never really been an issue for them.

At first, I felt guilty as hell living off their generosity. I'd been under their roof since I was thirteen, and even though they took me in without hesitation, I couldn't shake the need to earn my keep. During my first year of college, I got a job as a caregiver to help with expenses, as I was convinced I needed to contribute something. That brilliant decision nearly tanked my GPA. I was placed on academic probation, risking the loss of my financial aid and scholarship. I pulled through (barely) and, after a long talk (and an even longer crying session), I finally accepted the deal they'd offered.

They've never treated me like an outsider, never made me feel like a charity case. And every time I open the fridge to see it fully stocked or find an envelope of "pocket money" slid into my mail slot, I swear I could cry.

I'll never stop being grateful for what they've done for me. Not just the money, but also the way they welcomed me like family without hesitation or strings attached.

Eventually, the dopamine buzz from scrolling socials fizzles out, and like clockwork, I swipe over to my news app. No matter how grim or disturbing, I always end up here. It's a reflex now—compulsion dressed up as curiosity. It doesn't just whisper to me, it claws at the back of my mind until I give in.

There isn't much this morning—a couple of drug busts, some domestic disturbances, and a hit-and-run. Then, tucked between headlines about rising heat advisories and a city council debate, one article catches my eye.

Young Woman Found Fatally Stabbed Behind East Side Strip Mall—Identity Still Unknown

My thumb hesitates only a second before I tap the link.

The article is vague, which suggests that the case is still fresh, possibly even hours old. The body was discovered early this morning behind a cluster of dumpsters in a narrow alley, not far from a 24-hour smoke shop and a cash-only pawn store. The area is renowned for its vibrant nightlife and the diverse range of activities that thrive after dark.

No ID. No wallet. No phone.

The victim was estimated to be in her early twenties. Petite. Signs of recent drug use, according to an unnamed source. The coroner has confirmed multiple stab wounds, but no weapon was found. She was wearing black strappy heels, a black mini skirt, and a neon pink crop top when she was found—an outfit the article pointedly describes as "indicative of sex work." Just subtle enough to be judgmental.

There's no surveillance footage, no suspects, no motive—just a young woman with no name, discarded like garbage.

My chest tightens—not with fear, but something sharper. Anger. Someone did this and walked away. And unless someone cares enough to dig deeper, she'll be chalked up as another statistic. Another body in a city that's no stranger to bloodshed.

I sigh and drop my head against the headboard, rubbing my fingers through Max's short, silky fur. His tail thumps once against the mattress, like he's reassuring me.

My phone buzzes against my thigh, vibrating hard enough to jolt Max's ears. He lifts his head, blinking up at me sleepily while I glance at the screen.

KHLOE:

Do you and Tessa want to hang out today? I'm bored, and Marlena is too busy fucking Austin to literally do anything else.

A laugh bubbles up before I can stop it. That girl has no filter. I tap out a reply with a smirk.

ME:

Will Dutch Bros be involved if I say yes?

I watch as the little typing bubble appears, dances, then

disappears and reappears. After a few seconds, a message comes through

KHLOE:

I do owe ya one.

ME:

Yes, you do. Did you even finish that monstrosity????

KHLOE:

LOL No. I think I got about 3/4ths of the way before I had to throw it away 😆

ME:

😛

KHLOE:

😆

Anyways, what do you want to drink, and what are we doing?

ME:

Nutty Irishman, obviously, and come over here. I have snacks, and we can talk about boys while watching something cheesy, because Tessa might literally smother me in my sleep if I put on something murder-y.

KHLOE:

BOYS YOU SAY???? DEAL! Give me like an hour and I'm there!

I laugh again and toss my phone gently onto the bed, watching it bounce once before settling into the blanket folds. Max looks up at me and yawns before standing up. He shakes out the lingering sleep, then hops off the bed as I throw my comforter off me.

Time to make myself presentable before the Chaos Queen arrives.

I put in *zero* effort to look decent today. Khloe was about to get the bare minimum from me—overslept, under-caffeinated, and utterly uninterested in pretending I cared about appearances. I was exhausted, and if I wasn't leaving the apartment, then a bra was absolutely not happening.

I throw on an oversized purple t-shirt—soft, slightly worn, and perfect for a lazy day—and a pair of black leggings. My hair is twisted up into a messy bun with a claw clip, not for style but to keep it out of my face. That was as far as I was willing to go today.

Yawning, I shuffle out of my room, Max padding closely behind me like a loyal little shadow. The hallway opens up into the living room, where Tessa's voice greets me before I even reach the end of it.

"Morning, Sleeping Beauty," she calls, her tone light and teasing.

I roll my eyes but smirk as I head straight for the patio door. "How long have you been up?" I ask as I unlock it and slide it open. Max trots outside without hesitation, tail wagging like it's the best part of his day.

Tessa is curled up on the couch, legs tucked underneath her, a steaming mug of coffee balanced in her hands. She's wearing a pair of black spandex shorts and a burgundy butterfly Sleep Token t-shirt that's roughly two sizes too large for her. Her hair is braided and draped over her left shoulder, strands falling loose in that perfectly imperfect way she always seems to pull off without trying.

"About two hours," she says casually, bringing the mug to her lips.

I blink. "The fuck are you doing up so early?"

"Rae," she snorts into her coffee. "It's almost noon."

My brows lift as I blink again, like that might make time rewind. I slide my phone out of my leggings' waistband and check it—11:52 a.m. Well shit. Guess I got a little *too* into my morning doom scroll.

"Huh. I guess it is," I mutter, sliding my phone back into my waistband. "Anyway, Khloe's on her way over," I say as I lean out the door to check on Max.

"I know. She texted me like twenty minutes ago," Tessa says, eyes focused on the TV as she scrolls through the endless black hole of streaming options. "Said she's bringing caffeine and probably gossip."

Max eventually trots back inside, his tongue lolling from the side of his mouth as he pants happily. His tail wags like a metronome set to chaos, sweeping side to side as he heads straight for the couch like it's his throne. Without hesitation, he leaps up and circles once before flopping down beside Tessa, pressing his warm body against her legs with a huff of satisfaction.

Tessa smiles down at him and leans forward to set her coffee mug on the table. She eases back into the cushions and gently runs her fingers through Max's fur. He practically melts beneath her touch, his tail thumping softly against the cushions in lazy approval.

I watch them briefly before turning toward the kitchen. My stomach grumbles loud enough to be annoying, so I head over to make something simple. I rummage through the cabinets, grab the honey-roasted peanut butter and raspberry preserves, then pull a couple of slices of butter bread from the loaf. I'm halfway through spreading the peanut butter when a knock echoes from the front door.

"Hey, Tess, can you get that? I'm kinda elbow-deep in sandwich prep," I call out, licking some peanut butter from the knife without shame.

"Isn't it unlocked, though?" she replies, already pushing off the couch with a soft groan.

"Yeah, but she probably has her hands full or something," I reply as I return to my sandwich prep.

Tessa mutters something under her breath but shuffles toward the front door anyway. She yanks it open and pauses. "Uh… no one's here," she says, her voice colored with confusion.

I peek out from the kitchen, sandwich in one hand and the knife coated in the raspberry preserves in the other. "Seriously?"

"I swear, no one—wait, what's this?" She steps just outside momentarily, then returns holding a small white envelope. She closes the door behind her and eyes it curiously.

"What is it?" I ask as I toss the knife into the sink, then take a bite of my sandwich as I exit the kitchen.

"A card, I think. It was tucked under the welcome mat," she replies, flipping it over in her hands. "There's no stamp or return address. Just… a name."

"Whose name?" I ask through another bite.

Tessa looks up, brows knitting slightly as she holds it out. "Yours."

Del
F12
End
PgUp
PgDn
Home

EIGHT
RAELYNN

"MINE?" I ask, mid-chew, finishing off the last bite of my sandwich. Crumbs stick to my fingers as I motion for Tessa to hand over the envelope.

"Yeah." She passes it with a faint frown.

I wipe my hands against my shirt before taking it, turning the envelope over a few times. It's one of those cheap ones that come with dollar store cards. My name is scrawled across the front in jagged capital letters—rushed, sharp, the pen biting into the paper hard enough to indent. There's no return address. No stickers, no flourishes, none of the usual signs of a friend or family member sending something thoughtful.

A prickle runs down my spine. "Weird," I murmur. "The handwriting doesn't look familiar."

I'm just about to slide my finger under the envelope's seal when a sharp knock jolts both me and Tessa. We flinch, eyes snapping to the front door. For a split second, neither of us says anything—we just stare, as if expecting something (or someone) to burst through it.

Then Khloe's unmistakable voice cuts through the silence like a blade through tension.

"Ding dong, bitches!"

Tessa exhales a shaky laugh and shakes her head, a mix of relief and exasperation etched across her face. "God, Khloe," she mutters as she crosses the living room and pulls the door open without missing a beat.

Khloe struts in like she owns the place, a drink carrier full of Dutch Bros balanced expertly in her hands. She's dressed in peak comfort mode: a faded pink Nirvana smiley tee that hangs off one shoulder, black leggings, and tan UGG boots. Her hair is loose for once, her shoulder-length locks bouncing with each step she takes.

Max springs off the couch the second she's through the door, tail wagging furiously as he trots over to greet her.

"Sup," Khloe says breezily, nudging the door shut behind her with her foot as she bends down to give Max the attention he's demanding. "Hi, buddy," she coos, running her fingers behind his ears while he nuzzles her in approval.

She walks the tray over to the coffee table and sets it down before turning her attention to me. Her eyes catch on the envelope still in my hand, and one brow arches. "Whatcha got there, Rae?" she asks, her tone light but tinged with curiosity.

I'm sure the confusion's still written all over my face, heavy and unmoving. "A card," I murmur. "Someone left it on our porch a few minutes ago. No clue who it's from."

Max gives Khloe one last nudge of affection before trotting back to the couch, curling into the warm indent he'd left behind—content now that he's completed his greeting. Meanwhile, the envelope in my hand feels like it weighs a hundred pounds.

"Well… are you gonna open it or just glare at it like it insulted your outfit?" Khloe teases, her smirk not quite masking the edge in her voice. She snags a coffee from the tray and passes it to Tessa before grabbing another and walking it over to me.

Her smirk fades as she offers me the cup. "Here. Drink."

I take the iced Nutty Irishman, the familiar sweetness

coating my tongue when I sip, but it doesn't settle the prickle crawling up my spine. The envelope seems louder now, the edges sharp against my fingers.

Khloe folds her arms across her chest, her gaze fixed. "Rae."

"Alright, alright." I sigh and hold the coffee out to her. "Here—hold this before I accidentally spill it all over myself."

Khloe takes the cup without protest, her eyes never leaving the envelope as I slide my finger under the flap and ease it open. Inside is a store-bought card, the kind you'd find in the sympathy section of a grocery store. The front is soft blue with delicate white trim, and across the center, in looping cursive, are the words "Thinking of You."

My brows pull together as I stare at it, unease settling low in my gut.

"The fuck?" I mutter as I unfold the card.

The handwriting inside is the same jagged scrawl as the envelope, each stroke uneven and forceful.

You look just like her.

My stomach knots. Taped just beneath the message is an old newspaper clipping, yellowed with age and fraying at the edges. The headline, jaggedly cut from a 2008 article, jumps out at me like a slap to the face:

Local Woman Found Murdered in Alleyway—Latest Victim of The Butcher.

And just below that are another six words that have my breath catching in my throat.

Will your fate be the same?

The room tilts for a second. Behind me, I hear Tessa and Khloe talking, their voices rising with concern, but they barely register—just background static swallowed by the blood rushing in my ears. I know this article. I've seen it more times than I can count. I've studied, dissected, and committed every painful detail to memory.

It's the article about my mother.

But that isn't what freaks me out. It's the second message that leaves me uneasy.

Who the hell sent this?

I stare at the card, my eyes bouncing from the article clipping to the handwriting. Someone has to be playing some kind of joke on me. It isn't a secret that my mother was murdered, and anyone with a sense of mind could put two and two together with my last name and the fact that I am practically a carbon copy of the woman. But what did they mean by 'Will my fate be the same?' Was it a threat?

"Rae?" Tessa's concerned voice finally breaks through to me. I shudder and blink, my eyes shifting from the card to her. "What is it, Rae?" she asks, her hand resting against my shoulder as if grounding me.

"Someone playing a sick joke," I mutter as she eases the card out of my hands.

"Well, that is creepy as fuck." She looks it over before handing it off to Khloe. She doesn't even bother reading it before tossing it onto the coffee table.

"Someone just has a sick sense of humor, Rae. Don't give them the satisfaction." Khloe hands me back my coffee, her tone dismissive but gentle. I take a long sip, the icy sweetness doing little to untangle the knot in my stomach.

"They're just trying to get a reaction out of you," Tessa adds, her voice calm but firm. "They can't win if you don't let them."

My eyes drift back to the card on the coffee table, the message still echoing in my mind like an itch I can't quite reach. After a beat, I nod slowly. "You're right."

I cross the room and pluck the card off the table, holding it between two fingers like it might bite. I step up to the garbage can, tucked neatly beneath the kitchen counter. I press my foot on the pedal, and the lid flips open with a soft metallic creak. Without a second thought, I drop the card and watch it disappear into the trash.

The lid thuds shut behind me as I turn back toward my friends.

"There," I say, lifting my coffee again and taking a sip. "Out of sight, out of mind."

Khloe lifts her cup in mock salute. "That's the spirit."

"So," I ask, my voice lighter now, "what's the plan for today? Something fun, I hope. I could really use a distraction that doesn't involve creepy mail."

Tessa perks up, reaching for the remote on the coffee table with a spark in her eyes. "How about cheesy rom-coms and face masks?"

Khloe snorts and walks back over to the couch. She grabs a blanket, drops onto the cushion beside Max, and throws the blanket over her legs. "I was promised snacks and boy talk, thank you very much," she says with a smirk. "Rom-coms are fine as long as someone gets dumped dramatically or ends up kissing in the rain."

I laugh as I make my way back into the living room, settling into my spot on the couch beside her with my iced coffee in hand. "All of that sounds perfect—except maybe the rom-coms. I was leaning toward cheesy horror, but I know Tess can't stomach it."

Tessa shoots me a look, playfully defensive. "Horror *parodies* and low-budget ridiculousness are fine. As long as there's no over-the-top gore or jump scares, I can deal."

Khloe and I lock eyes, mischief blooming instantly. "Okay," I say, grinning. "*Killer Klowns from Outer Space* or—"

"*Scary Movie*," Khloe cuts in, practically bouncing with excitement. "Classic."

"Ooh, both good options." I nod, trying to gauge Tessa's reaction. "*Killer Klowns from Outer Space* or *Scary Movie*? Choose your fate."

Tessa groans dramatically. "Ugh, I hate clowns—so I guess *Scary Movie*. But if I have nightmares, I'm blaming both of you."

"Deal," Khloe and I chime simultaneously, grinning as Tessa passes me the remote, then rounds the coffee table and takes a seat beside me. She settles into the couch, folding her legs under her as I scroll through the apps on our smart TV.

After a few seconds, I find and click on Paramount Plus, waiting through the brief loading screen. Once it's up, I type "*Scary Movie*" into the search bar and hit play without hesitation. The familiar opening music starts, and I drop the remote into my lap before fishing my phone out from the waistband of my leggings.

"Alright, Khloe—snack commander, it's your time to shine." I hand her my phone, already open to the food delivery app.

She takes it like she's receiving a sacred artifact. "Death to your wallet, babe," she cackles, immediately diving into the app like it's her life's mission.

Twenty minutes into the movie, a knock sounds at the door.

"I got it." Khloe springs off the couch like she's been waiting for this moment. The sudden movement startles Max from his nap. His head jerks up, ears twitching as he blinks around in mild confusion.

I rise with her and whistle softly. "Max, c'mere," I call as I make my way toward my room. He lumbers off the couch, still groggy, and trots after me. "Sorry, buddy. You know how you get when food shows up," I whisper as he glides past me into the room. He hops onto the bed with a soft *fwump*, circles once, settling with a sigh. I close the door gently behind me and head back into the living room.

The sight that greets me stops me in my tracks.

"Jesus, what the fuck did you buy?" I blurt, eyebrows shooting up as Khloe, looking way too pleased with herself, starts unloading the bags onto the coffee table.

"She bought the whole damn app, that's what she did,"

Tessa quips, still curled up in her spot on the couch. Her laughter spills out as she sees the pure disbelief on my face.

Khloe snorts and flips her hair over one shoulder with mock offense. "Excuse me, I exercised *great* restraint. It's just Taco Bell, Crumbl cookies, and a few absolutely necessary survival items from 7-Eleven. You're welcome, by the way."

I glance down at the growing pile taking over the coffee table: six soft tacos, a pile of sauce packets, a large Crumbl box, several plastic bags filled with candy and chips, and three bottles of Vanilla Coke.

"That's your definition of restraint?" I raise a brow as I grab one of the tacos and peel the paper back. "Remind me never to hand you my phone while you're hungry," I say as I take a bite.

Tessa doesn't wait either. She reaches for two tacos, selects a couple of sauces, and pulls a bottle of Vanilla Coke from the bag, arranging everything neatly on her lap. "Shouldn't have trusted her with your phone, Rae," she says with a mischievous grin. "This is on you."

I roll my eyes, but there's no real heat behind it, and grab one of the bottles from the bag before flopping back onto the couch with the taco.

"Lesson learned," I mutter through a chuckle. I set my taco down in my lap and crack open my bottle, taking a long, satisfying swig. After a few seconds, I close the bottle and shove it between me and the cushion and take another bite from my taco.

Khloe hums happily to herself, then flips open the Crumbl cookie box like she's unveiling a crown jewel. The smell alone makes my mouth water. Nestled inside are six oversized cookies—two classic chocolate chip, two churro cookies with gooey Nutella centers, and two frosted pink sugar cookies that look almost too perfect to eat.

"Holy *shit*," I mumble mid-chew, eyeing the cookies like I've just been handed proof that heaven exists.

"You're welcome," Khloe replies smugly, plucking a churro cookie for herself and sinking back into the couch like a queen surveying her feast. She tugs the blanket over her lap again and grabs her drink.

I reclaim the remote from the arm of the couch and unpause our movie. The film picks up with the group of friends stripping the body of the man they thought they killed and tossing him into the water, the tone just as ridiculous and darkly hilarious as I remember.

We settle in again, laughter already spilling between bites of food and sips of soda.

By the time *Scary Movie* ends, we've polished off all the tacos, half the Crumbl cookies, and all the Vanilla Coke while the bags of chips and candy lie untouched on the table. After a short debate about what to watch next (and Tessa's puppy eyes), we queue up *Clueless*. The second it starts, the whole room softens, lulled by the nostalgia of it all. The face masks we'd talked about earlier? Completely forgotten. Too much work. We are content with being lazy, wrapped in fleece blankets, and gossip.

The boy talk kicks off about twenty minutes into *Clueless*, right after Cher strolls into class late, batting her lashes and somehow still managing to win over the teacher. Khloe, unsurprisingly, is the first to take the floor—and she does it with her usual dramatic flair.

"Okay, so listen," she says, sitting forward and flicking her ponytail like she's about to present a TED Talk. "This week? Chaos."

She launches into a rapid-fire rundown of every guy she's found hot this week, complete with unsolicited details about who she's slept with and where. There are zero filters—absolutely none. I swear the girl's libido has no off switch. She wears the term "hoe" like a crown. I seriously did not need to know that the frat boy from her Forensic Anthropology class had rearranged her guts with his "eight-inch cock."

"You're such a hoe," I mutter around a laugh, tossing a pillow at her.

"Proudly," she fires back as she catches the pillow. She hugs it to her chest and smirks at me. "Now spill it, Rae. Who's been on your mind?"

I fall quiet, gnawing on the corner of my straw. My Dutch Bros cup has been empty for a while now. I refilled it once with water but couldn't be bothered to do it again—or toss it out—so now I'm just chewing the straw for something to do. Something to keep my hands busy. Something to focus on that isn't the sudden heat creeping up the back of my neck.

"Oh my god," Tessa gasps, sitting up straighter. "There is someone!"

"No, there's not," I lie, very, very poorly.

"Bullshit," they say in perfect, suspicious harmony.

I shoot them a weak glare, trying to stall, but I know it's over. "Fine. If I *had* to name someone…" I trail off, hoping the sentence dies there, but Khloe's already leaning in like a bloodhound on a scent.

"Spill it, Rae."

I hesitate. The name is already at the front of my mind, uninvited and stubborn. Emilio Perez. The man who treated me like I was deadweight. Who laughed at my goals like they were a joke. Who looked at me like I didn't belong.

But also the man with golden eyes, forearms full of ink, a voice that made my stomach flutter in the worst (best) kind of way. And those lips…

"Emilio Perez," I mumble, defeated.

Tessa's eyebrows shoot up. "The grumpy hot cop?"

Fuck me for telling her about him. I knew it was going to bite me in the ass later, and yet I still spilled the beans about someone I found incredibly attractive, minus the damn attitude.

"He's not hot," I lie immediately.

Khloe shrieks, clapping her hands like she just won a bet. "I *knew* it! Girl, your face betrayed you *so fast.*"

"I don't even like him!" I argue. "He's rude, arrogant, and treated me like I was a complete waste of time."

"But would you climb him like a tree?" Khloe asks, deadpan.

"Absolutely," I blurt before my brain catches up to my mouth. I freeze. "I mean—ugh. Maybe. I don't know. My brain is broken."

They lose it. The room explodes with laughter.

We talk for a while longer—about everything and nothing. *Clueless* ends, and we throw on the first season of *The Rookie* as background noise. We eventually polish off the rest of the snacks, so I let Max out. He makes a beeline for the patio door, and I throw it open so he can do his business. When he returns, he goes straight for the wrappers on the coffee table like a food-seeking missile. He noses through the mess until I catch him trying to chew a Taco Bell wrapper, then, thoroughly disappointed, he settles on the couch behind Khloe, his tail thumping lazily against the cushions.

I gather up the trash and clean up the table. When I finally sit back down, Max stretches and rests his head in my lap like it's always been his place.

We continue to chat until the sky outside darkens and the soft buzz of fatigue starts to settle over us.

Tessa yawns and stretches. "I am hella tired, so I'm heading to bed," she mumbles mid-yawn before disappearing down the hall and into her bedroom without another word.

Khloe lingers beside the couch, already half-curled under the throw blanket.

"I'm too tired to drive," she mutters, voice thick with drowsiness. "I'm crashing here."

I smile and rise from the couch, grabbing one of the pillows from the armrest. "Wouldn't have it any other way."

I toss it her way, and she catches it with a sleepy grin.

"Thanks, babe," she says as she slowly gets up from the floor, clutching both the blanket and pillow to her chest.

"You're welcome, hoe," I tease softly as I head toward the hallway.

She snorts and flops down, the pillow now tucked beneath her head as she settles in. The blanket shifts with her as she curls into a cocoon, already halfway to unconsciousness.

I flick off the overhead light, the room falling into soft darkness, then call out, "C'mon, Max."

He hops down from his spot on the couch without hesitation, nails tapping lightly on the floor as he trails behind me. I glance back once, watching Khloe's chest rise and fall in a slow rhythm, her breathing steady. The apartment is quiet now, the chaos of earlier replaced by the kind of peace only late-night comfort can bring.

But my mind? It's anything but quiet.

By the time I push into my bedroom and close the door behind me, the cozy calm of the night is already slipping through my fingers, replaced by a low, thrumming tension that's been building all damn day. It pulses just beneath my skin, coiled tight in my stomach and burning low between my thighs.

Emilio. Fucking. Perez.

Just thinking his name sends a ripple down my spine. I grit my teeth.

I hate that he's in my head like this. Hate that every time I close my eyes, I see that stupid, smug smirk, those golden brown eyes, the tattoo inked across his arm that I keep imagining wrapped around me. His voice—deep, clipped, irritated—keeps replaying in my head like a song I didn't ask to like.

And the worst part? My body doesn't care that he's an arrogant asshole who treated me like an inconvenience. It wants him anyway.

I shed my clothes slowly, one layer at a time. The oversized t-shirt hits the floor first, followed by my leggings, then my panties, already damp with my arousal, which only pisses me off more. Max hops up, circles the foot of the bed twice, and settles with a sigh, chin on his paws. I slip beneath the sheets completely bare and let the coolness of the microfiber chase a shiver up my spine.

For a minute I just lie there, staring at the ceiling, listening to the faint hum of the A/C and Max's breathing. Once his breathing evens out, I reach into the bottom drawer of my nightstand and pull out my black rose-shaped vibrator. I long-press the button, and once it turns on, I readjust the covers over myself, the soft hum making my thighs twitch in anticipation.

I don't fight it anymore. I can't. I let my mind go exactly where it's been aching to go.

Emilio cornering me against a wall. Voice dark and low in my ear, telling me to shut up before he makes me. His hands on my waist. His mouth at my throat. That lethal gaze holding mine as he presses closer and growls that he's thought about ruining me for days. Since the first moment I opened my mouth and challenged him.

I press the vibrator against my clit and gasp, the contact electric, sharp, and immediate. My back arches, hips twitching as the pleasure rushes through me like a wave I've been holding back all day.

Fuck, yes.

Heat floods my cheeks, and I bite the inside of my lip to keep quiet. My fingers curl in the sheets beside me as I adjust the vibrator just slightly. My eyes flutter closed, and a soft, breathy moan escapes my lips as my mind gives in to the fantasy completely.

His left hand pinning my wrists above my head, dragging his mouth down my throat, growling things I shouldn't want to hear. Telling me how badly he wants me. How long he's imagined ruining me as his right hand slides between my legs.

His fingers circling my clit before slipping inside my pussy. His pace slow at first, then rough. Hungry.

My toes curl as my orgasm hits fast and hot, stealing my breath. I clamp a hand over my mouth, muffling the sound that escapes, and ride it out in silence, teeth sinking into my knuckles. My thighs tremble, and my chest rises and falls in uneven waves.

When the tide recedes, I collapse into the pillow and blink up at the ceiling. My heart beats loudly in my ears as I try to catch my breath.

God, I'm so screwed.

Because I don't just want Emilio Perez.

I *need* him.

And that was going to complicate things.

NINE
RAELYNN

STANDING in front of my dresser, I stare at my reflection like it might offer some guidance. I'm caught in that weird limbo of both dreading and looking forward to my shift today.

Rodriguez had called me yesterday afternoon, just before Tessa and I arrived at her parents' house—they had gently demanded that we spend our Labor Day with them, as it had been several months since our last visit—to let me know that I would be doing another ride-along. Who was it with? She didn't say, but my gut told me it was most definitely going to be with Officer Grumpy.

Part of me is excited—being back in the field, getting to observe real work, maybe learning something new, especially since I had spent my Thursday last week sorting through dispositions and arrest records and dusty ass files for five hours. But the other part? The part that still feels the sting of Officer Perez's dismissiveness and the fact that my horny ass got off to thoughts of him the other night? That part is dragging its feet.

Still, I get dressed—leggings, a red V-neck top, and my boots. Simple but clean. Professional enough for my internship, but comfortable enough to survive five hours in and out of a patrol car, but maybe not the heat. My hair goes into a high ponytail, and after a quick once-over in the mirror, I grab my bag, call a soft goodbye to Max, and head out.

The drive across town is quiet. The sun's just starting its climb, casting long orange shadows across the pavement. My car's speakers are loud, blasting my playlist, but my thoughts are louder—echoing with everything I should be ready for and everything I hope *doesn't* happen again.

When I pull into the Westside Division employee parking lot, my nerves start to kick in. The building stands before me—familiar now, but still a little intimidating. I park, kill the engine, and take a deep breath before sliding out of the car. I walk toward the back entrance, the rising sun warm on my back.

Time to face the day.

I make my way through the station at a steady pace, the echo of my boots muffled by the low hum of morning chatter. A few officers pass by, offering polite nods or distracted greetings, most of them too caught up in their own routines to do more than glance my way.

As I approach Roll Call, I spot Sergeant Rodriguez already stationed at the podium, her eyes fixed on her phone. She looks up when I enter, and her expression softens into a smile.

"Morning, Miss Carson," she says, her tone casual as she slips the phone into her pocket. "How was your Labor Day weekend?"

"It was great," I answer, settling into the front table. "Had a bit of a weird start on Friday, but nothing I couldn't handle."

She raises an eyebrow but doesn't press. "Glad to hear you had a good weekend. Mine wasn't too terrible either." After a moment, she steps around the podium, her tone shifting slightly as she approaches me. There's something more deliberate in the way she lowers her voice.

"Anyways, I wanted to touch base about something before

we start," she says, half-sitting on the edge of the table in front of me. "I'm aware of the incident between you and Officer Perez last week."

I blink, caught off guard. Not because she knows—of course, she knows, conflict between officers never stays hidden—but because the second she says his name, the wrong kind of heat creeps up my neck.

My stomach twists, shame tangling with anger. I press my thumbnail into the pad of my finger and look away, trying to keep my expression neutral. How the hell did I go from cursing him out in my head to touching myself to the thought of him pinning me down?

Rodriguez keeps talking, unaware of the firestorm inside my chest.

"I wish you would've said something," she adds gently. "But I understand why you didn't. No one wants to be that person."

I lean back in my seat and meet her eyes as I pick at my nails, a nervous habit of mine. "It wasn't worth escalating," I admit. "He wasn't exactly warm, but I didn't want to get anyone in trouble. I figured I could deal."

Rodriguez gives me a small nod, her expression thoughtful. "And that's fair. But this isn't about causing trouble, Raelynn. It's about accountability. That ride-along should've been a learning experience—not a test of patience."

My heart thuds a little faster, dread curling in my gut like smoke before a fire. I know exactly what's coming.

"This isn't a punishment for you not coming to me. It's a consequence for him," she continues. "He needs to learn to accept that there are going to be times when the job isn't how he wants it to be, which is why you'll be riding with him again today."

And there it is.

I swallow hard. It's like my body hears that before my

brain can even process it, because heat flashes beneath my skin again—an involuntary, traitorous response I don't want to admit. My throat's dry, my hands are clammy, and my brain short-circuits at the thought of being stuck in a cruiser with him again, not after Friday's events.

"I see," I say after a beat, trying to keep my voice steady.

Rodriguez offers a look of sympathy but stays firm. "He's a damn good cop, but not the easiest personality. Think of it this way—either he learns to work with people, or he keeps having to answer to me. And if it gets worse, I want to hear about it. He's been spoken to already, so he knows what's expected of him."

I nod slowly, exhaling a breath through my nose. "Understood, ma'am."

"Good," she says, straightening up as a few officers trickle into the room. "Keep your chin up, Carson. You're doing just fine."

"Thanks," I murmur, though the knot in my chest says otherwise.

Because now I have to get through another five hours sitting next to the man who made me feel like shit… and made me come so hard I bit my own damn hand trying to stay quiet.

Yeah. Just fine.

Rodriguez returns to the front of the room, her presence shifting the energy just enough to signal it's almost time to get serious. Around me, the low murmur of conversation picks up as officers begin filtering in from the hallway. The shuffle of boots across tile, the soft clatter of chairs being pulled out, and someone cracking a lazy joke that earns a few quiet laughs.

The usual stuff. Routine. Comforting, if I could actually feel comfort right now.

Some of the officers chat casually about Sunday's game, tossing around stats and trash talk like it's part of the morning warm-up. Others talk shop—weekend calls, scheduling headaches, and one particularly weird traffic stop someone had on the south side. The smell of strong coffee wafts in from a travel mug on the table nearest to me, mixing with the ever-present scent of worn leather and old paperwork.

Kline strolls in mid-conversation with another officer but breaks away when he catches sight of me. He offers a warm, easy smile, giving me a subtle nod as he heads for a seat a few rows back. I return the smile with a small one of my own—grateful, a little. At least someone here doesn't make my nervous system light up like a damn power grid.

And then Perez walks in.

He's the last one through the door, and he enters like a thundercloud about to break. There's no small talk, no smile, not even the pretense of civility. Just a heavy, brooding silence that seems to follow him with every step. His brow is furrowed, jaw clenched so tight it looks like it might crack. He moves with a purpose that's sharp and restrained—like he's holding back from punching something. Or someone.

His gaze sweeps the room, detached and disinterested.

And yet, when it passes over me, I feel it—sharp as a blade.

My spine stiffens like I've just been caught doing something I shouldn't.

Which, to be fair… I kind of *was*. Just a few nights ago. In my bed. Whispering his name into a pillow, thighs trembling, vibrator pressed so hard against my clit I saw stars.

God. What is wrong with me?

He barely said a kind word to me last time. Treated me like I was in the way. Laughed at me. Undermined me. And yet here I am, reacting to his presence like he's lit a fuse under my skin. Again.

I drop my gaze and pick at my nails as he drops into the seat directly behind me, and despite not seeing him, I feel the weight of him there—his presence, his tension, the unspoken frustration radiating off him like static. It prickles against the back of my neck and sends my heart into a frenzy. I force myself to keep my eyes forward as Rodriguez begins her morning briefing, her voice steady and practiced as she ticks through the day's agenda: units rotating out, coverage notes, recent calls, and admin reminders. But I barely register her words. I'm too aware of Perez behind me. He hasn't even said a word.

And still, he's *under* my skin.

Three minutes pass—maybe four—before Rodriguez wraps things up. "Alright, stay sharp out there," she says with a nod. The scrape of chairs follows, boots thud softly against the floor, and officers filter out in groups, murmuring quietly as they leave to gather their gear.

I stay seated, rooted to the spot, and so does Perez.

We sit in silence while the room empties around us, the background noise fading until there's nothing left but the faint hum of the overhead lights and the slow, steady drum of my pulse. The door clicks shut behind the last straggler. Then, finally, he moves. He stands slowly—deliberately—and steps around the edge of the table, his boots quiet against the tile as he comes to stand directly in front of me.

He doesn't speak right away. Just looks at me.

His face is unreadable, but not cold. There's still tension there, coiled beneath his skin like wire pulled too tight, but it doesn't feel angry this time. Doesn't feel like it's aimed at me. It's quieter. Careful. Measured in a way that makes the air between us feel heavier.

"I didn't say anything, just so you know," I offer, breaking the silence. My voice is low, calm, even as I meet his gaze. "I'm not a child who tattles to the boss."

His eyes hold mine for a beat longer than I expect. There's no flare of pride, no defensive retort—just a quiet nod. "I know," he replies, and his voice is… softer. Not warm, not friendly—but not biting either. "Rodriguez made that clear."

That throws me for a second. I expected more bite. A scoff. Maybe a snide comment. Not… this.

He exhales, raking a hand through his dark hair like he's been battling whatever the hell is going on in his head all morning and losing. "Your vest is already in the cruiser," he says, voice low as he finally turns toward the door. "Let's go."

With that, he turns on his heel and strides for the exit. I rise and follow, my boots tapping softly against the tile as I trail him out of roll call and down the corridor toward the parking lot.

Several cruisers are still parked in the lot when we step outside, their engines rumbling softly while officers finish final checks or retrieve gear from their trunks. The low thrum of police radios fills the air in uneven bursts, blending with the sound of boots on the pavement and the occasional slam of a car door.

Perez doesn't say a word as we approach his cruiser—the engine already running, headlights casting long beams across the pavement like it's been ready to go for a while. I open the passenger-side door and slide inside without a word. A better-quality observer vest, newer than the one from last week and not nearly as frayed, is folded neatly on the seat. I pick it up and drape it across my lap, feeling the slight weight of it settle there.

Outside, I hear the dull scrape of boots on pavement and catch glimpses of movement in the side mirror. Perez is conducting a standard walk-around, checking tires and ensuring everything is in place. His movements are practiced and methodical, and when he's satisfied, he yanks the door open and drops into the driver's seat beside me. He clicks his seatbelt into place, then finally glances over at me.

After a long moment of silence and uncomfortable looks, Perez finally breaks it. "Pick a call," he says, turning the MDT so it's angled toward me.

I blink at him. "You want me to pick it?"

He nods once as he shifts the cruiser into drive. My brows furrow slightly as I lean forward to examine the screen. The call log is a dense list of incidents waiting for response, each one tagged with priority codes and brief descriptions—everything from welfare checks to fender benders to reports of suspicious activity.

But one entry jumps out at me.

Priority Two: Possible body found in a wash near Blacklidge Dr and First Ave.

My finger hovers over the line for a second longer than it should, then I turn the screen back toward him. "This one. It sounds… interesting."

Perez's head tilts slightly as he gives me a sidelong glance, his expression unreadable. "You sure you're ready for a crime scene, detective?"

There's no malice in the word, not like before—just a dry edge of humor, the kind that doesn't bite.

I nod, firm. "Yeah. I am."

He studies me for a moment, eyes scanning my face like he's trying to gauge whether I'm actually ready for this. Whatever he sees must satisfy him, because he gives a curt nod and turns back to the screen.

"This is 2-L-17, show me en route to Blacklidge Drive and First Avenue," he says into the radio.

"Copy that, 2-L-17," dispatch responds, the voice crackling faintly through the static.

Perez replaces the mic in its holder, then flips the switch on the light bar. The cruiser floods with red and blue light, reflecting off the nearby cruisers and the concrete walls of the lot. A second later, the siren kicks in—low and mournful at first, then climbing to a piercing wail that cuts through the early morning stillness as we pull out.

The drive is only a few minutes long, but it feels like it stretches on. Tension knots in my stomach, twisting tighter with each block we pass. My fingers toy with the edge of the vest draped over my lap, and I force myself to breathe evenly. I've read case studies, watched body cam footage, and taken classes. But this is different. This is *real.*

Perez handles the cruiser with one hand on the wheel, eyes fixed on the road, expression unreadable. The only sound is the occasional chirp from the radio and the pulse of the siren.

When we turn onto First Avenue, I spot the yellow crime scene tape almost immediately, strung haphazardly between two dented metal posts near the edge of a rocky drainage wash. A white Community Service vehicle is already parked off to the side, and a small crowd has gathered behind the tape. Most of them are onlookers, but one woman stands apart—older, frail-looking, arms crossed over her chest. A golden retriever lies between her legs.

He kills the siren but leaves the lights running. "2-L-17 is 10-23," he announces into the radio. "We're on scene."

He's out of the car before dispatch can respond, rounding the front of the cruiser in long strides. He casts a quick glance over his shoulder and jerks his chin toward the tape.

"You coming or what?"

I snap out of my daze, unbuckle, and shove the vest over my head. The nylon clings to my shirt for a second before I adjust it and hop out. My boots crunch against the gravel as I jog to catch up with him as he approaches the older woman.

"Ma'am," Perez says, his tone calm but authoritative, "can you tell me what happened?"

The woman turns, her face pale and drawn. She gives me a wary glance before focusing on Perez. Her fingers tremble as she clutches her phone to her chest like it's the only thing keeping her grounded.

"I—I was walking my dog," she says, her voice thin and shaking. "He wouldn't stop barking near the tunnel. I thought maybe it was a rabbit or a stray cat, but then I got closer and… I saw *it.*" Her eyes fill with tears, and she presses a shaking hand to her mouth. Perez nods gently, softening his tone.

"You did the right thing calling it in. Thank you. Can you show me exactly where?"

She lifts a trembling arm and points toward the far edge of the wash, where the slope dips sharply behind a patch of overgrown brush and a rusted, half-collapsed fence. Through the tangle of weeds and broken fencing, I spot the mouth of a drainage tunnel. Lying partially in the runoff channel, caught on a cluster of rocks and debris, is a body.

From here, it's hard to tell much. But the position—half in, half out of the tunnel—and the awkward bend of the limbs send a chill down my spine.

"The rain must have carried them out," I murmur, more to myself than anyone else.

Perez follows my gaze, then steps forward, ducking beneath the caution tape. I follow behind, boots crunching over broken gravel and glass, my pulse loud in my ears as we approach the mangled remains of the fence that separates the wash from the back lot of a nearby strip mall.

The moment we reach the drainage tunnel, the smell slams into me.

It's like hitting a wall—a suffocating blend of rot and wet earth, with the metallic bite of old blood clinging to the air. The sour tang of decay hangs thick in the air, layered beneath the damp musk of stagnant runoff and weeds. My stomach lurches, and I instinctively bring a hand up to cover my nose, forcing slow, shallow breaths through my mouth as Perez takes in the scene.

The victim is a woman.

She's partially wedged in the runoff channel, her lifeless body tangled between jagged rocks and a length of rusted, broken pipe. Her clothing is soaked through, clinging to her like a second skin. The bright red of her low-cut top is now muted, stained with mud, grime, and something darker. The fabric is torn low in the front, revealing mottled bruises and deep gashes carved into her side. Her jeans are caked in dirt, ripped at the knees, and only one cowboy boot remains on her foot. Her blonde hair is tangled and streaked with filth, plastered to her face in wet strands. What's left of her lipstick is a faint, smeared line along her parted lips.

Perez pulls a pair of black vinyl gloves from his pocket and slides them on with practiced ease, the soft *snap* of each cuff slicing through the thick, unsettled quiet. Then he crouches beside the body, his boots grinding faintly against gravel as he lowers himself into position.

He doesn't rush.

His hands move with the kind of precision that only comes from repetition—efficient, careful, respectful. He pats the soaked fabric gently, checking pockets one by one, his fingers moving automatically. But there's a shift—small, almost imperceptible—when he gets a better look at her face.

His hands still. His breath catches—just barely—and something changes in the way he's crouched there, like the air's been sucked out of him.

He leans in slightly, brushing aside a damp strand of blonde hair matted to the woman's cheek. The makeup, the cut of her shirt, the red tint on her lips—it clicks all at once.

Recognition slams into him.

He forces out a breath, slow and strained, like he's pushing it past a boulder lodged in his chest.

"This is 2-L-17," he says into the radio, voice quieter than before, flattened out, controlled through sheer will. "Confirming a DOA. Notify Sergeant Rodriguez. We're going to need a CSU and a detective at Blacklidge Drive and First Avenue."

He releases the mic but doesn't move. His gloved hand lingers near the victim's shoulder as he stares, unmoving.

From where I stand, I don't need to hear his thoughts. I can see it.

The stillness in his face. The tightness in his jaw clenched harder than before, and there's something in his expression that wasn't there a minute ago—something brittle and distant. It isn't the kind of detached composure I've seen him wear before. No. This is different.

He knows her.

CRIME
OFFICER
STOP
STOP

TEN
EMILIO

IT'S THE BARTENDER.

Even under grime and the first ragged bloom of decay, even with bruises mapping her face like a bad roadmap, some things don't lie.

The red top—ripped and stained—is the same one she wore the night Kline and I hit Zeke's.

A week ago.

Fuck.

My jaw tightens until my molars ache as I look down at her. She's splayed in the drainage wash like a discarded ragdoll, limbs tangled in garbage and tumbleweed, hair matted to her forehead with grit and something darker. The smell hits me in a low, metallic wash that pushes bile at the back of my throat.

She served me drinks.

She joked with Kline.

She was so full of life.

Now she's just another body, waiting for a toe tag and a press release.

Behind me, I feel Raelynn watching. I turn, just for a

CRIME SCENE

second, and meet her eyes. There's something there that is not only sympathy. It's sharper: curiosity, intuition, suspicion.

She's probably watched enough crime shows, or something, to know the cadence of recognition when it lands on someone. She knows I recognized this woman. If she doesn't yet, she will once Detective Meyer arrives and the questions start to land.

I motion for her to follow and head up the embankment. Gravel skitters under my boots; each step throws up a dry, dusty cloud. Raelynn moves a few steps behind, breaths a little uneven, gaze fixed on the scrubby channel below like she's memorizing the angles of the scene. The wind plays through the barbed reeds, and the caution tape snaps like a small flag.

We barely make it to level ground when an unmarked black Dodge Charger rolls into the lot, its engine cutting as it pulls up beside my cruiser. The front door opens with that deliberate, practiced movement, and Detective Eliza Meyer steps out.

Auburn hair cascades in loose, polished waves down her back, catching the morning sunlight and glowing like embers. Her deep purple silk blouse is sleek and fitted, tucked neatly into tailored black dress pants that hug her frame with precision. The sharp click of her polished leather boots marks each step as she approaches, her badge catching the light from its place beside a matte black sidearm holstered on her hip.

Her smooth and naturally sun-kissed skin adds to the impression she always seems to give off—composed, focused, and completely in control.

"Perez," she calls as she makes her way toward the scene. "Fill me in."

Her eyes shift briefly to Raelynn. "Good morning, Miss Carson," she says, her voice level and professional, lips curving into a soft, polite smile.

"Good morning, Detective," Raelynn replies. Her voice is

calm, measured—but I can still hear it. That subtle waver beneath the words. She's not focused on Meyer.

She's focused on me.

And I can't blame her. She saw the shift in my expression the second I laid eyes on the body. She's sharp—sharper than most interns I've met.

I take a breath, grounding myself as the low growl of an approaching vehicle cuts through the heavy quiet. CSU rolls into view, its tires stirring up a small dust cloud as it eases beside the strip mall's edge. The doors swing open, and two techs step out, already pulling on gloves and hauling out camera equipment and evidence kits with familiar efficiency.

Detective Meyer stands a few feet from me, a calm silhouette against the chaos. She pulls a notepad from her back pocket, flips it open, and clicks her pen. Her eyes remain fixed on the drainage wash, the body barely visible through the tangled brush and caution tape. That quiet stillness in her expression—the steady detachment—says she's done this too many times. Seen too many people wind up this way.

"Victim is female. Mid-to-late fifties. Found partially submerged in a drainage channel. Signs of blunt force trauma to the head, multiple lacerations… possible defensive wounds." The details roll out cleanly. Years of saying the same things in a dozen different scenes smooth the edges into procedure, but my stomach still tightens with every word.

Meyer's pen scratches the paper. "Any ID on her?"

"No." I shake my head. "But—" I hesitate, jaw tightening with the memory. "She's a bartender at Zeke's. The dive bar off Grant and Campbell."

That catches her. Her stroke slows. The pen pauses. Her eyes sharpen like a lens focusing. "You know her?"

I glance toward the wash. Even now, her features are barely visible, distorted by bruising and grime. But I remember her. That red top. That gum-smacking smirk. Her southern drawl…

"Sort of," I say with a sigh, peeling off my gloves. "I went out for drinks there last week with another officer. She was tending the bar. I think her name was Vicky."

Meyer scribbles again, slower this time, then casts a glance back toward the wash. "Who were you with that night?"

I glance toward Raelynn, who's watching the crime scene unit set up, but I know she's still listening, eyes flicking between me and the techs like she's trying to absorb everything.

"Officer Jacoby Kline," I reply. "We met there after our shift. But the place was packed—other officers, civilians, regulars. Could've been anyone."

Meyer nods. "Anything stand out? Anyone giving her trouble?"

I shake my head. "Not that I saw. But I wasn't there long—an hour and a half, tops. She seemed fine. Friendly."

"Alright," she murmurs, wrapping up a final note before snapping the pad closed. She slips it back into her pocket and turns slightly toward the CSUs, who are now setting up the perimeter markers and prepping their gear.

"I'll follow up with Officer Kline for his statement. For now, that's all I need from you." She turns to Raelynn with a faint smile. "You and Miss Carson are cleared to return to patrol. I'll handle the scene from here."

"Understood," I say with a curt nod, casting one last glance toward the wash where the techs are zipping the body bag closed around what's left of Vicky.

I let out a sharp whistle to get Raelynn's attention. "Let's go," I call over, voice low and even.

Raelynn watches the techs lower the body onto the stretcher. The last glimpse of the victim—Vicky's face slack with demise, the red of that top a faded punctuation—seems to line itself in Raelynn's memory. When she finally turns away and walks toward the cruiser, there's a measurement in her face I haven't seen before—a quiet, fierce focus, like she's memorizing the way death settles into the edges of a scene.

When she finally turns and joins me beside the cruiser, I catch the edge of that look still lingering in her expression.

"You okay?" I ask, unlocking the doors.

She pauses, scanning my face with more intensity than I expect. "I'm fine," she says, voice steady. "Are you?"

"Not the first time I've recognized a body, Carson," I reply as casually as I can manage, though the words land hollow in my throat.

She studies me for another second—something unreadable flickering in her eyes—then opens the passenger door and climbs in. I follow and settle into the driver's seat, the door slamming shut behind me.

The crime scene burned through a solid hour and a half of the shift. As I turn the ignition, it's quiet for a beat, the low rumble of the engine filling the silence.

"This isn't the first time I've seen a dead body, either," she says softly, like she's not quite sure if she wants to open that door but knows she's going to anyway.

I glance at her, fingers resting loosely on the wheel. She's staring out the passenger window, her profile lit in the soft morning light. Lips pressed into a thin line. Still. Quiet. But the tension in her jaw—tight, unrelenting—says everything she's not yet ready to.

"How do you mean?" I ask, shifting the cruiser into drive and easing us away from the crime scene. Gravel crunches under the tires as we head back toward the road, the strobing lights from the CSU fading slowly in the rearview mirror.

She's quiet until we're a few blocks out, until the only sound left is the low hum of the engine and the occasional chirp of the radio.

"Last week," she says, breaking the silence, "you asked me why I wanted to go into homicide."

I glance her way. She's still staring out her window.

"I didn't tell you," she continues, voice tight. "Because you were an ass."

A low breath escapes me, equal parts guilt and regret. "Yeah," I admit. "I was. You didn't deserve that, Carson. I'm sorry."

She looks over at me, blinking like she wasn't expecting the apology. But she recovers quickly.

"No, I didn't," she says bluntly. "But that's not the point."

Her fingers knot together in her lap, white at the knuckles. When she speaks again, her voice is softer. Strained.

"I'm on this path because of something that happened when I was a kid. Something that shaped everything that came after. Something I never really escaped from." She hesitates. "Have you ever heard of The Butcher?"

My fingers go still on the wheel, tightening instinctively. That name slices through the air like a blade to the gut.

I was eleven when that sadistic son of a bitch carved his way through this city—seventeen years ago now, but it still feels fresh every time I think about it. My father kept the news on from morning until night, the volume turned up just loud enough that you couldn't escape it, even from the back of the house. And back then, every damn station was obsessed with The Butcher case, tracking every scrap of the investigation like it was the only thing worth talking about.

I heard things an eleven-year-old should never hear. Saw images that seared into my brain long before I was old enough to understand them.

It was always women. A string of them, one after another, each one found torn apart in ways that made even seasoned cops lose sleep. Slashed open like meat on a butcher's block—precise, deliberate, and horrifyingly clean. It wasn't rage, not in the messy, sloppy way most killers show it.

This was cold. Calculated. Like he was savoring every fucking second of it.

And the worst part? He never slipped. No prints. No

DNA. Not a hair out of place. Just bodies and nightmares, left behind like some kind of calling card only he understood.

Then one day—nothing. No more bodies. No more clues. No more news. He was gone.

But the last one… the final victim…

My stomach drops.

My gaze snaps to Raelynn, and she's already watching me. She sees the shift in my face—the recognition. The connection. She knows I've figured it out.

"I know what you're thinking," she says softly, voice brittle but steady. "And you're right."

A pause. Just long enough to sting.

"My mom was Elena Carson," she says. "The last victim of The Butcher."

I feel the breath leave my lungs from her confirmation. "Jesus," I mutter. "Raelynn… I'm so sorry."

She nods, but there's no emotion in it—just grim acceptance.

"I was six when she died," she says, voice distant now. "Nine, when I lost my dad. Car accident. At least, that's what the report said. But the truth is—he gave up. Couldn't live with me anymore. I was a walking reminder of everything he'd lost."

I stay silent, letting her speak, letting her bleed this out.

"The night she died… The Butcher didn't finish the job. The officers patrolling that night stumbled on the scene. They fired shots at him, but he got away, but not before he'd done enough damage to my mom. She bled out in the ambulance on the way to the hospital." She swallows hard. "My dad dragged me into the room that night, not realizing the damage. I saw her. In the OR. What was left of her, I should say."

I don't breathe.

"I overheard the officers talking," she continues. "About The Butcher. About what he did to her. I didn't understand it all then. But it stuck. Every word. Every detail. And when I was old enough to put the pieces together… I couldn't let it go."

She turns her head and meets my eyes. There's no hesitation, no flinch—just raw, steady honesty.

"That's why I'm here," she says, her voice soft but unwavering. "That's why I chose this path. It's not just about justice. I'm chasing closure—even if I never find it. I just… I don't want anyone else to go through what I did."

There's nothing I can say that wouldn't feel small compared to that. So I don't try. I just keep driving, my hands tightening around the wheel as her words settle in my chest like lead.

And all I can do is wonder how the hell someone with that much pain still manages to walk around like the weight of it hasn't crushed her.

ELEVEN
RAELYNN

FRIDAY CAME FAST, and I was grateful, and then I wasn't.

Despite my protests, I'd been roped into going out for drinks with the girls. Khloe had made it her personal mission to drag me out of the apartment, despite every excuse I threw her way. Something about "*needing to let loose, get the fuck out of the house, and maybe find some dick.*" Her words, not mine.

I'd reluctantly agreed (to the drinks, at least). The dick part? Absolutely not. No matter how hot he was. No matter how horny I was, I wasn't about to hook up with some random dude from a themed karaoke night at the Monkey Bar. Hawaiian luau, no less.

So now, here I am, a quarter after 9 p.m., standing in front of my vanity, adjusting the one dress I own that matches the theme.

It is a strappy halter that ties around my neck, featuring a white base with pink and yellow hibiscus flowers scattered across the fabric. It barely reaches mid-thigh; the end of the fabric barely covers the tattoo that follows the curves of my left hip, which I got a month before the semester started. I knew damn well one wrong bend and someone was getting a full view of my ass, the tattoo, and the sheer white lace panties I impulsively bought during a Victoria's Secret sale a few weeks ago.

And because I didn't own a strapless bra, I opted to skip it altogether. I'm not about to ruin the neckline with ugly straps.

I keep my hair simple, with a loose braid and a matching flower clip, and apply just enough makeup to conceal the exhaustion under my eyes. A layer of foundation to cover the bruised-looking shadows, a sweep of soft pink eyeshadow, and a matching lipstick to bring it together. I complete my outfit with a pair of white three-inch wedges, which makes me slightly regret every life decision I have made that led to this moment.

Satisfied (enough), I grab my bag and throw it over my shoulder, then step out of my room and knock once on Tessa's door before cracking it open. Khloe is already inside, perched on the edge of the bed, looking like a walking Pinterest board.

"Well, hello, gorgeous." She whistles as she stands up, revealing her outfit: a pink crocheted crop top with oversized bell sleeves thrown over a blue bikini top, paired with frayed black shorts and pink flip-flops. Her hair falls in effortless beach waves, partially clipped back with a rose gold butterfly.

Tessa, never one to be outdone, wears a dangerously low-cut romper printed with tropical leaves. The long sleeves give it a boho vibe, but the deep neckline makes it very clear that one wrong move would result in her breasts making an appearance for everyone to see. Her hair is twisted into a bun, secured with her signature paintbrush stabbed straight through the middle like a dagger.

Both girls opted for light makeup as their effortless beauty doesn't require much.

"I still hate you for making me go to this," I tell Khloe as Tessa slides into a pair of black sandals.

"You'll get over it after your first drink." Tessa teases as she walks over and throws her arms around me. She kisses my cheek with a grin. "I *do* have to agree with Khloe, though," she says as she pulls away. "You look gorgeous, babe."

I smirk, the tension easing a bit from my shoulders. "So do both of you."

Before we can say anything else, a knock at the front door echoes down the hallway, which sends Max into a barking fit. His nails click against the floor as he barrels toward the entryway—tail wagging like crazy, his fox toy clamped proudly between his teeth.

"It's open!" I call out, raising my voice just enough to carry down the hallway.

The door swings open a second later, and Marlena practically bounces inside, fingers laced tightly with Austin's. She's fully committed to the Hawaiian theme, as expected—wrapped in a strapless sundress splashed with leafy greens and blush pink florals. Her hair is curled and pinned into two playful space buns at the crown of her head, the rest spilling in glossy waves down her back. White wedges tap cheerfully against the tile as she makes a beeline straight for me—though Max intercepts her first, trotting right up with his squeaky fox held high like an offering.

"Oh my god, hey, Max!" Marlena coos, crouching just enough to ruffle his ears. Austin chuckles and scratches under his chin, earning a happy little squeak from the toy before Max trots over to the couch and curls up on it, his toy tucked under his snout.

Giggling, Marlena rises on her toes, the soft blend of honeysuckle and citrus in her perfume wrapping around me like a warm breeze as she presses a kiss to my cheek. The wedges give her just enough height to reach me without too much of a struggle, which says a lot, because Marlena is fucking *tiny*. Like, 4'11" tiny.

And I'm not exactly towering myself. I stand at a very average 5'4", while Tessa—blessed with long legs and effortless model energy—clocks in around 5'8" and Khloe at 5'6".

"God, Rae, you look hot as hell," Marlena says with a grin, giving my outfit a quick once-over.

I arch a brow, smirking. "What do I look like the rest of the time? A damn hobo?"

She laughs as she rejoins Austin's side, his arm already sliding around her waist. "Nooooo, babe. You just never dress up. We're all a little shook right now."

"I know," I say, chuckling. "I'm just giving you shit."

Austin wraps an arm around Marlena's waist, tugging her closer like he can't help himself, and gives us all a once-over. "Y'all ready to go?" he asks, keys in hand.

"Yep!" Khloe answers without hesitation, grabbing Tessa and me by the arms like we might change our minds. "Let's roll, sluts."

Austin, ever the hero, had graciously agreed to be our designated driver for the night, which meant no overpriced Uber or awkward small talk. Marlena tried to convince him to come with us, but he wasn't having it. Said this was girls-only territory, and he meant it. He just told her to call him whenever we were ready to leave, no matter what time it was.

We pile into his silver Chevy Equinox, Marlena riding shotgun while the three of us cram into the back. The moment the doors shut, Khloe cues up a playlist loud enough to shake the windows, and chaos erupts. Off-key singing. Laughter that borders on obnoxious. Tessa is yelling at Marlena for skipping her favorite part of the song. It's the kind of car ride that feels like a pregame all on its own.

Austin misses the bar twice, swearing under his breath that the Monkey Bar's entrance is practically invisible. To be fair, the place *is* tucked next to a rundown convenience store on the corner of Wilmot and 22nd. If it weren't for the neon beer bottle sign protruding from the wall, he'd probably still be looking.

Finally, he swings into the lot beside a greasy Filiberto's and pulls into a spot. The four of us climb out, shoes clicking and laughter trailing after us as we straighten out our outfits and fluff our hair. From here, we can already hear the unmistakable sound of someone absolutely butchering a Celine Dion song inside the bar.

Austin leans out the driver's side window, eyes scanning us one last time. "I don't care what time it is—just call when you're ready to bounce, and I'll come get y'all. Got it?"

"We will! I love you!" Marlena sings as she blows him a kiss and skips toward the entrance.

I glance toward the bar's glowing sign, take a breath, and follow the girls inside.

Inside, chaos is already in full swing.

A guy on the other side of the bar, where the karaoke is being held, is absolutely butchering a Slipknot song, the mic in his hand swaying like he's fronting a stadium tour. His voice is off-key, but the crowd doesn't care. A few people cheer him on while others throw back shots and laugh into their cocktails.

Khloe and Tessa immediately drift toward the singing area, heads bent over their phones as they scroll through the Karafun website, whispering excitedly about what song to queue up. Marlena trails behind them, already dancing to the beat.

Me? I head for the bar. If there's even a *chance* I'm singing tonight, I'm going to need a few drinks first. My sober stage presence is nonexistent. Zero confidence. Negative charisma. I'd rather be tipsy and shameless than clear-headed and dying of secondhand embarrassment.

I squeeze into a narrow opening between two guys dressed in matching dingy gray shirts and tan cargo pants. One is shouting hoarsely at the flat-screen mounted above us—some baseball game I can't pretend to care about. He's waving his beer bottle like it's a magic wand that might make the batter hit better. The other guy doesn't even glance at me; he's too busy nursing a double whiskey, staring into the glass like it holds the meaning of life. Neither pays me any mind, which is just how I like it.

The bartender—Cole, according to the crooked name tag pinned to the chaos of orange and blue hibiscus print on his half-unbuttoned Hawaiian shirt—glances my way and grins over his shoulder. His whole look is peak tropical dive bar: thick, black-rimmed glasses perched on a tan, round face, a light dusting of stubble that softens his jawline, and blonde hair slicked back with an absurd level of commitment, like he's moonlighting as a surf rock frontman.

The shirt is offensively loud, something you'd expect to find buried in the clearance bin of a beachfront souvenir shop—and yet, somehow, it works on him. He radiates effortless charm, and his whole demeanor exudes a laid-back, flirtatious quality.

"Hey, hon," he calls out, voice rising easily over the layered hum of conversation, clinking glasses, and a butchered rendition of a Lizzo song starts up from the karaoke stage. "Gimme one sec, and I'll get ya taken care of."

I offer a polite nod, resting one elbow on the sticky bar top and half-listening to the chaos behind me as he wraps up the current drink he is making. He garnishes the drink with a dash of Tajin, then hands it off to the guy at the end of the bar before turning back toward me, a grin stretched across his lips.

He leans over the bar, folding his arms atop the counter to get close to me. I can smell his cologne the moment he leans in. A combination of sandalwood, citrus, and coconut hit my senses, overpowering the multitude of scents that waft through the bar.

He flashes me a slightly crooked smile that showcases a chipped front incisor. "Alright, gorgeous," he says, voice low and playful. "What can I make for ya tonight?"

"What's the go-to tonight?" I glance at the laminated specials card wedged behind a plastic tiki bobblehead near the tip jar.

Cole chuckles, following my gaze with a smirk that's one part bartender charm and two parts mischief. Khloe would love this man.

"Blue Hawaiian's been the favorite so far," he says, his fingers tapping idly on the counter as I grab the card. "It's a fruity cocktail made with vodka." He winks. "But I can whip up whatever your heart's set on, darlin'."

I skim the card. On one side is a list of drafts, and on the other side are the cocktails and margaritas. "Blue Hawaiian it is," I say finally, setting the card back behind the figurine. "And throw in a Blue Kamikaze shot while you're at it."

Cole gives me an approving grin and pushes off the counter. "Coming right up."

He turns toward the wall of liquor with the easy rhythm of someone who knows every bottle by touch. As he starts pulling ingredients, the girls appear at my side in perfect synchronization. Khloe wedges herself between me and the whiskey guy and plucks the menu from its spot. Tessa slides in on my other side, looping an arm around my waist as Marlena lingers just behind them, her focus glued to the open Karafun queue on her phone.

"Song picked yet?" I ask, pulling my wallet from my bag. I slide my ID and debit card onto the bar as Cole tosses ice into a shaker.

"Khloe's doing 'Final Girl,'" Tessa says, nudging her shoulder with a grin. "Marlena and I are still debating—either Disney or pop. We'll see."

Marlena lifts her gaze, eyes glinting with playful amusement. "What about you?"

I snort. "I need at least two drinks before I even *think* about a mic."

Right on cue, Cole reappears, expertly balancing a tall, ocean blue cocktail with a tiny pink umbrella and a neon bendy straw, plus a bright blue shot glass that is filled to the brim. He places both in front of me with flair, then glances at my cards—but instead of reaching for them, he slides them back toward me with two fingers and that signature crooked grin.

"On the house," he says with a wink.

I blink. "Oh. Um… thanks."

"Anytime, gorgeous," he replies smoothly, already moving down the bar to take another order.

My cheeks flush warm as I snatch my cards off the bar and tuck them into my purse instead of back into my wallet, pretending not to notice the amused glances from the girls flanking me.

"Damn, Rae," Marlena teases, grinning like she's already decided this will be brought up again and again. "Got the bartender giving you freebies already?"

"Shut up," I mutter, laughing despite myself. I knock back the Kamikaze. It burns in a satisfying way, sharp and fruity, and I follow it up with a long sip of the Blue Hawaiian—sweet, boozy, and strong enough to soften my nerves.

While Khloe hangs back at the bar to order, Tessa, Marlena, and I weave through the crowd toward the small table they claimed near the karaoke setup. I settle into my seat and finally pull out my phone. I point my camera at the projected karaoke screen and scan the QR code at the bottom, clicking the link that pops up, and opening Karafun to finally scroll through the song list.

I debate for a minute or two, fingers hovering over a few options, before settling on "I Am the Fire" by Halestorm. It's fierce, bold, and a little angsty—the exact kind of energy I want to project tonight.

By the time I hit *Add to Queue*, Khloe's name is being called. She quickly rushes over from the bar, her drink sloshing over the edge of the glass, and squeals in excitement. She downs half of her cocktail in one dramatic gulp. The ice clinks loudly as she slams the glass on the table with a satisfied gasp, then struts over to the DJ.

He hands her the mic, and she steps up onto the stage and tosses us a look over her shoulder—a smirk tugging at her lips, one hand propped sassily on her hip like she was born for the spotlight.

"Let's go, Khloe!" we cheer in unison.

Tessa and Marlena are practically jumping out of their seats, cheering as the opening notes of "Final Girl" start. I clap along, laughing as Khloe begins to sing—no, *perform*—like she's the headliner of a stadium tour and we're all lucky to be in her presence.

While Khloe commands the mic with her signature sass and zero shame, Tessa grabs Marlena's hand and tugs her toward the bar. They disappear into the crowd, giggling like high schoolers sneaking off for something scandalous. I stay behind, swirling the ice in my half-empty Blue Hawaiian as I soak in everything around me.

Khloe wraps up her performance with a dramatic pose and a wink to the audience, her final note met with a wave of cheers. As she makes her way back to the table, Tessa and Marlena return too, carrying what can only be described as drink monstrosities. They were literal fishbowls of booze, vibrant blue, bubbling, and rimmed with a pineapple wedge and an umbrella. God only knows what was in them, but from the way Tessa nearly trips over her chair trying to sit down, I assume it was jet fuel with a hint of coconut.

"What the fuck is that?" I ask, blinking at the absurdity.

"Monkey Punch, baby!" Tessa announces, holding hers up like a championship trophy.

Marlena takes a sip from her bowl, only to immediately sputter and cough into her arm. "Holy shit, that's strong," she rasps between laughs, eyes wide and watering.

I laugh, shaking my head as I lean back in my seat. "That looks like it belongs at a frat party."

The girls settle in with their cocktails, and we spend the next hour watching other brave (or drunk) souls take their turn in the spotlight. Some are surprisingly good. Most are delightfully terrible. We cheer for all of them anyway.

Then, my name gets called.

My stomach does a little flip, but the kind that's more thrill than dread. The usual nerves that would have gripped me by the throat are barely a whisper, dulled by booze and the warmth of good company.

"Wish me luck," I say as I push back from the table.

"You got this!" Marlena beams. Khloe, on her way back from the bar, flashes me a grin and two thumbs up as she passes.

I make my way to the DJ, who hands me the mic with a knowing nod. As I take the stage, I turn to face my friends and flash them a smile as the opening beat of "I Am the Fire" by Halestorm pulses through the speakers—and that's it. That's all I need. One beat and everything sharpens. The crowd fades, the lights blur, and I step into something bold inside me that I didn't realize I'd been holding back.

I let the lyrics rip out of me, fierce and unfiltered. My voice rises, steady and strong, wrapping around every word like it belongs to me. I don't hold back—not for one damn second. I sing like I've got something to prove, and maybe I do, if only to myself.

From the corner of my eye, I catch the girls cheering—Tessa waving her straw like a flag, Khloe standing and clapping along, Marlena recording the whole thing on her phone like a proud mom.

And as the final note rings out, the room erupts into applause and cheers.

I step off that tiny stage with my pulse racing, breath shallow, and a grin so wide it actually hurts my face. I make my way back toward the bar, still riding the high, still buzzing from the rush.

"You killed it up there!" Cole says with a grin, tossing his towel over his shoulder, when I wedge into a space at the bar.

"Thanks," I reply, already feeling my cheeks warm, half from the praise, half from the alcohol.

"So, what can I get ya this time?" he asks, leaning on the bar.

"Sex on the Beach," I reply with a flirty smirk.

"Ain't no beaches around here, but I can always figure something out for ya," he replies with a wink.

"Oh yeah?" I laugh, and he leans in just slightly.

"Anything for you," he says, flashing that cocky little grin before turning to work his magic behind the bar. His hands move quickly, confidently, and in less than a minute, he slides the drink across the counter with a smooth flick of his wrist. A small, folded paper rests neatly underneath the glass.

"Can you add it to my friend's tab? We're covering it all together," I say, flashing him a smile as I pick up the glass and swipe the paper beneath it, briefly glancing at it.

"Of course." His eyes gleam with amusement as they follow my hand. His grin only widens when I slip the paper into the bodice of my dress like it's the most natural thing in the world.

"Thanks, Cole." I wink before slipping away from the bar to rejoin my friends.

Roughly another hour slips by in a blur of music, laughter, and clinking glasses. At some point, Khloe and I decide to wander off for a game of 8-ball. Big mistake—for her, anyway. I end up absolutely smoking her, sinking the eight ball with a smug little smirk while she groans dramatically.

"Sore loser much?" I tease, leaning on my cue stick as she mutters something about demanding a rematch.

She wants to go again, of course, but the pleasant buzz from my last drink is already starting to fade. I rack the cue and toss her a grin. "Later. I need a refill."

I weave my way through the crowd and head to the bar for the third time that night. Cole spots me instantly and flashes that signature grin of his—half flirt, half trouble.

"Back for more, huh?" he teases while he dries out a glass.

"You know me," I say, shooting him a playful smirk as I slide into an open spot at the bar. "I'm a glutton for punishment."

"What's your poison this time, darlin'?" He leans on his elbows.

"Same as before," I respond, my smirk never faltering. "Keep the good vibes rolling."

"You got it," he says as he gets to work on it. I distract myself with my phone, checking messages and anything else that has popped up. A minute later, he slides my drink across the bar, the condensation already pooling around the base. "Let me know if you ever want the real thing, gorgeous," he adds with a wink.

My cheeks flush, and I'm suddenly grateful for the dim lighting. "You're trouble," I mutter as I slide my phone back into my bag and grab the drink.

He just winks again and turns to the next customer.

Drink in hand, I head back to the table and plop down beside Khloe. She is back on the Karafun website looking for a song, her face twisted in concentration as she scrolls, so I take a sip from the drink and nudge her. After Cole's little offer, I knew I needed to tell her about the number.

"So… I've been holding out on you," I say.

She looks up, instantly intrigued. "Do tell."

I lean closer, lowering my voice. "Okay—but don't scream."

She cocks a brow. "Why would I—"

I pull the folded receipt from my bodice and unfold it just enough for her to see. Blue ink, messy handwriting, and a cheeky little winky face stare up at her. Khloe gasps so loud it turns heads.

"You did not!" she squeals, nearly knocking over her drink as she snatches the receipt from my hand. "You little *hoe*! Oh my god, Rae!"

Tessa and Marlena whip around in their seats like they've just been summoned. "What's going on?" Tessa asks, eyes darting between us.

Khloe thrusts the receipt into her hands like it's evidence from a crime scene, and my cheeks heat again. "Cole gave her his *number*!"

Tessa's eyes widen. "No fucking way! I *knew* something was up when he comped those first drinks!"

"Are you gonna call him?" Marlena asks, smirking as she peers over Tessa's shoulder.

I shrug, slipping the paper back into my bra. "He's cute, but I'm not *into* him like that."

"That's because you've got it bad for Officer Hottie," Tessa sings, wiggling her eyebrows. I don't even bother answering—but I can feel my cheeks betray me, glowing like a damn sunrise.

"If she's passing on the bartender, I'll take him," Khloe declares, reaching for the receipt again.

"He's more your type anyway," I say, laughing as I hand it over. "Go for it."

Khloe grins. "Cute, flirty, and totally fuckable? Say less," she says as she adds the number to her phone. I roll my eyes at her just as Tessa and Marlena's names are called.

"FYI, Rae?" Tessa says as she stands up from the table. I glance at her, my brows furrowing in curiosity. "You're terrible at hiding your feelings, babe. Stop pretending you don't like *him*," she says as she follows Marlena to the DJ booth.

"Okay." I mutter softly. Tessa knew me better than anyone. She knows what I am feeling, even before I do.

I watch as the two of them each receive a microphone, then step up onto the stage, their arms linked together as they bob their heads to the opening notes of "Monsters" by Ruelle.

As they start to sing, I take a long sip from my drink and stand. "I'll be right back," I murmur to Khloe, who pays me no attention, before slipping away from the table to head to the bathroom.

The bathroom itself is surprisingly clean for a dive bar. Flyers for old and upcoming themed karaoke nights, punk shows, and drink specials are taped over every inch of space on the walls and stalls. One of the lights above the mirror flickers with the persistence of a dying firefly, and the stall doors creak like they belong in a haunted house.

I step up to the sink and take a long look at myself. My cheeks are still flushed, and my eyes are a bit glassy from the alcohol consumption. My braid has almost completely unraveled, my hair now in soft waves that spill down my back. I adjust the flower clip that's somehow still hanging in there and run my fingers through the strands to fluff them out.

Tessa's words are still echoing in my mind. I'm not *denying* anything. I have already admitted to myself that I am attracted to Emilio. Hell, I masturbated to thoughts of him because of that attraction. But it was nothing more than that. The man is insufferable, and yes, kind of hot in a way that makes my brain do stupid things. He might have apologized for his behavior during our first meeting and been kind, but that doesn't mean I like him in the way Tessa thinks. I didn't really know the fucker. If anything, I just want to fuck him and satiate my body's needs.

I sigh and splash cold water on my face, hoping to cool both my flushed skin and my thoughts. I don't need to go down that rabbit hole again. One night of letting loose doesn't mean I'm suddenly catching feelings.

After a few minutes of drying myself off and situating myself again, I exit the bathroom, smoothing my hands over my dress. Thoughts of Emilio were still present in my mind but were now manageable.

I step out of the hallway. Tessa and Marlena had finished their song, replaced now by some guy royally butchering a song by Korn that my intoxicated brain can not remember the name of—drunk karaoke at its finest.

I do a sweep of the bar. The number of patrons has dwindled, leaving the bar top almost entirely open. Cole spots me from the hall as I look around and gives me a short wave, which I return before leaving the hallway.

And then I see him.

Emilio Perez.

He's sitting at a table a few feet from the bar, a bottle of Dos Equis resting loosely in one hand, posture straight and alert like he's halfway between off-duty and still on the clock. He's wearing dark jeans and a black fitted tee that clings to his well-defined abs just right. His badge and handcuffs are clipped to his belt—subtle but visible enough for anyone paying attention, and his off-duty weapon sticks out just slightly from the back of his jeans. His expression is unreadable as he listens to who I *think* is Kline, though I barely register that part.

Because all I can really focus on is the way something deep inside me shifts—like someone lit a spark and set it loose in my veins.

I wasn't expecting to see him here.

My steps falter, and I hover just outside the bathroom hallway like I've forgotten where I was headed. The combination of my thoughts just minutes ago and the alcohol has my heart already racing, my palms suddenly a little damp. The alcohol makes it easier to blame the warmth blooming in my chest, but I know it's more than that. It's physically seeing him that makes something stir low in my stomach.

And then he looks up, and his eyes find mine.

CRIME
OFFICER
STOP

TWELVE
EMILIO

AS SOON AS our eyes meet, the noise of the bar dulls into nothing. I forget what Kline was just saying—hell, I forget where I am for a second—because Raelynn Carson is standing across the room, staring straight at me like the world narrowed down to just the two of us.

Of all the damn bars in this city, I had to walk into *this* one.

She's standing just outside the hallway near the bathrooms, frozen for a beat like she's debating whether to turn around or come over. Her expression shifts somewhere between surprise and caution, and then—finally—she starts walking toward me.

With every step, more of her comes into focus.

That halter dress she's wearing accentuates every curve, the neckline dipping just enough at the front to tease the swell of her chest. Her hair's a mess of soft beach waves, a flower clip pinned near her temple. There's a flush to her cheeks that tells me she's been drinking—enough to feel good but not enough to be sloppy. And God, she looks *happy*. Relaxed. Lighter than I've ever seen her.

I shift slightly in my seat, trying to act like I haven't been staring. Kline lifts his beer to his lips and glances at me sidelong, clearly catching the sudden change in my posture.

But it's not until I catch the bartender watching her—that slow, hungry once-over, like he's mentally undressing her—that something sharp twists in my chest.

Jealousy.

I have no right to it, and yet it surges anyway. She's not mine. I know that. But the idea of anyone else having those thoughts about her makes my jaw tighten.

She stops just short of our table, her gaze flicking between me and Kline. She offers Kline a small smile—a silent greeting, and he returns it before setting his beer down on the table as she flicks her gaze back to mine.

"I wasn't expecting to see you here." she says, tilting her head slightly, her voice low and even despite the clamor of voices and music pulsing through the bar.

"I could say the same thing," I reply, leaning back in my seat as I drape my arm casually along the cool metal backing of the chair. "Who are you here with?"

She jerks her chin in the direction of the karaoke setup. "Just a couple of friends."

I follow her gaze to a table across the room where three girls are laughing over their drinks, eyes flicking between Raelynn and me like this moment is something they've been waiting for. The girl with shoulder-length blonde hair and a pink crocheted top spots Raelynn and waves enthusiastically, which earns another round of giggles from the others.

Raelynn waves back with a sheepish smile before refocusing on me. "I was roped into coming tonight."

I nod, swirling the last inch of beer in my bottle before taking a slow sip. I am due for another, but I have no intention of getting up—not with the bartender still eyeing Raelynn like she was the only thing on tap tonight. Every time the guy isn't pouring drinks, his gaze is locked on her. It is starting to piss me off, and if I go up there, I might end up punching him in the damn throat.

I glance at Kline, who seems lost in thought, his beer cradled between his hands like it might offer answers if he stared long enough.

"Kline, you mind grabbing me another?" I ask, not taking my eyes off Raelynn.

He blinks, coming back to the present, then nods. "Sure. I need another anyway." He sets his half-empty bottle down with a soft clink before pushing away from the table.

"Is he okay?" Raelynn asks quietly, her eyes following him as he makes his way toward the bar.

His absence shifts the air immediately. The bartender's focus moves with him, leaving Raelynn out of their direct line of sight, and I feel my shoulders loosen a fraction. I turn back to her. She's closer now—close enough that the faint trace of her perfume teases my senses. Jasmine and berries, subtle but warm. It's intoxicating. I find myself wanting to lean in, to breathe her in until the scent is imprinted on me. My fingers drum idly against the neck of my bottle, a poor substitute for touching her.

"Bad call today, that's all," I finally say. "He wanted to blow off some steam, so… like you, I got dragged out."

Her brow arches slightly. "Did everything with Detective Meyer get sorted out?"

That catches me off guard, pulling my focus. My brows knit. "What?"

"I overheard bits and pieces of that conversation the other day with that call we were on. You and Kline were at that bar where the bartender worked, right?" she asks.

"Oh. Yeah." I give a short nod. "No, everything's fine. Zeke's has exterior cameras and ones covering the parking lot. Footage caught Kline leaving not long after I did. The bartender was seen leaving after closing with another guy. They got a clear enough shot of him to put a name to the face. He was arrested that evening after she was found. He even made a full confession, too. Guess he didn't see the point in denying it once they had him."

"Oh, good," she says, when a voice behind me cuts through the brief reprieve between awful karaoke renditions—drawling, amused, and dripping with mischief.

"Is that a baton in your pocket, or are you just happy to see me?"

My brows arch in confusion, and I turn to find the blonde in the pink top standing a few feet away, a devilish grin stretched across her face. The other two girls in the group giggle behind Pink Top, their gazes fixed on Raelynn.

"Rae, you gonna introduce us to this *daddy* of a cop?" Pink Top teases, her eyes shamelessly scanning me up and down.

Raelynn looks both mortified and amused, flicking her eyes from her friends to me. I bite back a smirk and take the last sip of my beer, finishing it off before setting the empty bottle on the table and rising to greet them properly.

"Emilio Perez," I say, offering my hand.

"Khloe," Pink Top replies as she takes my hand. Her grip is firm, her gaze lingering longer than necessary—especially below the belt—before she finally lets go.

Next is a petite blonde with a bright smile. "Hi! I'm Marlena. It's so nice to meet you!" she says, shaking my hand with far more politeness.

"And I'm Tessa. Rae's told us *so* much about you." The redhead giggles as she shakes my hand quickly, releasing it with a wink.

I glance back at Raelynn, whose cheeks are turning pink. I raise a brow and let a grin tug at the corner of my mouth. "Oh yeah? What exactly has she told you?"

Tessa doesn't miss a beat. She smirks, looking past me at her flustered friend. "Oh, just how hot she thinks you are and that she'd totally fu—"

"Tessa!" Raelynn snaps, cutting her off with a glare sharp

enough to draw blood. Her face is flushed now, and I can't help the laugh that escapes me as I drop back into my seat. I knew what was going to be said, and truth be told, I've had the same thought more than once.

Kline returns then, beers in hand. He slows slightly when he sees we've gained some company, his eyes flicking between the girls before handing me my drink and sliding back into his seat.

Grasping for a safer subject, Raelynn turns to face Kline, her lips curled into a smile that was doing little to mask her embarrassment. "How are you doing, Kline?" she asks him as he pushes the lime into his beer with his thumb. Beer fizzles out the top, coating his thumb, and he pulls it out and sucks it off.

"Could be better. You?"

"Honestly, not bad."

"That's good. How about you ladies?" He turns his attention to Raelynn's friends. Khloe leans against the table, giving him an exaggerated once-over.

"Having the time of my life, baby," she purrs, her eyes shamelessly undressing Kline now. Raelynn groans quietly, covering her face with one hand as I chuckle behind the rim of my beer.

Kline chuckles, lifting his beer. "That's good to hear," he says, taking a slow drink, his gaze locked on Khloe the entire time.

"You here to sing?" he asks as he sets the bottle down, the glass clinking softly against the table.

"Mmhmm," Khloe hums. "We've already sung a few, but—" She leans across the table, elbows resting against the marble as her chest presses forward. The blue bikini top beneath her pink crocheted layer does little to hold her breasts in; they are barely hanging on, the curve of her nipples teasing the edge of the thin fabric. Kline's eyes drop, just for a second too long. His grip tightens around the bottle until his knuckles pale, and he subtly shifts in his seat.

"—I can always sing another just for you, baby," Khloe finishes, voice low and dripping with suggestion, punctuating it with a slow, sultry wink.

Kline nods, eyes never leaving Khloe's chest as he lifts the bottle and drains the rest like it's water. Two heavy gulps, and it's gone. The glass hits the table with a sharp *clack*, louder than it should be in the charged silence between them.

That was my cue.

The last thing I need tonight is to witness my partner pop a boner for a girl barely old enough to legally drink. I watch his eyes trail after her as she gives him one last wink, her glossy lips curling in mischief before she spins on her heel and follows her friends back to their table.

Kline doesn't even try to hide it; he stands up and stalks after her like a dog in heat, his eyes glued to the way her ass sways with each step. And with the way those frayed shorts barely covered her, he didn't have to use much imagination.

I glance over at Raelynn.

She's watching the scene unfold with thinly veiled discomfort. Her arms are loosely crossed, and her lips are slightly pursed like she is trying to decide whether to laugh or cringe.

I lean toward her, raising my voice enough for her to hear over the tone-deaf, drunk singing and indistinct chatter. "Want to get some air?"

She meets my eyes, her expression softening immediately. There's a flicker of relief in her gaze, like she's been waiting for an out and wasn't sure how to ask for it.

"Yeah," she murmurs with a slight nod.

She doesn't hesitate, just spins around and heads straight for the back exit. I follow close behind, tossing one last glance at Kline, who's now seated with his back toward me and Khloe in his lap. I pray he doesn't do something he'll regret.

The door creaks as it swings open, and we step into the cool embrace of the desert night.

Out here, everything feels quieter. The door shuts behind us with a solid *thunk*, sealing off the noise and the heat. The air is dry and crisp, tinged with the faint scent of cigarette smoke and asphalt. Somewhere nearby, a car engine hums in the distance, blending with the soft chirping of crickets hidden in the brush. The contrast to the suffocating bar is instant and welcome.

Raelynn drifts over to a worn bench just off to the side of the building and sits, exhaling like she's been holding her breath all night. I lean against the wall near the door, folding my arms across my chest as I watch her toe at the dirt with her wedge, grinding a cigarette butt into the gravel.

"Is she always like that?" I ask after a beat.

Raelynn sighs, a small, tired smile tugging at her lips. "Not always. Just when she's drunk and finds someone she thinks is hot."

She lets out a soft laugh and tilts her head slightly to the side, eyes glinting beneath the dim light above the door. "Honestly, she probably would've made a move on *you* if she didn't think something was going on between us."

I glance at her as she continues to grind more butts into the ground. "Why would she think that?" I ask, a hint of amusement lacing my voice.

Raelynn lifts her head, her eyes meeting mine with an unreadable look. There's a beat of silence. Tension crackles in the air between us, subtle but unmistakable. She sucks her bottom lip between her teeth like she's holding something back.

I don't stop myself. I have only known this girl for two fucking weeks, and already she was invading every single thought of mine.

Before I even realize what I'm doing, I'm crossing the space between us and dragging her to her feet, caging her body against the door with my hands pressed on either side of her head. Her breath catches. A combination of fear and lust radiates off her.

"Emilio," she breathes. "What are you—"

I don't let her finish.

My lips crash into hers. Hard, desperate, and reckless.

She makes a noise of surprise, her hands bracing against my chest. I half expected her to shove me off, but she doesn't. Instead, her fingers tighten in the fabric of my shirt, and she *pulls me in*, closing the space between us like she's been waiting for this just as long as I have.

My hands move off the door, my left hand slides up to cup the side of her face, thumb brushing the softness of her cheek. My right arm wraps firmly around her waist, drawing her body flush against mine. She melts into me as my tongue teases the seam of her lips, begging her to let me in, and she does. Her lips part with a low, breathy moan that goes straight to my fucking head.

Her tongue darts out to tease my lips, then flicks my tongue, playful and taunting, before retreating back inside her mouth. I chase after her, deepening the kiss, and she moans again—this time louder.

Raw.

Needy.

The sound vibrates between us and sets every nerve ending of mine on fire. It takes everything in me right then and there not to rip this damn dress off her. The taste of her, her moans, the way her body molded into mine, she is exquisite. I'd thought about kissing her more times than I could count. Hell, I'd thought about more than kissing her, especially with the way she looks at me when she thinks I'm not paying attention. And judging by the way she's grinding her hips ever so slightly against mine, she's been thinking the same damn thing.

I was a dick to her during our first meeting, and that didn't deter her. She craves me just as much as I crave her. I can tell from the way our tongues dance together, and the sounds she is making while her nails dig into my chest, that she wants this as much as I do.

I pull back, just for a second to breathe, and she lets out a soft whimper in protest. I can't help but chuckle as I bring my lips back to hers, brushing mine over hers before slowly moving down to press a trail of kisses along her jaw. She gasps softly and tilts her head back instinctively, giving me more access as her fingers slip beneath my shirt, tracing over my abs like she's trying to memorize every line. Her touch is slow, deliberate, and it makes my dick throb painfully against the inside of my jeans.

I continue to trail soft kisses under her chin and down to that sweet spot on her throat, sucking lightly, pulling another moan out of her that has my dick twitching again. I groan into her neck as her hand drifts down, fingers trailing along my V-line. When she brushes against my waistband, I snap. I slam her back against the door with just enough force to make her gasp, spreading her legs with my knee so she can *feel* exactly what she's doing to me.

"Fuck," she whimpers, and the sound alone almost undoes me.

One of her hands drags up my chest, nails scraping in a way that makes me hiss. The other lingers at my waistband, daring, almost teasing. I move my hand from her face into her hair and the other, which was wrapped around her waist, down the smooth skin of her left thigh, fingers slipping under the hem of her dress.

I pause and lift my head to look at her. Her cheeks are flushed, her chest rising and falling fast. Her eyes meet mine, flicking briefly down to where my hand rests on her thigh, then back up, full of heat. I slide my hand up higher, just enough that my fingers could tease with the edge of her lace panties, and she bites her lip. I smirk as I brush my thumb along her core. I can *feel* how soaked she is. She is just as aroused as I am.

"Shit, Raelynn," I whisper.

She whimpers when I press my thumb against her through the fabric, teasing her folds. Her hips buck into my hand, and her lips part like she's about to beg me not to stop.

But I do.

I pull back, slowly withdrawing my hand, and she lets out a needy sound of protest that makes me smirk.

I lean in, pressing my forehead to hers. "You're still drunk, Raelynn."

She blinks, confused. "What?"

"I'm not going to take advantage of you. Not like this," I breathe against her lips. "If we're going to do anything, it's not going to be behind a dingy ass dive bar. It's going to be when you're sober. When you *know* what you want. And when I can take my time with you."

Her breath catches again, not from shock this time, but something deeper. Her hands are still on me, her body trembling just slightly beneath mine.

I press a final kiss to the corner of her mouth, then step back, leaving a space between us that feels too wide.

She looks up at me, dazed and breathless, and I know this isn't over. Not even close.

Just… not tonight.

CRIME
OFFICER
STOP
STOP

THIRTEEN
EMILIO

I FELT LIKE SHIT.

Leaving Raelynn like that. Flushed, breathless, lips kiss-swollen from mine after teasing her the way I had… it was pure fucking torture. She didn't say anything when I pulled away and told her it wasn't happening tonight. But she didn't have to. I saw it plain as day in her eyes, the flicker of disappointment, the way her posture shifted, shoulders pulling back like armor, like she was trying to pretend it hadn't gotten to her.

But it had.

And so had I.

Still, I couldn't let it happen. Not like that. Not with the alcohol swimming in her system and her judgment dulled by more than just lust. I've seen too many guys cross that line, too many lives ruined by one bad decision. And no matter how much I want her—and *God help me*, I want her—I'm not going to be that guy, not with her. I have my morals. My mother raised me better than the scums that do that to women.

My attitude gets the better of me more often than I'd like to admit—but the one thing my mother made damn sure I'd never forget was how to be a gentleman.

Growing up, that wasn't something I saw modeled in my house. My father was a miserable bastard. Mean and cruel. Emotionally abusive to both of us from the start, and physically when he thought he could get away with it. He started with my mom first. Always her. But by the time I was old enough to stand between them, he started turning that rage on me, too.

My mother came to this country alone, crossed the border (illegally, mind you) without anything but a name and the clothes on her back. She met my dad not long after. A Mexican-American who helped immigrants once they crossed because his family had once been in their shoes. From what I understand, he wasn't always abusive. He was the only man she trusted in the beginning, so he took it upon himself to make sure she assimilated well enough. He taught her English, showed her around, and helped her get her Green Card. Eventually, they fell in love (or at least she did). After about six months in the States, they were married, and nine months later, I was born.

The physical abuse started when I was about three, but he was emotionally abusive before that. She knew nothing else, had no one else but me and him. He didn't like letting her out of his sight. His drinking got worse as I got older, and so did his temper.

The first time he put his hands on me, I was thirteen.

I stepped in between him and my mother during one of his drunken rages. He shattered a beer bottle against the wall, and some of the glass tore into my side when he beat me to the ground after trying to protect her. I ended up with two broken ribs and several lacerations from him and spent three days in the hospital. That was the turning point for her. The first time she truly saw how deep his anger ran. She finally found her voice and told the child safety investigator everything, and my father was arrested.

After my stint in the hospital, my mother and I wasted no

time moving out of my father's house. We didn't have much anyway, just a few suitcases of clothing and some toys for me were all we packed. Everything else belonged to my father. She filed for citizenship and divorce, and got a restraining order as soon as we settled. Life got better.

She raised me on her own after that. She wasn't willing to open herself up to another man. I was the only man she needed in her life, she would tell me. After graduating from college, I applied to the academy to stop abusive men like my father and make a difference in people's lives. She taught me to be the man I am today. She taught me strength, patience, and how to respect others, especially the people you love. And, yes, I have my flaws. I may not be the nicest person some days, and I may like to get a little rough in bed (because who the fuck doesn't), but I would never intentionally lay a hand on a woman.

But Jesus, just the *taste* of Raelynn. The way she melted into me, how her nails dug into my chest, the breathy little noises she made when my hands were on her… it had short-circuited every ounce of self-control I had. I am still reeling from it. My jeans are doing a piss-poor job of hiding just how painfully hard I am, and every step through this small hallway with her beside me feels like a punishment—my own private, slow-burning hell.

I don't move my hand from her back when we step inside and still keep it there when we emerge from the hallway. She doesn't pull away either. If anything, she leans into it just slightly, like the contact grounds her.

The table I'd been at earlier had been claimed by a couple now, deep in conversation and oblivious to everything else. Kline, of course, is still parked on the other side of the bar with the girls. Khloe is now fully perched on his lap, giggling with her head thrown back while his hand (not subtle in the least) is cupping one of her breasts. His other arm is tucked low, hidden beneath the edge of the table. I didn't want to know what it was doing.

Raelynn pauses beside me. I turn slightly, catching the way her gaze lingers on the scene. Her lip is caught between her teeth again, but this time it's not flirtation—it's quiet uncertainty. She doesn't look like someone who wants to join them in another drink or two. She looks done with the night.

And honestly? So am I.

"You want me to just take you home?" I ask, my voice low as I lean in close, my lips brushing her ear so she can hear me over the music and drunken noise.

She glances at me, then at her friends, and gives a small nod. "Yeah. I'd appreciate that," she says. "Let me just grab my bag and let them know."

"Alright." I nod, letting my hand fall from her back. "Go ahead. I'll wait here."

I watch her make her way across the room. Her stride is calm and confident, but I can tell, beneath it, something's still working itself out. She reaches the girls' table and leans down to speak to them, her voice low. I can't hear what she says, but I don't need to.

Marlena's face lights up like it's Christmas. Tessa does a mock gasp, one hand over her mouth. And Khloe, still firmly on Kline's lap, lets out a little whoop, her hands shooting into the air.

Oh, yeah. They're definitely talking about me.

Any trace of disappointment Raelynn might've felt seems to have faded. Whatever she just told them, it didn't hurt her. If anything, it empowered her. And maybe that's why she let me touch her the way she did. Maybe that's why she trusted me enough to *stop* when I did. Maybe she *gets* it. Maybe she respects me more for not letting things go too far.

The hugs start after that. Quick and affectionate. Marlena whispers something into Raelynn's ear that makes her laugh under her breath. All three of them give me lingering glances, some curious, some smugly approving.

Then she's back at my side, her Ghostface bag slung over one shoulder, and the smallest smile pulling at the corners of her mouth.

"All set?" I ask.

She nods. "Let's go."

We push back through the bar doors, side by side, the music and chatter fading into the background as we make our way down the ramp toward the lot.

I follow her to the passenger-side door of my truck and prop it open for her. The seat sits nearly level with her stomach, so climbing in is her only option. She flashes me a warm smile, grabbing the handle on the ceiling with one hand and the doorframe with the other. My hands hover just behind her, ready to help if she needs it.

As she hauls herself up, I get a clear, unfiltered view of her ass and the watercolor tattoo curling along her left hip—something I somehow missed earlier. I bite back a groan as she settles into the seat.

Once she's in, I shut the door and circle around to my side. With my height advantage, it's a quick step up into the Silverado. I slide into the driver's seat and take a second before starting the truck—just long enough to steal a glance at Raelynn. She's buckled in, hands folded in her lap, eyes fixed on the dashboard like she's not sure where to rest them.

I turn the key in the ignition. The engine rumbles awake, deep and familiar, and the rock station I always keep on blasts straight into the cab—Slipknot's "Duality" roaring through the speakers like it's ready to shake the bolts loose. Raelynn jumps in her seat, a startled gasp slipping out before she catches herself.

I can't help chuckling as I reach over and turn the volume down to something that won't rattle her bones.

"Sorry," I say, though I'm still smiling. "Forgot I had it up that loud."

She shakes her head, a small huff of a laugh escaping. "It's fine. Just wasn't expecting it."

"Where am I heading?" I ask after a few seconds, glancing between the windshield and her.

She rattles it off, and I punch it into the GPS mounted on the dash. Her complex pops up a few miles away, tucked off a quieter stretch of road.

The system chirps out directions, and I shift into reverse, easing us out of the parking spot. Raelynn keeps her gaze trained out the passenger window, fingers brushing absently over her knee, like she's replaying everything that happened tonight and trying not to let it show.

The drive to her apartment isn't long, ten minutes, maybe less, with most of the city asleep by now. Streetlights smear orange across the pavement, and the buildings loom like silhouettes against the night sky. Aside from the occasional car cutting through an intersection, the roads are empty—just stretches of asphalt and the low hum of the engine beneath us.

Raelynn stares out the window, one leg tucked up under her, the other bouncing lightly in rhythm with the alt-rock playing on the radio. Every now and then, I catch her sneaking glances at me, her lip rolled into her mouth.

I grip the wheel a little tighter, jaw clenched as I try to focus on the road instead of the lingering heat in my veins, or the scent of her perfume still clinging to my shirt, or the ghost of her lips against mine.

I want her—more than I've ever wanted anything.

After an agonizingly long ten minutes, I finally pull into Catalina Crest, Raelynn's apartment complex. Tucked just off a quieter stretch of Broadway Boulevard, the buildings are a warm, sandy beige with clean stucco and crisp white trim. The landscaping is neat and desert-friendly, featuring smooth gravel paths, well-placed mesquite trees, and a few flowering bushes that add a pop of color under the soft glow of the walkway lights. Everything looks maintained, cared for. Even the parking lot is freshly striped and free of trash, which is saying something for this part of town.

I follow her directions once the GPS leads me into the complex, rolling past the first row of buildings until the lot opens up toward the back. At her cue, I slow near the fire hydrant she mentioned and turn left, the headlights sweeping over parked cars and trimmed shrubs.

Her building is set back a bit, providing it with some extra privacy. It's a two-story structure with dark, sturdy metal railings and evenly spaced porch lights casting a warm amber hue across the balconies. It feels… quiet, but in a good way. Peaceful. Safe.

I roll past a row of clean sedans and newer-model SUVs, finally pulling into an empty space beneath a palo verde tree that sways gently in the night breeze. In the center of the complex, I catch a glimpse of the pool—clear water lit from the automatic pool lights, shimmering in the dark like a glass mirror. The gate is shut, the pool deck tidy, the loungers neatly arranged along the fence line. Someone clearly takes pride in keeping this place together.

It's the kind of complex people stay in longer than they planned, because it feels like home. And I don't hate that for her.

I kill the engine and lean back in my seat, exhaling slowly as I glance toward Raelynn out of the corner of my eye. She hasn't moved. Her body is angled slightly toward the door, but her hands fidget with the straps of her bag, twisting them between her fingers like she's trying to keep them busy.

I turn slightly in my seat, voice low. "You okay?"

She finally lets go of the strap and meets my gaze. Her teeth sink into her bottom lip (something she's been doing all night), and she gives a small nod. "Yeah, I'm good."

But I can hear the hesitation in her voice. I know there's a "but" in there, but she doesn't say, and I don't push.

After a few moments of silent eye contact, she breaks free and finally props open her door. I don't waste a second, and I'm out of the truck and at her side before she even has her bag on.

I hold my hand out to Raelynn in offering, and she takes it. I help her out of the truck, and she gives me a grateful smile. She probably knew that if she jumped out of the cabin while wearing these damned heels, she would end up twisting an ankle and eating the only patch of grass stubborn enough to grow through a sidewalk crack. Weeds and grass are resilient as fuck. They can grow out of everything, but god forbid you plant a flower or vegetable in the wrong type of fucking soil.

I let go of her hand once she's steady and close the door behind her, the heavy *thunk* of it echoing a little too loud in the quiet of the complex. She turns toward me, the words "thank you" forming on her lips, but I cut her off by gently retaking her hand.

"You can say it at the door."

She smirks, mouth closing, and we start walking toward her building. I'd parked as close as I could get, but we still have a bit of a walk down the path. Her heels click softly on the concrete with every step, the only sound in the stillness of the night.

After a few minutes, we are at her door, and I take in the area. A stack of plastic pumpkins is tucked in the corner, and fake spider webs hang from the stairs that create this little corner of privacy. Releasing my hand, she shoves it into her bag and fishes out her house key. It is attached to a Ghost-face lanyard, and I can't help but snort in amusement, which, to my surprise, she doesn't notice. She is definitely obsessed with the character (or at least the mask). Fisting the key, she jams it into the deadbolt, wiggling it until it finally clicks.

The second the door cracks open, barking explodes from inside.

Before I can react, a black labrador barrels toward us like a furry missile.

"Hi, bud!" Raelynn laughs as the dog launches himself at her, his whole body wiggling like he might fall apart from excitement. She crouches and smooshes his face between her hands, pressing kiss after kiss to his snout. "I missed you, too. Yes, I did. Yes, I did," she says in a baby voice.

I chuckle softly, and she looks up at me before releasing the dog's face. The dog immediately turns his focus to me, his nose sniffing away to ensure I wasn't a threat to his mother. Once he determines I'm not one, the dog jumps up, catching me off guard and nearly knocking me onto my ass as his wet tongue drags across my cheek.

"Max, no!" Raelynn giggles, grabbing his teal collar and pulling him back.

"It's all good," I laugh, wiping my cheek with the back of my hand. "I don't mind. He's a good judge of character."

She kneels beside him again, petting his head, and I join in. His tongue lolls out of the side of his mouth, and his tail thumps happily against the door frame. "Well, it's safe to say he approves of you."

"I'm glad for that. It would suck if he didn't like me."

She arches a brow. "Why's that?"

I watch her step inside briefly, setting her bag and lanyard on a small black entry table before joining me on the porch again. Max slips back into the apartment and leaps onto the dark gray couch. He spins three times before dropping down onto the cushions with a dramatic sigh.

"Because it would make coming to see you kind of difficult."

"Do you plan on seeing me again? Outside of work, I mean?" she asks, her head tilting and her cheeks flushing.

I take a step closer, reach for her hand, and bring it to my lips, brushing a chaste kiss across her knuckles. "Only if you want me to."

Her breath catches slightly. Then she closes the distance and cups my cheek with her other hand, before pressing her lips to mine. It's gentle, warm, and her mouth lingers on mine for a second longer than necessary.

"I'd like that very much," she whispers against my lips before pulling back with a soft smirk. She steps fully into the threshold of her apartment, fingers curling lightly around the doorframe. "Let me know when you get home?"

I scratch the back of my neck, a little sheepish. "I, uh… don't have your number." Why the fuck had I not asked for it sooner is beyond me.

She laughs, backing into the apartment. "You're a cop. I'm sure you can figure it out."

Before I can fire back, she grins. "Good night, Emilio," she says, and the door clicks shut behind her.

I stand there for a second, blinking at the teal door that separates me from her.

Well… shit.

FOURTEEN
RAELYNN

I PRESS my back against the door the second it clicks shut, holding my breath like that might quiet the frantic rhythm pounding in my chest. I can still hear him on the other side—his footsteps lingering, pacing maybe, or his fingers dragging through that perfect hair of his as he considers the challenge I just threw down.

I could open this door again. I could hand over my number and end the game. But where's the fun in that?

No, this is better. He left me needy, teased me just enough to drive me crazy, and now he gets to suffer, too. My body still aches with it, humming with the ghost of his hands sliding over me, the rough pad of his thumb brushing my cunt through my thin panties, his mouth hot and greedy against mine—before pulling away with that maddening, "Not tonight."

Fucking asshole. I hope he's suffering just as badly. Blue balls serve him right. Still, I can't deny I want him to do the exact same thing I'm about to—finish what he started.

Time is mercifully on my side. I manage to steal just enough of it to take the edge off—one toe-curling orgasm that leaves me trembling and breathless, muttering his name into the dark like a secret. Then it's cleanup mode. Fresh panties, a quick rinse of my face, and my oversized Johnny Cash sleep shirt that I stole from an ex years ago and never gave back.

I've barely settled when chaos comes storming through the door. Tessa and Khloe tumble inside, loud as hell, singing the last mangled lines of a pop song I can't even place. Their voices are high-pitched and off-key, bouncing off the apartment walls like some kind of drunken siren call. God only knows how many more drinks they went through after I left.

It doesn't take long for the noise to simmer into its usual brand of disorder. After a few attempts to shush them (because, hello, we have fucking neighbors and it was nearly 2 a.m.), Tessa plants a sloppy kiss on my head before retreating to her room, giggling all the way. Khloe, though, she doesn't even try. She just collapses face-first on the couch like a human pancake, limbs flung out in every direction, before grabbing the pastel butterfly throw and yanking it over her head like some kind of cocoon. Within seconds—literally seconds—she's out. Snoring.

I just stand there staring at her, baffled. What goddess blessed this girl with the ability to knock out cold the second she lies down? It's like she has a damn built-in switch that says horizontal equals unconscious.

Meanwhile, I have to cycle through *at least* seven different positions, stack three pillows in some complicated architectural formation, scroll on my phone until my retinas burn, and then bargain with whatever higher power will listen just to *maybe* fall asleep. And even then, my brain is a relentless little bastard, whispering things like, "Hey, remember that embarrassing thing you said in third grade? Let's think about that for the next hour."

Khloe? A fire alarm could go off. Max could bark himself hoarse. Hell, the world could end—and she'd snore right through it. A corpse sleeps lighter than her, I swear to god. Honestly, it's a miracle she makes it anywhere on time.

With a yawn, I retreat to my bedroom, nudging the door shut with my hip until it clicks softly behind me. My gaze immediately finds Max, already curled into his usual crescent of black fur near the foot of my bed. His sides rise and fall in a steady rhythm, each breath broken by a little snore that almost keeps pace with Khloe's distant symphony in the living room.

I roll my eyes, chuckling under my breath, and cross the room. The mattress dips beneath me as I slide under the covers, shifting until the familiar comfort settles into my bones. My body is just starting to relax when my phone dings on the nightstand.

I reach for it lazily, expecting some late-night chatter from one of my book group chats. But the second I see the screen, my stomach does a little flip. No name. Just a bare number I don't recognize.

My heartbeat quickens, fingers hesitating before I swipe it open.

Made it home safely, mi cariño. Sleep well.

The words blaze across the screen, and heat climbs into my cheeks. He actually did it. Emilio found my number. Part of me thought he'd brush off my challenge, leave it hanging in the air like one of those almost-but-not-quite moments. But here it is. Proof.

A smile tugs at my lips before I can stop it, giddy and impossible to shake. My thumbs fly over the screen, faster than they probably should at this hour:

ME:

I'm glad to hear that. Good night, Emilio.

I hit send, the message delivering with a satisfying *whoosh*, then immediately save the number in my contacts. Setting the phone back on the nightstand, I sink deeper into the blankets, my smile lingering even as I close my eyes.

EMILIO:

Good morning. I hope you have a great day Raelynn

I wake up to that message, and it fuels me more than coffee ever could. It's been years since a good morning text has left me grinning like a fool, cheeks hot, wishing that he was here in person instead of glowing on my phone screen. And yet, here I am—giddy as hell over a few simple words.

We don't talk much over the weekend. Just a few texts here and there, but I'm okay with that. Saturday morning, after his first *good morning* popped up, I asked how he managed to find my number. His answer? He had another officer, a buddy working graveyard that night, dig it up for him. *Cheater.* I told him that too, and he laughed, saying I never gave him any ground rules, that he was only using his "police skills." I called him a smart ass after that, but I had to give him props. I wasn't sure how I expected him to find my number, but I certainly wasn't thinking he'd phone a friend.

"Are you seriously still staring at that message?" Tessa's voice cuts through my thoughts, sharp enough that I nearly drop my phone.

I glance up to see her and Khloe making their way across the quad, fingers laced together, heading straight for where I'm perched on the low wall that borders the arboretum. The weather's merciful today—low nineties. Clouds covered most of the pale blue sky, promising rain later. Despite the humidity combining with the heat, it was bearable enough to sit outside with my lunch. On rare occasions, I decide that I'd rather indulge in one of the many other options the university has to offer for food instead of going to the Cactus Grill. Today I chose sushi. Not entirely sure why I decided on it, when Panda

Express or even pizza was available for god's sake, but it's hitting the spot.

"I can't help it!" I giggle, plucking a Philly roll from the tray with my fingers (yes, my fingers, because my helpless ass still can't figure out chopsticks) and popping it into my mouth.

"She's in looovee," Khloe singsongs, her voice dripping with her usual mischief, before going into a fit of giggles.

"I am not!" I protest, launching the chopsticks at her like the useless sticks they are. She swats them away midair and throws her head back into a full-bodied laugh when they smack into Tessa instead.

Tessa flinches and nearly spills the cup of water she snagged from one of the pop-up booths down the front of her shirt.

"Hey! Watch it!" she yelps, glaring at Khloe halfheartedly before tossing back what's left of the cup in one go.

"She started it!" Khloe cackles, pointing square at me. I stuff another roll into my mouth and throw my hands up in mock surrender.

They both laugh as they drop their bags against the wall, the dull thud echoing off the stone. I tug the tray of sushi into my lap just as they plop down on either side of me, their shoulders pressing into mine, the weight of their presence both grounding and comforting.

"You're not in love, huh?" Tessa teases, her smirk sharp as she leans just far enough to sneak a peek at my screen. Her eyes light up the second she spots Emilio's name—complete with the stupid little heart I placed beside his contact.

Heat floods my cheeks, searing hot, as I snap the phone against my chest like it's contraband I've been caught smuggling. "Okay, fine. I'll admit I like him. And maybe our shared kisses stirred up some shit. But that's it!"

Khloe's grin spreads, wicked and knowing. "So… when are you seeing him again?"

"Tomorrow," I blurt out way too fast. "At work."

She snorts, head shaking in mock disappointment. "No, you dumb hoe. I mean outside of work."

"Oh." The word slips out softer, my gaze flicking back to the glowing screen in my hand.

The unanswered question hangs heavy between us—an invisible weight pressing down harder than either of them. We haven't made plans. I haven't asked. And I don't want to look overeager. But still, the thought of him—of us—lingers, curling warm and tempting in the pit of my stomach.

I snag a sushi roll from the tray to distract myself, but Khloe doesn't let up.

"Well?" she presses, elbowing me just as I lift it to my mouth, nearly knocking the roll clean out of my fingers.

"I don't know yet," I admit, dragging the words out with a soft groan. "We haven't made any plans."

Tessa's grin sharpens, wicked as sin. "Well, make some. I think your vibrator deserves a break."

The sushi in my mouth goes down the wrong pipe, lodging halfway in my throat. I choke, coughing hard enough to send my eyes watering, smacking at my chest with one hand while trying not to die in the middle of the quad.

They lose it instantly. Both of them dissolve into unholy laughter, practically doubled over on either side of me.

Heads whip in our direction—some concerned, most annoyed. But Tessa and Khloe don't give a single fuck, as always.

"You're disgusting," I rasp between coughs, still trying to get my lungs back in order. My face burns hotter than the sidewalk underfoot.

"Disgustingly right," Tessa fires back without missing a beat, her smirk practically glowing.

Khloe leans in again, her perfume—sugary and bright—cloying at my nose as she pokes me in the ribs. "C'mon, Rae. Just text him. Ask him to grab coffee, or dinner. Hell, invite him over for Netflix and 'accidentally' end up in his lap.

Worst-case scenario? He says no. Best case?" She grins, devilish. "You're not sleeping alone tonight."

I roll my eyes but can't stop the small, traitorous smile tugging at my lips. My gaze drops back to my phone, still clenched in my hand like it's part of me. Emilio's name glows at the top of my messages, the little heart next to it mocking me.

My thumb hovers just over the keyboard, pulse picking up speed. My mind runs wild with a thousand possibilities—what I'd say, how he might respond, whether he'd even want to see me outside of work. It feels ridiculous, this rush of nerves, like I'm sixteen again waiting for a boy to text back after homeroom.

Maybe they're right. Maybe I should.

The thought lingers, heavy and tempting. My thumb presses just enough to make the keyboard light up—then the sky cracks with the low rumble of thunder.

The sound vibrates through the air, thick and warning. A cool gust sweeps over us, carrying the scent of damp earth and ozone, and I jerk my head up toward the sky. Dark clouds are rolling in fast, smothering what's left of the pale blue beneath their weight.

"Shit," Tessa mutters, already reaching for her bag.

Grateful for the interruption, I jam my phone into my pocket and grab the sushi tray. The three of us scramble to our feet, laughter bubbling as fat raindrops splatter against the pavement. Within seconds, the air is split between thunder and our hurried footsteps as we rush for cover.

CRIME
OFFICER
STOP

FIFTEEN
EMILIO

PEOPLE ARE FUCKING DUMB.

All it takes is a little bit of rain, and suddenly, half the city forgets how to operate a motor vehicle. Like clockwork, the first fat drops hit the pavement, and everyone collectively decides traffic laws are more like suggestions, and hey—why not spice things up with a couple rounds of bumper cars?

Since clocking in at 2 p.m., I've already been dispatched to three separate accidents. Three in four hours. Every one of them is the same damn story: slick pavement, careless drivers, and fender-benders that choke intersections like clogged arteries. No injuries so far, thank God—just a lot of insurance exchanges and pissed-off commuters. Still, the monotony wears thin.

Now I'm back in my unit, just past the halfway point of my shift, crawling along Speedway boulevard. The windshield wipers drag across the glass with that rhythmic squeak that grates after the hundredth time, pushing drizzle to the edges in uneven streaks. The rain's tapered off, leaving the asphalt slick and gleaming under the streetlamps. Drivers act like they're on a NASCAR track, cutting each other off, hydroplaning in their shitty sedans, half of them with bald tires. Every time I pass one, I half-expect to hear the crunch of another fender-bender in my rearview.

My coffee's gone cold in the cup holder, but I drink it anyway, chasing the bitter dregs to keep myself awake as I pull into an empty parking lot. I throw the unit into park and glance at the MDT glowing on the console, showing a stack of active calls. I scroll through them with one finger, half paying attention. Noise complaints. A "suspicious subject" who probably just looks homeless. Another fender-bender on Grant. The usual for a rainy weekday swing shift.

The radio chatters constantly, dispatch juggling units across the city. I keep the volume low, the steady hum of voices and static serving as background noise while I continue to sip the last of my coffee.

And for a moment, my mind drifts to Raelynn.

Roughly around the time I started my patrol, I received a text from her saying she wanted to see me when I was free next. I still haven't replied. Not because I don't want to, but because the day got busy. And now that I have a moment, I'm not wasting it.

Shifting in my seat, I pull my phone from my pocket, thumb unlocking the screen, and pull up our text thread.

RAELYNN CARSON:

Hey, um. So, I'm not very good at initiating things, but I was wondering when you'll be free next? I'd really like to see you outside of work.

I chuckle under my breath. I can picture her chewing her lip raw while typing that, probably debating whether to hit send a dozen times before actually doing it. I guarantee her friends egged her on.

I smirk, thumbs moving before I can second-guess myself.

ME:

I'm on the swing shift this week, so you won't see me at work anyway. But I'm free on Friday.

The message sends with a soft *whoosh*, and I keep my eyes fixed on the screen, imagining the exact moment she reads it. The way her face will light up. The nervous little smile she won't be able to hide. Hell, maybe she's chewing that lip again, right now, wondering what the hell to say back.

The thought makes me grin, but it's cut short when the radio chirps, sharp and insistent, snagging my attention and dragging me back to reality.

"All units, be advised—Priority One. Possible home invasion in progress at an apartment complex, 2400 block of North Stone Avenue."

The words snap me out of my thoughts instantly. My phone slips from my hand and lands on the passenger seat as I grab the radio.

"2-L-17, copy. I'm a half mile out. Responding Code 3."

I slam the handset back into its cradle, and my body moves on instinct—lights, siren, gearshift. The red and blue lightbar ignites the wet street, throwing warped reflections across windshields and puddles as the siren's wail tears into the night. I drop the cruiser into gear and floor it, engine growling as I push through traffic.

"This is 2-L-17. I'm on scene," I announce into the radio, voice clipped, steady, betraying none of the adrenaline already humming in my veins. "Standing by for backup. Beginning perimeter check."

I cut the siren but leave the light bar going—red and blue

pulses throb across the lot, washing the rain-slick pavement in color, bouncing off windshields, ricocheting off the tired stucco walls. Stone Ridge Heights towers above me. Six stories of weathered beige, paint bleached and streaked from too many summers, and chipped black trim curling like old bark. Rust chews through the fire escapes bolted to the face of the building, and water trails in thin lines down the metal, dripping onto the cracked sidewalk below. Under the pulsing light, the rust looks like dried blood running in rivulets down the walls.

The handset clicks back into its cradle as I shoulder the door open. My boots splash into shallow puddles, water spraying against my pant legs, the sharp tang of wet asphalt mixing with the heavy scent of motor oil hanging in the air. The mist hasn't lifted, clinging to everything, making sounds carry strangely and muffled.

Instinct takes over. My hand brushes the Glock at my hip, the weight familiar, grounding. But I don't draw yet. Instead, I unclip my flashlight and flick it on. The beam cuts through the mist in a narrow cone as I sweep the lot, forcing myself to take in every detail, one at a time.

A TV flickers through a half-drawn curtain on the second floor, the screen strobing blue and white. Somewhere below, muffled chatter leaks from a first-floor unit—casual, almost bored voices, like nothing's wrong. I'm rather surprised no one has peeked out their windows to see what's going on. People are inherently nosey. But then my light catches something that makes my jaw tighten: an open window on the fourth floor.

Purple curtains billow against the damp air, flapping faintly in the breeze. I shift my eyes, noting the fire escape ladder has been pulled down. Someone has recently gone up or down it.

I key the mic on my vest. "Dispatch, confirm—any additional calls from this location?"

Static hums back for a moment too long, making my pulse

quicken, before the line crackles to life, a woman's voice cutting through the quiet.

"Affirmative. Another call came shortly after the first."

My grip tightens around the flashlight. "What was reported?"

"Caller said they heard screams and what sounded like a struggle coming from an adjacent unit."

A cold knot twists in my gut. "Did we get a unit number?"

"Apartment 4018," Dispatch confirms.

I tilt my head back, beam aimed higher. The window gapes black now, swallowing the light whole.

I press the mic again, voice low and firm. "Copy. How far out is my backup?"

The reply is immediate.

"2-L-21 is two minutes out. Sit tight."

I exhale through my nose, jaw tight. Two minutes. Two long minutes. I force myself to keep moving, sweeping the light across stairwells, darkened corners, the narrow gaps between parked cars. Every shadow feels heavier than it should, stretched long by the pulsing red and blue, twitching at the edges of my vision like they're waiting to move.

Then, faint at first, I hear them—sirens. Cutting through the wet night, building fast. Relief and urgency spike in equal measure.

Headlights swing into the lot, tires hissing on wet pavement. Another cruiser rolls in hard, light bar already strobing. The beams of red and blue double mine, throwing the whole building into a violent wash of color.

The car brakes to a stop just a few feet from where I stand, and the driver's door pops open. Kline climbs out, jaw set as his eyes land on mine.

"Fill me in," he says, voice low.

I tilt my chin towards the fourth floor and holster my flashlight. "Possible home invasion. A second call came in, with a neighbor reporting screams and a struggle coming from Unit

4018. Noted an open window, and the fire escape ladder is down."

Kline grunts, nodding in understanding, and falls in step beside me. We both draw our weapons from our holsters and cut across the lot towards the back entrance, dimly lit by a dying lightbulb. With my free hand, I grip the handle and yank. The steel door ricochets off the wall with a metallic bang that echoes up the stairwell.

The door slams shut behind us as we breach the entrance.

Inside, it's colder. The smell of damp concrete and mildew clings thickly. The overhead lights flicker and hum as we stand at the base of the stairwell. Guns raised, we start the climb. Each step echoes off the walls, boots clanging against the metal treads, the sound multiplied and carried upward like it doesn't want us sneaking in quietly.

By the time we hit the fourth floor, my pulse is hammering steadily in my ears. The hallway stretches long and narrow, lined with faded green doors. The air is heavier up here, damp, sour, and pressing down on us, stenched with marijuana, mildew, and stale cigarettes.

I signal Kline with two fingers, sending him down one side of the corridor to cover while I move toward 4018. The door frame is scarred, paint peeling off in ragged curls, and the brass numbers dulled to a greenish brown.

I press myself to the wall beside the door, straining to hear anything.

Nothing. No voices. No footsteps. Just silence, thick and waiting.

Kline leans close, his whisper barely audible. "You hear that?"

I shake my head, keeping my voice low. "Too quiet."

I thumb the mic on my vest, speaking softly but firmly.

"Dispatch, 2-L-17 and 2-L-21 are at the apartment. Attempting contact."

"Copy, 2-L-17," Dispatch replies, voice steady over the static. "Proceed with caution. Additional units en route."

I swallow the dryness in my throat and glance at Kline. We nod once, then I raise a fist and knock hard—three deliberate raps that vibrate through the door frame.

"Police!" My voice booms down the hallway, sharp, commanding. "If anyone's inside, make yourself known!"

The silence that follows is deafening.

Then, a soft creak to my left. An apartment door cracks open, a sliver of light spilling out. A woman's face peeks through, her eyes wide.

"Ma'am, I need you to go back inside," I tell her, firm but not unkind.

"I was the one who called," she whispers.

"Once we know the scene is cleared, an officer will get your statement. Please go back inside."

She hesitates, then nods, retreating quickly. The door shuts with a muted click, leaving us in silence again.

Every nerve in my body thrums like live wires. I shift my stance, gun low but steady as I turn my attention back to apartment 4018, readying to breach. My eyes meet Kline's, and I give him a nod. Together, we move.

I draw back and kick hard. The frame splinters as the deadbolt rips free, the chain lock snapping loose and scattering gold-painted links across the tile. The door slams back against the wall with a violent crack.

Two things hit me first as we breach the entryway.

The sharp, metallic stench of blood.

And a cell phone lying face up on the floor, its screen spiderwebbed.

CRIME
OFFICER
STOP

SIXTEEN
EMILIO

BLOOD SPLATTERS across the cream-colored walls, a grotesque pattern painted in wide arcs that glisten under the thin light bleeding in from the kitchen to my right and the pale flicker of the television in the living room. The air is heavy with the sharp, metallic stench of it—so thick I can taste iron in the back of my throat.

At the center of the living room, a body lies crumpled in a pool of crimson. The blood has seeped into the wood grain, spreading outward in dark rivulets that reach for the furniture like grasping fingers.

I force my voice steady as I key my mic, though my pulse hammers in my ears.

"Dispatch, this is 2-L-17. We've got blood and a body. No signs of movement inside. Beginning room-by-room clearance."

"Copy that, 2-L-17," Dispatch answers, her voice sharp, urgency bleeding through the static.

My gut twists, but training keeps me moving. Every detail registers. Every sound, or lack of it. The creak of the floor under our boots is the only thing breaking the silence.

We clear the kitchen first. It's empty, nothing but dirty

dishes stacked haphazardly in the sink and an overflowing trash can—normal things in an abnormal scene.

"Hallway," I whisper, jerking my chin toward the shadowed stretch ahead.

Kline nods, his shoulder brushing mine briefly before we fan out.

The hallway yawns long and narrow, dim as a tunnel. A closet door hangs wide open, stuffed with a fake Christmas tree shoved into its box and a couple of cheap jackets dangling on wire hangers.

Two other doors wait at the far end of the hall. One is sealed shut. The other is slightly ajar, slivers of red and blue light filtering through from my unit's strobes outside.

My mouth goes dry. I nod for Kline to take the one on the right while I advance toward the open door.

Blood streaks around the knob, and my pulse climbs higher.

I raise my gun, draw a steady breath, and nudge the door open with my boot.

"Clear," Kline calls from the other room as I cross the bedroom, towards the partially open closet. Keeping my gun trained, I shove the closet door open the rest of the way in one quick motion.

A hiss erupts from the shadows, sharp and furious, as a calico cat launches itself forward. My heart jerks into my throat.

"Shit!" I bark, stumbling back a half step as the cat bolts past me, claws skittering across the floor before it disappears under the bed.

"Perez!" Kline yells, bursting into the room.

I suck in a breath, steadying. "I'm good, Kline. Just a damn cat. We're all clear."

But my eyes are already dragging toward the window.

The purple curtains we'd seen from outside flutter faintly in the night breeze. Blood smears stain the white sill. Whoever was here, whoever murdered the occupant of this apartment, was no longer here.

I holster my weapon and press the mic again. "Dispatch, scene is clear. We'll need CSU. Notify a supervisor and a detective."

"Copy 2-L-17," Dispatch replies.

Kline and I step back toward the living room. The body waits, the pool of blood expanding slowly across the floorboards. My hands move on autopilot, tugging a pair of nylon gloves from my pocket and snapping them on.

I crouch low, the smell of copper sharper this close, and brush sticky blonde hair away from the victim's face. Her features are pale, blood streaking down across skin that's far too young to be this lifeless. The pale blue tank top she wears is shredded, dozens of ragged punctures punched through the fabric, each one evidence of sharp force trauma. Too many to count at a glance. Rage simmers low in my chest.

Then recognition hits me like a bullet. I had only met her once, but I don't forget a face easily.

I stagger to my feet, ripping the gloves off, my throat dry and tight. "No." The word escapes me in a rasp, then again, harder. "Oh no."

Kline frowns, crouching to see for himself. "What is it?"

My fists clench so tight the gloves squeak in my grip. I wanted nothing more than to storm out of here, to release this anger out on something, to go to Raelynn because—god—she needs to know, but I can't. I can't leave until a detective takes over, and then there's the damn paperwork.

I force the words out between clenched teeth, jerking my chin toward the body. "Take a look for yourself."

Kline leans closer, squinting in the dim light. After a beat, he exhales heavily and slowly, rising back to his full height. His face says it before his words do.

"It's Khloe," he confirms.

The sound of her name rattles inside my skull, louder than

the hum of the strobes outside. I want to drive my fist straight through the blood-painted wall. Instead, I stand frozen, rage and heartbreak burning in equal measure.

What the fuck was I going to tell Raelynn? How the fuck was I going to tell her?

I grit my teeth hard enough that my jaw aches. "CSU and the detective need to hurry their asses up."

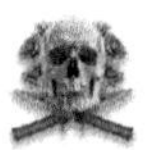

Several minutes later, the stairwell swells with bodies—CSU techs hauling cases that clatter against the steps, the medical examiner lugging his kit behind them, and extra uniforms squeezing into the narrow hall until the air feels stifling. And then comes Detective Martin.

Martin (or Fucktard, as I call him) strolls in like he owns the place. No urgency. No respect. Just that smug, lazy stride that makes my teeth grind. Meyer and I clash more often than not, but I'd take her clipped orders and sharp tongue over Martin's empty swagger any day. At least she gives a damn.

When he finally steps inside the apartment, it isn't reverence for the dead I see in his face—it's the self-importance of a man who thinks the world can wait on him.

I brief him on what we found, and he immediately dumps scene security back on me, because it is at this time that the damn neighbors decide they want to be nosy. Figures.

Doors creak open, whispers crawl up the hallway like a tide of insects. Because sure, the sight of half the damn department—cops, crime scene techs, a detective, and the ME—all cramming into a stairwell since the elevator's busted… yeah, that draws attention. But a girl screaming for her life? A cop pounding on her door before kicking it off the hinges? That didn't stir them from their holes. If they'd been nosy when it mattered, maybe Khloe would still be alive. I doubt it. But it's a lie I wish I could believe.

The murmurs grind on me, each one scratching against already raw nerves. People piss me off on a good day, and tonight isn't one of those. Kline must see the tension in my jaw, the stiffness in my shoulders, because he quietly takes over perimeter control, shoving rubberneckers back inside with the authority I'm about to lose.

It should buy me a moment, but it doesn't. Because just as I think I've got myself under control again, the ME crouches, seals Khloe into the black bag, and drags the zipper closed. The sound cuts through me like a blade—sharp, final, and it tears through me worse than the sight of her body on the floor. They cart her off as evidence instead of a girl whose laugh I can still hear in my head, still see teasing Raelynn just a few nights ago.

The rage comes back hot, bubbling over until I'm ready to walk out.

Fuck the paperwork. Fuck talking to the only witness we have. Fuck waiting for Detective Fucktard to permit me to leave.

Because Raelynn doesn't know.

She's home right now, blissfully unaware. She doesn't know that one of her best friends is headed for a slab in the morgue. And the thought of her finding out from the evening news—or from anyone but me—burns acid in my throat.

She deserves better than that. She deserves to hear it from me.

To my surprise, Martin waves me, Kline, and the extra uniforms off not long after Khloe is carted away. The neighbors finally retreat behind their doors, the hallway falling back into uneasy silence. CSU is still combing through every inch of the place, logging, photographing, and bagging what's left of the night. There's nothing more I can do here but write the report.

And I can't stay another second.

By the time I shove the building's door open, rain is coming down again, cold and relentless. It soaks through my uniform as I cross the lot, plastering fabric to my skin. I don't even care. My boots splash through puddles, and I climb into my cruiser, shutting the door on the storm. I flick off the light bar, jam the key into the ignition, and peel out of the lot, desperate to put distance between me and that apartment.

Hours blur together. It's past midnight by the time I finish the supplemental report, nearly one when I finally sign out at the station. My nerves buzz like static under my skin as I cross the empty lot to my truck. The rain has slowed to a mist, clinging cold against my face, but it does nothing to quiet the storm in my head.

I climb into the cab, twist the key. The engine rumbles awake, the radio sputtering to life with a burst of static. I snap it off immediately, leaving only the steady thrum of the motor and my pulse in my ears before throwing my truck into drive and pulling out of the lot.

The drive to Raelynn's apartment should take fifteen minutes. I shave it down to almost ten, speeding through the slick streets like distance alone is the enemy.

I wish I were pulling up under different circumstances. I wish I could be here to keep my word from Friday night and finally give us both what we wanted. Instead, I'm here to shatter her world. To deliver another loss she doesn't deserve.

By the time I roll into the lot, my chest feels tight enough to split. I kill the engine, step out into the damp air. Each step toward her door drags, heavier than the last. The closer I get, the harder my chest tightens—because I know what waits on the other side isn't relief, or comfort. It's heartbreak. And I'm the one about to hand it to her.

Finally, I'm there. Standing in front of her door, staring at the wood grain like it might swallow me whole. My hand hovers, useless for a beat as I pull in a deep breath, forcing my pulse to steady as I raise my fist.

And then I knock.

SEVENTEEN
RAELYNN

THE MICROWAVE HUMS LOW, its steady drone the only sound in the apartment. I lean against the counter, arms folded, eyes locked on the red digits ticking down. 0:39… 0:38… 0:37. The smell of buttered popcorn fills the kitchen, thick and salty, a small comfort in the silence. At my feet, Max waits like he always does, tail sweeping against the tile in slow, steady arcs, his gaze locked on me with patient hunger. He knows what's coming.

I should be asleep. God knows I need it with my alarm set before six. But sleep never comes easily anymore. My insomnia's a cruel bastard, showing up only when I'm bone-tired before kicking my brain into overdrive the second my head hits the pillow. So here I am—midnight creeping past—feeding the silence with junk food and reruns of *The Rookie*.

The timer hits zero and the microwave beeps. I pop the door open, and hot steam rolls out, curling around my face. I give the bag a few shakes to coat the kernels, before tearing it open. Max's restraint lasts exactly two seconds. He lifts a paw and taps my leg, his eyes wide and pleading as drool dribbles from the sides of his chops.

"Yeah, yeah, I see you," I murmur, laughing under my

breath. I reach into the bag, grab a single kernel. He leaps up, his nails tapping against the floor in dance. Drool flicks everywhere as he tap dances across the kitchen floor.

"Sit," I order, holding the piece above his head. He obeys, dropping his haunches to the floor so fast his tail smacks against the cabinet. "Good boy," I say, tossing the piece into his mouth. He chomps down with a happy snap, tail hammering the floor like he hasn't eaten in days. After a few seconds, he's back to pawing my leg, begging for more.

"Greedy boy," I tease, shaking my head as I yank a bowl from the cupboard and dump the rest of the bag into it. He follows me out of the kitchen, his nails clicking against the floor with each step, sticking close like my shadow.

Bowl in hand, I sink into the couch cushions, grab the remote, hit play, and toss it back onto the table. The TV flickers to life, blue light washes over the room as voices fill the quiet space. I let out a slow breath and pull the butterfly couch throw over my legs. Settled, I take a handful of popcorn and shovel it into my mouth. I'm mid-chew when Max freezes.

His ears perk, head snapping toward the door. His body stiffens, hackles rising along his spine. The sudden change yanks me upright.

"Max?" I whisper, but he doesn't look at me. His attention is fixed on the door, a low growl building deep in his chest.

Knock knock.

The sound echoes through the apartment, sharp and out of place at this hour. My body locks as Max's growl explodes into a series of harsh barks, loud and frantic. The door rattles under the force of the next knock—louder, heavier, more insistent. Each echo cracks like gunfire in the silence. My heart slams against my ribs. Every instinct tells me not to move, to stay still and let whoever it is give up and go away.

But Max won't stop barking. He charges toward the door, claws scraping the floor as he throws his weight against it.

"Max, hush!" I hiss, pausing the television.

I set the bowl down on the coffee table and toss the blanket off me before getting up. I step around the coffee table and over to the door and grab his collar to pull him back. He resists, barking again, his muscles vibrating with tension. I tug hard, pulling him back just enough that his front paws lift off the floor.

"Get back," I command, voice shaking more than I want it to.

He growls again and ignores my command, instead staying close, pacing at my leg as I edge closer to the door. The knocking stops. Silence stretches thin between each breath. My hand trembles as I reach for the lock, heart hammering so loud it fills my ears. I lean forward, rising on my toes to look through the peephole.

Emilio.

Relief hits first—then confusion. My breath rushes out in a shaky whoosh I didn't realize I'd been holding. Max is still huffing beside me, tail thumping in short, uncertain bursts, the fur between his shoulders bristled.

"It's okay," I tell him, palm on his head, thumb rubbing the soft spot behind his ear that always settles him. "It's just Emilio."

I slide the deadbolt back; the metal click feels too loud in the small entryway. My fingers don't want to work right. I turn the knob and pull.

"Emilio? What are you doing here?" My voice comes out softer than I expect, almost a whisper.

His eyes meet mine—and my lungs seize. Pain is carved deep into his face, raw and unguarded, the kind of expression no one wears when they bring good news.

"Can I come in?" His voice is quiet, almost fragile. His hands are buried in the pockets of his jeans, like he's bracing himself.

My pulse stutters. I step aside. He moves past me, closes the door softly with his palm, and stands there a beat, like he needs to make sure it's shut between us and the outside before he can speak.

"What's going on?" My voice barely makes it out.

He doesn't answer right away. His silence gnaws at me, every second stretching taut. "You're scaring me, Emilio. Just tell me—what's going on?"

"There's no easy way to say this," he begins, voice steady but weighted, each word deliberate. "But I wanted you to hear it from me. Not from the news. Not from anyone else."

He gestures toward the couch like he wants me to sit. I don't. I can't. I shake my head, and he exhales, stepping closer, his golden eyes darkened by whatever is weighing him down.

"I was called to a Priority One tonight. Possible home invasion at Stone Ridge Heights."

My stomach drops, and my pulse pounds so hard I can feel it in my ears.

"Another call came in after," he continues, eyes never leaving mine. "A neighbor reported screams and sounds of a struggle coming from Apartment 4018."

My breath catches, a sound tearing loose from my throat. I don't need him to say it. I know. My whole body knows.

Khloe.

"Oh god—no." The words splinter, broken and raw. My face is hot all at once and then cold, and the tears are there before I can blink them back.

"I'm sorry, Raelynn." His words crack at the edges.

"No, no, no—she's not—" My voice shreds apart before the word can finish.

"She was gone before we got inside." His tone is a soft finality.

The scream rips out of me before I can stop it—sharp, guttural, ripped from someplace deep. My knees give out. The world tilts violently, but Emilio catches me before I hit the ground, strong arms locking around me. I collapse into him, sobs tearing out so violently it feels like I might split apart. He lowers us to the floor, one hand cradling the back of my head, the other banding tight around my shoulders. I tuck in against him and shake until I can't feel where my body ends and the air begins.

"Rae? Rae, what's—" Tessa's voice cuts in, high and panicked, feet thudding down the hall. She rounds the corner, her eyes wide with panic.

She freezes when she sees me crumpled in Emilio's lap, my face buried in his chest, my body shaking so hard I can barely draw air.

"Khloe," I choke. Saying her name out loud feels like glass in my throat. "She's gone."

Tessa pales, her face draining of color. "What do you mean gone?"

Emilio's voice is steady but grim when he answers for me.

"She was murdered."

The words slice through me like a blade, sharp and merciless. Hearing them out loud makes it real in a way I wasn't ready for. My body convulses with another sob, my throat raw from screaming. I bury my face deeper against Emilio's chest, clinging to him like he's the only thing keeping me from shattering completely.

His shirt smells like rain, and faint traces of his woodsy cologne—comfort in the middle of devastation.

Tessa staggers back, one hand pressed to her mouth like she can shove the truth down her throat and keep it there. "No," she whispers, voice breaking. "Not Khloe. She—she can't be."

Her knees buckle. Emilio reaches out without letting go of me and steadies her by the elbow. "Sit," he says, gentle but leaving no room for argument. She drops to her knees on the other side of me, leaning into both Emilio and I as she sobs.

I can't breathe. It feels like cinder blocks have been set on my ribs. I drag in a breath, and it stutters and snags. Images of Khloe slam through my mind—her laugh bouncing off our apartment walls, the mischievous smirk she always wore, her incessant teasing, the midnight calls and texts she would have with us when we needed someone to talk to, the way her presence filled every space. They flicker too fast and then stop altogether, like someone yanked a plug.

Everything I loved about her is now…

Gone.

ME SCENE
CRIME S
OFFICER
STOP
CAU
STOP

EIGHTEEN
EMILIO

I HOLD Raelynn in my arms for what feels like hours, rocking her gently. Every sob rakes through her and hits me like a body shot. I've given death notices more times than I care to count—knocked on doors in the dead of night, watched faces crumble, families fracture, listened to them deny what I was telling them, refusing to accept that their loved one is gone. Those nights leave fingerprints on you. But none of them has ever come close to tonight. Delivering this to Raelynn felt like I ripped my chest open with my bare hands, tore my heart out, and stomped on it.

She's endured more than anyone should have to. Losing her mother, her father, and now Khloe… it's too much for one person. I know what it's like to lose pieces of yourself. I've buried people, carried caskets. I've dealt with my fair share of grief but not like this. Not this deep.

This is the kind of loss that carves straight to bone, and leaves scars that never stop bleeding.

Max doesn't leave her side—not once. He's a steady presence through it all, pressed against Raelynn like he knows she's breaking and can't stand to let her do it alone. His head rests on her lap, eyes lifted toward her face, quiet and patient.

Every few seconds, his tail moves—a slow sweep against the floor, the only sound in the heavy stillness. When her sobs start to quiet, when the shudders in her chest finally begin to ease, it's his warmth that grounds her. She knots one shaking hand in my shirt and the other disappears into his fur like she's afraid that if she lets go of either of us, she'll disappear with everything else the world's taken from her.

At some point, Tessa pulls herself up from the floor. Her face is pale, streaked with tears that haven't stopped since I told them. She doesn't speak—just slips quietly down the hall, her footsteps dragging, the door to her room clicking shut behind her. The silence that follows feels heavier. Like the apartment itself is holding its breath.

Still cradling Raelynn, I brush her hair back from her face with one hand, my thumb tracing the wet trails down her cheek. Her lashes stick together, clumped with tears. She's beautiful, even like this—especially like this. Vulnerable in a way that makes my chest ache. I lean down and press a soft kiss to her forehead, lingering there for a moment.

"Come on," I murmur, more to myself than to her. My voice barely works.

I shift under her, and she moves with me automatically, still hanging on. I stand, gathering her up as if she weighs nothing. She tucks herself against me, feet dangling, arms tight around my neck. Her hand knots in the collar of my shirt, refusing to let go. Max follows, his nails clicking softly against the floor as we move down the hall, never straying more than a few inches from her side.

Her room is dark except for the soft glow spilling from the hallway. Shadows stretch across the walls. Max jumps onto the bed as soon as I open the door. He circles once before curling up at the foot, his eyes locked on her, unblinking and protective. The soft thump of his tail against the sheets is the only sound that dares to exist.

I pull the comforter back and lower Raelynn gently onto

the mattress. She looks so small like this—fragile in a way I've never seen her. The fire that usually burns in her eyes is gone, replaced by something hollow and raw. Her skin is pale, streaked with tear tracks that glisten under the dim light.

Her hand slips from my shirt, the last bit of strength fading from her fingers as she whispers, barely audible, "Don't go."

Those two words nearly undo me. I sink down beside her, one knee on the edge of the bed. My hand finds her arm, thumb tracing slow, steady circles over her skin. "I wasn't planning on it, baby," I whisper. The word slips out before I can stop it, soft and natural. She doesn't flinch at it. Her eyes flutter, half lidded and tired.

I kick off my shoes and slide onto the bed beside her. The second I do, she finds me again, curling into my chest, her face buried against me like she's searching for something that feels safe. I pull the comforter over us both, wrapping my arms around her, and hold her as tight as I can without crushing her. She's trembling again—not from sobbing this time, but from exhaustion. Her hand rests over my heart, her fingers still tangled in the fabric of my shirt. Her breathing comes unevenly, broken by quiet hiccups that taper off one by one. I rest my chin on the crown of her head.

I can feel the rise and fall of her chest begin to steady, each breath syncing with mine. My own pulse slows to match hers, the adrenaline giving way to something quieter, heavier. I smooth a hand down her back, tracing the curve of her spine in slow, mindless passes. The warmth of her skin seeps into my palm. The weight of her against me feels like both a promise and a burden—one I'd carry without question. Every few minutes, she exhales a shaky breath, and I murmur something low and quiet—nonsense words meant to keep her anchored.

I tighten my arms around her, pulling her closer until I can feel every shallow breath. "You're safe," I murmur into her hair. "I've got you."

Her only response is a small sound, somewhere between a sigh and a sob. Max shifts at the foot of the bed, his head lifting for a moment before he settles again, as if he knows she's finally still.

Her breathing slows, and I feel her body start to relax against mine, exhaustion dragging her under. I stay awake, listening to the tiny sounds that fill the room—the hum of the air vent, the faint rustle of the sheets each time she moves, the steady rhythm of her heart under my hand.

If I could take this from her, I would. Every ounce of pain, every scar life has carved into her, I'd bear it myself without hesitation. I'd guard her from the world and everything waiting outside that door. Take every nightmare, every ugly memory, every flash of pain, and lock it away where it can never touch her again. Loss keeps finding her, clawing away at what's left. And I can't stop thinking how unfair it is—how wrong it feels to watch someone like her, stubborn and bright and braver than she knows, be broken again and again.

But in this moment, I'll give her everything I can—my warmth, my strength, whatever pieces of myself she needs to stay afloat because the world has taken too much from her already.

And I'll be *damned* if I let it take anything more.

NINETEEN
RAELYNN

THE SHRILL BLARE of my phone alarm drags me out of sleep in a panic. My body jolts upright, lungs clamped tight, heart jackhammering against my ribs as if it's trying to escape. I fumble blindly across the nightstand, knocking into a water glass I forgot existed, and the edge of a book, before my hand finally smacks down on the glowing screen. The sound dies, leaving the room in a heavy, aching silence broken only by my ragged breaths.

For a moment, I just sit there, blinking into the washed-out gray of early morning pressing through the blinds. Thin streaks of light cut across the room, painting everything in pale, cold stripes. My brain claws for purchase, scrabbling to stitch together where I am, why I feel so wrong, so hollow. Max is curled against me, his solid weight stretched across my thigh, his body warm, breaths slow and steady. My hand finds his fur, fingers sinking into the softness automatically, clinging to the anchor of him.

Last night comes back in fragments. I remember making popcorn. The opening credits of *The Rookie* flickering across the TV. Max's sudden barking at the sharp knock at the door —loud, frantic, insistent. And then—

It hits me.

Like a freight train at full speed, slamming into me with the force to shatter bone.

Khloe.

Her name detonates inside me, ripping me apart from the inside out. The air leaves my lungs in a broken rush, a sound tearing loose from my chest that doesn't even feel human. Emilio's voice echoes in my head, replaying itself mercilessly: low, heavy, cracked around the edges. His words last night weren't just words—they were claws. The memory of my scream, of collapsing into him, of his arms locking around me because the floor couldn't hold me—it all crashes back in suffocating waves.

A sob bursts out of me, raw and jagged. My hands fly to my face, and hot tears spill fast and relentless through the cracks of my fingers. My body shakes so violently that it feels like I might splinter apart.

"Emilio?" The name slips out, splintered and desperate, almost a plea. My voice is hoarse, shredded by grief. Panic lances through me when the silence answers back. Louder this time, my chest heaving, I cry out again. "Emilio!"

Max whines, lifting his head, nudging insistently at my side, sensing the panic ripping me apart. His warm body leans harder into mine, a steady weight trying to tether me, but the storm raging inside me is too wild that I barely notice my bedroom door flying open, the knob cracking hard against the wall when it makes contact.

"Rae?" His voice cuts sharply through the air—urgent, frantic, but laced with softness when his eyes land on me. Emilio is there in an instant, filling the doorway, then crossing the room in three long strides. His presence changes the air itself. Those golden brown eyes lock on me—shaking, broken, clinging to scraps—and soften with something so achingly tender it nearly undoes me.

The mattress dips under his weight as he sits beside me.

His arms wrap around me before I even realize my body has moved toward him. I collapse into his chest, burying my face in the solid heat of him, my fists twisting in the collar of his shirt like it's the only thing keeping me from drowning.

"I thought you left," I choke out, the words muffled against his shoulder, my entire frame trembling like a leaf trapped in a storm.

"Baby." The word falls from him like a vow, his lips brushing the crown of my head. His voice is steady, warm, the kind of surety I don't have in me. "I told you I wasn't going anywhere. I just went to make you coffee and breakfast." His arms tighten, pulling me closer, as if he could shield me from the world outside these walls. His heat seeps into me, a lifeline in the cold wreckage of grief.

The sobs still come, but they soften, losing their jagged edge. It's like he's siphoning the worst of them from me just by holding me. My lashes lift, blurred with tears, and I catch his face close to mine—jaw flexing, expression carved with guilt and tenderness all at once.

"Baby?" I whisper the word trembling on my tongue, like I'm testing it, unsure if it's real.

His jaw flexes, guilt flickering across his face. "Sorry—it just slipped. I won't—"

"Don't be sorry." I shake my head quickly, swallowing hard, fighting through the thickness in my throat. "I… I like it."

Something flickers in his eyes then, like a storm cloud breaking just enough to let sunlight pierce through. He cups my face in his calloused hands, his palms warm, his thumbs brushing away the hot tracks of tears on my cheeks. The smallest chuckle escapes him, rough but real, and it tugs one out of me too, weak and tinged with sorrow, but there all the same.

"Does that make us official then?" he teases gently, trying to lighten the ache hanging between us.

My chest aches, my grief still raw and jagged, but the thought of him wanting me—claiming me—plants something small and steady in the wreckage. "Yes," I whisper, the word trembling but certain.

His mouth finds mine, and the kiss is desperate, clinging, soaked in salt from my tears. His warmth presses into me like he's stitching me together with every movement. For a moment, there is no storm, no death, no weight of the world. There's only him, and me, and the fragile spark of light between us.

When we break apart, his forehead rests against mine, his breath warm against my lips. "I'm going to finish making your breakfast, okay?" he whispers, easing me gently back against the pillows.

I nod, words lodged in my throat. My chest still feels like it's caving in, but at least now, there's his warmth in the cracks.

When he leaves the room, the scent of bacon and coffee drifts in from the kitchen. It's so ordinary, so achingly normal, it almost feels cruel. I force myself to reach for my phone, notifications crowding the screen—Discord, Instagram, Facebook—all buzzing with noise I can't face. I swipe them away until only one thing matters: Sergeant Rodriguez's number.

It only rings twice. "Rodriguez here."

"Hi, ma'am, it's um Rae—Raelynn Carson." My voice trembles, but I force it steady. "I just… I'm calling to let you know I can't make it in today."

There's a pause, then her tone softens, all business stripped away. "I figured as much. Officer Perez called me earlier and explained. I'm very sorry for your loss, Miss Carson. Take all the time you need."

Of course he called to let her know. She was his boss after all. I'm just grateful he saved me from having to explain my situation because I wasn't sure how I was going to accomplish that.

"Thank you, ma'am."

I hang up and set the phone aside, dragging myself from the bed. Max hops down with me, sticking to my heels. At the end of the hall, the kitchen glows with soft yellow light, Emilio's silhouette moving over the stove as bacon hisses in the pan. The smell of coffee curls through the air, almost mocking in its comfort.

I turn away, my feet carrying me to the opposite end of the hall. I lift my hand, knuckles brushing against Tessa's door in a soft knock.

"Come in." Her voice is quiet, weak.

I crack the door open, peeking in. She's curled on her side, cocooned in her comforter, her phone tossed carelessly beside her. Her eyes are swollen, rimmed red, the kind that tell me she didn't sleep at all.

"I texted Marlena," she whispers hoarsely. "Told her to come over. I couldn't… I didn't want to say it over the phone."

"Good." My voice softens as I step inside. "She needs to know, too."

Tessa pushes herself up slowly, hair tangled around her face. Tears brim again, spilling over as she chokes on the words. "It doesn't feel real. I—I texted her, like I always do, and then I remembered—" Her voice cracks, shattering, and her hands press hard against her face.

I climb onto the bed beside her, wrapping her into me before she can collapse entirely. "I know," I whisper, my own voice splintering. "I know."

The grief rips through us both, and we sob together. The sound is unholy, raw, filling the small room until it feels like it might burst apart. When her sobs taper to shudders, she pulls back, wiping her swollen face with trembling hands.

"Is Emilio still here?" she asks quietly.

I nod. "He's in the kitchen making us breakfast."

Her lips twitch into the faintest ghost of a smile. "That's… sweet of him."

"Yeah," I whisper, before sucking my bottom lip into my mouth, hesitation buzzing in my chest. "I know this isn't the best timing and all." I dig my teeth into my lip as she looks at me with confusion. She gives me a signal to continue, and I release a breath. "We, um… we made it official."

Her brows lift, and a smile stretches across her face, the grief in her eyes softening just a fraction. "Well, it's about damn time. Ever since Friday night, he's all you've been able to think about."

I manage a weak laugh, shaking my head. "That is *so* not true."

"Is too," she argues softly, a smirk ghosting across her lips. "Just… do me a favor. If you two decide to fuck, put a sock on the door or something so I know to drown you out. I'm too sad to be horny and get off to you two."

"Tessa!" I gasp, startled into laughter, even through tears.

"What?" she shrugs. "Sad fucking exists, Rae. It's right up there with hate fucking—it's distraction 101."

I press my hands to my face, still laughing weakly. "I know that," I say. "I just wasn't thinking about *that*."

She smirks faintly. "Well, now you are."

I roll my eyes, sliding off the bed with a soft shake of my head. "I'm gonna go check on breakfast. You coming?"

"I will in a little bit. Just save me a plate."

I nod and kiss the top of her head before sliding off the bed. "You got it."

"Thanks," she whispers, curling back under her comforter as I slip out.

After breakfast, Emilio and I end up tangled together on the couch, the apartment swallowed in an uneasy quiet. The TV hums in the background, some sitcom rerun flashing across the screen, its canned laughter and snappy dialogue bouncing uselessly around the room. Neither of us is watching. My head rests against his chest, the steady thud of his heartbeat syncing with the slow rhythm of his breathing. That sound—the rise and fall, steady and certain—is the only thing keeping me tethered. His arm is wrapped around me, heavy and warm, his thumb absentmindedly drawing slow lines along the skin of my arm. It's grounding, and I cling to it more than I want to admit.

The soft slap of Tessa's panda slippers drifts out of the hallway. She shuffles into the kitchen, her hair wild, and her eyes still heavy with sleep. She doesn't speak, just gives me a faint, worn smile before tugging open the microwave. She pops in the plate of bacon, eggs, and pancakes I left waiting for her, the light buzzing faintly as the food spins in slow circles. When it beeps, she pulls the plate out, grabs a fork from the dish rack, and pads back to her room without a word, shutting the door behind her, cutting us off again.

I don't know how much time passes before Emilio's voice cuts through the quiet. It's low, careful, almost hesitant.

"Tell me about Khloe," he says softly. "How did you two become friends?"

The name squeezes my chest. I shift against him, the words sticking before they can form. His thumb is still brushing over my arm, patient, waiting, and finally, I let out a breath.

"I met her not long after I moved in with Tessa's family," I say slowly, each word dragging. "I was still… figuring out how to breathe again, I guess. Everything in my life then was upside down, raw and jagged, and then there she was—loud, unfiltered, the kind of girl who refused to let anyone sit on the sidelines. She had been this burst of sunlight I didn't expect. She didn't treat me like I was broken or fragile; neither did Tessa. Those two made living possible again."

A tiny smile tugs at my lips before it falters. "From then

on, it was always the three of us: me, Tessa, and Khloe. We stuck together like glue. Middle school, high school, college—we went through everything together. First crushes, heartbreaks, skipping class, sneaking into movies. Khloe was there for all of it." My throat tightens, but I keep going, because stopping feels worse. "She wasn't just a friend. She was family in every sense but blood, like Tessa."

Emilio doesn't say anything right away, just lets the silence stretch. His chest rises beneath my cheek, steady, constant. Then he presses a kiss into my hair, murmuring, "I'm glad you had her."

The ache in my chest doubles. My eyes sting, and I press my face harder against him.

For a while, the silence stretches thin between Emilio and me, only broken by the flicker of the television fading into nothing. I feel like I'm sinking deeper into him, exhaustion winning its quiet battle. My eyes slip shut, my body lulled by his warmth, the soft drag of his thumb across my arm, the rhythm of his breathing beneath my cheek.

At some point, I must drift. The next thing I feel is Emilio shifting beneath me, slow and careful, as though he's trying not to wake me. His hands slide around my waist, gentle, coaxing me off his lap. My lashes flutter, a quiet panic sparking in my chest as my fingers curl into his shirt, holding tighter, like I can anchor him here if I just don't let go.

"I wish you didn't have to go," I murmur, my voice hoarse with sleep. My chest aches at the thought of him walking out the door, leaving me behind in this too-quiet apartment.

Maybe if I hold on tighter, he'll stay. There are plenty of cops to cover him, right?

"I know, baby." His voice is low, warm, his breath brushing against my ear as he leans down to kiss me. The kiss is soft, lingering, almost reverent, and it nearly undoes me all over again. "I'll come check on you tonight, okay?"

I force myself to let go, my lips tugging into a pout I can't stop. He rises, stretching just slightly, before making his way toward the door. He pauses to crouch down and scratch Max behind the ears. His tail thumps a steady beat against the floor, and his eyes close with contentment.

Emilio glances back at me before leaving. His expression shifts, tightening into that firm, protective look I've come to know too well—the one that says he's already running through a dozen worst-case scenarios in his head. "Anything happens, call me. Got it?"

I nod, my throat too tight to speak.

He watches me a moment longer, then the sternness in his face softens just enough. The corners of his lips twitch upward, and the words slip from him in a low rasp, deliberate, sure. "Good girl."

The phrase lands in me like a spark to dry tinder. My body reacts before my brain has the chance to catch up, a shiver rolling through me, heat flooding beneath my skin despite the grief that weighs on me like a second body. The words echo in my head, clinging, twisting, sending my thoughts down a path I shouldn't be wandering.

The door clicks shut behind him, leaving me alone with the apartment's stillness, staring at the empty space where he stood moments ago, my heart racing for reasons that have nothing to do with panic.

I press my palms to my face, dragging in a shaky breath. My thoughts circle back to Khloe, unbidden, sharp. The way she would have teased me right now, her grin wicked, her voice bright with laughter. Tessa was right earlier—Khloe always said grief made people do strange things, made them reach for the living in desperate ways. She would have laughed at the idea of "sad sex," and yet the thought doesn't feel as far-fetched as it should.

TWENTY
RAELYNN

ALL DAY, Marlena, Tessa, and I huddled on the living room floor, knees tucked beneath us in a tangled fortress of blankets, surrounded by mountains of crumpled tissues and mugs of tea, abandoned half-empty, their steam long since vanished into the heavy air. Grief weighed down the room like a storm cloud that refused to break. We cried until our eyes stung and swelled, until our throats turned raw and our ribs ached with every shaky inhale. And then, in fragile gasps between sobs, came laughter—jagged, unexpected, almost guilty. We stitched Khloe back together from scraps of memory: her snorting laugh that filled every space, the way she stole fries with shameless glee, the dramatic hand gestures she used when telling even the smallest story.

Each memory was a shard of glass—cutting deep, yet impossible to let go of.

By the time the sun bled itself into the horizon and shadows swallowed the house, grief had hollowed us out, leaving exhaustion in its wake. Marlena lingered after dinner, arms wrapped around me so tightly I felt rooted for the first time all day. But eventually, she slipped away into the night. Tessa and I couldn't stomach the thought of cooking; we ordered takeout that went lukewarm on the counter before we picked at it. Later, we curled up on the couch, Max sprawled heavy across our feet, his warm body a fragile anchor. We tried to lose ourselves in a movie, but halfway through, Tessa gave in to the need for solitude and shut herself in her room. That left Max and me, the flickering TV, and the silence pressing in around us.

It's close to one in the morning when a knock sounds at my door. Soft, but sharp enough to slice through the stillness and make my heart leap into my throat, despite knowing exactly who it is.

I open the door without hesitation. Emilio fills the frame, leaning against it like he's been there a while. His navy shirt clings to him, stretched over the hard lines of his chest and shoulders. His hair is damp, curling slightly at the ends. His eyes—those golden eyes—catch mine, sparking warmth I didn't know I was capable of feeling tonight.

"You came," I whisper, the words slipping out like a breath I didn't know I'd been holding.

"I told you I would," he says, his voice low and steady, carrying the weight of a promise.

Max barrels up to him before I can even move, his whole body wagging as he shoves his toy into Emilio's hand. Emilio laughs softly, kneeling to scratch behind his ears, stealing the toy with a mock tug before tossing it toward the couch. Max skitters after it, claws clicking against the floor.

Emilio steps inside and shuts the door behind him; the dam inside me breaks. I'm in his arms before I can think. My chest collides with his, my arms winding tight around his neck. His scent surrounds me—citrus, coffee, rainwater, and the warm bite of cedar—and I breathe it in like oxygen. His embrace is immediate, fierce yet careful, one hand sliding into my hair, the other anchoring me close as his chin dips against the crown of my head.

For the first time all day, the tension in my body eases. The grief doesn't vanish—it never could—but it softens, edged out by the heat of him pressed to me, by the steady rhythm of his heartbeat under my cheek.

"I missed you," I murmur against him.

"I missed you too," he breathes, his voice brushing hot against my ear, sending a shiver racing down my spine.

I tilt my head back, and his gaze hooks mine. There's still pain there, shadows clinging to him the same way they cling to me, but beneath the darkness burns something hotter—an intensity that mirrors the ache coiling low in my belly. His thumb strokes along my jaw, slow and reverent, as though I'm something fragile, something sacred, before his mouth finally finds mine.

The kiss begins soft, hesitant, careful—like he's offering me an escape. But I don't want one. I clutch his shirt tighter in my fists, dragging him closer, pressing harder, devouring him like I've been starving for this all along. His lips part, and the kiss deepens, heat surging between us with relentless force, quick and consuming until the air itself feels flammable.

When he pulls away, it's only to whisper against my lips, his breath rough and uneven, "Tell me to stop, and I will."

I shake my head, my voice shaky but resolute. "Don't stop."

His eyes darken, hunger eclipsing the sorrow. Then his mouth claims mine again, with raw, unrestrained need. His hands roam over me like he's memorizing every curve, sliding down my sides, over my waist, tugging at the hem of my sleep shirt until his fingers graze bare skin. The touch rips a shudder through me, every ounce of grief in me alchemizing into hunger.

In one fluid motion, he lifts me into his arms. My legs wrap around his waist instinctively, holding on as the world around us blurs—the hallway, the shadows, the grief dissolving into nothing but him. Each step he takes toward my bedroom rattles me, a slow burn unfurling low in my belly, until I feel like I might combust. His lips trail down my throat, sucking lightly, his teeth grazing the sensitive skin at the base of my neck before his tongue soothes the sting, leaving fire blazing along my pulse.

My back hits the doorframe, and I gasp, his hips grinding into mine. The hard length of him presses against my core through his jeans, the friction making me writhe, a needy moan spilling from my lips before I can stop it.

When he finally lowers me onto my bed, it isn't rushed. It's deliberate, careful, like he's giving me one last chance to change my mind. But I don't want distance—I want to drown in him. The mattress dips beneath us as he follows me down, his weight pinning me, his mouth devouring mine with frantic worship.

His hands roam everywhere—palms flattening against my ribs, fingertips skimming my waist, tugging my shirt inch by inch until I raise my arms, surrendering it to him. The fabric is gone in an instant, tossed somewhere unseen. Cool air ghosts over my bare skin, pebbling my nipples, but the heat in his gaze sets me ablaze. His eyes linger, reverent and hungry, as if he is searing every part of me into his memory.

"God, Rae…" His voice is rough, ragged, breaking under the weight of his desire. "You're so damn beautiful."

Heat blooms across my cheeks, but I don't shy away. I want him to see me. I want him to want me the way I ache for him. My hands fumble with his shirt, shoving it up until warm, solid muscle is bared to my touch, until the ink stretched across his chest is revealed—desert flowers winding around the hollowed skull of a bull.

"What does it mean?" I whisper, my fingers tracing the Roman numerals etched into the curve of the horn.

His gaze softens, shadows shifting into something more vulnerable. "November 20, 2010. The day my mother and I left my abusive father." His voice is low, steady, but the weight of it presses into me.

My throat tightens. “I’m sorry you had to go through that.”

He catches my hand, pressing his lips to each of my knuckles, slow and deliberate. “Don’t be. It made me who I am.” He releases my hand only to claim my mouth again, a kiss laced with both vulnerability and fire.

I taste it—his grief, his strength, his need—and my tongue pushes deeper, tangling with his as his hands continue to roam over my body. His hands move to my breasts, cupping and kneading them before toying with my nipples. I moan into his mouth and grind against his hard length protruding from his jeans. My hands go to his belt, fumbling with the buckle, desperate and clumsy to free his cock from its denim prison, but he catches my wrists, stilling me. He breaks the kiss, his golden eyes smoldering but tender as they lock onto mine.

“Patience, baby,” he whispers, letting go of my wrists.

A pout forms on my lips, but it dissolves when his mouth trails lower, down my throat, leaving marks—his marks—as he nips and sucks. He dips into the valley of my breasts, capturing one in his hand while his tongue circles my nipple then pulls it into the heat of his mouth. My back bows off the bed, a sharp cry spilling out as his teeth scrape lightly, teasing. His free hand glides lower—fingers ghosting down my stomach, brushing the waistband of my panties, then retreating, tormenting me with the promise of more.

“Emilio…” My voice cracks on his name, a plea and a prayer all at once. My hips buck against him, begging for friction.

He lifts his head, lips glistening, eyes dark and feral. “Tell me what you want, baby,” he rasps, his voice guttural and thick with need.

“I want you,” I whisper, trembling beneath him. “All of you.”

His fingers toy with the edge of my panties, brushing the

damp fabric but never dipping lower. My breath stutters, my body arching toward him, desperate.

"Please," I beg, raw and shameless.

His mouth curves into a smirk—wicked and tender at once—as he pins my wrists above my head with one hand, holding me down. This shift in him should terrify me, but instead it ignites me. His mouth trails lower, kissing, biting, worshipping, until he reaches the lace clinging to my hips. With his teeth, he tugs at the edge, his gaze flicking up to mine, daring me to look away. I don't. I can't.

I won't.

His free hand slides between my thighs, fingers pressing against the soaked fabric. I gasp, thrash, but he only presses firmer, rubbing slow circles that have my body trembling and spreading my legs wider without thought.

"Fuck, you're so wet for me," he growls against my hip, the words vibrating against my skin. "So ready."

When he finally hooks his fingers in the waistband and drags the panties down my legs, the cool air kisses the heat of my core. He doesn't wait. His mouth replaces his hand, tongue sliding through my folds, slow, deliberate, savoring me like he's starving and this is the first meal he's had in days. My cry shatters the silence as my body bows, my hands straining against his hold above my head.

"Emilio—" My voice splinters into a sob of pleasure as his tongue circles my clit, flicking, then sucking, the rhythm relentless until my thighs are quaking around his head.

He releases my wrists, and I claw into his hair, anchoring myself to him as he devours me. I can't help myself, I grind against his face, willing his tongue to go deeper.

"So needy," he groans against my pussy, the vibrations sending shivers down my spine.

I moan out a response, my hold in his hair tightening. He chuckles and flicks his gaze up to me as he slides a finger into my pussy, then two, curling them just right until I cry out. He pumps them in and out, steady at first, then faster, while his mouth latches back onto my clit. Heat coils fast in my belly, winding tighter with every thrust of his fingers, every suck of his mouth.

"Oh god—" I gasp, my thighs clenching tightly around his head. "Please, don't stop."

The pressure builds, higher and higher, until the world narrows to nothing but the feeling of his fingers and the heat of his mouth.

The pressure inside me builds fast, unbearable, like a storm swelling with no release—until it finally detonates. My orgasm rips through me, violent and all-consuming, wave after wave crashing over me until I'm screaming his name, my body splintering apart in his hands. Emilio doesn't stop. He keeps working me through it, his tongue and fingers merciless, wringing every last drop of pleasure from me until I collapse against the sheets, trembling, wrecked, breathless.

He doesn't give me time to recover. He climbs up my body, his lips glistening with the evidence of my release, his golden eyes blazing.

"You taste divine," he groans.

He presses his slick fingers to my lips, and my mouth parts without hesitation. My tongue curls around them, tasting myself on his skin. I suck them into my mouth, moaning around them as I clean him off, and the guttural sound that rips from his chest makes my pussy clench all over again.

His hips grind against my sensitive core, denim rough against my bare heat, and I whimper into his fingers. The sight of him—his broad chest heaving, his pupils blown wide, his fingers buried in my mouth—has me aching, throbbing, desperate for more. My hands fumble at his belt again, clumsy with need, and this time he doesn't stop me. His eyes stay locked on mine, molten and unblinking, as I free him from the confines of his jeans.

His cock springs free, hot and heavy in my hand. He's

massive, thick, the length of him daunting, pre-cum already glistening at the tip. My breath catches. I wrap my fingers around him, stroking once, twice, my thumb smearing the pre-cum along his velvety skin. His head tips back, a deep groan tearing from his throat, his hips bucking into my hand like he can't help himself.

He pulls his fingers free from my mouth, leaving a trail of saliva glistening down my chin, and grabs my thigh, hiking it high on his hip. With his other hand, he positions himself, dragging the swollen head of his cock along my slit. The friction makes me shiver, makes my breath stutter as he coats himself in my arousal, pausing just long enough to circle my clit until I'm whimpering beneath him, begging without words.

"Ready?" he asks, voice low and guttural, his restraint a thin thread I can see unraveling in his eyes.

I nod quickly, biting down on my bottom lip, nails digging into his shoulders. And then he pushes forward. Slowly. Deliberately. Stretching me open, inch by thick inch. The fullness steals my breath, the burn sharp, almost overwhelming, but it feels so fucking good—like he was made to fit inside me.

"Fuck, Rae…" His voice breaks, a growl torn from deep in his chest. His grip tightens on my thigh as he sinks deeper, bottoming out with a shudder. "You feel so fucking good."

My nails rake down his back, desperate. "Move," I whisper, then louder, pleading, "Please, Emilio. Move."

He pulls back slowly, dragging against every nerve ending before he slams back into me hard enough to rattle the bedframe. A strangled cry bursts from my throat. He sets a rhythm, each thrust harder, deeper, more brutal than the last, pounding into the spot inside me that makes my vision spark white.

Our mouths crash together again, messy and fevered, tongues tangling. His groans bleed into my moans, the sound of us filling the room, drowning everything else out—grief, silence, the world beyond these four walls.

He catches my hand mid-thrust, slamming it against the pillow above my head, his fingers entwining with mine as his pace grows rougher. His eyes blaze into mine, wild and unyielding.

"You're mine," he growls into my mouth, the words vibrating through me. "Every." *Thrust.* "Fucking." *Thrust.* "Part of you." *Thrust.*

"Yes," I gasp, my pussy clenching around him. "I'm yours."

His free hand slides down between us, fingers finding my clit. He circles it in time with his thrusts, the double assault sending my body spiraling, every nerve ablaze, every muscle straining. I am unraveling fast, the coil in my belly tightening with each stroke, each touch, until I am right on the edge.

"Emilio—" His name breaks from me, ragged, strangled, as my second orgasm tears me apart. It hits like lightning, violent and consuming, my body arching off the bed as I clamp down on him, screaming into the night as I shatter for him again.

He doesn't stop. He pounds into me, relentless, driving deeper with every thrust. His rhythm falters into something raw, ragged, desperate, until his control snaps. With a guttural roar, he buries himself to the hilt and comes undone inside me. His entire body shudders against mine, muscles tight as steel as he empties himself, his breath breaking in harsh, uneven bursts.

For a long moment, he doesn't move. He stays pressed against me, heavy and unyielding, our chests rising and falling together in a chaotic rhythm. I can feel his heart hammering, wild and uneven, until gradually it begins to slow, syncing with the beat of mine.

His lips brush my temple, the faintest ghost of a kiss, and I close my eyes, breathing him in—cedar, citrus, sweat, and something entirely his. I want to memorize it, brand it into me.

After a while, he eases out of me, careful, almost reluctant, and I whimper at the loss. He murmurs something soft against my skin, a curse, a prayer, maybe both, before pulling back just enough to look at me. His golden eyes are still dark, but the hunger has faded, leaving behind something quieter, deeper.

"You okay?" he asks, voice hoarse, roughened from growls and groans.

I nod, throat too tight for anything more. My thighs still quake, my body humming from the aftershocks, but it's a sweetness I never want to end.

He brushes the damp strands from my forehead, his thumb lingering against my cheek. "Didn't hurt you?"

"No." My voice comes out soft, but firm. "You could never."

The tension in his shoulders loosens. He dips down to kiss me again, slow this time, tender, lips lingering over mine in an unhurried promise. Nothing frantic, nothing urgent. Just him, giving and gentle.

When he finally rolls to the side, he doesn't let me go. His arm hooks around me and pulls me with him until I'm tucked against his chest. The sheets are tangled, the air thick with heat and sex, but his body wraps around mine like a cocoon. My cheek rests over the steady thud of his heart, and for the first time in forever, the world feels still.

Max's claws click faintly on the floor outside the bedroom door, a reminder of the world still spinning, but inside these four walls, there's only us. Emilio's fingers trace slow patterns across my spine, lazy circles that send tingles down to my toes. Each stroke calms me, lulling me into softness, my body slackening against him.

"I meant what I said," he murmurs into my hair, his

breath warm against my scalp. "You're mine. Every part of you. Not just your body."

His words settle deep, wrapping around something fragile inside me. My eyes sting, but the tears that rise aren't jagged this time—they soothe.

I press my lips against his chest, tasting salt, heat, him. "Then don't ever let me go."

"I won't." His reply is steady, resolute, carved into the air like a vow.

The silence that follows hums with warmth, threaded with the echo of everything we just shared. His hand keeps moving over my back, protective, constant, until my body slackens completely, exhaustion pulling me under.

For the first time since Khloe's death, I let myself drift. Not into the emptiness that waits in the shadows, but into him. Into us.

TWENTY-ONE

THEY NEVER LOOK UP.

That's what always astounds me. People drift through the world like prey animals who've forgotten they're prey. Heads down, eyes glued to glowing screens, laughter spilling out into the night without the faintest thought of what could be lurking just beyond the streetlights.

The couple in front of me is no exception.

The boy—tall, broad-shouldered in a dark gray t-shirt and jeans—walks with that arrogant ease of someone who thinks his strength alone makes him untouchable. His arm brushes the girl beside him, her crimson braid swaying with each step they take, his laugh cutting too loud through the air, careless, like nothing could ever go wrong.

The girl clings to him, her petite frame dressed in a yellow sundress, pressing against his side like he's her shield. She trusts him. She trusts the light. She trusts the illusion of safety.

But shields splinter. And safety is a lie.

I trail three paces behind, slipping between shadow and light as the streetlamps buzz overhead. The hum of traffic drones from Fourth Ave, neon spills from bars, students stumble out of doorways in clusters. But all of that is background noise.

None of it matters.

Only them.

I've been following them for blocks now, watching and waiting, and it baffles me how completely unaware they are of their surroundings. Not a single glance has been thrown over their shoulders. Not a flicker of suspicion. They've moved through this city like they own it, like nothing bad could possibly touch them here—prey with no awareness of the predator trailing them.

If it weren't for their tie to *her*, I'd drop this hunt altogether. They're boring—laughing, oblivious, predictable. I don't do boring.

Khloe wasn't boring.

I can still see it—the way her body froze when the text pinged her phone, her hesitation before answering, the exact moment her pulse spiked. The way she tried to convince herself that the open window was her mistake. She ignored her instincts, like they all do. That's why it was so easy to slide out of the hall closet, the blade already in my hand. She was distracted, cornered. Perfect.

The memory smolders, feeding me, coiling hot in my veins as my gloved fingers curl tighter around the knife hidden in my hoodie pocket. Anticipation hums like electricity under my skin. This is the best part—when stalking shifts into the hunt. When the fear sets in. Fear makes the blood sweeter.

I tug my mask down over my face—white, smooth, the absence of everything—and the world narrows to the cold void of that blank face. Identity vanishes under the mask like chalk under a rainstorm. The street becomes an audience, and tonight I am the show.

I step into the intersection's shadow and pull my knife free from the confines of my pocket and press the tip against the rough brick wall.

The steel shrieks as I drag it down the stone. A piercing scrape that claws through the quiet street, splitting the night open.

They freeze.

The girl stiffens, her laugh cut off mid-breath. Her head whips around, wide eyes locking on me. The boy's jaw snaps tight, his cocky grin evaporating as soon as he sees the mask.

I tilt the knife, a lazy wave, mocking. Then I drag it again, harder. Sparks spit into the dark like fireflies.

"Run, run, run as fast as you can..." I croon, my voice lilting, a twisted nursery rhyme, as I take two long, deliberate steps toward them.

"Bailey, go!" the boy shouts, panic shredding his voice. He shoves her forward, nearly sending her to the ground. She stumbles, then bolts, her white Vans slapping against the pavement. He's right behind her, dragging her into motion.

Perfect.

I lengthen my stride, my boots pounding the pavement, each step steady and deliberate. They bolt down the side-blocks, turning corners with the confusion of people who don't know the ground beneath them, desperate to outrun me.

But they don't know these streets like I do. I've memorized every artery.

Bailey slips at the end of the block, her shoulder slams into brick and the world tilts. The boy crashes into her back, sending them both to the ground, clutching at each other. And for the first time they look up with the terrified pleading eyes of prey.

The scream that is equal parts frustration and fear rips out of her throat the moment she realizes...

The alley is a box with three walls and no exit except the one they entered in.

A *dead* end.

"Fuck!" she cries, voice splintering apart as she spins around just in time to see me step into the alley's mouth.

The dull glow of the streetlight outside halos my mask in pale yellow. My blade glints in the light, serrated edge catching each flicker.

The boy plants himself in front of her, shoving her back. "He can't get us both, baby. When I say run, you run." His voice shakes, but he still tries. Still thinks he has a chance. I tilt my head, smirking behind the mask. They always think they can fight.

"I'll hold him off, okay. Go, get help."

"Liam, no, I'm not leaving you," Bailey cries, her hands gripping tightly around his bicep.

"I'm not asking, Bailey. RUN!" he snaps, shaking her off.

She falters, fear freezing her in her place before she finally catches on to what she should be attempting to do. It's cute, thinking they'll get away from me.

Before she can even move, I free my other hand and reach for the .45 tucked against my waistband. The suppressor drags against my thigh as I pull it free, cocked and ready.

The shot is almost polite—a near-silent crack from the suppressor, but not gone. The sound tears a raw edge into the night. Bailey's scream is immediate and animal, the pitch of it splitting the air.

The bullet tears through her calf, ripping flesh and splintering brick behind her. She collapses, clutching her leg, blood painting her fingers as it pours hot between them.

"NO!" Liam roars, fury ripping out of him as he lunges. His fist cracks against my shoulder, jolting the gun from my grip. Pain lances down my arm, but I welcome it. Gripping my knife, I step into him and drive it upward, burying it beneath his ribs. The resistance of bone grinds along the edge as I twist and rip it free.

The sound he makes is guttural, wet, like air forced through water. He staggers back, crimson blooming fast across his shirt as his hands claw at the wound.

"Liam!" Bailey's voice cracks as she tries to drag herself up, blood streaking her leg.

He drops to his knees, eyes huge and emptied of the plans he'd made to be a hero. I don't give him the mercy of recovery.

I stalk forward, blood dripping from the blade's edge, and grip his shoulder tightly, steadying him before plunging the knife into his chest. Once. Twice. Each thrust brutal. His body jerks as I rip it out, then ram it through his throat.

His eyes go wide, blood bubbling from his mouth, gurgling as it spills past his lips. His hands clutch weakly at his neck, but he's already collapsing, crimson pooling beneath him as his body hits the ground.

"Your turn," I growl, my attention shifting to Bailey as I step around Liam.

Bailey's wail slices the night open. She scrambles backward on her hands, dragging herself across the asphalt, pressing her back to the far wall like stone could save her. Tears streak her face, mixing with sweat and blood, her hands flailing blindly across the ground for something—anything.

"Why are you doing this?!" she screams, desperation splitting her throat.

I crouch low, my mask inches from her face, and trail the dull edge of my knife along her cheek. She whimpers at the touch.

"Because I can," I whisper, and the words are the coldest thing I offer all night.

When I move, it is violent and purposeful. The blade sinks into belly flesh, the sound of it entering and exiting a rhythm of its own. Her body jolts. Eyes wide. Mouth gasping. She rasps it out through bloodied lips, broken but defiant, "F—fuck you."

Then something burns sharp into my clavicle, white-hot and furious, crudely thrust, like the alley itself has teeth. Pain flares and for the first time tonight I feel a momentary, furious surprise. I snarl, ripping the object free.

A syringe. A filthy, discarded syringe.

"You bitch!" I roar, fury burning hot.

I drop it, and with one hand, clamp her throat, dragging her up the wall. Her feet dangle, her nails claw at my glove as her screams shred into nothing. I tighten, crushing her trachea, savoring the way her strength falters.

My other hand finds the knife still in her gut. I don't pull it free. I drag it upward, sawing through skin and organs, splitting her open until the fight drains from her body. Her arms fall slack.

Only then do I let go.

She crumples to the ground in a heap.

For a moment, I stand perfectly still, listening—letting the silence settle thick in the alley. It clings to me, broken only by the faint drip of blood hitting pavement. My eyes skim over what I've made, the stillness of their bodies painted in red.

My masterpieces.

I crouch slowly, deliberate, and scoop up the syringe, holding it carefully between my gloved fingers. Nothing gets left behind. Nothing that could point back to me. It disappears into my pocket, along with the knife, its edge still slick.

A few steps carry me back to where Liam sprawls, his chest painted in crimson, his mouth slack with the last attempt at breath. I crouch again, retrieve the pistol from the ground, and slide it smoothly back into my waistband. For a moment, I just look at him. The boy who thought he could fight. Who thought love and bravery might make a difference.

From my back pocket, I pull a crumpled slip of paper. I unfold it, glance at the words once more, then crush it into a ball with one hand. Carefully, I pry open his stiffening fingers, press the note into his palm, and curl his hand closed around it. A gift for the ones who'll find him. A breadcrumb left on purpose.

Then I rise, step back, and leave the alley behind me—my shadows stretching long across the walls as I melt into the night.

CRIME
OFFICER
STOP
STOP

TWENTY-TWO
EMILIO

NO MATTER how many crime scenes I work, it never gets easier.

The weight settles the same way every time—the copper stink of blood in the air, silence clinging to the brick and asphalt after violence has screamed itself hoarse, and the inescapable truth that someone's selfish choice just ripped away light, laughter, and future from another human being. I can already see what it means for the people waiting at home. Parents who will never hear their child's voice again. Brothers, sisters, and friends left staring at a space in their lives that should be filled with birthdays, arguments, late-night phone calls, and stupid inside jokes—but instead holds nothing but absence.

The void violence leaves behind feels endless, but still, I carry it. Because if not me, then who?

I know violence will never disappear from this world. Humanity's been tearing itself apart since the beginning of time. But every time I stand in the aftermath of it, I can't stop asking: what fractures inside a person that makes them cross that line? What hunger, what void convinces them they can strip the life out of another human being?

The alley reeks of hot metal, piss, and rot—so sharp it settles on my tongue, clinging in my throat. Red and blue strobes from the cruisers bleed across graffiti-tagged brick, flashing off shattered bottles, glinting glass, and trash that litters the narrow passage. Fast-food wrappers and crushed cans grind beneath my boots with every step I take toward the carnage waiting at the end.

"Elcot," I call, my voice low and steady, despite the way my stomach knots.

He's stationed near the far wall, posture rigid, one hand resting on the butt of his weapon like he's waiting for something else to lunge out of the dark. He doesn't look at me at first, doesn't take his eyes off the bodies sprawled at his feet. Like if he doesn't blink, he won't have to accept what he's seeing.

"Perez," he finally answers, his tone clipped and professional. "Scene's secured. CSU and a detective are en route." His throat works with a hard swallow, betraying what he doesn't want me to see. He feels the weight, too.

I force myself forward, my eyes sweeping the alley. The first victim, male, maybe early twenties, is sprawled only a few feet to my left. His gray t-shirt is shredded, stained nearly black, spiderwebs of blood blooming across his chest. His face is contorted, frozen in the last moment his body failed him. His pale lips are parted, his teeth streaked with red, dried blood pooling at the corners of his mouth like he drowned in his own breath.

The second victim is farther down, slumped against the graffiti-smeared brick. A girl. Petite, no older than him. Her sundress is torn and clings to her frame, the once-bright yellow fabric now blackened with blood. A bullet tore her calf apart, the muscle mangled, and blood congealed thick around her ankle, staining her white Vans a deep crimson. Her head tilts against the wall, hair spilling like a macabre halo across the brick. The faint bruises circling her throat are fresh enough to stand out beneath the harsh light, proof that her death wasn't quiet.

The silence hangs heavy, broken only by the occasional static crackle from our radios and the low hum of traffic bleeding in from the street, a reminder that the world is still moving outside this space.

"Who called it in?" I ask, voice low.

"Anonymous tip," Elcot answers. "Dispatch said they left no name and that the call came from a burner. All they gave was the location and said that a murder occurred."

I grit my teeth. Anonymous tip my ass. I guarantee the killer called it in. Why be anonymous about it if you weren't the one who committed the crime or felt you'd be suspected of it?

Before I can voice my thoughts, the low growl of a van cuts through the suffocating silence. A white CSU vehicle rolls to a stop, headlights flooding the scene before they snap off. Doors slam, and three techs step out, lugging heavy kits and camera cases. They duck under the tape, and gloves snap into place, their motions automatic, practiced.

"About damn time," Elcot mutters, but I catch the faint drop of tension in his shoulders as they arrive.

The team fans out quickly, efficient in their movements. One sets up portable floodlights that bleach the alley in harsh white, stripping shadows from every corner. Another snaps cameras together, shutters clicking in rapid bursts, each flash burning the victims into momentary still frames. Evidence markers drop beside trash and pools of blood. Swabs dip into dark stains. Bags crinkle as gloves gather anything that doesn't belong.

I step aside, giving them room to work, but my eyes keep tracking every move.

One tech kneels beside the male victim, methodically working over him. They measure the depth of the wounds, swab the streaks of blood crusted on his cheeks, camera popping with each adjustment. Then, another burst of flash reveals something in his left hand—a crumpled wad, clutched tight in rigor-stiffened fingers.

"What's that?" I ask, crouching closer, nodding toward it.

"Not sure. Let's see," the tech says as he works carefully, prying each finger loose until he pulls the object free—a wad of paper, tacky with semi-dried blood.

I pull out a pair of gloves from my pocket and slide them on as the tech gently starts unfolding the paper. The paper sticks to itself, nearly tearing as he unfolds it, but he manages to flatten it before slipping it into an evidence bag.

He seals it, then hands it over.

I grasp it between my thumb and index finger and examine it.

Blood has smeared most of the ink, but enough remains for me to piece together what was intended. I slide my duty phone out of the pocket of my vest and open the camera. Lying the bag across my knee, I snap a photo, then read the message.

She may not have been my first, but she will be my last.

The message slams into me like a gut punch. My stomach twists, breath catching in my throat. Whoever wrote this isn't taunting. They're confessing. Claiming. Promising.

And worse… there's a part of me that feels like I know who "she" is.

I ease my truck into a spot outside Raelynn's building, the dash clock glowing just past 12:45. The lot is a patchwork of sleeping cars and long, thin shadows; the only sound when I cut the engine is the faint tick of cooling metal and the distant hum of a transformer. For a beat, I sit there, hand on the wheel, watching the thin slit of light under Raelynn's blinds.

She texted back that she was up, but that little notification of hers doesn't calm the coil in my chest. If anything, it tightens it — dread with an edge of purpose.

I know this visit isn't just to hold her; it's because the alley and the smeared handwriting are still stuck under my skin.

Finally, I step out, boots hitting the pavement. The night air is cool, brushing over the sweat at the back of my neck as I stride up the narrow path toward her building. Most of the windows are dark, the whole complex sunk in silence, but hers spills a sliver of yellow light through the blinds, a quiet beacon that pulls me forward. When I reach her door, I can't help the faint curve of a smile tugging at my mouth. She's added more decorations, and we're not even halfway through September yet. Yellow crime scene tape crisscrosses the frame, fluttering lightly with the breeze. Plastic spiders cling to the cotton webs she hung weeks ago. Where the pumpkins used to sit, she's propped up a makeshift body—a black trash-bag torso stuffed with old bottles and rolled paper, duct-taped in a laughable approximation of mortality. It's dark and cheeky and exactly the kind of thing Rae would do to mock the world into submission.

I knock, my knuckles brushing against the tape.

The deadbolt slides back almost immediately, and the door opens. Raelynn stands in the frame, lit by the warm glow inside. Her hair is damp, still dripping at the ends, leaving dark spots on the shoulders of her purple *The Nightmare Before Christmas* sleep shirt. The oversized fabric hangs loose, brushing her thighs, and the matching black shorts barely peek out from beneath the hem. They ride high on her hips, short enough that when she shifts, a glimpse of bare skin flashes at the curve of her ass. The sight alone makes my pulse jump, my carefully built composure threatening to unravel right there on her doorstep.

"Hey, baby," I murmur, my voice rougher than I mean it to be.

She doesn't answer—not with words. She steps forward and wraps her arms around my neck, and I pull her in like I might suddenly lose her if I don't. I close the door behind us with my hip and tuck the deadbolt in before anything else. Her face buries into my neck; coconut shampoo and the warm, clean smell of her skin fills my nose. For a flash, there's nothing but the small, steady life of her against my chest, and it's a temptation I don't try to fight.

When she finally leans back, her eyes glint up at me, wide, searching. I catch her chin gently between my fingers, tilt her face up, and kiss her. It's slow, deliberate, lingering. Her lips are soft, pliant, a balm I didn't realize I'd been desperate for all night.

"Hi," she breathes, and the single syllable thrums through me.

For a single, stupid heartbeat, I want to forget everything else—to melt into her, to let the apartment swallow the world and keep us safe in the small space between our bodies. I could stand there forever, let the heat of her press me flat, and pretend the alley and the words on that smeared scrap of paper were someone else's problem. But I didn't come here only for that. The other reason—the one that's been gnawing at me since I left the alley—is pulling at the edges of my focus like a hand you can't ignore.

I drag my thumb along her cheek, the motion gentle because she's fragile with this news already. "Rae," I say, and the word has the kind of gravity that makes her shoulders stiffen. "We need to talk."

She blinks, brows knitting hard and fast. "About what?" Her voice is small, taut. There's a thread of iron under the fear, the way she always answers when she thinks she needs to be brave.

I run a hand through her damp hair, exhaling slowly, like dragging the words out of me will hurt less if I pace myself. "There was another murder tonight. Two victims." My voice is level, but the words have weight; I can feel her arm clamp around mine like a second skin, fingers digging in hard enough to leave an imprint. "Something was left behind that… doesn't sit right with me. I'll explain it, but first, I need to ask you something."

She goes rigid, the inhale stealing the breath from her lungs. For a second, I fear she'll crumble. Instead, she swallows like she's buckling herself and nods once. "Okay," she whispers, the single word already hollowed out with too many possible meanings.

"Do you know Liam Carter and Bailey Gilbert?"

Her face changes before she answers—a micro-expression I've learned to read: recognition, then recoil. "I… yeah. I dated Liam my freshman year," she says, voice uneven, thin around the edges. "And I know of Bailey, but we weren't close. I'm not close with either of them, to be honest. Why?" She drags the word out, already bracing. I can tell by the way her eyes search mine that she doesn't need me to answer, that she's already connecting the dots. "Oh my god." Her breath falters, her hand flying up to her mouth. "They were killed, weren't they?"

"Yes," I reply grimly. "And CSU and I found this."

My jaw clenches as I reach into my pocket and pull out my phone. I've already forwarded the CSU photo to myself; the duty phone's camera doesn't flatter anyone under normal circumstances, but it captured the message at the scene. I hand it to her.

She takes it with trembling fingers and zooms, her lips mouthing the words to herself. For a moment, she just stares, her brows furrowing, lips parting like she doesn't want to believe what she's seeing. Then she hands it back quickly, like she doesn't want it in her hands a second longer.

"What the hell is that supposed to mean?" she asks, sharp and raw now. The line between curiosity and panic splits her words.

"I don't know for certain," I say, my jaw taut, "but I've got a gut feeling. And my gut's never steered me wrong."

She folds in on herself for a breath, then shakes her head like she can dislodge the thought. "That's—what? Who even says that?"

I close the distance and exhale slowly through my nose, my thumb finds the hollow beneath her ear, brushing the line of her jaw. "Whoever left that note… it wasn't random. Killers don't leave words like that unless they want them seen. They're telling us something, *claiming* something. And if I'm right, it means this wasn't about Liam, Bailey, or even Khloe. It's about the person they're circling."

Her eyes search mine—hungry for certainty, for a way to refuse the worst. "You think that person is me?" Her voice is paper-thin.

"I don't *know* yet," I admit, "but look at what's already happened. Your best friend was murdered. Tonight, two more people you know were killed in a similar gruesome manner. That's not a coincidence, Rae. That's a pattern."

She shakes her head, the motion quick and desperate. "That doesn't mean it's about me." Her reflex is bravery, bargaining. I hear it, and I hate that she has to say it.

"Maybe not," I say firmly, "but until we know for sure, I'm not willing to gamble with your life. This person isn't just killing. They're taunting us. Sending messages. And I don't give a damn if you think it's paranoia—" I lean closer, my voice dropping lower, harder "—there is a psycho fucking killer on the loose and you are *not* safe."

Her lips press tight, her mind spinning—but then, suddenly, something flashes in her expression. Her eyes widen, recognition and fear.

"Wait," she whispers before taking off down the hall.

My brows crease together in confusion, and I follow. She pushes her bedroom door open. Max perks up on the bed when he sees me and jumps down, his whole body wiggling with excitement. I pet him as Rae rummages through her desk drawers, fingers scrabbling through a jumble of notebooks, old lecture notes, and stray pens. The cheap wood rattles as she throws things aside—her motion is urgent, frantic. Then she pulls up a white envelope, creased and stained tan around the edges with her name written across the front.

"What is that?" I ask, my brows creasing.

Her hand trembles as she fully withdraws it from the drawer. "A card," she says, her voice thin. "I got it a few weeks ago. At first, I thought it was a dumb prank, and I almost threw it away. Actually, I did. But something… I don't know. I retrieved it from the trash a few nights later and kept it in the drawer. Just in case."

She peels back the already torn flap like someone defusing a bomb. From inside, she withdraws a light blue card, which bears the words "Thinking of You" printed across the middle in soft cursive. She hands it to me, and I unfold the card. The first thing that catches my eye is the yellowed newspaper clipping, the headline in bold, faded black letters. The next thing my eyes catch is the writing above the cutout and the one below it.

"Tell me you don't recognize the handwriting," she says, eyes wide, breath shallow.

I pull my phone out, bring up the photo of the note from the scene, and lay it beside the card. The two samples sit together like mirrors.

My stomach drops so hard I have to steady myself on the desk's edge. The letters line up. They're the same jagged capitals I've seen two times now: angry, quick, like the writer was punching the letters into the paper. The quirk on the R, the long slash on the T—the same brutal signature stretched across two different pages. The realization slams into me like a fist.

"Jesus Christ," I mutter, not really sure what else I can say in this moment.

Her eyes are wide when she meets mine. "So it *is* about me."

I fold the card back into its envelope as if the motion could erase the truth it carries. "Whoever wrote this," I say, every word weighted, "they've been watching you longer than we realized."

A silence swells between us, thick as storm clouds. She crosses her arms tight around herself, as if she can physically keep her body from unraveling. Her shoulders tremble under the strain. I step forward before she can fold too far into the shadows of her own head, pulling her into me. Her frame collides with my chest—small, fragile, shaking. Her pulse beats frantic against the side of my throat, wild and erratic like a bird desperate to escape its cage. I hold her tighter, steady, because right now it's the only thing I can offer.

"We'll figure this out," I murmur into her hair, the words low, rough, absolute. "I swear it. But until we do, you need to understand something—whether you want to believe it or not, you're a target. And I'm not about to let you become his last."

Del
F12
End
PgUp
PgDn
Home

TWENTY-THREE
RAELYNN

"WHY IS THIS NECESSARY?" I exclaim, breathless, as my ass smacks the mat for what feels like the hundredth damn time tonight.

The dull thud reverberates through the nearly empty gym, stealing the air out of me. I gasp, arching my back, sweat beading and tracking down the hollow of my spine. Loose strands of hair have escaped my ponytail and cling stubbornly to my temples. My palms sting from catching myself wrong—again—and a curse slips through my teeth as I roll to the side, glaring up at him.

After Liam and Bailey were killed, after we found out that someone had been stalking me for longer than we thought, I (begrudgingly) agreed to this whole self-defense thing. Because apparently, in Emilio's words, I "couldn't fight my way out of a paper bag." *Fuck you too, Emilio.* But the bastard wasn't wrong. My self-defense skills are absolute shit. I know I need to work on them if I ever want to make it as a detective, but hearing it out loud stung, and every slam onto the floor tonight feels like him grinding it in.

"I told you not to go easy on me," I snap, shoving up onto

my elbows, my chest heaving. "Guess I should've specified don't toss me around like a ragdoll either."

Emilio looms above me, lips curved into that infuriating smirk that makes me want to slap him almost as much as kiss him. His navy shirt clings to him, plastered to his chest and shoulders, the fabric darkened with sweat that highlights every solid line of muscle. His curls are mussed, damp, sticking to his forehead. Even under the flat glare of the fluorescents, which bleach everything in the room, he looks criminally good —like a sin wrapped in sweat and muscle.

He extends his hand towards me, his palm rough and calloused from years of use, and I take it. His grip swallows mine, hauling me to my feet with no effort at all. He holds me there a beat longer than necessary, his thumb brushing against my knuckles before he finally steps back. His stance resets instantly—shoulders squared, knees bent, ready for me to come at him again.

"You want me to take it easy?" His tone is low, patient, too damn calm for someone who just flattened me. "That's not how this works. Out there, no one cares if you fall hard. They won't stop until you're down and bleeding. You need to know how to fight back—with or without a weapon."

The station's gym is deserted at this hour, just like he wanted. Past midnight, the overnight shift barely trickles in here. The gym is half lit by fluorescent lights and half by natural light: one bank of bulbs buzzes, casting harsh, white rectangles across the mats; the rest of the room smolders in softer shadows. The mats beneath us are scarred with years of use, rough against my palms every time I hit the floor. The smell in here is a mix of disinfectant, sweat, and old rubber from the stacked dumbbells and weight benches along the wall. Treadmills and ellipticals sit across the room, their screens still glowing faintly from whoever last used them. Resistance bands hang from hooks, a jump rope coiled lazily nearby. Every sound—the squeak of our shoes, the snap of the mats under impact—feels amplified in the emptiness.

I roll my shoulders, trying to ease the ache that's settled deep into the muscles. My lungs burn with every breath, heat coiling under my skin, made worse by the cling of my shirt, which is plastered to me with sweat. My sports bra holds me steady, but it doesn't stop the flush creeping higher under the weight of Emilio's gaze.

"You just like knocking me down," I mutter, circling him.

"Maybe." That dangerous grin curves his mouth, slow and deliberate. He flexes his hands and motions me forward with a tilt of his chin. "But that's not the point. I need to know you'll fight. That you won't freeze if someone corners you."

"And what if they've got a knife?" I shoot back, frustration boiling over. "What then?"

His eyes narrow, and his voice comes out hard, unflinching. "Then you don't hesitate. You fight like your life depends on it, because it does. Eyes, throat, groin, wherever you can strike. You make them regret *ever* thinking they could put a blade near you. You take the opening, Rae, no matter how dirty it feels."

The words land hard, heavier than I expect.

My jaw tightens as irritation and adrenaline collide in a single, reckless surge. I lunge, aiming the way he showed me. He registers the move quickly and sidesteps with infuriating precision, catching my wrist and spinning me so fast the room tilts. My back slams into his chest, hard muscle absorbing the impact as his arm bands around me, pinning me in place.

His breath ghosts the shell of my ear when he murmurs, "Again." The word vibrates through me, low and commanding, and my stomach flips traitorously.

I squirm, jamming my elbow back, but he shifts effortlessly, catching every move before I can finish it. My pulse spikes, not just from the fight, but from the solid wall of his chest pressed against my back, the heat rolling off him, the rough sound of his breath against my skin.

"Let me go," I pant. My voice comes out thin, breathless, lacking the bite I want.

"You think an attacker's going to let you go because you asked nicely?" His tone drips with mockery, lips grazing my ear again, and the fleeting contact sends a shiver ripping down my spine I can't hide.

I freeze—just a second too long—and that is all he needs. His grip tightens, sweeping my legs out from under me, and I crash down hard. My knees skid across the mat, the burn sharp, and then he's on me again, and though he never crosses the line into hurting me, the control is his.

"Fight, pretty girl," he orders, voice rough and uncompromising. "Don't stop until you're free."

I push back with everything I have, muscles straining until they shake, and for a breath, he lets me think I've gained ground—before slamming me flat again. My back bounces off the mat with a jolt, the breath ripped out of me.

In a blink, he's straddling me, pinning me beneath the solid weight of his body. Sweat drips from his jaw onto my chest, hot and tangible, while his breath stays maddeningly steady as mine tears ragged from my lungs.

And then—his shirt is gone, stripped off in one fluid motion and tossed aside without care.

My breath hitches. My eyes rake over him, greedily drinking in every inch—the broad planes of his chest, the rise and fall of his ribs, the tattooed ink stretched over taut, sweat-slick muscle. The way his arms flex when he pins me harder to the mat. Heat and shadow, power and want—that's what he is, hovering over me, and my body responds before my mind can catch up.

The gym hums with silence, the fluorescents buzzing overhead in a steady rhythm like a pulse. My world narrows to this: the weight of him above me, the feeling of his sweat sliding where our bodies nearly touch, the uneven drag of my own breath breaking apart in my chest.

My hands twitch against the mat, restless, itching to grab hold of him. His stare pins me even harder than his body, those molten eyes daring me to break.

"Are you waiting for permission?" His voice drops low, smooth and dangerous, threaded with challenge.

Heat spikes through me, sharp and unstable. I bare my teeth, trying to sound sharp, but the words falter, coming out softer than I mean them. "You've got me pinned, asshole. What do you want me to do—sprout wings?"

His smirk curves, slow and devastating, like a fuse catching fire. "I want you to prove me wrong. Show me you can take control—even when you don't have any."

I twist under him, trying to buck him off, but his weight shifts with mine, relentless. His thigh slides between mine, grazing where I'm already throbbing. The accidental touch sends sparks ripping through me, white-hot, and my breath stutters. His eyes sharpen, darkening like he felt it too.

The silence thickens. The hum of the lights overhead grows louder, every sound sharper, every breath deeper. My pulse thrums so fast it drowns out all thought, too loud in my ears. He's so close that the heat rolling off him licks across my skin in waves, suffocating and intoxicating.

"Still think this isn't necessary?" he murmurs, dipping until his lips hover a whisper from mine. His breath is hot, taunting, close enough to taste.

I should shove him off. I should spit out some smart remark. But I don't. My hands betray me, sliding up, palms skimming the ridges of his abs, tracing the taut muscle under sweat-slick skin. My fingertips tremble, but I can't stop. His abdomen tightens under my touch, his jaw flexing as his eyes blaze, hungry and raw.

The tension snaps.

His mouth crashes onto mine, all heat and teeth and desperate hunger. The kiss is savage, consuming, like he's been starving and I'm the only thing that could sate him. His tongue tangles with mine, fierce and demanding, and I meet it with equal fire, fisting his dampened hair to drag him closer.

He groans, guttural, the sound vibrating through me as his hips grind down, his cock pressing hard against my core through his shorts. The pressure is unbearable, perfect, and I writhe beneath him, every nerve lit.

I gasp into his mouth, tasting salt, heat, and something purely him, arching into him with greedy desperation. His hands are everywhere—rough, certain, claiming. They slide up the flat of my stomach and grip my waist hard enough to leave bruises. He tugs at the hem of my shirt until the fabric peels away, sticky with sweat. Inch by inch, he bares me, impatient, until the shirt's gone completely and I'm left raw under his stare. His calloused fingers slip beneath my sports bra, searing hot against damp skin, and I bite back a moan when his thumb skims the underside of my breast.

"Emilio—" His name tears from me, pleading, breathless.

He doesn't give me the chance to say more. His mouth abandons mine to trail fire down my throat, biting, sucking until sharp pain blooms into aching pleasure. His hand cups me through the bra, squeezing hard, before he shoves the fabric aside and takes my nipple into his mouth. The scrape of his teeth, followed by the wet drag of his tongue, is unbearable in the best way, and a strangled cry rips free before I can stop it.

"Fuck, baby," he rasps when he finally lets go, my nipple slipping wet from between his lips. His voice is shredded with need, ragged like it's costing him to hold himself back. "You're gonna drive me insane."

My hands fumble desperately at his waistband, trembling with urgency. But he beats me to it—shoving his shorts down far enough for his cock to spring free, heavy and hard, pre-cum already slick at the tip. My hand closes around him instinctively, stroking, marveling at the heat and thickness. His body shudders, his groan rumbling low in his chest.

His gaze drags down the length of me sprawled beneath him, then back up, hot and hungry. But something sharper flickers in his expression, darker.

He moves before I can think. One hand clamps around my wrists, pinning them above my head, the other snatches up my discarded shirt. In a single rough motion, he bunches the damp fabric and presses it hard against my mouth, stuffing it between my lips until my protest comes out muffled.

His eyes blaze, feral and possessive as he growls, low against my ear, "Your screams are mine and mine only. No one else gets to hear them. Not here. Not ever."

The words hit harder than his grip, raw and absolute. The shirt muffles my gasp, turns it ragged, and somehow makes the fire inside me burn hotter. My body writhes under him, caught between desperation and surrender, and he feels it all.

His free hand yanks my shorts down in one brutal sweep, baring me to the cool air. He shifts, the swollen head of his cock dragging through my folds, smearing my slick arousal. Teasing, testing. I buck up instinctively, seeking more, but he growls low in his chest, the sound vibrating against my spine.

"Yeah," he rasps, pressing just enough to make me whimper into the gag. "That's it. Beg me without words. Show me how bad you need it."

I writhe against him, the gag swallowing the sounds I want to make. My body does the pleading for me—hips snapping upward, thighs trembling, nails clawing at the back of his hands as if I can force him deeper. He only presses the head harder against my entrance, circling cruelly slow, never breaking through. Each brush makes me hotter, needier, until frustration burns through me like a fever.

"Good girl," he growls, and then with one savage thrust, he buries himself to the hilt.

The stretch is sharp, exquisite, splitting me wide. My scream tears into the fabric gag, muffled and raw, my nails biting into his trapped hand. His cock fills me perfectly, painfully good, and every nerve in my body lights.

"Fuck," he snarls, forehead pressed to mine, his grip punishing on my hip. "You feel so fucking good—so tight."

He pulls back, then slams into me. Again and again. Each thrust harder, deeper, until the mats beneath us squeak with the impact. His rhythm builds fast, brutal, and relentless. The obscene slap of our bodies collides with the slick drag of him inside me, filling the hollow gym with the sound of us.

Pinned beneath him, gag muffling my cries, I arch and writhe, every nerve ending lit. His hand clamps my wrists tighter, and I strain in his grip, but the restraint only makes the heat coil tighter inside me. I can't get away, I don't want to. His cock stretches me perfectly, hitting that spot over and over until my vision sparks white, his body driving mine into the mat.

His breath is ragged in my ear, hot and harsh. "That's it, baby," he growls, voice shredded with need. "Take me. Take all of me."

His free hand slides down, thumb circling my clit in ruthless rhythm with his thrusts. The dual assault wrecks me.

Pressure builds quickly, unbearable, my thighs shaking around him. I scream into the gag, high and muffled, my body arching as the orgasm slams into me. It's violent, tearing through me in waves that leave me shaking apart under his weight. My pussy clenches tight around his cock, milking him, and he groans deep in his chest, guttural and raw.

"Fuck, Rae—" he rasps, driving harder, chasing it. "So fucking tight, so perfect."

His thrusts grow ragged, desperate—each one harder, rougher—until with a final, guttural growl, he sheathes himself fully inside me and comes completely undone. His body shudders violently, every muscle locked tight as he spills deep, his moan fractured and raw where it muffles against my shoulder.

For a heartbeat, for several, everything goes still. The only sound is the faint creak of the mats beneath us and the harsh drag of our breathing. His weight bears down heavily, grounding me, pressing me so close I can feel the wild thunder of his heart, each frantic beat syncing with mine. My lungs burn around the gag, each shallow breath scraping through me until at last he reaches up, grabs the damp shirt, and yanks it from my mouth. He tosses it aside carelessly.

I gulp down air greedily, each inhale shaky, like I've been underwater too long. My chest rises against his, trembling.

His lips brush my temple—soft, reverent, a stark contrast to the raw brutality from moments ago. "You okay?" he asks, voice rough, threaded with something gentler now.

I nod, my throat too tight for anything more. He kisses me once, slow and steady, then carefully pulls out, leaving me sore and trembling in the aftermath. His arms wrap around me instantly, pulling me tight against the heat of his sweat-slick chest. His palm strokes lazy circles into my back, steady and soothing, until my shivers start to ease.

"Good girl," he mutters against my hair, his voice ragged but quiet. "So fucking good for me."

We stay tangled on the mat longer than we should. The air is heavy, thick with sweat and the sharp musk of sex, clinging to my skin. The world outside these walls presses closer, reality reminding me how easily someone could walk in, how precarious this bubble we've built really is.

He moves first, his touch practical but tender. With a careful hand, he adjusts the strap of my bra back into place, then tugs my shorts up over my hips with a quick, practiced tug, his knuckles brushing against my thigh. There's no rush in him, only care, as if making sure I feel put back together matters more than anything.

When we finally stand, my legs threaten to buckle beneath

me, but his hand is there instantly, steadying me without a word. He bends, scoops up both of our shirts from the mat, slings them over his shoulder, then threads his fingers through mine. His grip is firm, warm, unshakable—leading me out of the heat and mess of the gym, still tethered to him.

Del
F12
End
PgUp
PgDn
Home
P
L
K
M
N

TWENTY-FOUR
RAELYNN

AFTER THREE MURDERS, the university doesn't feel like a place of learning anymore. On paper, it still wears its familiar skin—red brick warmed by the sun, stucco facades threaded with ivy—but the surface is a lie.

Under the heat and the greenery, everything has been hardened into something defensive and raw—a battlefield disguised as academia.

Security checkpoints choke the main entrances where students once streamed freely. Now, ID cards flash under suspicious eyes, and bags are thoroughly examined. The rhythm of campus life has slowed to a crawl—impatient lines stretching down sidewalks, bodies pressed shoulder to shoulder, the air full of shifting feet and muttered complaints. Uniformed officers scan each face with deliberate precision, their gazes sharp as glass.

Campus police stand in pairs at every corner, their hands resting on their belts, their eyes hard and sweeping as if they're waiting for the killer to reveal himself in broad daylight. A few city cruisers sit parked along the main quad, their hoods catching the sun, lights off but presence heavy. The officers stationed near them don't move, don't blink, until you realize their eyes are tracking every motion with a predator's patience.

It's all meant to reassure, but it doesn't.

The air feels stretched too thin, brittle with unease, and the silence between footsteps always feels a second away from snapping. Three murders are proof enough that promises of "increased security" don't mean shit. Locks, buddy systems, ID checks, badges, flashing lights—it won't stop a determined killer who has already picked their prey.

The entire atmosphere of campus has soured. The chatter that once layered the background—gossip about who hooked up at the last party, debates over football scores, the endless buzz about Greek life—has been stripped away. In its place is something sharp, jagged. Conversations are cut short when someone gets too close. Students move in packs now, shoulders brushing, eyes flicking toward every sound.

Even the bulletin boards look like they've been through triage. The neon flyers for rush week and improv nights, the profuse posters for film club and intramural sign-ups gone. In their place are black and white handbills stapled in neat rows—counseling hotlines, phone numbers for campus safety escorts, photocopied vigils with time, place, and an urging to "come together." Someone has laminated a map of well-lit routes with arrows and the words "STAY SAFE" printed in block letters. Dorms now have printed lists taped to their doors: "If you witness something suspicious, call 911; report it to campus safety; do not approach." Little prayer candles and hastily arranged bouquets lean against a corkboard like failed attempts to hold back the bleed.

I can still hear Emilio's voice in my head as I push through it all, like a recording on repeat. He'd told me last night, while we lay in bed, what the detectives were saying, in a voice that tried to stay calm but didn't quite manage it.

"Forensically, what CSU can link is the wound pattern," he'd said, hands steepled together as if he were holding the blood itself. "They're seeing the same trend through all three scenes: same blade type—long, serrated; same stroke depth and angle; same right-to-left trajectory, which suggests a right-handed attacker using a downward, oblique motion. Defensive wounds on the victims' forearms show similar parry patterns. It's—" he paused, thumb tracing an invisible line in the air "—consistent enough that the detectives believe the same person committed all three."

And enough to convince the media that a new serial killer has started stalking the streets. A serial killer they have tastelessly named Ripper Incarnate.

The phrase is a notch in the hum under my skin as I move across the quad. It feels like a mockery—a Victorian nightmare stitched onto our modern walkways—a monster named before anyone's been brought to justice. The name spreads through the feeds, the group chats, and the water-cooler gossip with all the speed of a flame on dry grass. It makes people look at strangers like they might be a costume and a devil at once.

I hitch my bag higher on my shoulder and weave into the slow-moving crowd toward the Koffler Building. The early sun cuts across the quad, white-hot, turning the glass walls of the science buildings into blinding mirrors. Heat presses down, dry and sharp, carrying with it the faint tang of asphalt already baking. My boots crunch against stray gravel scattered along the walkway. Each step echoes too loudly in the taut hush; a rhythm that keeps time with the small, repetitive questions flitting through the crowd.

"Did you know them?" a whisper brushes by me.

"I'm not walking home alone tonight," someone else says.

"They caught someone, right? They had to have by now."

Same questions, same hollow answer—silence. The current of whispered worry tangles around my shoulders like static.

My book bag thumps against my hip with each step I take

as I climb the concrete steps to my lecture hall. At the landing, I pause, gaze sweeping across the quad—half expecting to catch someone staring. I can't stop the thoughts that come. What if he's here? Hidden among the sea of students, watching me or looking for his next prey.

The thought sends a shiver down my spine, and I push it out before it can take root and force myself forward. The heavy metal door groans as I tug it open, swallowing me into the shadow of Room 204.

The dimly lit room slopes downward in half-moons of fold-out desks, rows that climb like bleachers. Usually, this space hums with sound—gossip traded across aisles, friends shouting greetings, the crinkle of snack wrappers, and the clatter of iced coffees set down too hard. Today, it's hushed. Barely half the seats are filled, and even those who came look unsettled, their pens scratching without focus, their eyes sliding often to the doorways and corners of the room.

The low murmur of conversation bounces faintly off the whiteboard at the front. A few students tap on laptops, their faces lit in cool glow, but their eyes don't linger on the screens for long—they flick toward the doors, the aisles, the backs of the room, like prey waiting for a shadow to shift.

I slide into my usual seat midway down. Marlena is already there, her face pale, shadows bruised under her eyes. She forces a small smile, the corners of her mouth twitching up without conviction. Her hand brushes mine under the desk, the minute I pull it down over my lap, fleeting but firm—one squeeze, a wordless reminder that she's here, that we're still here.

Austin sits on her other side, posture slouched but gaze sharp. His usual lazy grin is absent, replaced by something quieter, more intent. None of us says anything at first. We don't need to. The silence speaks enough.

When Professor Henley walks in, the room seems to shift. His stride is steady, composed, not a hair out of place. His slacks are pressed, his shirt sleeves rolled just enough to show forearms that suggest ease without effort.

He sets his messenger bag on the desk, arranges his papers into neat stacks, and finally looks up. His gaze sweeps the room once—calm, unreadable—before it settles. On me. Just for a second. Long enough to stir the prickling heat across the back of my neck.

"Good morning," he begins, voice calm and evenly pitched. It carries easily without strain, yet is deep enough to demand focus without needing to be loud. "I realize the past week has been… difficult for many of you. Three lives lost in such a short span—classmates, friends, members of this community. That weight is not something I overlook." He pauses, allowing the silence to thicken, then continues, his tone softening just slightly. "Please remember there are resources available to you—counselors, peer support, and my office hours if you need them."

The silence afterward is heavy. A few students shift uncomfortably, and someone coughs near the back, but no one speaks.

Then, with a click of his mouse, the projector flickers to life, splashing pale light against the screen, and his voice falls back into lecture mode, smooth and steady, the rhythm of normalcy.

Except it isn't.

The seconds stretch until Henley's words blur together, bleeding into a low hum that doesn't quite touch me. My pen scratches nonsense patterns into the margin of my notebook, shapes looping and curling without meaning. My body is in this chair, but my mind is outside—back in the quad, in the heavy air, under the glare of watchful eyes. Waiting for a shadow to break away from the corner and move toward me.

When dismissal finally comes, it's like a valve releasing. Chairs clatter as they snap back upright, bags zip open and closed, the sound sharp and chaotic after an hour of forced stillness. Conversations ignite instantly, buzzing and fractured, spilling into the aisles and swelling into a static hum that follows us out the door.

Marlena falls into step beside me without a word, her presence steady but taut, and Austin lopes up on her other side, his easy grin muted by the weight that hasn't left the air in days. The three of us move with the tide of bodies through the narrow hallway, the crush of shoulders and backpacks pressing until we finally spill out into the open quad.

The sunlight outside is brutal, bouncing off red brick walkways and the pale sandstone buildings that frame the courtyard. Heat radiates upwards in shimmering waves off the pavement, making me already regret my all black attire. Marlena threads her fingers through mine and Austin's, holding us tight like we're kids again playing safety-in-numbers—even though we all know that hand-holding won't stop anything.

We cut across the quad, weaving through clusters of officers in uniform and the booths that have sprouted up since the start of class. Student organizations have lined the walkway, their folding tables covered in neat stacks of flyers, banners fluttering weakly in the breeze. Some hand out slips for tutoring sessions and study groups, others advertise hiking trips, art clubs, or trivia nights at the union. A few try to pass out candy with their pamphlets, bright smiles plastered on their faces, but even those smiles don't quite hold. The entire effort feels forced, thin, and hollow, like stage dressing slapped over a crumbling set.

Still, I can't blame them. Maybe that's what people need—something to look at that isn't fear.

We stop at the stone bench tucked beneath the arch that frames the path to the Student Union. Marlena sits between Austin and me, her posture squared and firm, but her grip tight, fingers digging into mine like she's afraid I'll slip away into the tide of bodies. She turns to me, her voice soft, curious in a way that makes me pause.

"How are you doing, Rae? How are things with that cop?"

Her voice is gentle, almost teasing, but the question lands heavier than it should. She doesn't know about the card. Or the note. She doesn't know most of it. Only Tessa and Emilio do. I've kept the rest locked down, tucked into the shadows of my chest where the weight sits constant. But the weight of her gaze tugs the words loose anyway.

I manage a small laugh, thin but real. "Things with Emilio are good. Great, actually." A flicker of heat creeps into my cheeks. "The sex is amazing." Marlena snorts softly, shaking her head, but I press on, quieter now. "But… he's worried I'm being targeted."

Her expression sharpens, confusion flashing across her face. "Why would he think that?"

I let out a breath and lean forward, elbows braced against my knees. My gaze shifts down toward the gravel underfoot, and I nudge a piece with the toe of my boot. I'm hesitant, like rolling gravel or not looking at her, won't push her to keep asking.

So I give in and kick the gravel piece away before bringing my eyes to hers. "Because of this card I found on my doorstep a few weeks ago that I thought was some kind of prank, and this note Emilio found at Bailey and Liam's murder scene… they're written in the same handwriting."

The smirk fades from her face entirely, replaced by something brittle. "Rae… are you being threatened?"

"Yes and no." I drag a hand through my hair, frustration hot in my chest. "The note never mentioned me specifically. But on the card… I got asked if my fate would be the same." I pause, the memory of that line sharp and sour. "So… I don't know. Emilio doesn't want to take any chances. He wasn't exactly thrilled about me going to school today, but I reminded him that he won't always be around to protect me. I have to be able to stand on my own, or there's no point in him teaching me self-defense or how to shoot a gun. Besides, he can't just abandon his job to babysit me. I'd rather he be out there catching criminals and looking for this killer than hovering over me every second."

Marlena blinks, then quirks a brow. "He taught you how to shoot a gun?"

"Yes," I answer, my lips twitching at the corners, "and self-defense. Although… the self-defense training was a lot more fun." I wink.

"Oh?" she questions, but then her eyes light up as she figures the answer out herself. "Ohhh." A laugh bursts out of her.

I nod, biting back my own grin, before laughing with her.

"The thrill was wondering if someone was gonna wander in on us," I admit.

Her jaw drops, then she squeals, smacking my arm. "You did it in public, too?! You kinky bitch."

"Semi-public," I correct quickly, giggling with her. "It was during the overnight shift at the station. There weren't a lot of people in at that time."

Before Marlena can tease me further, the sound of my name cuts through the air.

"Miss Carson."

I glance up, startled, and find Professor Henley standing only a few feet away. He moves toward us with that same deliberate stride I've come to expect from him—measured, controlled, as though every step has already been mapped out. His expression is calm, composed, but his eyes… his eyes are too intent.

He stops directly in front of us, and his gaze finds mine first. It lingers, steady and unblinking, and I shift uncomfortably on the bench.

"I wanted to offer my condolences," he says, his voice even, smooth, carefully pitched to sound sincere. "I know

Khloe was your friend, and I'm deeply sorry for your loss." His attention flicks briefly to Marlena, acknowledging her presence, before returning to me with the same unwavering focus. "And Liam, Bailey… such senseless tragedies. I'm glad to see you back in class, despite everything."

Beside me, Marlena stiffens, her fingers brushing my arm like she's anchoring me to the bench.

"Um… thank you, Professor," I murmur. My voice feels caught in my throat, paper-thin. He inclines his head, but he doesn't step away right away. His gaze lingers, weighted, as if there's more he wants to say but won't.

Marlena squeezes my hand once more, the unease lingering between us as Henley walks away.

The library doors swing shut behind Tessa and me, and for the first time all day, the air feels bearable. It's cooler now, quiet in that late hour way that makes every sound carry. We stayed way later than we planned—one hour of studying turned into three, most of which had nothing to do with studying and instead was spent talking to get our minds off the chaos that has erupted in our lives (or more specifically mine). Anything to stop thinking about everything that's been happening lately—the deaths, the tension, the big possibility that a serial killer is hunting me.

I hitch my book bag higher and scan the courtyard. The broad lawn is mostly empty. Lamps cast pale circles across the brick paths, and the buildings sit dark except for a few classroom windows still lit. A patrol car idles near the edge of the quad, lights off, engine a low hum. The police presence has thinned now that the campus has emptied for the most part. Almost everyone has either left for their off-campus homes or returned to their dorms for the night, thanks to the new curfew the university set, because they're convinced it will help.

A curfew will solve jack shit.

An officer stands near the library steps. I tip my chin; he sweeps the trees and the walkway, not us, and gives a distracted nod. Tessa falls in beside me, and we cut across the brick toward the student union. My boots scuff the brick, and Tessa's sneakers whisper beside me. A couple of stragglers cut across the far side of the lawn with heads down, bags slung tight. The university banners hanging from the light poles snap once in a weak gust and then go still again.

"What do you want to pick up for dinner?" Tessa asks as we pass the alumni plaza and the shuttered food court.

"I don't know, Mexican maybe? If the birria place is open, maybe we can get that," I reply with a shrug.

"I'm pretty sure they are. I'll call and place an order for pick up," she says as she digs her phone out of her purse.

I nod, but my focus has drifted. The hairs at my nape prickle, and I slow without meaning to. Every few paces, I look back. The walkways behind us are empty—just the line of trees, the benches, the soft wash of light from windows where the lights were left on. No footsteps. No voices.

Still, the feeling clings.

I stop at the corner where the Greek houses start, the big porches and columns gone quiet for the night. I scan the sidewalk, the hedges, the shadowed gaps between buildings. Besides the cruiser creeping down the road with its lights flashing, I see no one. And that's what bothers me. Whatever I'm feeling, it's not like whoever *might* be following me would make themselves known.

Although now would be their chance.

If this fucker could take down two people in the middle of downtown without anyone knowing, I'm sure Tessa and I are no issue. But somehow I don't think I'm on the menu tonight.

"Rae?" Tessa's voice pulls me back. I blink and turn to

face her. She's already a few steps ahead, frowning back at me. "You okay?"

"Uh, yeah," I say. "Just thought I saw… something. Probably nothing."

She studies me like she doesn't quite buy it, then glances back at her phone. "Okay, well, I called the restaurant. I guess they are closing soon, so they couldn't get an order in for us."

"Damn." I blow out a slow breath. "Well, we can do Chipotle if you're good with that."

"Chipotle sounds delicious." Tessa smiles. I try to match it despite the continued uneasiness I'm feeling.

We angle toward the underpass. The road above hums with steady traffic, and the tunnel drops in front of us, long and low—the lights along the ceiling stutter in a few places. I sigh and grip the straps of my bag tightly as we walk through the underpass. Our steps echo off the concrete. A car crosses above, and the sound rolls through the passage like a wave.

I keep glancing at the openings at either end, counting breaths, counting seconds.

We pop out the far side and jog to the crosswalk. The Highland Avenue structure rises in tiers of concrete, open railings along each level, stairs spiral upwards at the corners, and elevators in glass shafts on both ends. The ground floor is mostly empty now, save for a few cars.

I jab the call button and rock on my heels as we wait. Tessa is still going on about something, but it's all noise. My focus is tuned in to everything else around me: the crickets, the sounds of cars rolling past, sirens wailing in the distance. I'm still uneasy and can still feel the sensation that someone is watching me. After what feels like a damn lifetime, the elevator dings and the metal doors slide apart. We step in. The panel light for "3" gives a tired glow when I press it. The car hums and lurches when it starts its ascent. My reflection stares back at me in the warped stainless steel wall—eyes too wide, mouth a hard line. I blink and force my shoulders down.

When the doors part on the third floor, the level is almost bare—just a few scattered cars, the concrete lanes yawning between them. Night presses in from the open sides. I step out and drift toward the waist-high wall, that same bad feeling tugging me forward like a hook in my ribs.

"Keys," Tessa says behind me. "Where'd you—Rae?"

"Hang on."

I plant my palms on the rough concrete and lean over, peering down to the ground floor. The area around the entrance isn't well lit, but it's enough that I can still make out that someone is down there.

He stands just beyond the mouth of the garage, centered in the gap. All black. Face hidden behind a white mask that erases everything human.

He's already looking up at me.

Waiting.

My stomach drops. For a second, I can't pull air.

His hand lifts, metal glinting in the light as he gives me a slow, almost friendly wave. It's then that I catch what he's waving. The metal takes shape as the light whispers over it. He's waving a knife, taunting me.

"Tessa!" I call, turning towards her. She stops a few feet ahead, her face contorting into confusion.

She's a few steps ahead and whirls around, confused. "What are you—"

"Someone *was* following me," I choke out.

"What do you mean someone was following you?"

"Look for yourself," I say, pointing down below.

She comes to the wall, frowns, and leans over with me. "There's no one there, babe."

I blink and snap my head back. The space below is empty. No mask. No figure. No *knife*.

"The fuck do you mean there's no one there?" I mutter, looking below again. "I swear to God he was just there."

"What did you see?" she asks, her tone soft.

"Someone in black clothes and a white mask. He was just standing there, looking up at me, and then he waved his knife at me." I scan below, looking at every corner I can see. I shift my gaze towards the stairs, run over to them, and peer over the railing. Nothing. "I know he was there. I'm not crazy."

Tessa checks again, slower, eyes working corner to corner. "I believe you saw what you did," she says, when I rejoin her side. "He's probably hiding somewhere you can't see." I nod as I peer over the wall again. "You should definitely tell Emilio. He'll want to know."

"I will." I peel away from the wall, every nerve burning. The empty space where he'd been feels worse than if he were still there. At least then I'd know where he was.

Tessa hooks her arm in mine, and we move quickly towards my Kia. I shove my hand into my purse and yank it out, metal clicking against each other as my hands fumble with the fob. The lock chirp echoes too loudly off the concrete. I hand the key to Tessa, and we slide in fast, doors slamming. I thumb the lock button twice and keep my eyes on the open side of the level. Nothing moves. Tessa's hands are tight on the wheel even before the engine turns over.

Tessa pulls toward the exit, checking mirrors, checking again. I stare out over the edge until the sightline breaks and the ground level drops out of view. Only then do I let a breath fall out of me.

Express Newspaper
FEAR GRIPS CITY AFTER DOUBLE HOMICIDE NEAR UNIVERSITY. POSSIBLE WORK OF A SERIAL KILLER?

TWENTY-FIVE
RIPPER

Fear Grips City After Double Homicide Near University. Possible Work of a Serial Killer?

THE HEADLINE BLEEDS across the front page, letters bold and black, daring anyone to look away. They never do. Fear is magnetic—more potent than sex, than hunger, than prayer. People devour it with their morning coffee, let it stain the edges of their tongues as they pretend the world hasn't tilted. I savor that. I savor how the name tastes in mouths I will never meet.

With three murders under my belt, the media has since named me Ripper Incarnate. A modern-day legend reborn, stalking the cracks of this desert city while the sun burns high overhead. It's fitting in a sense. I'm not ridding the world of trash or filth.

I'm instead after something much more important—a legacy character in this horror story.

It has been several days since I tore apart that bitch and her boytoy, and I'm still seething. I can still feel the pain from that mistake. I've never let anyone get the drop on me before, and it will never happen again.

Pride will get you killed; sloppiness will get you caught, and I don't want either.

As much as I enjoy stalking the streets like the ripper they claim me to be, there are too many variables where something could go wrong, and that was proven with Bailey and Liam's murders.

I prefer to plan and take my victims by surprise, have them believe that just because they are behind locked doors, they are safe, when in reality, they are far from it. Locked doors have never stopped me. Fourth-story apartments have never stopped me. I was in Khloe's apartment before anyone could suspect anything, and getting out was just as easy with the fire escape.

Detail is the backbone of survival.

Tonight is no different. While extra police patrol the university, they often overlook the fact that the rest of the city still exists. They think my territory is the campus because that's where three of them fell. Cute assumption. My target has nothing to do with the university or its students.

It's someone worth more of my time, and eventually, I will get to her, but until then, I'll enjoy playing with my food and inflicting psychological pain. Psychological pain is as much an art as the physical act.

I could easily end this game, but where's the fun in that? Where's the artistry? The story? One best friend and two side characters are only a prologue. I doubt she's even figured out that all of this is because of her. Perhaps tonight, she will.

The screen fights me for a beat—metal fibers rasping under the tip of my knife, a small, stubborn argument before it gives. I press the blade harder, levering at the corner until the frame pops free with a brittle snap that sounds louder than it should in the hush. I hook the mesh, pry it free, and toss the useless thing aside without bothering to look where it lands.

The window itself yields without effort. There's no click of a lock, no stubborn resistance. She didn't lock it, such a stupid move on her part. People are always so careful about the visible things—the deadbolt, the chain—then leave a hairline seam of invitation and call it safety. That little seam is the honest betrayal, the private faith people hand to glass and a plastic catch and then forget. They curl up with their phones, comfort themselves with streaming noise, and assume nothing will test that sliver of trust. They never imagine a hand on the other side of the glass.

They never imagine me.

Pocketing my knife, I press my palm against the window frame and ease it open. The pane slides up with a faint groan. I slip through the gap in one smooth motion, landing on the carpet below. It swallows my boots completely, the thick plush material muffling the sound before it could even form. I stay still for a moment, letting my eyes adjust to the dark. The only movement comes from the faint flicker of light bleeding through the open doorway ahead. It spills across the floor in pale stripes, flashing weakly against the wall each time the television changes scenes. The sound reaches me in waves—laughter, bright and hollow, clashing against the quiet. It rises, falls, then bursts again, a loop of synthetic cheer masking the truth that the house is otherwise dead silent. It's the perfect kind of noise. Mindless, and loud enough to drown out almost anything—even her last scream.

I move with patience, sliding across the floor like a shadow. My body tilts forward, each step deliberate and placed with care, weight spread across the balls of my feet, the soles pressing into the softer edges of the floorboards where time hasn't made them shift and groan. The air hums faintly with static from the television, and snippets of songs, people advertising stupid shit to gullible buyers, a man attempting to tell a story too fast. Scroll. New voice. New song. Again and again.

I stand in the doorway between the living room and the hallway and find her immediately.

She's curled up in a recliner, body small and soft against the fabric. One leg is tucked under her, and her chin dips toward the glow in her palm. The blue light traces the delicate hollow of her throat, flickers across the curve of her cheek, and catches the faint sheen of her lip gloss when she bites down in concentration. Her hair—black streaked with washed-out pink—slides forward, curtaining half her face, leaving one pale shoulder exposed to the lamplight. She shifts, and the fabric of her oversized pale pink t-shirt rides up slightly, revealing smooth skin above the waistband of her matching shorts. Her foot taps against the recliner leg in a steady rhythm—tap, tap, tap—a small, absent sound that punctuates the muffled laugh track coming from the TV. She's completely absorbed, lost to her glowing screen, scrolling through an endless feed of meaningless faces, songs, and jokes.

She's completely unaware of my presence looming in the shadows of her living room.

I watch her. I let the sight build, stretch, and pull tight inside me like the string of a bow drawn, waiting to release. She's still lost in her little world, and I can see the rise and fall of her shoulders, slow and even—completely at ease. My pulse, on the other hand, beats steady and deep, every thud echoing through my skull as I wait for the moment.

Patience. That's what separates me from the rest.

The art isn't in the kill—it's in the waiting, in the build-up. The longer I let it stretch, the sharper the moment will feel when it finally breaks.

She shifts in her seat, the phone's light flashing across her cheek. That's when I step closer, silent but no longer hiding, my shadow spilling long across her shoulder. The knife slides into my grip, weight balanced. I flex once, just to feel the give of my glove against the steel. I take another step just as the TV coughs out a burst of laughter. The floorboard beneath my boot complains, a single sharp creak that snaps through the air just as the laughter quiets.

Her head jerks up.

The look that blooms in her eyes is the exact thing I've been waiting for—confusion collapsing into fear that ignites so fast it's almost beautiful. One moment, she's locked inside her little private world, thumbs moving like a metronome over the tiny glass screen. Next, her pupils blow wide, and I can see the exact second her brain scrambles to rearrange reality around the fact that she is not alone in this house.

The first sound she makes is not a civilized noise. It rips out of her, half a bark, half a sob, the raw animal alarm that leaves the throat before the mind can make sense of it. She jerks upright so fast the recliner rocks back; her phone skitters from her hand and bounces across the floor. A mug upends and explodes against the hardwood, ceramic shards scattering across the floor in a constellation. The spilled coffee spreads in a slow, uneven pool, its scent sharp in the air.

She moves like someone yanked the floor out from under her—pure, blinding motion—hands and feet a mess of impulses.

"What the fuck?" she spits, a string of disbelief and protests.

The knife flashes as I shift my grip, the lamplight accentuating the serrated edge. Realization slams into her then. She knows now. There is no parsing it away.

I move. My steps are measured, patient—every motion designed to close the distance without giving her time to find logic. She's frozen in fear, and I take the opportunity and lunge.

My blade whistles through the air in a clean arc. She twists, and the steel bites into the couch where her shoulder was a breath before. The sound of fabric swallowing metal with a muffled thud—and it snaps something in me. The miss is a little thrill—frustration braided with joy.

The chase is its own intoxication.

She scrambles, her bare foot coming down hard on a shard of porcelain hidden in the rug. The scream that rips out of her is sharp and unfiltered, a burst of pain and panic that fills the room. She collapses to her knees, one hand clutching the floor for balance while the other presses against her heel. Blood wells up fast, a dark streak crawling down her skin and spreading across the fibers beneath her.

For a split second, everything narrows—her pain, her breathing, the ragged sound of it tearing through the air. It's all I hear. I rip the knife free from the couch, the fabric sighing as the blade slides loose. The sight of her struggling to stand sharpens everything.

I can almost feel her pulse in the room, wild and erratic.

She pushes herself up, trembling but desperate. Her body jerks into motion, fueled by instinct more than thought. She bolts toward the hallway, each step slapping against the runner, the trail of her blood marking every footprint she leaves behind. The sound is chaos—her gasping breaths, the wet drag of her feet, the squeak of the boards beneath us.

I lunge again. My hand snags the sleeve of her shirt, fingers curling into the soft cotton. She twists hard, the fabric tearing as she wrenches herself free with a strength born of panic.

I don't hesitate. I move with her. The knife comes down, fast and certain.

The blade bites into her side, slicing through fabric and skin in one motion.

She jerks mid-stride, her cry breaking apart before it becomes a scream. Blood wells and darkens the cotton, a spreading stain that slicks her fingers when she presses them uselessly against the wound. She staggers, her breath coming in broken gasps.

Her scream finally comes, then—high, shrill, and raw. It bounces off the narrow walls in jagged echoes.

She runs anyway, limping, the hand at her side trying to staunch what she can as she claws for the next inch of distance. Every footprint she leaves is a red thumbprint on the runner, a messy breadcrumb trail that tells me exactly where she's been and where she's going.

I follow, staying close enough to hear the hitch in her breath, the way her sobs tear into words that never form. Her palm smears blood along the wall as she scrabbles by; the print gleams, bright and impossible against the pale paint. She flings herself at the nearest door, fingers scrabbling at the knob like a drowning woman at a lifeline.

I am at the door in two strides and meet the frame with my shoulder just as she secures the lock. The impact is solid; the grain groans.

She braces the other side, her body pressed against the panels. I slam into the door again before driving my knife through the splintered wood. She screams and loses leverage. I yank the blade free, then drive my boot into the edge, ripping the lock from the frame. The panel snaps with a hard, obscene crack, and the door bursts inward, timber exploding into the room in a scatter of splinters. The door ricochets off the wall; pieces of wood rain across the threshold like broken teeth.

The bathroom is small and bright, its innocence almost laughable. The shower curtain still ripples from the burst of air when I broke the door open, a faint tremor lingering in the room like it already knows what's coming. I am very much looking forward to redecorating with the spray of her blood.

Fear has her backed into the corner, trapped by the walls and by me. One hand clings to the sink for balance, the other pressed tightly to her side in a futile attempt to slow the bleeding. The blood slips through her fingers anyway, trickling down her arm in a steady line, dripping onto the tile and spreading in uneven streaks that pool near her feet. The tremor running through her body rattles the bottles on the edge of the sink, a nervous percussion that fills the room.

Her eyes flick between me and the doorway, wild with desperation, searching for an escape that doesn't exist. The panic in her gaze is electric, thrumming through the space, feeding something deep and primal inside me.

It's almost beautiful, the way terror transforms a room.

Almost enough to make me take my time.

"What do you want?" she gasps, voice breaking, eyes darting wildly for anything she can turn into a weapon.

Her hands scramble over the counter, closing around whatever she can reach—a bottle of mouthwash, a ceramic soap dish, the plunger. Her fingers shake so violently that the bottle slips, sloshing blue liquid across the sink before she hurls it. It bursts against my chest, soaking through my jacket, splattering across the mirror behind me. The soap dish follows, cracking against my shoulder and exploding into pieces that scatter around her feet. She's screaming again, a hoarse, panicked sound that tears at the edges. The plunger comes last, swinging wide, clumsy, and desperate. I sidestep it easily, a scowl of disgust forming under my mask, and watch it bounce uselessly down the hallway.

Rage warms me in a different place than the plan. Her flinging hands are volatility—improvisation—and for a breath I appreciate the sound of her trying.

But I've had enough.

Her breathing breaks apart, uneven and sharp, every inhale a fight. The sound wavers between a sob and a gasp, filling the small room until it drowns everything else out. She presses her back against the cold tile, eyes wild, searching for an escape that doesn't exist. Her bare feet slip on the wet floor as she tries to keep her balance, one hand clamped tight over the wound at her side. Blood seeps through her fingers and runs down her arm, dripping to the tile in thin, uneven streaks. The other hand gropes backward, feeling along the wall as if she could somehow make it open, as if sheer panic might force it to give her a way out.

I take a step closer. The space between us closes fast.

Her eyes find mine—wide and frantic as they dart between the knife and the exit. "Please," she manages, voice small and shaking. "Please, don't—"

I move before she can finish.

The knife cuts through the air, glinting under the harsh bathroom light before it sinks deep into her abdomen. Her whole body jerks. A guttural noise tears from her throat—half a gasp, half a sob. I push forward, driving her back until her hips slam into the edge of the sink, the force making bottles topple and rattle around us. Her hands are everywhere—grabbing at my jacket, clawing for my arms, pushing against me with every ounce of strength she has left. Her nails catch my skin through the fabric, frantic and useless. Then one hand lunges upward, catching the edge of my mask. She yanks it off in a desperate pull.

For a moment, our eyes meet. Her eyes widen—recognition, shock, and disbelief flickering through them in quick succession. A question forms on her lips, but I cut her off by pulling the knife out, splattering blood across my sweater and surrounding surfaces. I drive it into her again. The second thrust penetrates between the ribs, and the third buries the blade to the hilt below it. I can feel the steel scrape against her rib as I twist, slicing through viscera. Her body convulses with each hit, her strength fading fast. She's still trying to speak, to scream, but all that comes out is a soft wheeze, a wet, rattling sound that fills the space between us. I drive my knife into her once more, right between her breasts. She gasps, coughing up blood as she collapses against me, heavy and limp. I hold her, a smirk curled on my lips as I watch the life in her fade away.

I pull my knife free slowly, the wet sound it makes when it leaves her flesh is music to my ears.

Her body stills, and I let go, letting gravity take her. She slides down the wall, smearing blood in uneven streaks as she goes. She crumples into the tub, hitting the porcelain with a hollow thud. The hollow impact echoes around the small bathroom. The shower curtain jerks, the plastic rings snapping one by one until it tears from the rod and falls with her. The fabric envelops her body, tangling in her limbs, except for the one leg that hangs over the edge of the tub. Her head lolls sideways, eyes half open and glassy.

Blood seeps fast, pooling beneath her and spreading along the seams of the tub floor. The color dulls as it mixes with water left from her earlier shower, smearing into the grout. The mask she tore from me still hangs from her hand, fingers stiffening around it. I look at it for a long moment, then decide to leave it. Let them find it. Let the media put a face (albeit a mask) to the carnage I am responsible for. Her blood is already smeared across the plastic anyway, and I've prepared for a moment like this. I have another for incidents like this, just in case.

I crouch beside her, my chest rising steadily as I watch the life drain from her. It truly is a beautiful sight. Not just the blood, but the whole masterpiece. There is something truly gratifying about knowing that I held her life in my hands and got to decide when it ended and how.

Smirking, I dip my gloved fingers into one of the new wounds, feeling the warmth of the blood before I pull away. Then I stand and press those fingers to the wall, dragging them across the tile in thick red strokes.

YOU CAN'T SAVE RAELYNN. NO ONE CAN. SHE WILL BE MINE.

The letters gleam wet under the bathroom light. The words stand out stark against the pale wall. I wipe the blade on the pink towel beside the shower, then slide it into my pocket. I take one last look, my eyes shifting between her body, the blood, and the message, and step into the hallway. The noise of the sitcom blooms again in the living room as if nothing had happened, as if the world had already decided to move on. I head back to the room I had entered, just a few feet from the bathroom, climb out the window I came in, and melt into the night.

SCENE
CRIME
SCENE
OFFICER
STOP
STOP

TWENTY-SIX
EMILIO

THE SCENE within the house is chaotic. Ceramic shards crunch under my boots, littering both the living room and the bathroom floor. Coffee has puddled and dried tacky across the hardwood. Blood drags through the hallway in broken streaks and handprints, a morbid map of whatever hell this poor girl went through. In the bathroom, a bottle of mouthwash has spilled across the tile, blue liquid mixing with dark pools of blood until it runs in thin ribbons into the grout. The air is suffocatingly thick with a mix of the metallic stench of blood and mint.

The bathroom looks like a slaughterhouse. Blood is everywhere—on the floor, speckled up the vanity, cast across the shower tile. The pattern pulls the eye to the tub, to where she took her last breath. She's half in, half out—left leg hanging over the rim, while the rest of her is tangled in the shower curtain that came down with her. In her right hand, caught tight between stiff fingers, is a white vinyl mask smeared with dried blood. She most likely yanked it off during a struggle. But why didn't he grab it? Is there a reason he left it? My brows furrow as I take in the rest of the bathroom. But what stops me cold isn't the body, the blood, or the mask…

It's the message written on the wall.

The letters are still wet when I read them. Eleven words—each one a slick, brutal cut—and they land in my gut like punches. For a second, the room tilts and my hands go numb. Those eleven little knives written in blood, wake something old and violent inside me. The same blind fury I carried as a kid when my father beat my mother, then turned on me, is nearly the exact same rage I'm feeling reading these eleven fucking words smeared across the wall, and it makes my vision narrow to that smear of red and nothing else.

CSU threads around me, moving with careful choreography. Cameras pop every few seconds as they photograph every piece of evidence. I barely register when one ushers me out of the bathroom so they can collect the rest of the puzzle pieces that could hopefully help us catch the fucker that did this, starting with whatever they can hopefully get from the mask. After swabbing the mask, they move to her fingernails. They swab the nail beds and scrape under them. Every scrap is handled, every droplet photographed, labeled, sealed. They put numbers next to footprints, measure the smear patterns, and photograph the angle of the wounds.

After several minutes, a black bag is brought in and laid out across the floor. My fists tighten as I watch them lift the girl out of the tub. The shower curtain—tacky with blood where it clings to her skin—peels away as they wrestle the plastic from her. The curtain comes off in one sticky sheet and is folded, catalogued, and bagged like everything else. Everything necessary and valuable is tucked away for safekeeping—except for the message on the wall. That still sits there, drying into the seams of the tile.

He's full on taunting me now. Taunting her. This message only confirms my suspicion. A psychopath is after Raelynn, and it's only a matter of time before he decides he's psychologically tortured her enough, broken her down enough, that he finally moves in for the kill.

But the thought of him touching her, of her being next, makes something dark and violent rise in me.

My nails dig into my palms until I feel the sharp sting of skin breaking as anger surges through me. My fists clench tighter, blood rushing hot behind my eyes as they zip the bag closed, sealing up another person within Raelynn's circle. The second the team wheels the body past, I turn on my heel and push through the doorway, the hinges rattling behind me. The night air does absolutely nothing to cool the fire in me. I pace, breathing hard, trying to keep myself grounded, but every breath only fans the flames higher. I slam my fist into the stucco wall beside the door. The crack of impact echoes across the yard. Pain flashes up my arm, followed by the sting of torn skin, and I welcome it. Blood wells up through my knuckles, running down to my wrist.

Kline's voice drifts over the yard. He's standing a few feet from the porch with the roommate who found the body. The poor girl looks traumatized. Her McDonald's uniform is rumpled, the name tag hanging sideways. Tangled strands of strawberry blonde hair stick out of her bun. Mascara runs down her freckled cheeks in messy black streaks, and her hands—stained red—are shaking so hard she can barely hold onto her phone. There's blood smeared across the front of her uniform from when she tried to help but then realized too late that her roommate was long gone before she got there.

Her swollen red eyes fix on me, then to the blood dripping from my knuckles, before dropping away, lip trembling. Kline angles himself to block her view of the door and whatever she might see behind me.

He murmurs, something comforting or reassuring, is my guess, and gives her bicep a gentle squeeze before glancing towards me. "Give me one minute," he tells her softly. "I'll be right back." When she nods faintly, he gives her a small smile before stepping away.

He turns toward me and climbs the porch steps. His eyes sweep over me once, lingering on the blood spattering between my boots. My hand is already swelling, the skin split wide open, and my knuckles raw. The adrenaline in my veins has my heart pounding so hard I can hear it.

"Emilio," he says—my name carrying both a warning and a question.

"I'm fine," I mutter, even though I can't bring myself to unclench my fists. He gives me a stern look, definitely not buying my lie. I am practically vibrating with unspent rage.

"You're not fine. What is it?" he presses.

I drag my uninjured hand through my hair, the motion jerky. My breath shakes as I try to steady it. "He left another note," I say finally, voice low, rough. "This time addressed to Rae."

Kline's face hardens. "What did it say? I've kind of been occupied out here since arriving on scene."

"He's taunting us," I answer, jaw tight. "Said I won't be able to save her. No one will, and that she's his."

"Fuck." The word comes out on a breath, his jaw locking as he looks past me toward the house. "They're going to want to talk to her," he says after a beat. "You know that, right?"

"I know," I mutter. I don't want that for her. She's been through enough. But now that she is being personally named, they're going to want to wring every ounce of information out of her to understand why people she knows are dying and why she is being hunted.

He sighs and rests his hand on my shoulder. I know it's meant to be comforting, but my muscles tense instead.

"Go," he says, voice steady but soft. "I'll handle shit with the detective. You need to be with her, make sure she's safe and not alone. I'll tell them she'll come in tomorrow to give her statement. That'll buy you some time." He gives my shoulder a firm squeeze before pulling back.

I nod once. "Thanks."

Kline's mouth lifts in a half-smirk that doesn't reach his eyes. "You owe me, amigo," he teases quietly. "Now get that hand wrapped and go see your girl."

A dry laugh escapes me, more breath than sound. I glance down at my hand. The skin is already swollen, streaked with blood that keeps dripping in steady drops to the porch. I flex my fingers, wincing when the skin pulls, but the pain helps clear my head. I honestly wasn't expecting Kline to take over for me. But I sure as fuck was appreciative of it.

Out by the curb, the block is painted in red and blue light. Patrol units idle at both ends of the street to hold the perimeter, engines rumbling low. Lights pulse over the dark windows of nearby houses. A few neighbors stand behind the yellow tape, faces pale and drawn, whispering to each other. Some record with their phones, screens glowing ghostly against their faces. A news van creeps around the corner, slowing as it approaches the scene like a vulture spotting prey, their logo gleaming in the wash of headlights. I ignore it all and start toward my cruiser. Gravel crunches under my boots, every step pulling me farther from the house. The message on the wall burns behind my eyes, refusing to fade.

I don't care what this fucker thinks will happen. I *will* not let him have her. I *can* save her. I will be by her side, making sure she is safe, because it does not matter if the door is locked, if the city puts on a curfew, or you're in public, *he* has proven nothing will fucking stop him. Safety is a fucking illusion to a serial killer. Where there is a will, there is a way.

And he seems to always find a fucking way. I'm done with it. I'm done with this fucker.

I'll stand at her side. I'll break rules, burn bridges, risk my badge, whatever it fucking takes. If it costs me everything to keep her safe, then so be it. Let him come, let him test me. He's picked the wrong woman to haunt and the wrong man to bait. This bastard is playing a game he doesn't understand. A game I will make sure he fucking loses.

I swear to God, on my fucking life, he will not get her. Not while I'm still breathing.

Del
F12
End
PgUp
PgDn
Home

TWENTY-SEVEN
RAELYNN

EVERY DOOR, every window in this damn apartment is locked—and I still don't feel safe.

When Tessa and I got home, I took Max for a quick walk, not daring to go farther than the end of the building. My nerves were still shot, my pulse a constant drum beneath my skin. I kept my taser in one hand, my kubaton in the other, and Max's leash looped tight around my wrist. Pepper spray sat ready in my jacket pocket, though it would probably blind me before it did anything to him because the fucker is wearing a mask.

After a *very* long pee, Max and I *finally* headed back to the apartment. Knowing I was still on edge, Tessa and I tore through the apartment like we were prepping for a siege. Every lock, every latch, every goddamn window was secured. I checked the kitchen and bedrooms twice while she went over the living room and back door. Then we switched and did it again, just to be sure. The blinds are shut tight. Curtains drawn. We secured the screen door, the front door, the patio door, and even jammed the broom handle into the sliding track so it can't be forced open. And when that still didn't feel like enough, we dragged the entry table over and stuck it in front of the door.

After seeing him following me at school, the feeling that he would come here—try something—hasn't left. I keep telling myself I'm overreacting, but that voice in the back of my head won't shut up. I also couldn't shake the gut-deep certainty that someone was in danger tonight. Maybe not me, not yet—but someone. And there's nothing I can do to stop it. That helplessness gnaws at me, sharp and constant, like it's digging under my skin and taking root.

I did what I could. I texted Marlena to let her and Austin know to lock their doors and windows. She responded quickly, assuring me they would. But once I put my phone down, I realized I couldn't think of anyone else to warn, and that hit harder than I expected.

There are so many people who are a part of my life in some way: friends, classmates, study partners, and those I grab coffee with on occasion. Someone is picking apart my life, murdering people I know or am close to, just to torture me. And the thought that one of them might not wake up tomorrow makes my stomach twist. I keep wondering if I should've done more, said more, reached out to more people. But the truth is, no matter how many locks I check or texts I send, it won't change what's coming.

Nothing has stopped him up to this point.

The shrill ring of my phone slices through the heavy silence like a blade, jerking both Tessa and me awake. My heart slams against my ribs, pulse pounding in my ears as I look around the darkened living room, confused and disoriented. It doesn't take long for my brain to catch up and remember tonight's events. I guess, at some point, after securing the apartment to the best of our ability, Tessa and I must have fallen asleep.

Tessa stirs beside me on the couch, a groggy sound catching in her throat. "What the hell…" she mutters, rubbing at her neck.

The phone's glow cuts across the room in rhythmic flashes. Emilio's name burns on the screen, his contact photo flickering with every vibration. My stomach sinks. I snatch the phone off the table, nearly dropping it in my haste.

"Emilio?" My voice comes out rough, the sleep still clinging to it.

"Hey, baby," he replies, voice low. There is a tightness in his voice, one I have begun to recognize as something has happened, and it typically isn't good.

"Hi," I reply softly, pulling the phone away just long enough to glance at the time. It is nearing midnight. My pulse quickens. "What's going on?"

There's a pause on the line, a soft exhale, like he's trying to decide how to word something he doesn't want to say. "Nothing good," he finally says. "I'm heading your way soon and will explain, but until then, do me a favor."

My chest tightens. "Okay…?"

"Lock your doors. Don't open up for anyone. I'll call when I'm there."

My eyes shift between the patio and the front door. The blinds are drawn, but because of the missing strips (due to their poor quality and Max's roughhousing), there are several spaces where anyone can see through. The broom handle is still, however, wedged in the track, and the entry table is still pressed tight against the front door, but looking at them now, they suddenly feel useless.

"They're already locked," I say, though my voice sounds unsure even to me.

"Good," he replies. "I had to grab a few things from the station, but I'll be there as soon as possible."

Before I can respond, Max lifts his head from where he's sprawled on the rug. His ears prick forward, and then he growls—low, deep, rumbling through his chest. The sound freezes me.

"Baby?" Emilio's voice comes through the line, edged with concern.

"Hold on," I whisper, rising from the couch. Max follows instantly, his growl growing louder, more urgent. His hackles rise, body rigid, eyes fixed on the sliding glass door.

Tessa sits up, her brow furrowed as her eyes shift between Max and me. "Rae? What's wrong?" she asks, her voice barely above a whisper.

"Rae, talk to me," Emilio demands. "What's happening?"

"I think—" I swallow hard. "I think someone's out there."

"What?" both Tessa and Emilio exclaim, their tones equally alert.

Tessa sits up as I tiptoe across the room to the light switch beside the door. My hand hovers over the light switch, my breath shallow. Max's growl turns into a low snarl, lips curling back to show his teeth.

The moment I flip on the light, Max explodes into barking, lunging toward the patio. His claws scrape against the glass, the sound sharp and frantic. Just beyond the glass stands a figure—tall, motionless. The porch light flickers over him, and for a heartbeat, the world narrows to the expressionless, white mask.

It's the same mask I saw at the parking garage.

"Emilio!" I scream into the phone, my voice breaking as I stumble backward. "He's here!"

The man tilts his head slowly, studying me from behind that blank façade, unfazed by Max's aggressiveness, then reaches into his pocket and pulls out a knife. The light glints off the silver blade, accenting every groove of the serrations, as he raises it and waves it tauntingly. My heart slams against my rib cage as he moves—rounding the patio and vanishing from my line of sight. But I know where he is going, and so does Max. He bolts to the other side of the room to the front door just as several loud metallic bangs sound off. The screen door rattles violently. Another hit follows, metal shrieking under the force.

Tessa scrambles to her feet, knocking into the coffee table as Max's barking fills the room. "Oh my god, Raelynn!" she cries, stumbling backward and crashing to the floor.

The pounding stops. For one dreadful second, there's silence, the only sounds filling the space are mine and Tessa's heavy breathing, Max's low growls, and Emilio's voice coming through my phone's speaker.

"Rae!" Emilio's voice booms from my phone, still clutched in my hand. "Talk to me! What's happening?"

"I-I don't know," I reply softly.

But after the words leave my mouth, I hear it. The slow, creaking sound of the screen door being forced open—metal groans, hinges screech, and my stomach drops.

"He's trying the door!" I scream into the phone, panic lacing every word. The front door shudders under a heavy kick. *THUD.* Then another. Each kick rattles the chain and jolts the entry table forward a hair.

"Listen to me, baby," Emilio orders, his voice firm despite the urgency. "Go hide. Get your room, the closet, somewhere you both can lock yourselves in. I'm almost there, and I'm calling for backup."

"Please hurry!" I cry into my phone as I rush toward Tessa and pull her up by the arm.

The door shudders again. And then, like a nightmare made real, a knife plunges through the wood, splintering it. One strike. Then another. The sound is deafening.

Tessa's screams echo mine as I pull her back; she clings to my arms, her nails digging into my skin. Max's barking becomes wild, frenzied. He lunges at the front door, claws scraping against the hardwood. After the third hit, everything stops. The silence stretches, broken only by my ragged breathing. Max's barks quiet to low growls as he begins pacing the living room in restless, protective strides.

"Where did he go?" Tessa sobs behind me, her voice breaking the fragile stillness.

I shake my head and step back, tugging her with me toward the hallway "I don't kn—"

BANG.

The explosion of sound rips through the air, so loud it feels like the walls shake. The patio door shatters inward in a rain of glass. Shards fly across the room, scattering like glittering knives. I throw my arms up on instinct as screams tear out of both of us.

Max yelps, caught in the blast, then bolts behind the couch with a terrified whine, and my phone slips free from my hand.

"Run! Run now!" I scream, shoving Tessa down the hall the moment I see *him* come into view.

CRIME S
OFFICER
STOP
STOP

TWENTY-EIGHT
EMILIO

THE SHARP, deafening sound of a gunshot splits through my phone's speaker, and a second later, glass explodes into the darkness with a sound that shreds the quiet. Raelynn's scream rips into my ear, thin and animal and full of panic, and my chest caves.

"RAE!" I scream into the speaker, but the line answers me with static and the faint tail of her voice echoing away.

For one terrible second, she's there and then nothing but a silence so loud it hurts.

"Rae!" I shout again, almost a plea this time, fingers tightening until my knuckles protest against the cheap plastic of my phone. Fury and cold fear war in my chest, and I let the anger win for a second. "FUCK!" I drive my injured fist into the passenger side of my truck. A dent forms in the metal beneath my knuckles, and red beads up between the seams of the bandage. The pain grounds me, and I draw in a breath, listening to anything else I can hear. Nothing but silence comes through.

I pray to the fucking gods she's hiding in a good spot, somewhere to give her a good fighting chance, because I don't know what I'll do... no scratch that, I know exactly what I'll fucking do if she is hurt. I'll hunt the bastard down and kill him myself if something happens to her.

He'll get a taste of his own medicine as I rip him to fucking shreds.

I press my forehead to the window, the cool glass steadying me for a moment. "Baby," I breathe into the phone even though the call's gone quiet. My voice drops, tight and raw. "If you can hear me, help is on the way. I'm coming…" I let the word hang there, then twist it into a promise and a warning as I lift my head off the glass. "And if you can hear me, *Ripper*," I pause, spitting out his name like it's acid on my tongue, every syllable a curse. "Touch her and it'll be the last thing you ever fucking do."

Ending the call, with shaking fingers, I dial 911. It rings twice, twice too fucking many, before Dispatch answers. I don't even give them a chance to speak before I cut in, willing my voice to steady as I yank open the passenger door.

"This is off-duty Officer Emilio Perez, badge number 48274. I need immediate assistance at Catalina Crest Apartments, 9306 E Broadway Boulevard, apartment 151. Home invasion in progress as we speak, suspect is armed and dangerous!" I say quickly as I toss the folders that I had tucked under my arm onto the passenger seat.

The dispatcher's tone sharpens instantly. "Copy that, Officer Perez. Units are being dispatched now. Is anyone injured?"

I slam the passenger door and round the front to the driver's side. "Not that I know of," I say through gritted teeth. "But someone will be if *she* is."

I climb into my truck, jam my keys into the ignition, and twist. It roars to life, the radio spitting out some song. I quickly switch to Bluetooth. The moment my phone connects, I toss it onto the passenger seat and throw my truck in reverse, and back out of the station, gravel spitting from the tires.

"Are you on the property now, Officer?" the dispatcher

asks. Her prying questions are starting to grate on me, but I know she's only doing her job.

"No," I snap, my grip tightening on the steering wheel. "I was on the phone with my girlfriend, Raelynn Carson, when she told me someone was trying to break in. I lost contact with her after I heard gunshots." I take a hard right onto Speedway Boulevard, tires squealing. "Just get someone there fast!" I yell before ending the call.

The city blurs past in streaks of amber light and shadow, every streetlight a heartbeat I can't afford to lose. My pulse hammers in my ears, keeping time with the low snarl of the truck's engine as I push past eighty. Red lights flash ahead and I barely slow, rolling through intersections when they're clear, every nerve locked on the road, on the distance shrinking between me and her. The tires hiss over the wet pavement, the whole truck trembling as I weave through the empty streets. Every second that passes feels like another piece of her slipping away.

I hit the turn for her complex in under ten minutes. The parking lot is dark, except for the distant glow of a few porch lights. I kill my headlights before pulling up as close as I can to her building—to her apartment.

Then I see it.

The patio door, or what's left of it. The glass is gone, blown inward, fragments glittering across the cement like frost. My chest seizes, the air leaving me in a sharp, silent gasp.

I throw my truck into park and pop the center console. I take my Glock, check the magazine and chamber, then grab the flashlight and slide out. My Vans scuff the pavement as I move, flashlight in my left hand, gun up in my right. I cautiously step toward the front door, and my pulse beats erratically at the sight of the split wood. I try the door, noting it's still locked and round back towards the patio. I draw in a breath as I push open the patio gate. It creaks, the sound too loud in the quiet as I slip through. My flashlight drifts over the porch and into the living room, glinting off the shards strewn across the living room floor as I cross the threshold. Glass crunches underfoot as I move further into the room.

A low whimper breaks the quiet. I pivot toward it, gun up, beam low. Max lies crumpled by the couch, panting heavily. His flank glistens wet beneath the light.

"Shit," I mutter, dropping to a crouch beside him. "Hey, buddy." He whines when I touch his head, the sound weak and broken. There's blood slicked around his hind leg, just above the flank. "It's okay, Max, good boy. Save your strength," I drag my palm along his fur once before forcing myself back up.

Turning away from Max, I sweep my flashlight through the rest of the living room and into the kitchen before moving towards the hall. Sirens wail in the distance, growing closer with each passing second.

"Police!" I call out. "If anyone is in here, make yourself known!" I move down the narrow hall on tiptoe, flashlight in my left hand, Glock high in my right. "This is the police," I call out again. "Come out with your hands up!"

Something creaks, and the hair on the back of my neck lifts. I swing the beam toward the sound just as a voice cracks through the dark.

"Emilio?"

My heart jumps at the sound of her voice. "It's me, baby," I answer, lowering my weapon just enough.

A door opens slightly at the end of the hall. Raelynn partially steps out with Tessa clinging to her arm.

"I-Is he gone?" Tessa's voice trembles, eyes wide and glassy.

I open my mouth to answer, but the closet beside me explodes open, and I'm immediately met with something cold that punches through my shoulder with enough force to steal the breath from my lungs. Everything goes wrong in a single, brutal second. My Glock slips from my hand and clatters across the floor. Rae and Tessa scream and retreat into the room, slamming and locking the door. My back slams into the opposite wall, and I gasp for breath. Pain flashes—a hot, immediate line from the joint up through my neck.

"Fuck," I hiss, looking down just long enough to see the hilt buried deep in my shoulder, blood soaking through my gray shirt. My eyes flick up to the person holding it. A white mask stares at me, tilted, as if curious, and I swear I can sense the grin forming behind the emotionless vinyl.

He shoves the knife deeper. I scream, my good hand flying to the wound, trying to stop him from twisting it. He yanks it free with a wet sound that makes bile rise in my throat. Blood splatters his mask. I stumble, slam my hand over the wound, hot liquid leaking between my fingers.

"You weren't here for her, were you?" I grind out, voice strangled.

He lunges again, blade flashing toward my chest. Pain screams through my shoulder, but adrenaline burns away the rest. I throw my body sideways, hit him with my full weight, and drive my knee up—hard. The impact connects square in his groin. He grunts, a harsh, muffled sound behind the mask, and drops back a step.

I dive for my gun. My fingers brush the grip, slick with my own blood, and I snatch it up. I twist, aim, and fire. The shot rips through the apartment, deafening. He dodges, and the bullet lodges in the wall just above the couch, drywall spraying from the impact.

Screams erupt behind me, and my attention briefly shifts to them, but it's a moment too long, because the second I turn back, the bastard is already running out of the living room. I fire again. The bullet rips through the tail end of his black coat, but he doesn't stop. He slips through the shattered patio door and into the night just as my backup arrives.

My arm trembles. Blood runs down to my wrist in steady

drops. Pain blooms hot and bright where the blade chewed me open. I drop to a knee and press a hand to the wound, fingers slick with blood I can taste. Outside, red and blue lights strobe across the glass shards littering the floor. Sirens crescendo, boots thud on the porch, voices calling. Somewhere, a radio crackles, someone yelling for scene control.

I force air into my lungs and turn toward the hallway. "RAELYNN! TESSA!" My voice is hoarse, but it carries. Backup floods through the door, shouting commands and sweeping the apartment, but all I can hear before everything goes black is her wails, her voice splintering apart from the end of the hall.

TWENTY-NINE
RAELYNN

I'VE NEVER BEEN inside an interrogation room before, and I hate every second of it. The walls feel too close, the air too sterile, the hum of the overhead light too loud. It's cold—clinical, almost—and the metal chair under me does nothing to help. My leg bounces uncontrollably beneath the table, and no matter how hard I try, I can't stop it. My heart hasn't slowed down since the moment the cops pulled me out of my apartment.

I know I'm not in here because they think I'm involved—not directly, anyway. I'm in here because they're trying to make sense of the chaos orbiting me. Four people I know are dead, all killed brutally, and the one thing connecting them all… is me. They're asking the same questions I am. Why them? Why me? Why the hell is The Ripper leaving notes addressed to me?

And why did he break into my apartment tonight—not to kill me—but to wait for Emilio?

The problem is, I don't have the answers they're looking for. Hell, I don't even have them for myself. How the fuck should I know why a serial killer is obsessed with me? Why he's picking off the people around me one by one? But deep down, in that quiet, ugly part of my mind that I can't shut up, I already have an idea. It all circles back to the first note I received—the card with the old article taped inside. My mother. Her death.

The metallic *click* of the door handle makes me flinch. The door opens, snapping me out of my thoughts.

"Evening, Miss Carson."

I look up from the water ring I've been staring at for the last ten minutes and meet the eyes of a woman I've only met once—Detective Meyer. Her expression is polite, but her eyes are sharp, calculating. Her auburn hair is pulled back in a ponytail, but strands have fallen free and frame her face. She looks as if she has aged several years since I last saw her just a few weeks ago. But I guess a gruesome serial murder case such as this one will do that to you.

"Evening," I mutter, my voice coming out hoarse.

She shuts the door behind her with a soft click. "I understand tonight has been a traumatic experience," she says, her tone sympathetic, as she moves around the table. She carries a file tucked under one arm, a notebook in her other hand. When she reaches the chair across from me, she sets everything down—right on top of the water ring—and sits. "I'll make this as quick as I can, but I need to ask you some questions first. Can you handle that?"

I nod, though it feels mechanical. "Yeah." My voice barely carries.

I sit back, the metal chair creaking under me, and fold my arms across my chest for two reasons. Reason one, I don't want to be here, and I want to make that perfectly clear. Reason two, it is fucking cold in this room. The thin sleep shirt and shorts I'm still wearing offer little warmth. I didn't exactly have time to change my clothes when the night turned into hell. There's also a smudge of blood on my forearm that I can't rub off. It's not mine. Emilio's, maybe. Or Max's. I don't know, and I can't decide which option makes me feel worse.

"Cold?" Detective Meyer asks, her eyes flicking up from her notepad to study me.

"Is it that obvious?" I ask, forcing a small, humorless smile. That was a dumb question. Of course it's obvious. My nipples are literal mountain peaks in this fucking shirt.

She chuckles softly, the sound surprisingly warm against the sterile silence of the room. "Hang on," she says as she stands, pushing her chair back with a scrape. I watch curiously as she strides to the door and cracks it open. "Hey, can someone grab me a blanket and some coffee, please?" she yells into the hallway.

She closes the door again and returns to her seat, the faintest smile curling on her lips. I give her the best smile I can manage, considering everything going on, and lower my arms.

"He's going to be fine, you know," she says, her tone gentler now. "Rodriguez called in before I came in here. She said there is no internal damage, so they're stitching him up. He'll surely be sore, but he'll be released tonight."

My breath catches in my throat. "You're sure?"

She nods. "Positive."

A shaky exhale slips from me, part relief, part exhaustion, and I try to cover it with a halfhearted laugh. "Is this a detective thing? Knowing what I'm thinking?"

She chuckles and leans back in her seat. "It's part of the job. You learn to read people—their emotions, their tells. Yours are pretty loud, sweetheart." She studies me carefully. "Right now, they're screaming that you're scared and worried. And you should be. But I meant what I said—Emilio's okay. And your friend's with your dog, making sure he will be too."

Before I can respond, the door opens behind me. I turn slightly as an officer steps in—a tall guy, young, holding a Styrofoam cup in one hand and a folded blanket in the other.

"Thanks, Elcot," Meyer says as he sets them down on the table.

He gives me a brief nod before slipping back out without a

word. Meyer slides the cup toward me and drapes the blanket over the edge of the table. I reach for it immediately, wrapping it around my shoulders. The fabric is thin, like hospital-issued fleece, but it's better than nothing. I lift the coffee to my lips and take a sip. The bitterness hits instantly, and I grimace. Black coffee. Yuck.

Meyer laughs under her breath, clearly amused by my reaction. "It's all they had."

I set the cup down and curl deeper into the blanket. "Figures."

Her amusement fades as she flips open her notebook again. "Alright, Raelynn. Let's get through this, yeah?"

"What do you want to know?" I ask, ready to get this shit on the road so I can finally leave and check on Emilio at the hospital. "What can you tell me about your relationship with the victims?"

My stomach twists. The word *victims* feels clinical, detached, like it strips them of who they were.

"Khloe is—" I pause, swallowing hard "—my best friend and has been since middle school." The correction catches in my throat. "Was." My gaze drifts to my lap, where my fingers have started picking at my nails—a nervous habit I can't seem to shake.

"I wasn't close with Liam or Bailey. I dated Liam for a couple of months my freshman year, but it didn't last. We stayed friends for a while but eventually stopped talking. Bailey… I barely knew her. Tessa was closer to her than I was. Alexis, though…" I exhale slowly. "We had classes together. This semester and last. We were pretty close friends."

Meyer's pen moves steadily, the faint scratching filling the heavy silence between us. The sound is rhythmic—almost soothing—if not for the tension wound tight in my chest. I can tell she's giving me space to gather myself, but all that space does is let my thoughts spiral deeper.

Emilio never got to tell me what happened to Alexis, as he

wanted, because everything went to hell before he could. Instead, I had to find out what happened to another friend of mine through Kline. Every brutal, gory, stomach-turning detail. I asked, of course. I needed to know. Needed to see the complete, awful picture, no matter how much it hurt. Because not knowing felt worse.

That's when Kline told me about the note The Ripper left for Emilio. Every word written in blood—a promise—telling Emilio that no one will be able to save me. That I was *his*. The words burned themselves into my head like a brand.

I think the bastard severely underestimates what Emilio is willing to do to protect me. He wanted to prove something, to twist that message into reality. To make sure I understood that even Emilio couldn't stop him. With Emilio gone, I was free game. That's why he broke into my apartment. He wasn't there for me. Not yet, at least. The Ripper knew Emilio would come to see me. Even with every nerve on alert, every instinct sharpened, Emilio still got caught off guard. And it's my fault. I distracted him. If I'd just stayed where I was, if I didn't call out to him…

My stomach twists violently. Emilio wouldn't have been hurt if I had used my fucking brain…

"Raelynn."

The sound of my name cuts through my spiraling thoughts. I blink and look up, startled. Meyer's watching me with a slight frown, concern etched between her brows, her pen tapping lightly against the notepad.

"Sorry," I whisper.

She shakes her head gently. "Don't be. You've been through more than most people could handle."

I shift in my seat, pulling the blanket tighter around me. "What was the question again?"

She glances down at her notes. "Why do you think he went after your friends?"

The answer forms easily, even if saying it feels like

coughing up glass. "To hurt me," I say quietly. "To break me down. To make me suffer. There's about a thousand reasons I could give, but they all come back to that."

Meyer nods slowly, her eyes never leaving mine. "And why do you think he's after you specifically?"

I swallow hard and pick up the coffee cup; it's warm against my fingers. "I don't know. Maybe…" My voice trails off. "Maybe it has something to do with my mother. You know what happened to her, right?"

Her expression softens, and she nods. "I do. She was the last known victim of The Butcher."

I nod faintly, staring down into the dark surface of the coffee. The bitter smell turns my stomach. "Yeah. That's why I think this is connected. Why else would someone target me like this? I've never done anything to deserve it. But it's more than a hunch—it's what he's *telling* me."

Meyer raises an eyebrow. "How do you mean?"

I take a breath. "A few weeks ago, someone dropped a card off on my front porch. My name was printed on the front. When I opened the envelope, the card inside was like one of those get-well cards you get at the store. When I opened it, I saw that taped inside was the headline from an article about my mother's murder seventeen years ago." I pause, the memory scraping raw. "Written across the top it said, '*You look just like her.*' And below the article—'*Will your fate be the same?*'"

Meyer's pen stills. "And you're certain that card pertains to this case? That it wasn't someone playing a cruel joke?"

"That's what I thought at first," I admit. "Until Emilio showed me the note left at Bailey and Liam's crime scene. The handwriting was identical." I shift forward, my voice sharpening. "Speaking of handwriting, why has every method of communication been different? Why wasn't anything left with Khloe that actually ties him to her?"

She exhales slowly, setting her pen down. "It's actually a

fairly common practice among serial offenders. They shift their patterns to avoid detection. If the evidence doesn't match from scene to scene, it's harder to connect the crimes legally."

I nod in understanding.

"Khloe was the first murder," she continues. "No note was left, but we did recover a string of text messages sent to her just before she died. The number traced back to a burner, so there was nothing we could get from that. In my honest opinion, I think the message he left *was* Khloe. She was your best friend, and whoever killed her knew this."

I frown, leaning forward. "Wouldn't you think he'd kill the person closest to me *last*? Draw it out for maximum damage?"

Meyer's eyes flick up to mine. "Normally, yes. But this guy doesn't follow convention. He started with Khloe because he knew it would *wreck* you. That was the first punch. The rest—Liam, Bailey, Alexis—they were the kicks that followed. He's not just trying to destroy your world, Raelynn." Her tone softens. "He's trying to destroy *you*."

The room falls silent again, heavy with the weight of her words. Four people are dead, and Emilio is at the hospital for a stab wound, all because of me.

THIRTY
RAELYNN

BY THE TIME Detective Meyer finally lets me go, the first bruised shades of dawn are bleeding into the horizon, turning the sky a washed-out blue gray. I step out of the station and into the early morning chill, exhaustion sinking deep into my bones. My entire body feels like it's been wrung dry—muscles aching, nerves frayed, brain buzzing like static. Hours of sitting under harsh fluorescent lights in that freezing interrogation room, answering question after question about every terrifying detail, have hollowed me out completely.

All I want is my bed. To crawl beneath the blankets, bury my face in my pillow, and pretend tonight never happened.

But my bed is inside an active crime scene. My apartment—my sanctuary—is now sealed off behind yellow tape, swarming with officers and crime scene techs. And there's no chance of rest, not while Emilio is still in the hospital. I need to see him, to touch him, to know he's really okay.

The second I slide into my Kia, I grab my phone. My hands shake as I fumble with the screen. I call Tessa first. She answers after a few rings, her voice thick with exhaustion.

"Rae?" she says softly.

"Hey. How's Max?"

"He made it through surgery," she says, and I hear the relief in her voice. "They're keeping him overnight for observation, but the vet said the wound missed anything major."

The tension in my chest loosens just a little, enough for my breath to hitch. "Thank God."

"Yeah," she exhales. "He's a tough boy. I'm gonna pick him up tomorrow and take him to stay with me at my parents, unless you want me to bring him to you?"

"As much as I want to be with my baby, we're not in the clear yet. Both you and Max will be safer far away from me." I sigh.

"You don't gotta lie, babe. If you want the space, all you gotta do is ask."

Even through the fatigue, I hear the smirk in her voice. "Tessa—"

She laughs softly. "Oh, don't act like you don't need it."

I roll my eyes, but I can't help the tiny smile that tugs at my lips. "Goodnight, Tess."

"Night, Rae. Hang in there."

When I hang up, I call Emilio immediately. He, of course, answers after the first ring.

He's still at the hospital, waiting for his discharge papers. The doctors stitched up his shoulder and offered him pain medication, but the stubborn bastard refused them. Said he didn't want to be stoned in case The Ripper decided to make another move tonight, which I completely understand.

Still, I can hear the fatigue in his voice, the way the exhaustion bleeds through even when he's trying to sound steady. He's been stabbed, nearly bled out on my living room floor, and yet he's more worried about me than himself. That thought alone twists something in my chest—equal parts love and guilt.

Because I keep replaying the night in my head, over and over. The chaos, the screaming, the glass shattering. The way I froze when I should've acted. Every ounce of my self-defense training with Emilio evaporated the second fear took over. I thought I was at least somewhat prepared for something like this, but the truth is, when it finally came, I was useless.

By the time I pull into the hospital parking lot, the sky is soft gray, the kind that comes before sunrise. The fluorescent lights outside the emergency wing glare against the dewy pavement. I park crooked between two spaces and don't bother fixing it.

When I step out, the air is cold enough to make a shiver skitter down my spine. The hospital doors slide open with a sterile *hiss*, and the scent of antiseptic hits me immediately. My slippers squeak against the polished tile as I make my way down the corridor, past nurses and patients and the distant beep of machines.

Then I see him.

Emilio stands near the nurse's station, his arm wrapped in a fresh bandage and resting in a sling. His gray t-shirt is stained dark where blood once soaked through, his black jeans scuffed, his hair messy. His expression is tight, a mix of exhaustion and barely contained anger. However, the moment he looks up and sees me, that hard edge softens just a little.

"Hey," I breathe.

I don't even realize how fast I move until I'm in his arms. His good arm wraps around me and pulls me close, his body warm and solid against mine. I sink into him, the metallic stench of blood, sweat, and antiseptic cling to him, drowning out the familiar scent of cedarwood and citrus I normally find comfort in.

"You okay?" he murmurs into my hair. His voice is rough, low—half worry, half relief.

"I should be asking you that," I whisper against his chest.

He pulls back enough to look at me, his golden eyes flicking over my face like he is making sure I am real, that I am actually here. "I've had worse," he says, though his voice doesn't match the words.

He brushes a thumb along my cheek before letting his hand drop. "Come on. Let's get out of here."

Outside, the sky has started to pale, streaks of light pushing through the clouds. I lead him toward my Kia, fumbling for my keys, the exhaustion making everything feel slower, heavier. I unlock the doors and slide into the driver's seat, but before I can start the car, Emilio opens my door.

"Move over," he says, his tone leaving no room for argument.

"Emilio, you just got out of the hospital," I protest.

His gaze darkens—not angry, just that he's-not-budging look he's perfected. "Rae. Change seats."

I hesitate for a second, wanting to fight him on it, but the set of his jaw tells me it isn't worth it. With a sigh, I climb over the console into the passenger seat, pulling the blanket from the station into my lap. He slides into the driver's seat and immediately removes his sling, tossing it into my back seat.

"Seriously?" I mutter.

"It's fucking annoying," he says, flexing his fingers with a wince before shoving the key into the ignition.

The engine hums to life, and as he backs out of my crooked parking job, his free hand finds mine. His skin is warm, his grip steady—solid, grounding.

"You've been staring at those files nonstop for three days, Rae. I think it's time to step away and come back to the land of the living."

Emilio's voice cuts through the quiet, low and edged with concern. I glance up as he walks out of the kitchen, the soft clink of his coffee mug breaking the silence.

After I picked him up from the hospital, he took a detour to my apartment to trade my car for his truck, insisting I wouldn't need it for a while. He wasn't planning on letting me out of his sight, and, I didn't argue. What I didn't know was that the other reason he wanted his truck was that he had somehow managed to smuggle copies of the case files from each murder for me.

So here I am, three days later, drowning in them.

Every report, every photo, every transcript is spread across his coffee table, overlapping in chaotic layers—a crime scene of its own. Names, dates, autopsy details, time stamps—they blur together until I can barely tell one from the next. Khloe. Liam. Bailey. Alexis. Their faces stare up at me from glossy photos, their smiles frozen in time, their stories ending in blood.

I trace their timelines again and again, my fingertips brushing over the ink like I can will a connection to appear. Something the detectives might've missed. Something that explains why this fucker is after me. But the longer I look, the more it all unravels—the details smearing together until all I can see are smudged shadows and the thin, splintered lines in the table's varnish.

"I can't," I murmur, voice rough from disuse. I flip through Khloe's file for probably the hundredth time and scan the same paragraphs I've already memorized. My eyes burn, but I keep flipping through the pages anyway.

Behind me, I hear Emilio sigh. The sound is low, a warning cloaked in patience. "Give me one good reason why you can't."

I don't even look up. "Because you almost got killed, Emilio. Because of me." The words crack in my throat, raw and sharp, every word laced with guilt. "All four of these people—" I snatch the files up, the paper edges cutting into my skin as I shake them in my hands "—are dead because of me!"

He exhales slowly, the sound dragging out between us. "It's not your fault that this sick bastard is after you, baby."

"Yes, it is!" I snap, slamming the files down hard.

The papers scatter across the table, crime scene photos of faces I can't bear to look at slip loose and land face-up. My trembling fingers gather the pages again, trying to rebuild the order, but it's useless. Everything's a mess—on the table, in my chest, and in my damn head.

I pull Alexis's file up to the top, flip it open, and start thumbing through it, but the words swim uselessly before my eyes.

Behind me, I hear him move. The dull scrape of ceramic on tile tells me he's set his mug down. I glance up from the open file on my lap, curiosity flickering despite myself, and watch him disappear down the hallway toward his room.

I drop my gaze back to the file. For a moment, I think he's giving me space, but then I hear the creak of the floorboards again—his footsteps returning. When he re-enters the living room, I look up and silently curse.

The bastard is fucking shirtless.

The sight knocks something loose inside me. The light from the table lamp brushes over him, casting soft shadows across his torso and highlighting the hard lines of muscle beneath the fading bruises scattered along his ribs. A white bandage runs diagonally across his left shoulder, taped carefully over the wound that nearly took him from me.

His eyes meet mine, and the world narrows to just that look. Dark, steady, unreadable—but something is burning beneath the surface. Something I feel before I can name it.

He crosses his arms over his chest, the movement pulling at the muscles in his abdomen, and when he speaks again, his voice is lower, firmer. "I'm only going to ask you once. Put the files away, Rae."

The warning in his tone makes my pulse stutter.

"And if I don't?"

The corner of his mouth curves—a dangerous ghost of a smile that makes my stomach flip.

"Do you really want to find out what happens if you don't?"

The truth is, I do. God help me, I want to know. Because I know exactly what he's doing, he's trying to distract me—to pull me out of my own head, away from the endless loop of guilt and what-ifs. Maybe that's exactly what I need: to stop thinking, stop analyzing. Maybe if I let him, it will clear my head. Or maybe my mind will be so foggy from whatever he has in mind that I'll stop worrying about the threat looming over my life, even if it's for a minute.

"Don't make me ask again," he warns, the quiet authority in his voice sparking heat low in my belly. Deciding to play his game—to test him—I ignore his warning and keep my eyes on the papers, feigning focus, pretending his presence isn't unraveling every ounce of resolve I have left.

The silence stretches. Then—his sigh. Long, sharp, full of restrained irritation. It slices through the quiet, and I can't stop the small, defiant smile tugging at my lips.

It lasts all of two seconds.

The file is ripped from my hand and thrown across the room. I gasp, looking up just as his shadow falls over me, and before I can even process what is happening, his hand is at my throat, not squeezing, just firm enough to startle me, to command my full attention as he hauls me off the couch.

"You'll regret ignoring me, pretty girl," he murmurs, his breath hot against my ear, voice low enough to crawl under my skin.

Before I can form a reply, the world tilts.

He lifts me like I weigh nothing, slinging me over his shoulder in one fluid motion. My hands press against his bare back, the heat of his skin seeping into my palms. A startled laugh escapes me—half protest, half disbelief—swallowed quickly by the sound of his footsteps thudding down the hallway.

"Emilio!" I squeal, somewhere between outrage and laughter.

He doesn't answer. He only tightens his grip, his muscles shifting under my hands like coiled steel. My laughter dissolves into breathless protests, but even I can hear the lack of conviction in my voice.

"Put me down!"

"Oh, I plan to," he rumbles, his tone dark and thick with promise.

His hand swats once against the curve of my ass. I yelp, my body jolting from the contact. My skin burns where his palm lands, the heat spreading like wildfire through me. The sound of his low chuckle follows, dark and satisfied.

By the time he reaches his room, I've stopped pretending to struggle.

He drops me onto the bed without warning, the mattress catching me in a bounce that sends a gasp tearing from my throat. I push myself up on my elbows, ready to throw some kind of comeback at him—but the look in his eyes stops me cold.

There's a storm brewing in them, a quiet, intense warning that sends a thrill of anticipation and fear coursing through me.

He's on me before I can think—knees braced on either side of my hips, his weight pressing me into the mattress. His fingers thread through my hair, the grip firm and controlling, as he tips my head back. His mouth crashes into mine, and everything else disappears.

The noise in my head. The fear. The guilt. Gone.

The kiss is rough, desperate, and consuming. His tongue finds mine, and I melt beneath him, answering with the same hunger. My hands find his shoulders, fingers digging into warm skin and the edge of the bandage. He winces when I squeeze, but he doesn't stop. He kisses me like he's drowning, like I'm the air he's been denied.

When he finally pulls back, I'm gasping, the air between us charged and heavy.

"Still think you can ignore me?" he murmurs, voice roughened, his breath ghosting across my lips.

I don't answer. I can't. I can only look at him. My thoughts are gone, scattered like the papers he threw.

He smirks, leaning in until his mouth grazes my ear. "That's what I thought."

His hand slips from my hair, tracing down my throat and chest to the hem of my shirt. He takes his time lifting it. The movement is unhurried, deliberate, every inch designed to unravel me. His knuckles graze my skin, the faint rasp of his calluses leaving a trail of goosebumps in their wake. The air seems to thicken, hum with energy. I shiver, my body caught between surrender and the heat that's building under my skin.

When he finally lifts the fabric, the soft brush of cool air kisses my bare skin and hardens my nipples to stiff peaks. His fingers skim the base of my throat as he pulls the shirt over my head, and the small contact makes my pulse jump against his touch. He chuckles—a low, rough sound that slides down my spine—as he tosses the shirt aside.

His eyes meet mine, and for a moment, he just looks at me. The weight of his gaze is almost tangible, tracing the shape of me in reverent silence. "I'll never get tired of looking at you," he murmurs, voice husky.

Heat blooms across my cheeks, my pulse tripping faster. I suck my bottom lip into my mouth. My fingers drift down the planes of his stomach, his skin warm beneath my touch. My fingertips trace the lines of his Adonis belt and stop at his waistband. He watches me, a smirk ghosting his lips as I pop the eyelet of his jeans.

I am halfway done with his zipper when he stops me and catches my wrists, his grip gentle but firm.

"Always so eager." He tsks as he pins them above my head, pressing them to the headboard.

The laughter that bubbles out of me fades the second I feel something cool and solid brush my skin. And then the soft, unmistakable sound of metal clicking breaks the quiet. My head snaps up, my mouth slack. The fucker handcuffed me.

I glance up at him, disbelief and something else mingling in my chest. "So that's what you were doing when you walked in here," I whisper.

He chuckles and nods as I give the cuffs a soft tug, my pulse spiking.

He leans close enough for me to see the glint of amusement in his eyes. "Tell me to stop," he says softly, his thumb brushing under my jaw, voice low enough to vibrate against my chest. "And I will."

I shake my head, voice barely a whisper. "Don't."

His lips curl into a devilish smirk, and he pulls back just enough to look at me properly, his gaze lingering on the metal around my wrists, then on my face. "Good girl," he murmurs as he rocks back onto his knees. I watch as he finishes what I set out to do and slides his zipper down the rest of the way.

I suck my bottom lip into my mouth as he shoves both his jeans and boxers down, freeing his already hardened cock, pre-cum already beading on the tip, and I clench my legs together, but he shoves his knee in between them, forcing them apart. I whimper softly, my fists clenching as he slowly begins to stroke his cock.

"Open that pretty little mouth of yours, Rae, I want to see that tongue of yours be put to good use."

Heat blooms across my cheeks as I obey, opening my mouth. He angles himself closer, tracing my lips with the tip of his cock, smearing his pre-cum over them before he slides into my mouth. He groans as he pushes deeper, slowly, coating the length of his shaft with my saliva.

I gag when the head of his cock hits the back of my throat, his balls resting against my chin. He holds it there for a few seconds before pulling out, a string of saliva connecting to the tip. He smirks at me again and wraps his hand around his shaft and strokes it again.

"You want this?" he asks me, and I nod, pulling on the cuffs. "Use your words, baby," he muses as he continues to stroke himself.

"Yes, please," I whimper out.

He chuckles darkly and positions himself at my mouth again. My lips part, and I slide my tongue out and flick it over the tip. I lean forward and wrap my lips around it and swirl my tongue around. Impatience gets the best of him, and he pushes in. I drag my tongue along his shaft as I take him deeper. He lets out a low groan and slowly starts to thrust, quickly picking up pace. I gag each time his head hits the back of my throat. After several seconds, he slows, then holds himself deep in my throat. Then he abruptly pulls out, leaving me gasping.

The minute I catch my breath, his lips crash against mine. He kisses me ferociously, his tongue invading my mouth, claiming every inch of it. I moan into his mouth, which only seems to drive him madder. He nips at my bottom lip, then begins to trail hot kisses down my jaw and over my throat, nipping gently as he goes. He continues to move further down until he stops at my breasts. He palms both, kneading them between his hands as his tongue alternates between nipples. His tongue flicks over both hardened peaks before sucking one into the heat of his mouth, and I arch beneath him, a moan escaping my lips.

My nipple pops free from his mouth, and he looks at me, his golden eyes dark with lust. "Who do you belong to?" he asks me, his voice low. His thumb brushes the nipple that just left his mouth.

"You," I breathe out.

"Mmm, that's right, and don't forget it." He chuckles as he presses his lips between the valley of my breasts. His tongue slips free, and he drags it down my stomach, his hands following the curve of my waist, until he reaches the waistband of my panties.

"You're so wet for me, Rae," he murmurs, his thumb rubbing at my folds over the fabric.

I squirm and buck into him, need coursing through me. "Please," I whimper.

"Please, what baby?"

"I need you," I beg, bucking into him again, the handcuffs clinking against the headboard.

He smirks and tucks his fingers into the waistband of my panties. The sound of tearing fabric fills my ears, and I squeak. He pulls the torn panties off me, then waves them briefly before tossing them aside. His fingers immediately return to my pussy. He slowly and agonizingly drags two fingers between my folds, coating them in my arousal, before slipping them inside me. They curl, instantly hitting that sweet spot, and I let out a shuddering moan, my body bowing off the bed.

"Fuck," I gasp as he pumps his fingers in and out of my pussy.

My thighs clench around him, but he forces them apart and brings his lips to my clit. He flicks his tongue over it before sucking it into his mouth, doubly assaulting my throbbing cunt. He pumps his fingers faster, his tongue working in sync. I moan and squirm, yanking at the cuffs, my body on fire with need. He holds me down, his assault relentless.

"Emilio!" I cry out, the cuffs biting into my wrists as I pull. My thighs clench around his head, my body shaking from the pleasure. He slows his assault, then slides his fingers out and brings them to my lips.

"Open your mouth and clean yourself off me," he demands, his voice rough. I obey. My lips part, and I suck his fingers into my mouth, my tongue swirling around each finger as I clean myself off of him.

He returns to my pussy, his tongue sliding up my slit before diving deep inside of me. I let out a shuddering moan and buck into him, grinding into his tongue as it thrusts.

"Mmmm, that's it, baby," he groans against my pussy, the vibrations sending shivers down my spine.

Heat coils fast in my belly, winding tighter with every thrust of his tongue. The pressure builds higher and higher, my body quaking around him until finally I can't hold it anymore and I break. My orgasm rips through me in violent waves, and I scream his name.

"I will never tire of the taste of you," he says, his voice husky with lust as he climbs back on top of me and grips my thighs as he shoves my legs apart to position himself between them. The head of his cock rests against my entrance, the tip pushing past my folds just enough to drive me insane with need.

"I'll never tire of you," I reply breathlessly.

"Good, because only death will get rid of me," he growls, his nails digging into my thighs as he slams into me with enough force to lift my ass off the bed. I scream from the sudden fullness, my pussy clenching around him. He continues to slam into me, his left hand moving from my right thigh. He grips the space between my cuffs, anchoring himself, while the other stays on my other thigh in a bruising hold.

My back arches off the bed, my fists clenching tightly until my knuckles turn white. "Oh god, d-don't stop!" I cry out as he pounds into the spot that has my eyes rolling back into my head. He lets out a guttural groan to my pleas and picks up pace, the bed frame creaking in tune with each thrust.

He drops his hand from my cuffs and closes it around my throat, applying just enough pressure for my brain to fog, and all I can think about is the feel of him as he continues to relentlessly fuck me.

My body convulses around him as I feel the pressure of another orgasm building.

"Be a good girl, Rae, and cum for me," he orders, his voice rough, and that is all it takes for the dam to break and a second orgasm rips through me.

He releases my throat, and I let out another scream. His thrusts continue, milking every ounce of my orgasm out of me. Then he slows and buries himself to the hilt and comes undone inside me. His entire body shudders against mine as he empties himself, his breath breaking in harsh, uneven bursts.

For several moments, he stays in me. The air between us is thick and quiet, filled only with the sound of our breathing. His forehead rests against mine, slick with sweat, our exhales mingling in the stillness.

"You okay, baby?" he murmurs, his voice rough around the edges. His hand comes up to cradle my cheek, his thumb brushing a slow path along my skin. I nod against his hand, a small laugh catching in my throat.

"You always ask me that," I whisper, teasing lightly, though my voice trembles with exhaustion.

A faint smile touches his mouth. "I always ask because I never want to hurt you," he says softly. His thumb drags over my lower lip before he presses a kiss to my temple, then leans down and captures my lips in his. "At least not intentionally," he says when he breaks the kiss.

He pulls out of me, the sudden loss of his warmth making me shiver. He leans over the edge of his bed and reaches for his jeans. He slips his hand into his pocket and pulls out a small key, then drops his jeans again and undoes the cuffs. The moment they fall away, he immediately brings my hands to his lips, brushing a kiss over the faint red marks before rubbing slow, careful circles into the tender skin.

Then, without a word, he pulls the blanket up over us both. The sheets are still warm, heavy with the heat of our bodies. He lies back and opens an arm, guiding me into the space against him until my head finds its place on his chest.

His heartbeat thrums steadily beneath my ear. One of his hands settles on my back, the other in my hair, fingers moving in slow, soothing strokes. I breathe in his scent, a sweet mixture of sweat and the faint traces of his cologne and feel the last of the adrenaline slip away.

"Better?" he whispers into my hair.

I hum in response, too tired to speak, my hand curling lightly against his ribs. He tightens his arm around me, pulling me closer until there's no space left between us.

Del
F12
End
PgUp
PgDn
Home
P
L
K
M
N

THIRTY-ONE
RAELYNN

I THUMB through the files spread across the coffee table again, the edges of the papers soft and curling from how many times I've handled them. I've been at this all day, since waking up in the late afternoon, burning through hours circling the same details, retracing the same lines, waiting for something to finally give. The only light in the apartment comes from the lamp beside the couch, its warm glow pooling over photographs and reports.

After last night's events (thank you, Emilio), my head is clearer. The storm that had been tearing through my thoughts has finally calmed, the chaos settling into something quieter and more focused. Not gone though, just contained. For now.

He wasn't exactly thrilled that the first thing I did after waking up—post-shower and scrounging up something to eat—was dive back into the files. However, he didn't try to pull me away or tell me to stop. Instead, he stayed by me.

Throughout the day, he took care of me in ways that never demanded my attention. A fresh mug of coffee would appear beside me when the last one went cold. A glass of water pressed into my hand when he noticed I hadn't taken a single sip in hours. Food nudged within reach when time slipped by and I forgot to eat altogether. A blanket adjusted around my shoulders when I started to shiver without realizing it. He never interrupted my thoughts, never asked what I was looking at or what I'd found. He was just there—steady, patient, and unwavering.

He sat with me—or rather, I sat on him—pulling me into his lap every chance he got, and I wasn't one to complain. His presence grounded me, anchored me to something solid while my mind stayed buried in the past. It was comforting, calming, and just distracting enough to keep me from spiraling. His fingers drifted through my hair in slow, absent-minded passes, a quiet reminder that I wasn't alone in this, even when the weight of the files threatened to pull me under. And honestly, I wouldn't have had it any other way.

I lift my mug off the table and take a sip, savoring the sweet flavor of the hazelnut and mocha. I go back in for another sip but freeze mid-swallow when I realize something.

Emilio feels it immediately. "What's wrong?"

"I've been ignoring the biggest fucking clue of them all," I mutter as I set the mug back down on the coffee table.

"How do you mean?" he asks, shifting under me. I half turn, and his brows pull together. "Rae? What is it?"

I drag in a breath that trembles at the edges and stare down at the faces on the table. "The clue is me, Emilio."

"I don't follow."

I slide off his lap and stand, restless energy fizzing in my legs. "Me. They all knew me."

"We already know this, baby…"

"Yes, but how does *he* know that?" My voice snaps sharper than I intend. I gesture to the photos. "Khloe was my best friend; she was always around me. But Liam? Bailey? I barely talked to them. Hell, Liam and I haven't said more than four words to each other since we stopped being friends a couple of years ago. The most that has been said was 'Hello,' and that was in passing! How the hell would someone know to target them, unless they knew something about me that I didn't tell anyone?"

Emilio lifts a file, thumb tapping the paper's edge. "You think he's watching you," he says slowly. "That he's been watching for a while."

"He *has* to be," I say, the words spilling faster now, my pulse thudding in my throat. "There's no other way he could know about Liam or Bailey. I didn't post about them, I didn't hang out with them in public—hell, I didn't even mention them to you until after they were killed!"

He straightens, the file forgotten in his hands. "So either he's digging into your life through someone on the inside, someone with access to reports, records…"

"Or he's close enough to have seen it himself," I finish.

His jaw works. "Or he has access himself," he adds, quieter.

For a moment, neither of us speaks. The silence presses down, thick and suffocating.

Finally, Emilio stands, his decision made in one swift motion. "I'm taking this to Rodriguez and Meyer. Now. They need to know."

I nod, gathering the files into a stack even as dread crawls up my spine. The realization sits like lead in my stomach. There's a possibility that whoever this is, it's someone I know. Someone I trust, someone within my circle… or it's someone who has been standing just outside it where I never thought to look.

I hug the files to my chest and nod, though dread crawls up my spine like cold water, and follow Emilio as he starts down the hall to his room. I set them down on the dresser, open it, and grab a pair of leggings from inside. They are halfway up my thighs when Emilio turns to me.

"No, you're staying here."

I blink, then haul them up the rest of the way. "What? No. Fuck that."

"Rae, listen to me," he says, his tone clipped and controlled. "If he's out there watching you, I'm not risking it. I'll take the files, talk to Rodriguez, and come back. It shouldn't be more than an hour tops."

I take a step towards him and fold my arms over my chest. "If he's watching me, then he already knows where I am. You're just as much a target as I am, maybe more, because he knows you won't let him get near me. So no, I'm not staying. You'll have to handcuff me to the bed again if you want to keep me here."

He hesitates—just long enough to tell me he's considering my argument.

"If he's been waiting for a chance, separating us is what he'd want," I say, softer.

His jaw flexes, and after a tense beat, he exhales a sharp, resigned breath. "Fine. You win. But you're not leaving my fucking sight. Get your shit."

I nod and grab a pair of socks from the drawer, tugging them on with shaky hands before slipping into my boots. The leather creaks softly as I lace them, the sound swallowed by the hum of the air conditioner and the low thud of my heartbeat. I sling the files under my arm and follow Emilio out of the bedroom.

He's already by the door, sliding his gun into its holster. Without a word, he grabs a sweater off the coat hook and tosses it to me, and I pull it on. My bag waits by the door—one of the few things I was able to gather from my apartment before coming to stay here—I pick it up and shove the files into its front pocket before slinging it across my shoulder.

As Emilio locks up behind us, a ripple of unease crawls under my skin. The parking lot is nearly empty, save for a few cars and a single flickering streetlight that throws light in erratic bursts. Every shadow feels like it's breathing, and the sound of Emilio's keys jingling is deafening in the quiet.

He unlocks his truck and opens the passenger door for me,

and I slide in. The leather seat is cold, stiff beneath my legs. He closes the door, rounds the front to the driver's side, and climbs in. He jams his key into the ignition and turns it on, and the low rumble of the engine fills the silence. For a few moments, neither of us speaks.

The city fades behind us in streaks of orange and white, the glow of the streetlights thinning into long stretches of dark asphalt and the occasional neon sign buzzing in the distance. The roads are mostly empty, the world reduced to the rhythmic sweep of headlights cutting through the night. I count the pools of light as they pass—one, two, three—anything to keep my mind from slipping back into fear.

Then I feel the shift. Emilio's posture stiffens. His grip tightens on the steering wheel, the leather creaking under his palms.

"What's wrong?" I ask quietly.

He doesn't answer right away. His eyes flick up to the rearview mirror, then back to the road. He does this several times. "Someone's following us," he says finally, his voice low and tense.

A chill rushes through me. I twist in my seat, peering out the back window. Headlights glow faintly several car lengths behind us. "How can you be sure?"

We were only a couple of miles from his apartment, and this was a relatively busy road, albeit not at this very moment, but still.

"I'm not sure yet," he mutters, scanning the road ahead. "Let's find out."

He takes a sharp right turn onto a side street. My shoulder slams lightly against the door from the sudden motion. I watch through the mirror as several seconds later, the headlights follow. Emilio's jaw tightens. He takes a left, then another right. The headlights mirror every turn.

My heartbeat drums against my ribs as we take another

hard right, only for them to be right on our fucking ass again. "Emilio..."

"I see them," he says, voice clipped. "Hang on."

He speeds up, tires squealing as he weaves down a narrow side street lined with closed shops and shadowed alleys. The headlights stay close, just far enough to taunt us. Emilio takes another turn, then another, faster this time. The world outside blurs—a jumble of yellow streetlamps, broken fences, and the gleam of wet pavement.

He finally pulls into a narrow lane behind a warehouse and cuts the lights. The truck idles quietly, its engine ticking as we sit there, the sound of our breathing loud in the cabin. I twist in my seat again, looking out every window I can.

Nothing.

After another minute, Emilio exhales, the tension bleeding from his shoulders. "I think we lost them."

I don't know if I fully believe him, but I nod anyway. He drives slowly through the side streets, looking into every space big enough to conceal a vehicle. He eases the truck forward again, crawling through side streets until we emerge back onto Speedway Boulevard. The traffic lights ahead cycle through their colors for no one. Emilio's gaze flicks between the mirror and the road as he accelerates.

"Emil—"

Blinding headlights surge toward us, and Emilio's name dies on my tongue. The impact hits like an explosion. Metal whines and glass bursts around us like a hailstorm, glittering in the dark. My head slams against the window, the seatbelt biting into my shoulder as the truck rolls—once, twice, then again. Each rotation steals the breath from my lungs.

When it finally stops, we're upside down. The world has gone eerily quiet except for the hiss of the engine and the slow drip of leaking fluid. My ears ring so hard it feels like a scream. I can taste blood, metallic and sharp, on my tongue.

“Rae!” Emilio’s voice cuts through the haze, frantic but alive.

I turn toward him, heart hammering. Blood trickles down his temple. “Emilio,” I cough out.

“Hold on, baby, I’ll get us out of here,” he says as he fumbles for something in his pocket.

Something slips from his grasp, clattering against the crushed roof above us. “Shit—” He reaches again, fingers scrabbling for it. When he finally grasps the object, he opens it, revealing a pocket knife. He quickly saws through his seat-belt, dropping heavily to the ceiling, then cuts mine loose.

The second I fall free, he grabs me and pulls me close. “It was him,” I rasp, tears brimming in my eyes. “I know it was him. He didn’t leave. He was waiting.”

“I know, baby. I know, but we’re still not in the clear,” he says as he brushes the tears away. “Are you in any pain? Can you walk?”

I quickly flex every joint and nod. “I-I can walk,” I reply.

“Good, because we need to get out of here right fucking now.” He lets go of me and pushes toward the driver’s side window. “Okay, come on, baby,” he says, reaching back for me.

I follow, glass biting into my palms as I crawl across the roof of the cab. My breath comes in short, ragged gasps. I’m halfway through the window when the night splits open with a single, deafening crack.

A gunshot.

“Emilio!” I scream, his name tearing through my throat as I twist, trying to find him. “Emilio!” I call out again, panic lacing my voice.

No response. Only the groan of the wrecked truck and the faint hiss of leaking fuel. My chest tightens until I can barely breathe. I crawl back inside, searching blindly for anything—a weapon, a phone, anything at all. My fingers close around a shard of glass, my hand shaking.

Then I hear it.

The sound of footsteps and crunching glass outside the wreck. A low whimper escapes my lips. "Emilio?" My voice breaks.

The footsteps stop just outside the shattered window, and everything in me goes still. My heart slams so violently against my ribs that for a moment, I swear it's trying to escape. The figure bends, and the weak glow of a distant streetlight catches its face—no, not a face. A mask. *His* mask.

A strangled noise tears from my throat. I scramble backward, my hands slipping over glass and blood-slick metal. My legs hit the backseat, and I push myself between them, desperate, half blind with panic. I am barely between the seats when a gloved hand shoots through the window, fingers closing around my ankle like a vice.

I scream, kicking and thrashing, but he doesn't flinch. The grip only tightens, dragging me backward inch by inch. I kick again, connecting with something solid—his arm, his shoulder, I don't know—but it proves absolutely useless as he continues to pull. My fingernails rip through the leather seat as I claw for leverage, for anything to hold onto. He yanks hard, and my grip slips.

"No, no, no, no, please no!" The words tear from me in a half sob, half scream as I am dragged through the cabin, my body scraping across the broken glass scattered through the wreck.

Shards bite into my skin, slicing fire across my stomach and arms as I am hauled out of the truck completely.

ACKNOWLEDGMENTS

This book would not exist without the people behind it. The ones who were here lifting it up, shouting about it, and loving it even on the days that I don't.

I struggled most days with writing and life in general and constantly had this feeling that this book wouldn't be good enough, that no one would be interested. But I kept at it because I wanted to prove to myself that I could do it, that sometimes your book may not be for everyone, and that's natural.

Honestly, if it weren't for the incredible support of my team, friends, family, and the people who were just interested from the start, this wouldn't be out in the world, so I want to personally thank a few people who have helped me along the way.

The ones who were there through it all, hyping me up, supporting my dream, and were just always there when I needed them. So thank you to my incredible beta team who helped shape this book: Ariel, Nicole, Morgan, Michelle, and Belle. And special thanks to a few others who were always there supporting me as well: Ash, Tori, Katie, Sunshyne, Celeste, Mario, Marie, Beckie, Jackie, Courtney, Torie, my mom, and my wonderful boyfriend, Gabriel.

Thank you for keeping me on track, for seeing the vision even when I couldn't some days, and for showing up with your whole heart every single time. I am endlessly grateful for your patience, your hustle, and your belief in me.

THANK YOU

Thank you so much for taking the time and care to read A Killer's Obsession. This story marks my debut as a published author, and knowing you chose to spend your time with these characters and this world means more to me than I can express. Writing this book was an intense, emotional, and incredibly rewarding experience, and I truly hope you enjoyed reading it as much as I loved creating it.

Your support—whether through reading, reviewing, recommending, or simply holding this book in your hands—helps me grow, learn, and continue doing what I'm passionate about. I hope you'll stay with me as I continue this journey, develop more stories, and bring even darker, deeper worlds to life.

Thank you, from the bottom of my heart, for being here.

ALSO BY DR BROOKS

A Killer's Reckoning: Book 2 in the Killer's Game Duet is currently in development! More information on that to come!

FOLLOW DR BROOKS

Please follow me on one of my socials!
IG: @author_drbrooks
Threads: @author_drbrooks
Tiktok: @authordrbrooks

www.ingramcontent.com/pod-product-compliance
Lightning Source LLC
LaVergne TN
LVHW010630110826
845149LV00014B/2821